the WALNUT TREE

the WALNUT TREE

MARTHA BLUM

Edited by Geoffrey Ursell.

Cover image, "Street in Chernivtsi," by George Hupka.
Cover and Book Design by Duncan Campbell.
Author photo by Hans Dommasch.

Printed and bound in Canada.

Canadian Cataloguing in Publication Data

Martha Blum, 1913–
The walnut tree
ISBN 1-55050-154-2

I. Title.

PS8553.L854W34 1999 C813'.54 C99–920144–1
PR9199.3.B556W34 1999

COTEAU BOOKS
401-2206 Dewdney Ave.
Regina, Saskatchewan
Canada S4R 1H3

AVAILABLE IN THE US FROM:
General Distribution Services
4500 Whitmer Industrial Estates
Niagara Falls, New York, USA 14305-0368

The publisher gratefully acknowledges the financial assistance of the Saskatchewan Arts Board, the Canada Council for the Arts, the Government of Canada through the Book Publishing Industry Development Program (BPIDP), and the City of Regina Arts Commission, for its publishing program.

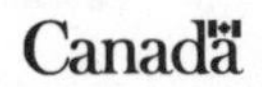

To Irene

Then Jacob kissed Rachel
And broke into tears.
– Genesis 29:11

I would like to emphasize that this is a work of fiction. Characters in the foreground are fictitious in their entirety. Similarities to individuals living or dead are strictly coincidental. Historical events are as accurately drawn as I could recall them. Any error, historical or other, is my own, and in no case was there a deliberate falsification.

– M.B.

TABLE OF CONTENTS

Czernowitz 1921-1943

Saskatoon 1951

Czernowitz 1941 Saskatoon 1961

Czernowitz
1921-1943

Süssel

The Legend

"YES, THIS IS THE MOST HOLY LEGEND OF THE Romanian people," Ileana starts, taking me on her lap and into her Romanian motherhood where a five-year-old would find her sweetest home. "Come, Jewish child, come sit with me, night is falling, a dusk as long and as beautiful as my story."

I always long for this hour, when Ileana's work is done and it is in-between times. Not yet dark, yet there is shimmery silence. The end of things before the end. Stories as bloody as the one I am hoping for make me settle into Ileana's mighty breasts with that slight horror of delight. That in-between feeling, in dusky in-between times. A child of five knows better than all the clever adults of things possible yet untold. She does not think. She knows of this hour where fears spring from the gut, taking not yet imagined, true, shape. And this is the holy story of Master Manole, so often promised to me for good behaviour, for washing behind my ears, or not bringing my bitten-into apple back from kindergarten. It is a promise coming true; as stillness settles, no one moves, except her bosom and me in it.

"Master Manole," she starts with a hushed voice, worthy of

that holy moment. Oh, it is totally ours, this moment. Ileana and I know that Father and Mother have gone down to the wine cellar for the evening glass of wine, for the cigarette taken from a silver case, burnt hazelnuts, and a chat with neighbours. Maria the cook is off, and who cares about my big fat brother, at this time. Playing soccer maybe. It is all ours, time, the kitchen bench, and the stove still glowing with slowly dying coals. Dusk, our time.

"Yes, this a holy story," she starts. "It is about the great Romanian holy man, Master Manole, and it is about God. You see, there is Manole. He can do anything with stone. He is a master builder, a mason. He can chip the stone with a chisel, his fingers, or any piece of sharpened-edge stone. He can fit stone into stone like our forebears, the Romans, did. We come from them, you know, my child. They could build bridges like none other at their time to bring water from one corner of the world to another, or span mountain ranges, or roads. They made arches of stone, which hold through the ages, without a touch of mortar. Imagine! But of course they could build of brick and mortar also, and so can our master Manole. He can build anything like them, but he is also a Man of God, a holy man. And God knows.

"One night Manole hears the Voice. There is only one Voice and Manole hears it: *Master, build Me a house of prayer, contemplation, and learning,* God says. *A home of glory.* Manole, awestruck, trembling, falls to his knees, makes the sign of the cross. He understands. He has been chosen. God has found him worthy among all His Romanian children to build to His glory a monastery, right here in the beautiful Curtea de Arges. And he goes to work. Assembles all he needs, utensils, stone, wood.

"A master of the art, a mason like Manole had help from his villagers. They revered Manole, for God had chosen him. The work went very well, foundations were laid, and he slept well in the great hope of completing the holy work. But somewhere, sometime, around when he started on the small turrets for the side chapel, things began to go wrong, and whatever he had built in the daytime would crumble in the night. He would pick up his stones in the morning, put one on top of the other with much more care, thinking he had been careless in his work. But lo and behold, the next morning, he would find all he had built with so much love and vision broken on the ground.

"Master Manole prayed and prayed. Neither could he eat nor sleep and he kept away from his beloved wife, like a monk. Oh, I see," Ileana said, answering my unspoken question. "It means to be alone, at night as well, to do penance, for he feared he had failed God and he was searching within himself for that failure. And then, one day, when he was deep in thought, the answer came. He heard the command, the unmistakable Voice. God asked of him the highest sacrifice: *Take what you love best and offer it to Me. Take what you love best to the monastery and wall in what you love. With your skilled hands, Master Manole, put stone on stone until the wall is closed around what you love. Then the house of God will be built. Then I will know my true servant.*

"The Voice had spoken. It was Manole's task to finish the Lord's dwelling. And he went to what he loved best. He took his beautiful wife, set her into the side chapel with a little bread and water, and started to set stone on stone. And before the last stone was set, he heard her scream for air for the first time. So he set the stone fast, fast, so as not to weaken in his service to God. And now the Curtea de Arges stands in its glory forever and ever...."

"Let her out," I shout. "Let her out, Ileana! I do not want her in there, she has no air, she can't breathe! I don't care about your terrible monastery, let her out, Ileana." And I jump from her lap to the kitchen floor and I flail my arms and legs about. "Let her out, let her out!" I scream.

"You stupid Jewish child, you understand nothing holy. I'm wasting my time. Get up!" Ileana is angry. She tries to hold me still with her two mighty arms, tells me there is no way a Christian can be made out of a Jew. I will not hear of anything, I sob on the kitchen floor until I hear my parents' footsteps.

My glorious mother, smelling of burnt hazelnuts and cigarettes, picks me up and holds me tight. And slowly, on the brown leather sofa in the salon, she hears the story of Master Manole and what it was that I wanted so desperately to be let out. "Nothing," she assures me, "could ever happen to that lovely Lady Manole. She may have slipped out somewhere, Süssel. God is good."

"No, no, Ileana said no, the monastery would crumble then. And Master Manole wouldn't allow that to happen."

"So," my mother goes on, "you are a Jewish child. Remember the story of Abraham, your forebear. He also heard the Voice of God and was to bring his son Isaac as a sacrifice, and you remember well that at the last moment, as Abraham's arm was raised to slay his son, God held his arm and spoke: *It is enough, you have shown that you are my faithful servant!* So you see, my sweet, God would not allow for Isaac to be killed."

Oh, not to have to be a Christian was so good, so comforting! God would not have permitted Lady Manole to die. She had slipped away.

And I chew my brown hazelnuts, which Mother has brought from the cellar. They are such funny hazelnuts. They look like peas in a pod, being rolled by the sixes into strips of paper. Our parents always bring them home after their wine-hour to both of us, my brother Felix and me. So I unroll them, count them to make sure there are six, chew and chew until overwhelmed by sleep.

Dearest Jehoshua! Or Iesus, as Ileana would call you. I have not slept a wink, for night after night I am awakened by that last scream. You know, the unbearable one I hear and you must too. The one before the closing of the wall. My heart races as I wake and slowly all things close in on me. The walls move, everything, but the hat stand first. You know, the one that stands in the corner of my and my brother's common bedroom. Near the window, which opens towards the west. My favourite one with the broad windowsill, where I sit evening after evening to see the night green under the setting sun. But it is a very black window now, cut by a cross in four. There it usually stands, that hat stand with Felix's hat on top, his coat hanging, trailing low, the arms like a scarecrow's. It is the first to move, before the desks, the chairs, my dolls on the sofa, and is the most dangerous. It raises its arms, there is a dark grin under the hat. I feel my heart beating in my temples, sweat in my palms. I want to shout and can't.

The walls move in, stone by stone. I can hear Master Manole working faster, praying against his will. As he lifts the last stone I hear her screams. I scream and shout and run, before my air is taken, into the bedroom of my father and mother. Crying, sweating and shaking, inconsolable. Until my mother's red hair falls upon my face, and I smell the Houbigant *parfum* and nestle against her lacy nightshirt. Peace, safety.

He does not want me there of course, my father. I would have run to him, as much as to my mother, lain in the hollow of his arm, alongside his flank. But he does not want me there, I know that. I am nothing to him, just a screaming five-year-old. What he wants is my glorious mother. Her hair and perfume. I hear them sometimes at night when those walnut twin-beds-so-close-to-each-other creak and wake me.

Here is my question to you, dearest Jehoshua: Why did the stones that Master Manole had laid in the daytime crumble at night? And how did the screams of the lovely lady strengthen the stone to stand firm until the monastery was built? I am just a stupid Jewish five-year-old, as Ileana says, but I cannot enter your house. All the stones will scream, they will echo through the Curtea de Arges. The scream holds the walls up, it is her soul that is the mortar. I want none of it. It would be with me as I sleep and wake and no lullaby could pierce it at night.

Dear Iesus, is it possible that Master Manole was not a pious but a wicked man, who wanted to kill his wife, from the first day? A wicked, wicked man who did not love her? Who despised her black hair, her smell of onion, how she rolled the meat-rice mixture into the cabbage leaves and wiped her hands on her apron, or her fingernails dark with earth. You see, Master Manole was a master-builder, clean in his work, accurate in his measuring, and silent. She may have been messy, have talked too much, or perhaps she sometimes wanted him to kiss her and he couldn't. And when the first stone fell the first day, he trembled, but on the second and the third he knew it was her fault. God wanted her within his wall. And he thought it was she whom God loved best. Dearest Jehoshua, if you are God, as Ileana says, or His only Son, as Ileana says – why did You – or did You – command Master Manole to take the breath of his beautiful wife and build it into your stone?

MY MOTHER SINGS GERMAN TO ME, and I sing a third up or a third down. She sits on the edge of my new adult bed and I terrorize her by not letting her leave the room I share with my brother. I do not want him there. Another song, another song, sweet German sounds, a lullaby for a prince – *Schlafe mein Prinzchen es ruhn* – and we harmonize until I drop into sleep.

No, I do not want Felix there. I like a corner of my own and he is everywhere. So big and so fat. The shadow he casts moves as if alive, with a will of its own, an animal occupying every bright spot. We are on the third floor of my grandfather's house. Windows like wings fly out to the west, doors are carved walnut, and inset glass is crystal.

A corner bench helps me to reach the windowsill. I touch, stroke the often-caressed wood, brown chestnut, mellowed with time. At the age of eight a girl likes to feel the naked wood against her thigh, she likes to sit and wait. For the sun to set, the greening of the sky as the sun descends from its orange sea. A waiting for something fearful – wonderful – to happen. And my hand moves from the heated chestnut to my inner thigh. It rests and waits.

Of course, the big shadow will move in, will shout, will ruin my moment. No girl should have a big fat brother. He is everywhere, though, asserting his dominion over me. He teaches me Latin. He cuts my cake in two and steals it before my eyes. And mother gives him the juiciest cutlet, "because he is growing." I hate him. But sometimes he does intriguing, interesting things. Today, curious to know what he is up to, I follow Felix to the attic and hide behind the linens spread out to dry. It's a real attic, on top of our three-storey stone house, its small rooms secured with big locks hanging on makeshift doors. Just like the adults, all knowing things and not telling. The attic smells of garlic and mushrooms, wreaths and wreaths of them. Oh, the waiting. My heart stops and I hold my breath. Here they are: my brother Felix, another boy, perhaps Hans, and Ileana the Romanian maid, who wakes me in the morning, feeds and washes me, makes my *Butterbrot,* and sends me off. Ileana, no! I see it all, it happens very fast. Oh, life is hard.

I love Ileana. She stinks of onion, her hair is greasy, and she paints her lips with red crêpe paper. She has breasts of gold with highlights of darker gold, mountains of gold I stare into when she is on her knees washing the kitchen floor. Doing housework, she tucks her skirt under her belt – a Romanian *brâu,* a big wide loomed belt with stripes in all colours. An ancient belt, I was told in school, a Celtic ornament, of which the poet Ovid speaks. She looks funny down on all fours, with her skirt up, on her naked knees. But when she dances on her floor brushes, a brush held on each foot by a strap, she is much funnier yet. Those glorious breasts shake and jiggle as she dances to shine the oak parquet. Oh, I want to kiss them, Ileana, let me kiss them. She smacks me hard, but her throaty laughter is my reward. She is beautiful, I think, and I love her. But she should not have lain with the boys.

My mother never rises in the morning to send us to school. We children do not see her until she kisses us at one o'clock for dinner, smelling heavenly of Houbigant, hair piled up high in a chignon, catching the red. I could die in that hair. I want it to fall, cascade over me. Her black Spanish turtleshell-inlaid comb is my personal enemy. I never see my mother late at night or early in the morning, only at dinner, beautifully dressed and coiffed and everything so in order.

The dinner table is silky damask with shining tulips, white on

start, kids running, coats being thrown on hooks, and books smashed to the ground. Then the sun rises, and all magic dispels.

But not yet. This is our moment. Tanase limps for me to slow time down, freeze it to stand still. He hugs me and takes my satchel and we walk, lovers, into the empty classroom. I help him with the wood – he is awkward with his crooked spine, and we pile the split wood in front of all the stoves, until we come to my own classroom. There we light the fire and he sits down next to me on my bench, a four-seater hard bench and desk, watching the glow dance on the dark walls.

There is a rhythm in the crackling sound of the fire, and rays of black pirouette and mingle with the gold. "Sing to me, my sweet," he says, "sing to me." And I sing above the rhythm, enfolding it, accommodating it, missing a beat just to feel the stillness.

Then the gate crashes down and the stamping army of girls arrives, and our moment is over.

Tanase is my winter lover, but oh! My summer lover. Spring breaks in with a fury in my mythical childhood town. No early warnings, sweet violets and snowdrops, just water tumbling down suddenly from the Carpathians, swollen with glistening gems and the sounds from the end of all time. The drowning sound of the true stream, that band of silver carving its bed through pine underbrush and stone. This is the river I see in every river.

Up on the hill sits the Archbishop's Residence, holy and mysterious, of red brick with gold-and-green lacquered stones in roof and walls. I see it from my grandfather's house, blocking the evening sun. Eleven years old, I sit on my windowsill, with the back of my eye filled with its Moorish encircling walls, slowly losing themselves in the coming dark.

The Residence is off limits for everyone except the Greek Orthodox priests and their young seminarians. It is certainly off limits for a Jewish child with wild Hasidic dreams, jubilant in Jewish laws, joys, and penance. But I long for knowledge of that unknown other, for the limning of the contours of the forbidden.

There always is a brick or two at the bottom of the Moorish wall that can be loosened to give me a narrow space – entrance to the off-limits, the forbidden. Here on my walks among pine grottos, small Moorish fountains, and geometrical forms, I find my summer lover. He strides weightily in the black soutane of the seminarian, still young. Book in hand, he passes me without a glance. "Come back," I address my Adonai, "come back and sit by me so I can see the dark shine on your upper lip." He turns – did he hear me pray? – and asks for permission to sit by me.

And so it is, day after day all summer long, that I loosen those bricks from the Moorish wall and crawl through the hole to my wonderland. My wonder world of beauty and fear, my forbidden world. Of course he knows I shouldn't be there, but the knowledge only strengthens the alliance between us, two penance-seekers.

I am always there early, after matins. The same hour, the same cast-iron bench, a dwarfed pine at our back. My name is Sweetie, I tell him. Well, not really. It is Süssel in Yiddish and so they call me Sweetie.

Oh yes, a Jewish child, he says. He speaks of mystery and reads aloud, my black guardian angel, speaking of the risen God and redemption of all sin. I do not understand the word *redemption* well enough, but his soothing voice teaches me things that mere cleverness couldn't.

I tell him I would like to know why our parents keep children indoors at Eastertime, during the candle-processions and singing of *Christos has risen,* answered in counterpoint by *Indeed He has risen.* I want to know why we children are quarantined and told there is danger in the streets and murder for Jewish children. I let my summer lover read and read, in an abandon as sweet as sleep. I imagine Jerusalem, familiar yet strange. His soutane, black and to the ground, roughens my thigh, my leg, as he turns. *Come down into my face,* I pray, *come down and let me just –*

He turns the page, gathers the cloth around him as if it were a shield, raises his voice to a gentle edge, and says, "Tomorrow, Süssel, I'll read to you of the wondrous wedding."

A wedding, he said – what wondrous wedding?

Oh, I will grow and be your bride, and under the *huppa* you will lift my veil to sip the wine from the Kiddush cup. And I will hear you say: Look up my bride and sing, oh sing! Shabbat is in the heavens!

Look up my bride and sing
My dove, my soul, my neshamah
Oh, sing my dove!

My dove has wings of silver
They fly through doors
All windows open
My dove has wings of silver.
Oh, sing my soul!

My soul has wings of gold
They fly through dreams
Through nights and days

My neshamah has wings of gold.
Oh, sing my neshamah!

My beauty, soul and bride
Your eyes are heated wine
To flow and fill the rivers
Your hair a flame of red
To burn my head and heart
My dove has wings of gold!

Look up my bride and sing, oh sing
Shabbat is in the heavens!

The third summer is our last. It is full of sorrow. My breasts haven't grown like other girls' breasts, they are small and boyish. There is no shine of red hair in the forbidden places – such deep sorrow. And I have never felt my summer lover's fine down against my face.

"I'll Marry Her –"

I GO DOWN THE RESIDENZGASSE ON A JUNE DAY towards the Residence of the Greek Orthodox Archbishop. The chestnuts are in bloom, their pink and white candles upright, lit it seems, nearly holding the clouds; they guard the Evangelical church on both sides of the entrance. I pass the University grounds, Austrian looking, sombre but fanciful enough not to subdue my step. At the crossroads I see the fountain, its iron-old hand lever swinging.

She sits on the rim of the fountain. I'll marry her, I think, and get it over with. I'm impatient, but can't go with the boys to the whores. My twin brother wakes me this morning at five o'clock and whispers conspiratorially, *get dressed fast, we are going out....* We are fifteen years old and I tremble. You go, I say, and I'll wait. No, I am not afraid, but I'll wait. You're a coward, my athlete-brother says, and a sissy, and you'll never learn how.... All I want is sleep, and perhaps to go down the Residenzgasse as far as the fountain, or the old stone house at the corner. Farther up, the street slowly rises, not perceptibly, but it slows your step as the Residence rises increasingly powerful before you, walnut and chestnut trees above the roofs.

I like to rest near that stone house. It has flying angels carved into its gate by Italian craftsmen brought to the city at the turn of century. Sometimes she stands there, with her lithe legs and red hair, knit and knotted like yarn, falling from the crown to the shoulders, half into her face, barely revealing the green of her eyes. A wild thing.

Across from the old house is the school principal's house, heavy-bourgeois, ugly, but with a perfect hiding place to observe her. There are too many children in the old house, pouring out onto the Residenzgasse, shouting, surrounding her. I'll marry her – I'm not going to the whores. I'll cover up for my twin, put a pillow underneath his blanket, as if he were just cuddled inside. Let him go with the others, there is no use for me to go. I am the laughingstock of the gang anyway. With an undistinguished penis, which all but disappears on cold days. Let them go. I want to marry her. I'll wait. Next time, when standing in my hidden corner across from the old house, I'll catch her alone, without the rowdy gang of cousins that always hold her in their midst like a precious prey.

From across the road I can see her hair streaming, flying like all the wings-spread angels in the carved gate. Above the gate, set into the stone, is a single devil, carved from darkened marble. Its face ominous, its tongue thrust out, as if out for my heart's blood, two symmetrical horns, and wicked eyes within a foliage of wild profusion. Not Jewish and not Christian, but pagan – Greek really, more like Pan. Who conceived this image, the split hoofs, horns, tails, the nimbus of lechery? Who and when? My Jewish grandfather would smile and say, "Ah Mordechai, God is good, His creation awesome and of the highest, why would He – blessed be He – invent such a stupid monstrosity just to scare you? Come

Bubbale, let me hold you and maybe you find something in my pocket – just look!"

And my Lutheran mother would say: "It's wicked Catholicism, they invented it all! Forget the nonsense. Yes, one does mention Satan at baptism, to make sure.... Oh, well, sweetheart, go on with your work. Go help Moritz split the kindling."

From across the street the devil draws my gaze to it and I hear it say: *Watch out, don't enter this gate, think twice. Have you ever seen her eyes?* No, I haven't seen them, and I must, before I bind her with my ring. I play with a green-mottled marble in my pocket, as I always do when fearful or cowardly. But now it begins to feel like a wedding band to me. It curls itself inside index finger and thumb. How foolish the heart....

Lots of *braggadocio* from the boys, everyone a hero: how many times, how hard the penis, how big, laughter and demonstrations! My twin is the wildest. Half an hour older than me, he knows everything better. He can open any lock by looking at it almost, by knowing and undoing the law of the object. He looks at a thing, sees what it is made of, guesses its secrets, and, with huge shouts of war, conquers it. And he opens the cupboard, where a sliced torte has been stored, and takes from every piece a fine cut, so the number – well counted by our fiercely just mother – remains the same. Closes the cupboard elegantly, with the gentle swish of wood against wood, and hides the hoard, passing out small pieces to me for bribery and bargaining. For services too, but mainly for complicity. At the age of seven or eight, you can bribe any boy with sweets, especially me. But I tremble. I am just as criminal as Moritz, my brother. I am Max. The two of us a famous pair of unruly no-good-but-not-so-terribly-bad-either kids. Of course, M and M is what they call us. We do have respectable Austrian names – Siegfried and Franz Peter. But Max and Moritz is what we are, inescapably.

Moritz knows where the young toads are when in season and he drags me along to the river Prut on the northeast side of town, where there is a bridge above a small island where all the toads collect and croak. He taunts me, calling me *Hasenhertz* – cowardly bunny-rabbit-heart, to get me to hurl the stones that we have brought with us at the innocent young things. Green and red mingles. I faint, as usual. This is what I always do, I do mischief and I faint. Taking hold of my feet, Moritz pulls me down to the bank to revive me with river water. The first thing he says, when I open my eyes: "Max, don't you tell, or you'll faint for good."

No need to warn me. I fear our mother. She is just, but it is not my kind of justice. There is a hazelnut rod on display in the vestibule, sharp and slender. I always have to bring it to her and let my pants down for just punishment, the ten strikes on the behind. Across her knees. Only me.

Moritz appears virtuous. He never gets caught. But neither does he give his shoes or his *Butterbrot* away to a miserable barefoot boy, nor does he lose his mittens, hats, and gloves. He is virtuous and I get the rod.

I love Moritz. We bathe together. He fashions a Spanish Armada, sailboats made out of walnut half-shells, with matches as masts, flying cotton flags, insignia clearly displayed, fighting the British fleet. He commands both forces, playing general for both sides, all in the bathtub. Oh, my hero! He washes me and rubs my back and helps me button up pants and suspenders. Lots of buttons everywhere and I have two left hands. He often covers one of my misdeeds and then I have to carry his satchel to school for a whole week, as I did when I once stole hot peanuts from a peanut vendor. But they smelled heavenly, roasted on coals, such a delicacy on a cold winter day.

Fiery little ovens are everywhere on market days, with peanuts, roasted chestnuts, or popped corn – the Romanians call it *Floricele,* the little flowers. I am a greedy boy at seven or eight, with no money, and I grab a handful of searing peanuts and run. The man shouts: So young and so wicked. My mother will be informed. Of course I faint. And here Moritz was at my side saying: "Carry my books to school for a week and I'll protect you."

And protect he did. He fought off the bullies, the toughs on the school grounds. He would plant his two legs wide, his fists ready, and shout: "Max, run!" And he would stand his ground. He had to – they would beat me to a pulp otherwise. So he looks after me and I gladly pay the price.

Such a hero, my brother. And what he can do on a horse or on the rings. How he flies across the skating rink! Like a bird he flies, in pirouettes, jumps, as if carried by the winter wind, not earthbound. And I sit on the wooden benches, laugh, clap my hands, and shout with joy to be allowed to love him and have my name linked to his for all to see, M and M.

But not at fifteen. It started a little earlier. We had a sweet neighbour of ten or eleven and chasing her one day, Moritz caught her, squeezed her against the entrance door, and kissed her. She let it happen, because no one can resist my brother. But I, this time, resented it. "She did not want it," I said. "You should not have done it."

"So, tell mother, go tell, I'll deny it! You, dear Max, have become very uppity and preachy of late, you're not interested in any of the things we all do and talk about. Are you normal? Don't you want girls? To see what they look like under their skirts, and feel them up? What is the book in your hand, anyway?" The book was about Kepler, Johannes Kepler's mother. A story of her trial. She was accused of witchcraft to burn at the stake. And of how Johannes succeeded, through his fame as an astronomer, to free her.

My brother Moritz flings the book out of my hands, turns with disdain to me, and says: "You're different now, you're no fun anymore." True, I'm no fun anymore. There is a kind of inertia, a laziness in my movements, stopping me, holding me back. Not knowing the next move, my muscles stall. I'm lankier now, my legs have stretched, my feet are too big, my belts too loose. All these are hurdles to take, and I don't jump them easily, or do not wish to. I'd love the wind to cool my cheeks. They burn and my heart races. But my steps are cautious, small, as if there are puddles of water or boulders in my path.

I just want to walk down the Residenzgasse and stand in my hidden corner across from the old house with the angelic-devilish gate and wait. With anxious heart, paralyzed body. Will I see her today? The marble devil in the foliage above the gate looks straight at me, winks by closing the wicked eye – his left of course, it is no accident that *sinister* means *left.* He winks and the foliage moves in turmoil around his face and horned forehead.

A sudden flash, a page from a schoolbook. A fifteenth-century print of Vlad the Impaler – Romanian hero, defender of the faith, Vlad Tepes, alias Dracula. In moments of fear it is always there, haunting me. I see the whole page, butter-spot and all, translucent. I see Vlad – his enemies impaled through their bellies around him – enjoying his dinner. Heads rolling, hatchets, hands, feet in disarray, and the dark face of Vlad, moustache covering his nonexistent upper lip. Will I hang on that lance...my stomach turns. I ask permission to leave the classroom.

I swoon when my eyes meet hers. She has seen me for days, standing there. Now she is just at my level, our eyes locking. Green they are and wide apart, slit; almost without eyelashes, just a line of pink around them, and a black, black hole in the centre. I hear Vlad-Dracula, the devil above the gate, call to me: *You'll never sleep again. Never.*

As dark as the hell in the green pools of those eyes is her mocking voice: "What's your name, stranger? Are you a statue made of stone, or something with blood in its veins?" And she laughs, striking my face with the back of her hand.

"Max," I say, and run now, no boulders or water puddles holding me back. I am propelled by fear, the deep embarrassment of having been caught at my forbidden thoughts. Or caught stealing hot peanuts. Unarticulable, indefensible thoughts. Robbed of the illicit pleasure of watching through keyholes. Of waiting. There they were: eyes and voice, materialized out of the ether of my wishes. Seen and heard, real. Will I never sleep again? *Macbeth shall sleep no more.* At fifteen all things are forever. The day stretches into no end and when sleep comes, it comes like murder.

I STAND IN MY CORNER, under the eavestrough-overhang, early. Whistling, watching, waiting for Süssel. To go to the mountain with her, if she can or will. Lights go up in her west window and my blood beats against the temples. I whistle an ancient tune of the German peasant wars, Florian Geyer leading the mob. It is ours. I whistle and Süssel replies with a third, fourth, or fifth up. And I know, no matter how much time she'll take, it will be joyful, just to hold those long fingers in mine. Going down to the village Rosh first, then always a different road up the holy Cecina.

Cecina is holy as all mountains are holy, wooded to the top, water springing from every crevice, trolls, elves, and lovers lurking in dark branches, and clearings suddenly upon you with a sun as loud and yellow as a trumpet.

And we talk as only Süssel knows how. Of her Jerusalem, her longing to go there. From Passover to Passover: next year in Jerusalem, in dead earnest. Some rescue will come from there, she says, from the dry sands, the emaciated seer. New texts will be found. They reside there, eons pass in the sands, they keep the past. She says, "Max, our common roots are there. Christianity comes from there. It is ours as well as theirs. We know too little. We have to go there to learn. I will. And if not I, you must."

We return late that evening. Foolish and dangerous. "You're my fiancé, maybe husband-to-be, who knows?" she says, turning her cheek toward mine, without kissing. And I fly with the angels in the carved old gate, unearthbound. Back in my corner, I watch her turn the key and close the gate.

There is heaven on earth for seven days. A total vacuum of power from above, a disorientation. Eating whatever is around, not going to market, no work routine, no colleagues, no envy. Suspended, hanging in the air. Family a little closer, but not much talk. Eyes and bodies meeting, questioning wordlessly. My mother serves the soup. Seven around the table, roasted chicken, potatoes. No fresh vegetables, no fruit, because the peasants haven't come to town.

A walnut torte. Yes, walnuts, there are always walnuts. This is walnut land. Walnut and chestnut trees grow to heaven here. I'm the greediest of them all for sweets. "Max," my father calls, "come have my share." But I don't want any walnut torte, and I do not hasten, as I would at other times, and we all disperse. I walk to the Residenzgasse, feeling the sweet abolition of value, duty, and moral obligation. A wait is in the air. A promise of things to come.

These were my seven days. Süssel sometimes replied to my Florian-Geyer whistle, and sometimes she did not hear or see me in my corner. Came out of the gate, with a fast step. Wearing silk stockings, flesh-coloured, patent-leather shoes, a new suit, the costume of Pepita, salt and pepper, her red hair restrained by a fashionable *herrenhut* in brown velvet, an emerald cravat matching her eyes. Up the Residenzgasse towards the Archbishop's Residence, purposefully stepping out. I followed at a safe distance, along the Moorish wall towards the "Heights of Hapsburg," the garden behind the Archbishop's Residence. And down to the birchwood, where she sat down. If next to anyone, I could not tell. Fearful, I imagined the birch branches reaching down, the hazelnut rods thickening, and a single fir turning into a black man.

Ashamed of my watching-at-the-keyhole ways, yet comfortable in them, like all criminals a single-farer, a lawmaker of his own realm, I forgive and postpone. And I lie, with a twisted double-mind that sees, smiles, and does not wish to change. Lies rescue, lies help: *She was alone, the birches were in the way, she was with a girlfriend, I did not see clearly, the light was wrong.* A keyhole has a strange distorting shape. It throws shadows, covers movements, makes arms look like legs. *Did they kiss? No, no, there was no one there. She is my fiancée.*

Step by step, looking down at my feet, pushing the pebbles, I would not retrace my steps. Wavering between shame and certainty, I forced myself to go on. I took the west walk behind the Residence, to the promontory to the west-southwest that overlooks the whole southern river valley. The dust of high summer shimmering, making arrows out of sun rays, pure beaten gold! And I came to rest without eavestrough or other cover. No mountain ranges promising shelter, no cool caves to hide in. Just the open sky facing me, and Süssel in her stepping-out long silken leg, intent and purpose in every movement. All done up in front of her armoire trifold-mirror, where she looked at herself with the conviction of invincibility.

I know her now. I know her two-piece costume from the expensive Herrengasse shop, the tailors of the upper-handful. And her hubris, her confidence in conquering whom she chooses. She walks with me, holds my hand, laughs at my looking for symbols – shortcuts, signposts for turns in thought or road. She laughs at me, mocks me, strikes my face with the back of her hand. Endearingly, she says; mockingly, I would say. I don't dare kiss those lips for fear of the back of her hand, so I just stand there, eyes welling over, full of her beauty. Others will kiss her, others who dare.

Early the next morning, whistling my medieval tune, I approach the old house, and she is out there before me. She stands in my corner waiting, wearing nothing but a blue coat over her nightgown. She leans against the inner wall, on the few stones that I have built up to have a better view; she whistles back before I reach her. She gives me a mocking hug, brings my face close to hers, and I divine the pressure of her tiny breasts through the summer coat. It seems as close to a kiss as we will ever come. She jumps down from the pedestal and simply says: "Max, I've seen you. Don't follow me. No one will conquer me. It is I who conquer.

"I am the one who chooses, Max. I have promised to marry you, and truly, no one could love me with such perseverance, but

I just may not. We have the same rhythm when walking, I swing to your tunes. You're tall and thin, one hand of mine can hold your waist. I love your skies, your joy to *know,* it's all over your face. And above all, I know you'll always be here for me. But I have wild ways. I'm my own master and I won't be possessed by anyone.

"Look, the sun is almost above the horizon. From here in your little private cave you can see the whole eastern side of the old house, the three tall windows on each floor going up in flames. The image sears my heart and binds yours. But Max, I can only give you what I can, the rest is mine alone. Don't follow me, or you'll be hurt." And she looks up to the old gate, towards the marble devil. "You know, I've never noticed him before, just the angels in the gate. But today, from here, I suddenly see him. Is he winking at me? Is the foliage around him moving?"

Then, with a whispered warning, *do not follow me,* she tightens the blue coat around her waist and runs across the street to the stone house, the gate shut banging behind her. I remain rooted. It's hard to get caught.

WE SIT ACROSS FROM EACH OTHER in a café, for the first time, on a Sunday afternoon. It is the last time that I will see her until the day that she will appear like Gabriel with a paper flag to save me from the hands of bullies. The afternoon late-August sun has made us too drowsy to go walking, even in the treed and foliage-intertwined public gardens on the southeast end of town.

She tells me, "Wait here Max, just for a few minutes. I'll run up and pretty myself a little, and we'll go to a café, sit across a table from one another. We've never done that, we're always running up the mountain, lying in the fields, eating picnics at the river. Let's just be civilized and go to a café!" We will go to Kucharczyk, the Polish sweet-pastry shop. Nobody bakes like the Poles – such a fanciful mixture of Vienna tradition and Slavic flair! A real *konditorei,* a café with newspapers – one of them the *Vorwärts,* the social-democratic daily of her typesetter-uncle Saul. *Kaffee mit Schlag,* all the coffee heaven imaginable, whipping cream, a glass-covered counter, plates heaped with walnut crescents, Moor's-heads resting on paper doilies – right off the Herrengasse.

She steps out of the old gate, as she does for others, smart, black-and-white print hanger dress bound around her neck with black ribbon, pumps in black inlaid with white. High heels, flesh-coloured silk stockings, seam at the back. For the first time she dresses for me. My heart sinks: I feel the parting. Yet she is doing it for me, now. Until now I have only known her in heavy hiking boots, her hair tied up high, carrying a rucksack to climb our Cecina, to our meadows.

Grown up, she steps out, locking the gate. She takes my arm, and we head toward the Corso. Past the Evangelical church, the two chestnut-cerberus watching the entrance, their candle-blooms extinguished now, past the University grounds, through the Ring-platz, the centre square, city hall on the right, and up into the Corso-Herrengasse. Gauche and awkward, I try to step into her rhythm, but it is she who adjusts to mine. The childish joy of walking in step and the corporeal nearness of someone so desirable, so unachievable, makes me feel all men are watching my swinging arms and unsure gait. Uncomfortable in my unaccustomed self-consciousness, I stiffen. Yet, having outwitted all the world, I wear her like a medal on my lapel, colours flying.

Around the corner, to Kucharczyk. I wonder if she will

remember this August afternoon? If not for me, perhaps she will for the late summer sun. "I'm born of a burning August sun," she says. "There is no cheating or hiding behind sweet shadows." She confronts everything head-on, and shows little pity for the suffering creature. I am the one who hides in every hollow, to watch, contemplate, and doubt. Jerusalem is for you, I think, not for me.

Stepping into the café, we are warmed by the roast-almond-coffee-vanilla aroma, welcomed by smiles. People lean across the tables, whispering gossip or love. The whole room is pink and cream, lamps and curtains, everything. We find a table in a darkish corner against the wallpaper roses. We order Moor's-head *Krapfen* – a chocolate-covered sweet bread, and hot chocolate with cream. But I cannot eat. I watch her across from me with intense joy, watching her greedy bite, whipping cream oozing. She wipes her mouth with the back of her hand, not having noticed the linen serviette. I love her desperately, knowing, fearing, that this silken-leg elegance is a kind of parting gift. I reach over the table to touch her hand, but mine is hot-wet and I take it back quickly.

"Oh Max," she says, "do eat your Moor's-head, it is extraordinary today. Come, the world hasn't ended. I can see you're on your famous tragic bent. Your eyes are watery, your hands are sweaty, you're not saying much." And she says something else. She calls me her "stalker-voyeur-lover."

"You live your life in hiding, looking through keyholes, watching Moritz's life. You're a watcher, a postponer of life, you find words to avoid living. You stand in that awful corner among the ants, the mice, the spiders, you stand in the rain beside that awful Mr. Schultz's house." The hated Mr. Schultz, the school principal. He once made Süssel sit on his lap, when she was just seven years old, telling her he was the honeybee and she the nectar, so she would let him kiss her. And she ran to her mother, who said, "Hush my child, it is nothing, don't worry." I remember that story so well!

What else did she say, across from me at Kucharczyk's, that laced my hot chocolate with a drop of vermouth so bitter that even now my mouth feels dry? She took my hand, held it a moment, our knees touching under the table, and she looked up from her cake, her green eyes meeting mine.... She said: "Yes, I know I said I'd marry you, when I was fifteen it was nice to think I had a fiancé. I promised to marry you after you pulled me out of the river, but Max, it was kid's stuff."

Have you ever seen a black August sun? The world stopped. But Süssel just held my hand a little longer, then went on: "Max, do something for me. When you're grown up, go to Jerusalem. Something portentous will come out of that desert. We will find the scripts there, that tell us that we are one tree, that show the deep Judaic roots of Christianity. The scripts will be found, they're waiting there. I don't know if I'll ever go there, but you, my sweet friend, you will. For me." And she squeezed my wet trembling fingers and I felt the sudden pressure of her knees around mine. My spirits rose and I promised, "Süssel, I will go there for you."

I took her home the way we had come, past the church, the Ahi fountain gleaming with a last ray of the sun. I saw her flit inside the old gate, a turn of her head, a shimmer of red in her hair, a smile for goodbye, and I knew, love is forever.

Süssel

Fetters Fell

BROTHER FELIX, NO LONGER THE BIG FAT BROTHER, but handsome and beauteous now: *Hübsch und Schön.* My Felix grown to a svelte, slender-in-shoulder-and-hip young Apollo. Hair: a brown-gold wave lying loose around his ear and neck – daring for the time. Eyes set far apart, with my father's upward-turned obliqueness, almost free of eyelids, gold-brown eyes against the clearest white.

Out of all that fat grew a chiselled jaw and a magnificent head set haughtily on his shoulders. His shirt open, his hairless body set off by shirts dyed a vivid citron-yellow. Felix and the serving maids, boiling big cauldrons in the cellar kitchen to get the right colour. He stayed in the cellar for hours on end, the maids catering to his every whim. Poor, sweet Ileana, who taught him and his classmates whatever they knew about – call it love. And who was made to suffer when it was discovered.

"You will leave the house!" my mother shouted. And all of us crouched in despair, recalling the Romanian horror-lore that we loved and feared. "It is enough of walled-in wives of madmen."

Ileana, her golden breasts shaking with sobs: "Where am I to go?

My parents' house has burned, there is no crop planted, there will be no harvest, not even squash lying in our fields. Where am I to go?" My handsome and beauteous brother, who had lain upon her breasts from early boyhood, begged Mother to let her be, at least through an unforgiving winter, and she was allowed to stay for a while. After she left, Marusja took over her duties in the house.

I loved Ileana, for the rhythm of her body. So often as a child I had wished to have been born a boy, to enter that body, felt jealous of the calm and glow on the young men's faces after they had lain with her.

As Felix grew into manhood, we became enamoured with each other. No, we won't marry anyone! – we'll have lovers on the side, we said. We'll make a house of the two of us, pool our inheritance, build a mansion, and – first of all things – a ballroom the size of Versailles. With mirrors, bright and modern, light from all sides doubling and quadrupling in their silvery surfaces. A glass dome to reveal the sky above, clouds passing in sweet or monstrous shapes. Parquet laid in diagonal stripes of old oak, shiny honey, to recall our grandfather's floors, our endless hours spent tossing jacks along the boards.

We would have windows looking west. We would sit on the mythical Heights of Hapsburg, spinning yarns of interweaving dreams threaded with childhood's chosen pearls. There we sat holding hands, chaste, yet puerile and guilty. Felix, too, like our inlaid-honey floor, is of honey, dark gold in his yellow shirt, with pants of maroon plush. I touched the fabric and I shivered with fear.

We were at the end of the twenties, and taking on the spirit of the thirties: a sensuous lightness of heart, Versailles-castles in the air, and dance floors. And we danced. A new wave of *crêpe geor-*

gette, dresses in kerchiefs, triangles, like fairy-fringes hanging, the belt at the hip. My hair was still long, hennaed, curled up on top – the equal of my mother's. My muslin dress both concealed and revealed, falling from the open neck past the knee. Beige. The new beige, sometimes a hint of grey in it, the famous *greyge.* So Felix and sister went dancing. Felix, a swish-swing in his hip, yet with the elegant gaucheness of the upper class, was the most loose, yet most intimate, dancer to hold. My left arm rested lightly on his velvet coat, his movements intimating, not commanding, a unison of rhythm.

My brother Felix: the girls went wild. I held on to my possession with a ferocity I never showed later with any lover. This was different; I was his also. He looked and I turned, swirled in two-step, three-quarter waltz, or the four-step polka. No, we will not marry. As my eyes rested on his perfection, I would hear the upper notes from *Der Nussbaum:* A walnut tree is greening.... Schumann. Unforgettable.

We had to practise the piano, as children, for hours on end. But as we grew to be dancers we also became singers. Just as yellow as his shirt was the sun in his voice – bright yellow, cutting to the heart. My grandfather's house was a haven, the Bösendorfer grand piano displaying duty and the virtue of art; there we sat after sunset. The Archbishop's Residence darkening, the sky gone, we gathered, the two of us. We played and sang, our parents hushing away, proud of their success. We went through page after page, four hands, or Felix on the keyboard and my mezzo voice. Slowly others joined us for a song – trios, quartets, omitting the parts that were too difficult. And then, we ran down the three floors into the garden to the walnut tree. The old shelter, grown now to full height.

Where will we build our castle? Behind the Archbishop's Residence, of course, facing the western sun. We're rich, we'll buy the whole wooded garden behind the Moorish walls and build our house. Good night, Felix my brother, I said, and I ran fast, before I kissed him.

When Ileana left, Marusja took over her duties in the house. Marusja, a svelte little Ukrainian woman, lived in the cellar with her husband Dmitry. Illiterate Marusja was gentle and soft-spoken, so different from the brutish, loudmouthed Dmitry. But Dmitry helped Marusja clean house and polished the brass handles on all the doors as if his life depended on it. The handles shone, reflecting any glint that came their way. But we never knew when Dmitry was in a good mood and when he was sullen, sulking or cursing Marusja. She giggled, laughed it away. "He loves me," she said, and ignored him. "Look, Süssel, how he loves me! But what would you know, a young spoilt rich girl!"

Before Ileana left, I would watch Ileana and Marusja sitting together, their heads close in complicity. The complicity of the servant who knows the master, plotting a little, reviling him or her with impunity. But also, like Marusja, I took a shivery delight in Ileana's Romanian horror-lore. The peasant-lore – medieval or coming from God-knows-where, inherited old fears, stories of walled-in women – excited Marusja's imagination. She pressed Ileana: "Tell us the Manole story – or the Impaler-Vlad-story –" Or on another occasion: "Ileana, come to the bench under the walnut tree tonight, my wonderful Dmitry is out in the fields helping his father...."

I envied them. I was excluded from their intimacy, being both the master and a Jew. But, wickedly, I played up the master role, making them do things for me, in revenge for their intimacy. You haven't polished my shoes, Ileana, or I would say, I'm cold Marusja, we need more firewood from the cellar. I made them run and do unnecessary things just to show them who paid the piper. It was wicked and they did not like it. Especially Ileana, who was a domineering character herself and rebelled in her serfdom, she got back at me with curses mainly, heavy Romanian curses that only she knew how to utter between the teeth. But she knew her place on the rung. So different from Marusja, who outwitted her masters with girlish giggles, as she did her many brothers or her jealous Dmitry. Who would sometimes want her *now,* and would raise his voice to her, so that I trembled.

"He loves me. This is how he shows it, I would not know otherwise." And she took his fist-in-the-face, when he was drunk, justifying it with the same argument. "He loves me." And perhaps he did, but to a Jewish girl, who does not know about fists and obeys a mere look from her father, it was strange indeed.

"Don't interfere," my mother said. But I ran down one day, when the noises from the cellar were echoing through the staircase, and saw Marusja's smashed face. I felt indescribable rage. *I'll kill Dmitry. I'll kill him.* He was snoring on their bunk bed, sleeping out his drunkenness. An indelible picture, to return life-long.

Marusja too loved Felix. Every woman did. She, too, stood in the wash-kitchen with the other maids to dye his shirts the right yellow or please him with a flirtatious turn at the waist. But, she would not have dared kiss Felix or permitted any other intimacy. Not with a husband like Dmitry, whose property she considered herself to be. Of course, there was always "upstairs and downstairs" talk, putting blame on the other party, the "downs" doing the "ups'" dirty work, noting their undercurrents, intrigue, and small jealousies, taking comfort that in spite of all that dressing-up in silk and satin, we were the same as they were. Bound to necessity. And forgiving in the end one another as the day follows the day before.

MOTHER AND FELIX. Two of a kind. To beauty born, of a playful disposition, they laughed at the same things. Both found the world a piece of theatre. Theirs was a love without terror, without domination, looking for sweet raisins to pick from the cake. The two of them read Goethe, Mörike, and Mathias Claudius. They read the French, Mother better than Felix, Baudelaire and Rimbaud, for the longing for the far away. She wanted Felix's voice and let him read aloud, corrected him here and there. Theirs was a love without matter, commuted, distilled into beauty. As Felix danced with me and by the slightest change of step I moved to his wish, so Mother answered a throw-away line or hint with a cascade of laughter. They were at one in disposition, with a taste for the trivial, the decorative. Two enchanted children.

"Read," she said, "read to me." Oh, she loved that light voice, yellow-tinged like his shirt. The opening of *Faust,* prologue in heaven, the chimeric figures entering. She often urged him to read it aloud, in the evening before night fell. But most of the time it was banter, idle chat and slightly derogatory joking about the maids – the Slavs, the Romanians. They chatted about these Slavs with earth in their fingernails, the Slavs, the golden souls. Well, some killings, when they're drunk, the knife sits loosely when in vodka. Mother and Felix, exchanging servant stories, talking with gentle disdain of these poor creatures bound to the ground, or as the Romanians said, glued to the soil. The word they used was *lipit.*

Mother: "Yet there is distinction among those Slavs, there is separateness. Poles are Poles, they are proud of their image as master craftsmen." Of course, mother's only knowledge of Poles was from the working people around her.

Felix and Mother, with their assuredness, their superiority of speech, clothes, poetry, and perfume, and the blueblood money gives, made light of life; their derision an escape. Drudgery, work, the mundanity of every day, was not for them. Yet when the rules changed they accepted them with the same shrug of the shoulder. There was pain, of course, just as intense as mine or Father's, but also that shrug, a symbol of their superiority.

It was supreme theatre working its way inward. Felix and Mother adopted stances to distance themselves, creating private enclaves, fortresses to withstand onslaught. Felix's, and my father's too. Felix loved my father, but love was fissured by enforced authority, male domination of a young male, his inheritor to boot. There was strife: "You're not studying, Felix, you are playing the piano, you are playing Schubert and Brahms. You are lying on the sofa, Felix, reading Karl May, Winnetu on the warpath." And Father tearing all his penny-books pamphlet-nonsense through the middle – just violently tearing them, to keep from launching into Felix. "These are not my books – they are an exchange-loan from my friends." To no avail.

I trembled in the corner. The voice of my father had none of Felix's gold, just straight iron, when he spoke to Felix. Not when he spoke to me, and certainly not when he spoke with strangers or servants. And never with beautiful women. I heard my father – rarely, but I heard him – court other women at a party. Little girls recognize fast and with certainty a sound, a shade of tone, that has not hit their sensibilities before. Felix had a respect for Father's overwhelming strength, his lack of self-pity, and his work. No one ever saw Felix cry. He doesn't and Mother doesn't. Not in front of anyone, at least. Except, yes, I once heard them, both Mother and Father, in an undervoiced but intense exchange:

Mother: Felix found this letter. Here it is.

Father: What letter?

Mother: An anonymous letter.

Father: What about? Anonymous letters ought not to be read. They're garbage mostly, people seeking to blackmail.

Mother: The letter gave an address and a time of day.

Father: What of it?

Mother: For me to go there. It is in the lower part of town. Not respectable.

Father: To do what there?

Mother: To find you in the arms of Marie. One of your workers in the plant. You were there, the letter says, and you are there at certain hours on certain days and you are never home or at the lab at these hours, on these days.

Father: Are you spying on me? Let's not continue. I hear the children come and I must go to the lab.

Felix and I, we both heard them. We heard her pent-up shout, a sob, and we both stormed the bedroom door into her arms. And I had always thought he wanted only her, her fabulous sensual hands, her flame-hair.

As a child, fleeing into their bedroom chased by hat stands and advancing walls, by a childish terror universal yet unexplained and never the same, fleeing into their bedroom to be safe, I always thought: *He wants just her, her beautiful hair, like a blessing, a waterfall.* So I thought. And then we saw the letter. Felix took it from the postman, though it was addressed to her. Awkward writing, bad spelling, in pencil and pen. He broke the seal, convinced there was danger. I advised him not to tell Mother; he thought differently. How difficult, how complex, the world for a young girl, with buried passions, inherited fears of things unknown! A bewildering world. No easy order or transparency, no simple laws to govern it. I was approaching puberty. As a very, very little girl, on pious grandmother's hand, I had lived easier.

Well, Felix and Mother. She had to know, he said. But of course it was blackmail, by the rooming-house matron, we found out. And we never regained our innocence. We also knew Katja, a lovely German woman, from the village Rosh, just a twenty-minute walk down the Schillerpark. She was his worker, and a good one. Willing to her boss, who was like no other boss – humane, generous, and discreet. Not to call it secretive; but all of that. We avoided going to the lab, for a long while. But finally, wanting to work there, we just looked the other way. Who knows who else had shared Father's off-hours? Since gentlemen of that time owed no account to anyone.

Fetters fell from my wrists. I was seventeen. A new feeling of strength, of self and separation, loosened the fetters of religion, law, and stricture. A pious, singing child, adoring God, loving the commandments, the Law. The holy tongue, the Hebrew, had no workable use for me of any sort but jubilation. Grandmother Esther would take my hand and we would walk down to the Jewish quarter, the poor old Turkish quarter, where Turkish baths, old fountains, and low sunless houses huddle close together, doors giving straight onto the cobblestones. Onions and garlic and the smell of poverty – it was a different world from uptown, where water came out of faucets, stoves were of blue-green or burnt-orange ceramic, or of silvery-grey slate, and houses were tall with stone stairways.

This was a world of poverty and singing. A world unworldly with its own tongue. A tongue of wonder and magic, describing nothing real, no table, no spoon, no shoe, no bed, no stomachache or toilet, no doll or game or ball. A tongue of sound, of herald, of glory. "Sing, oh sing, my child, if you sing the holy words you will be strong and grow to be a beautiful woman." Esther holds my hand and takes me to the court of her rabbi. We sit in the outer court with all the other women, not allowed into the hallowed presence with his disciples, except on special occasions. I had longed for this moment with such intensity that when the day came – and it was before *Simchath Thorah,* the day the children of Israel received the Law through the hands of Moses – I fainted. But the rhythms of the chants sank deep into my heart.

They were about beauty, delight beyond measure, they were about the grandeur that I, a little girl of no significance, was allowed to touch.

Against the wishes of my father, a modern man, Esther took me there. And we always left home like accomplices, ready for crime, before Father could forbid it and hold us back.

It is the Word. The commanding power of the Word. It speaks of something we can't comprehend. It speaks in sounds that mark us, that brand us, with a knowledge as intimate as conception. It gives us a self, a belonging, distinct. Fertile chains, Hebrew sounds link in mysterious underground ways, and run to lead you to God within you. A little girl understands this. She sings with abandon, of knowledge beyond knowing. It is the Word. It prepares and strengthens her soul for bitter days to come.

Yet at seventeen fetters fell from my wrists. There was a smashing of the old, the familiar, the conformist. A doing-away with dos and don'ts, with eyes spying, noting, reporting deeds and misdeeds. Eyes, all-seeing, once revered, dismissed now. A stepping-out of the mystical hold, rabbis and their courts, true and false. Another road of glory lay before me, stretched like a silver band. A fearless self stepping out of her father's house. A different soul, another body.

In the huge mirror of the armoire – carved walnut, Venetian glass – I saw myself for the first time. A different body faced me, a stranger of such beauty it stopped my heartbeat, my breath. Flaming red hair fell down to my shoulders – my mother's coveted hair, green eyes, almost slits – not entirely my father's, and a hue of apricot on cheeks and throat. Limbs grown slender, a shapely leg above an ankle as subtle as the wrist. Someone else's body and soul. And it showed its fury. It demanded silk stockings and patent leather pumps, tailor-made *Herrenfaçon* – costumes in stripes of white on navy blue or grey on grey, like pepper on salt. It demanded a *Herrenhut* in brown velvet and an Italian silk cravat for the shirt-cut blouse. It demanded and received. A rich man's daughter simply had to go to town and order and choose. And she stepped out on to the Corso in the Herrengasse – it seems to be all about *Herren,* or masters, in German – with a fast, self-assured step. *Jeunesse dorée* at her feet.

The break came so suddenly, born from the passing image in the mirror and the glass of the bookcase, unleashed a strange inner desire, that had lain submerged and unsuspected. It was a bold breaking-loose, a smashing of the chains. No need for shelter, tribe, or fold, the world was mine.

"Dead, dead, dead!" I screamed, throwing books, Greek or Latin, across the dining-room table, where conjunctions and declensions were my daily fare. "It's dead, all dead." And I took all three floors of the stone stairwell in a wild dash to freedom. I ran like mad up the Residenzgasse to my solace-garden. It lay beyond the Archbishop's Residence, on the very hill, but jutting out far into the plateau above the valley. The Garden – the "Heights of the Hapsburgs," or *Habsburg's Höhe* – hugged the back wall of the Moorish Residence of the Archbishop. Full of blue-black pine, mouldy creeping juniper, lurking trolls. Gently trembling woods of aspen, where every twig tossed and turned, the air shimmered, and even sun rays seemed to move, seemed to change grey-green leaves to gold. And finally my birch wood over the abyss. A sharp precipice and a wide look into the river valley, where I came to rest.

He was sitting on one of the backless benches, overlooking the intercutting surfaces of land against land and banks against the river. I sat next to him. Fortyish and balding, Germanic looking but short-necked and somehow stunted, he looked up as I sat down.

Like my summer lover, he was there, every time. But he spoke not of Jesus, of unearthly goodness, of heaven on earth, of the orthodox, the true faith, but of Johann Sebastian, as he called Bach, his church. The glory of the opposing, counterpoint, joining sounds in harmony. A tongue, a world. Speaking through itself directly to the heart, he says, with no one in between, no rabbi, no priest. And he draws the running lines on his sketch book. Of course I could read music, I learnt it from the age of six, but the heaven of Johann Sebastian I learned from my handsome "lad born out of a tear." Eyes of beauty! Prince, I thought, Prince. And next day and the next and the next, I went there at the same hour and found him there.

Fat Frumos din Lacrima, "the beautiful lad born from a teardrop," the Romanian Prince Charming. No white horse, just born from a tear. And born from a tear he was, my prince. He had lost his wife to mental despair: a beautiful thing she had been, who ate oranges with peel, without feeling the sting of volatile oils in the orange skin. One day she went up into the attic, put herself into a trunk, and closed the lid. He took me to this flat of his, where he had lived with her for ten years, the rooms marked with her Berlinese taste. And I gave myself to him with such savage abandon as if to God. It was new to him. He had to both learn and teach.

I saw a man's body fully naked for the first time. *Uncovering nakedness is possession. The sight alone carries the unconscious power of marriage;* the sin of Lot and his daughters. A taboo of that force, deeply embedded in a Jewish girl's consciousness, empowered by purity and sin, needs no worldly controls.

I lay next to my lover, frightened and still. But like a prayer before a meal, it was a savoured single moment, for I knew the onslaught to come, from within me, from my ardour to search and gain a world forbidden. A Christian world, feared and desired. I looked into the blue of my lover's eyes, at his squat, fat-around-the-middle forbidden body, and my heart went out to him with such a fury I thought I would never feel again. So I kissed his mouth and hairy chest and asked him gently to cup, to hold, to kiss my breath, my giving body. "Do not worry, it won't hurt," he said. But it did. And I know now that all of us are born from a tear.

Days and days and days of taking and giving our bodies. In search of the skill to unlock the unknown. And then days of rest, distended, and questioning of a very different sort. Of "Who are you? Where are you from?" Of Mother, Father, love, or first prostitute? What God?

"Oh please, do not come to me with your Jewish arrogance of the abstract, the unseen, the not-to-be-fashioned God," he says. "We reach Him the way we reach Him, by the myriad ways of the imagination. Everything will do. Why this disdain of wood and clay and object? It is not what it is. We transform this object, imbue it with meaning, wishes, and magic." And he holds me close, for fear I will cry. "I once stood in front of a young Mexican boy viewing a Pietà," he continues. "Christ across his mother's lap, the head reclining, the left arm dangling elegantly, as if alive. He stood for a long time, then slowly approached the body and touched the tips of Christ's fingers, stroking the hand finger by finger, the palm, the wrist, up the forearm and upper arm, and then returned to touch his own fingers, the palm of his hand, and so on, touching all of Christ's fallen body and his own, a deliberate, intimate, slow stroking. It took all morning. I walked out of the church *de la Guadeloupe* in a trance. I had seen God."

My lover looks with tenderness at me, blue-eyed: "I know, you Hebrews, you named Him. Yes, it is the Word, the word that made Him, the word that linked thought, commentary and the famous Hashem, the name you-mustn't-take-in-vain. Your God is the Voice, your desert-prophets hear it and you tremble in fear and adoration. The word, the sound. It speaks, and it is the distinguishing mark of humanity, our divine mark. Yes, *this* it is. But God is multifold. His manifestations are as varied, coloured, and complex as is our ability to grasp them. My Mexican youth heard his God through touch and so, Sweetie, the Word is not the only way there is.

"My sweet child, I hope – oh, just forgive me. But let me, please, think it through a little: You revere the pure, the spiritual, I know that," he says. "But why this disdain of the material? Don't *you* take the letter for an icon, don't *you* touch the holy books with reverence?

"Sweetie, come, you're clever. Look at the Lord in Johann Sebastian. The language he uses is yours and mine. For us to cherish. It speaks of God. Sound speaking, sound touching the eternal without, beyond words of sorrow and elation. What place for arrogance, then? Come, sweet child, let's sing." And he takes a two-part invention and we join our voices, reading it from the page. More, more, and one more time! All arrogance leaves me. Such rest! Such comfort! My mother stands before me. I am her voice, her marvellous correct intervals of third, fourth, or fifth, as she sings, sitting on the edge of my childhood bed before nightfall. "Sing, my sweet Jewish child," he says, and his baritone-coloured tenor meets my mother's warm voice.

It seems that everything that is beautiful is walnut. The broad shiny leaves set opposite one another, with a seventh leaf to crown the fan. The branches of our walnut tree, heavy with green fruit to the top, sheltering us children beneath. Leaves, thick with wax, shining, polished by rain. The tree so big it took three children to hug the trunk.

His piano is of shiny brown walnut, the round swivel piano stool of darker walnut, rubbed smooth with time. A turner's loving handiwork. One can swivel it up, high up on its pivot. It is his childhood piano stool, he tells me, from when he was three years old in Berlin. The joints, filled with dust, are hidden in the form, absorbed by it. I sit free of shame and memory of shame, my nakedness on its inner hollow, and move it gently on its axis, facing my lover, stretched out with Morpheus, God of sleep, in his arms. Stilled and wishless. He is not beautiful, my prince born from a tear. I sit on his piano stool, warm walnut under my inner thigh. And memories of heated wood against my little girl's body, gentle strokes with fingers and palm to find the yet unknown, take my breath away. And I go back to him, into his bed, and take his sex with tender hands into my mouth to wake him.

I see him everywhere, with the rise of day, at breakfast, at the laboratory table where I have just started my apothecary's apprenticeship – in any free moment and in moments stolen from work. I run out to find him. He may just be entering the bank where he works, or coming out of there. A little glimpse of him I take away, as a gift from destiny. And I watch him walk away with his dancer's step. Short, but slim in the hip, he moves with an inturned toe, his well-ironed crisp trousers falling upon his fawn-brown shoes, straight into the centre of it, *Lege artis,* Berlin. This what he is to my seventeen years: Berlin. The great German world, of freedom, letters, boulevards, young witty sharp tongues, frivolity, and the street eroticism of cabaret. Standing under his window, I wait. I see him chatting with his colleagues, living his life. Moving away from me, with that swivel in his hip, with lightness of sole; I watch him cross the square and enter a wine-and-cheese shop for lunch. I am crushed.

My father's face was earnest during dinner and I did not like it. I had passed my *baccalaureat,* the entrance exam to the university, with the highest marks in all subjects except physical education and drawing, and expected praise. Instead the mood was subdued, Father looking into his plate, raising his eyes now and then, trying to find mine. I knew his searching looks and that there was always something unpredictable to follow. Just the three of us at the table now, Father, Mother and myself; brother Felix away to study chemistry in Vienna. I did not like dinner without Felix, who brightened the table, chatted with mother, exchanged wisecracks, puns, and simple banter. It helped get me through it. Without it, as lovely as the meal was (Sunday was always special with chocolate pudding at its end), all I wanted now was to run, when I heard my father in his gentle bass say, "Come, Süssel, into the salon, we'll talk." I hated that tone. Neither did I like his *pluralis majestatis,* his royal *We,* which he used to give gravity to what was to follow. He rose, came in my direction, put his arm over my shoulders, which I always cherished, looked forward to, but not today. Mother, of course, in the know, said smilingly, "Go, Sweetheart, it's just a friendly talk, to congratulate you on your achievement." But I knew better.

We sat down on the brown leather couch. He took his time. Lavender-musk-tobacco filled the air as he lit his pipe and leaned into the cushions. He spoke in his *paterfamilias*-style that I once loved and now disliked. "Süssel, I expect you to make a pharmacy degree first and then go into post-graduate work in biochemistry. This is where the future lies. Wonderful things are happening; you, both you and Felix, live in the most exciting scientific times. I need you by me to continue my work and take it over. Of course, the choice of universities is yours. Felix chose Vienna." And father looked at me now. Full-faced, straight into my eyes. I couldn't help but think how beautiful he was. But no, he should at least have asked me what I wanted, if only *pro forma.* I knew what *he* wanted. And I had been in his pharmacy and in his lab all through my high school years, put to work, doing this or that. I knew, and Felix knew, we were being groomed for succession. The two of us, behind his back, often poked fun at his polite but clear orders, afraid to contradict him openly. But not today. I wouldn't take it from him. I had graduated, had passed my entrance exams to university with highest praise, had been honoured as the top student in science and language, and here I was being treated as a child expected to take orders from above.

My cheeks burned with anger. I lowered my voice, as he did when angry, and I said slowly and deliberately, "Father, you haven't asked me what *I* want to do."

He took my hand fast, said, "Yes Süssel, what is it you want to do, other than pharmacy?"

"Nothing else, I will do pharmacy, it interests me. I have always loved to be by you in the laboratory. But I do want to study Slavic languages on the side and this is why I will choose Prague first. Then I'll go for the French. To both universities, Strasbourg and Paris." He was satisfied, wanted to hug me, and I kissed him fast on both cheeks before I cried. His face looked pained and drawn, worried. How much or what does he know about me? I wondered. Does he look through me? I have lain with my lover. Does he know? Perhaps. Who can fool him about anything, and my passionate ways are his. So he must know. We sat a little longer, hand in hand on that brown couch, neither of us wanting to rise first, but when he took his hand from mine to extinguish his pipe and said "Good luck, Süssel my daughter," then I was free to go.

I registered by mail at the Charles University in Prague, and was accepted. I was a proper university student now. My exhilaration knew no bounds.

Prague Summer 1933

Sweet Prince,

The air was full of coal, black particles in the eyes and hair, passengers with babies coming in and going out, no place to stretch your limbs, heads falling on other people's shoulders, feet resting on suitcases, a whole night. Over Poland to Czechoslovakia. Border checks, passports.

How silly we all are. Once in possession of a seat, we are a sudden tribe, behaving like one body, conspiring to keep any new man out of our conquered territory by unanimous tribal behavior. Funny what one learns about oneself! I too, in a tribe of total strangers, keeping an old lady, desperately in need of a seat, out of the compartment. Oh, well, I better learn the ways of the world which seem to be mine. Coffee never tasted so good as it did after that nearly sleepless night.

Prague. Suitcase in hand up the Vinohrady – the vine-covered hill. I fell in love. With my youth, with the grey morning stone city. Almost my grandfather's house. A stone staircase, a façade down to the trottoir, the oak entrance carved. Old-fashioned creaky bed in a spinster's inherited quarters. And out into the streets. In love. With the big square, rectangular in shape, Saint Václav presiding, and the river. At home. Stone houses, tall, ageless, and rivers to wash the shores. Smetana and Dvorak in the streets, everywhere.

Sweet beloved Prince, not just Johann Sebastian, whose law and soul, whose majesty, we seek, our daily bread like no other, here the soul is in the streets. Here the soul is offered, breathed with the air. It jumps at you from Smetana's river and Dvorak's dance. Walking up from the train station it was there, in their faces. People hurrying to work, whistling in the Slavic minor key. A young man, calling after me *slecna, slecna*, wanting to carry my suitcase, but I hurried on, to find that room to rent from the old demoiselle with her family-heirloom feather beds.

You taught me Johann Sebastian, but I will bring you the tear you came from. The singing soul of all the nameless street singers. I know I am a bad, bad Jewish girl, my sweet old Christian lover who knows everything from counterpoint to the great message. I am a bad, bad sort. No message, not today. No message to displace the wanderings of the heart, the new web to be spun from the yarns lying in your path. Forgive, beloved, there is no one like you. But let me sing, soar. You will punish me for it when I am again sitting across from you on your childhood piano stool. You won't let me undo the buttons on your shirt, the six buttons I so love. And the four, or are they five, below the belt. I know you won't let me. You will say, "You can't have them or me." You will punish me, with stricture, blue eyes and all. And I tremble with anticipation of that punishment. But, sweet Prince, never forget you're mine. You're my master, but also my felled game. I brought you down with bow and arrow as you sat on the birchwood bench on the *Habsburg's Höhe*. I brought you down. My trophy. Will you forgive me, for I have sinned?

At night next day.

Ideologies run wild, each one with its own promise. Kill, kill! Bring the bourgeoisie down, heads must roll, blood must flow in the gutter, freedom, freedom. And all I want to do is sing.

A Russian appears at my spinster's door, asking for me. Thick accent, tongue curled in the throat. Ns like onions and Ls liquid like a lute. Speaking broken German, limping, bearded, skin of marinated olive, inner palm the silver of its elongated leaf. Frightening and handsome. Pants torn to fringes, heavy sweater, black on a hot summer's day. Eyes of coal. He enters, sits on the single rocking chair, and talks incessantly of the great world to come, of the promise. Of equality, workers' rights, being paid according to one's needs. Of Russia, the genius of the five-year plan, socialism in one single country, and the West. We must make our own revolution under the leadership, guidance, of the Great Leader.

He rocks himself, his voice and his crippled leg in rhythm. "At six o'clock in the morning be at the shed of the *Rudé Pravo,* the communist *Praguer* daily," he commands. After he leaves I find the *Inprecorr,* the forbidden International publication printed on silk-paper, on the night table. I do not go to classes, I am reading the *Inprecorr.* What a world to come! Not beyond, but here on this earth and now. With my help, and without God. My head spins. I walk on air, sweet Prince. Immense power invades my heart. I don't eat, drink, sleep, see anyone, I read the *Inprecorr.* Political, new, something to live for and die for. Russia, heaven on earth, beleaguered, to be defended. Like you, sweet Prince.

Beautiful Russia, like Christ. Russia assaulted, and my summer lover's sacrificial lamb. Never, never, my sweet Prince. It is in my power to forbid it! To see Man and all the sons of Man to hang on the cross again – no.

I am there at six o'clock in the morning sharp. We are conspiratorial comrades. There are decisions to be made and implemented. He, my limping God, names me leader of a cell of five. We are to meet regularly, devise strategy, logistics, in the discipline of the military. Can you fathom, sweet beloved, the ecstasy of the empowered? I ask myself, what power and what authority to impart it to me? Yet it was given, like the blessing of the wine on Friday night, from above. Chemistry? Who needs it? Revolution, revolution! All injustice extinguished. Women partners, full partners to men. And why would women then sell themselves in the marketplace for a farthing, if the world be just? Poverty will be abolished.

I am leading my cell, strategically placed at the worker's meeting. We are among the Škoda workers, looking for direction from the head table. My limping God presides. We clap on coded command, lead laughter, derision, insults, and shouts as ordered. The resolution gets through almost by acclamation. With the linking of arms and the singing of the "*Wacht auf Verdammte dieser Erde*" – "arise ye damned of this world" – in Czech and German, we leave. Sweet Prince, don't look at me like that! I told you the truth, but I will lie to my father. For he will say to me, you're manipulated, stupid child, by powers, interests, and money which aren't yours, you're a mannequin dancing to foreign tunes and hanging on a wire. And he will use a Ukrainian proverb: you are so, so clever that you are dumb. I must lie to him then, because never ever have I felt so free, so wonderful, and above all, so right.

Next day.

We were out last night, on the Pancrac, past midnight. Pasting slogans and leaflets on the newly-built Worker's Housing Complex. We're out in force, my own cell of five and a few more young men and women who I haven't met before. There is no need for formal introduction if you serve. There is a tacit communion of goal. It is church without the nonsense and God is one. We carry pails of flour-water paste, brushes, suitcases with materials to distribute and paste up. Exhilarated, we work silently, bonded to each other and our purpose. Individual identity dismissed, we are as one.

Have you ever seen those enormous brushes, with handles two metres long? One of us dips it into the pail of paste, the other holds the printed sheet against the wall, and with a fast stroke glues a metre-long sheet to the wall on the side of a house. Physical too, exhausting, perhaps because I am just such a pampered rich man's daughter, used to having her nose in books and totally unaccustomed to what you would call work. I am so tired and long for my forgiving mother. What if I am wrong?

Second letter from Prague. No date. In a hurry.

A sleepless night at the police station. Prostitutes, molesters, and ordinary drunks sleeping it out, next to me.

My father's daughter and your Jewish child. I have to leave the country without delay. My room has been searched – for weapons, printed material, or God knows what. The party is legal but foreign students have no rights, it seems. A policeman came with me, to collect my exam papers, pack my bags, and get me to the train. They will post this letter, they promised. I will never be allowed back into this beloved country, unless the future holds victory.

Will you take me back?

Return from Prague – Summer 1934

I have returned to the windowsill of the western window, that broad wooden almost-seat of little girls. But I look westward to the sky behind the Residence with very different eyes. I have returned from the big world out there. And my childhood world has changed. Moorish forms, the enamelled roofs, the chapel's many-layered Greek cross, are dark, catching the night. My summer lover is gone. I have been abroad. I look across to the principal Schultz's house: I expect Max to be there, to look up to my window and whistle. He was always there, in his under-the-eaves-trough cavern, waiting for me. He studies abroad now: physics, astronomy, God knows what, mathematics. No, he is not there and I am saddened by the passing of time. Yet his love will always be. I search across the street for my own childish exuberance and the longing face of Max. But I have been abroad. I have run thousands of steps up and down in the Golden City, Zlata Praha. I've run after Kafka, to all the flats he lived in as his parents moved more and more uptown. I've run across the Karlsbrücke with its crucified figure of Christ and *holy, holy, holy – kadosh, kadosh, kadosh* in Hebrew letters, above it. All covered in gold by the Jews of Prague as payment for something to the masters of the church.

And on the banks of the Moldava one can sing like nowhere else. I sat with the local toughs playing their accordions, and I went with them to the taverns to drink their Pilsner beer and to choke on Prague ham for the first time. Hard to swallow a piece of ham, it makes you tremble. But I was there for the big world. I had slept with my Christian lover, I knew what these men looked like inside their pants, and I drank and danced and ate pork.

I love the accordion. I was always forbidden to play it. *This is no instrument,* I can hear my mother say. So I grabbed one from one of the boys to show them "what I can do," smashing all commandments. Everything seemed possible, and I took it fast. I had one of my own the next day. Leaving chemistry class, I climbed to the Hradcany, sat on its steps, on the Moldava's edge. Little did it matter that there was within these Czech songs a Yiddish heart. Another youth and one more; rounds and canons we sang to my accordion.

Of course I will lie. Never tell your mother of accordions, Czech crowns thrown at you. *Like a gypsy,* she might say. One lies easily to parents. They forgive.

I've run after Rilke. A poet of the woman's heart, he knows all about us, writes in a German of delicacy, of the senses. *Das Marienleben,* the life of Mary. The Mother to be, expecting Him, the Promise in the womb. All mothers, all sons born to them. Only Rilke can write of the heart above the womb, only Rainer Maria Rilke, the Prague-German poet, who lived uptown in a world so distinctly separate from the lower-class Malá Strana of Kafka. Both now are mine. They melt into one, separate as they are.

I sing the *Marienleben* to the accordion. Of course it does not work, not with Hindemith's music, it is too heavy with clustered sound. Poor accordion – too much is asked. But I have beaten my beautiful mother's commandment, revelled in the forbidden, fetters have fallen from my wrists and ankles. I am afraid and thrilled.

So I have returned to my grandfather's old house. Returning at night for the first time, I take all stone steps in a dash. I'm a sudden stranger outside the old house, that lies silent and dark like a sphinx, in the Residenzgasse and around the corner Balschgasse. Fearing a new janitor, I hesitate to ring the nightbell. But Marusja, who comes, sleep in all movements, to open the gate, says, "Oh, it is you, Fraülein Süssel." And I hug her and am glad.

It was good to sit at the table the next day, eat walnut torte with Turkish coffee to tone the sweetness down. It was both the same and not the same. I spent a short quarter-hour with just the two of them, brother Felix still in Vienna. But I was impatient. Hardly noticing Father's delighted smile or Mother's urging me to please take another slice. I left the table with a hurried kiss and ran to find my Prince. He was not home and I stood and waited on a rainy summer day, hidden by the mighty chestnut covering the front door. Finally I saw him approach, pensive, toe inward, polished brown shoe, as is his Berlinese custom. I did not step out until his key was in the lock, then I whispered his name. He turned, delighted and perhaps not. He had aged, I thought.

Every day I came, if only for an hour, as long as the summer lasted. And I talked of all my plans. Of French, my hobby, and of my studies, of Strasbourg, the half-German-half-French city, and of Paris, and of the fact that we would part again. He loved me, with a tenderness and a care I had not remembered. "No children 'out of flowers,' as the Romanians put it," he said, smiling. And I will always love his Johann Sebastian beautiful fingers.

Strasbourg – Late summer, 1934

Thank you, sweet lover, for the argument from the other side of the barricade. And for the last kiss. It lingers still, and my lips retain the imprint of your fingers, Prince. You never thought me beautiful, but the design your left-hand index finger drew along the heart of my upper lip was of beauty that was mine. Detected by you, enriched, and given back to me. No, it will not go away. It has a memory, it sits in every cell, and I call it back as the train cradles, jerks, and sounds the locomotive. It is between lips and lips, fingers and lips, where memory lies. And I take the index finger of my clumsy left hand to redraw the line, in tears. It brings it all back, but with the tear you came out of. That pain of birth and passing, with such small time in between, flighty, ephemeral, soon gone. Having no existence other than the tip of my index finger on the upper curve.

There is wild commotion around me as the train approaches the French border, but my mind is elsewhere. You have descended, entered into me. The train has rocked your memory to life. I tremble with memory and do not understand the officer before me. He wants my passport, obviously. We enter France, but it has no reality, it is meaningless to me. I am still alongside my Prince in ritual closeness, hands knowing where to kindle, stroking on their own with learnt wisdom. Or not learnt, more guessed at and discovered to be true. Along the spine you want it, as you turn away from me to preserve the illusion of the inner self and suspend the body. To dismiss its weight, presence, and need. Just along the spine you want it. With my fingertips, down to the last of your vertebrae, where it touches the lower cleft. I love the look of your turned-away back, the side dipping into the hollow of your hip, covered by the bridge of your resting arm. Naked, almost hairless, except for a gentle hint of fur, ending in those Johann Sebastian fingers, full of sound. And when you turn to me, aroused and ready to cover my body, with hands on my face, I go before called. As the train jerks into Strasbourg station, you have not left me.

Coming from the train station, I meant to check into a students' residence for well-off girls. It had everything that I like: a small stream in front, the Ill; windows facing the river; medieval backstreets, narrow and dirty; ancient carved walnut doors, cracked in spots, speaking of the past; and handles of polished brass gleaming like displaced suns. Against the front door stood a boy, a gentle form, it seemed to me. But he forbade me entrance. "You're just a Jew, I know you," he said. "I will have you right here. I'll open my fly, pull your skirt over your head, smear you with the Aryan gift of God, and you will bear my son and be my Jewish Mary Immaculate."

I ran in terror, along the river. It was a hot summer's day, windows were open, and all the radios were blaring one voice. I heard this voice, it followed me from one open window to the next, until I reached a grassy piece of land, the orangerie maybe, and fell on the ground. That voice, German it seemed, had a rhythm, a music, so alien to my middle- and eastern-German ear that only the open fly of the gentle boy, his promise of carrying the gift of God, had meaning.

And I hear the strangest French here, so different from my schooling, with heavy weight on first syllables, French, yet German. Faces too looking like all their past, poised between murder and accommodation. Goethe loved this city. Approaching the inner town, I see the single-towered Münster. Sweet Prince, just a last kiss.

I rush to the Münster early next morning. Her staff is broken, her head is bowed, her eyes blinded and bound. She faces the triumphant Church, the crowned Queen, staff and world at her command, her brandishing cross. The two women flank the south entrance. There I stand with my spirit robbed, my dress in tatters, my head to the ground, defeated on the first morning. Robbed of my law. Read with a slant and sold as true. Is this how you want me, Prince? Bound and barefoot as the synagogue at the south entrance of the Münster?

Across the Münsterplatz those curious sounds again! I go into a café, smells of burnt beans, brewed coffee, golden croissants, French crusty baguettes, and German *Brötchen*! Chipped crockery, roosters decorating the plates, handleless coffee cups that look like soup bowls. Orange roosters climb the walls between the cracks, are embroidered on the plush seats, hang from the ceiling. How will this day begin, with a broken staff, among the roosters? I am surrounded by early-morning faces, dreamy with sleep, speech unrecovered yet. Everyone writing letters or essays around their coffee bowls, or simply staring. An eerie time of day.

I pay my bill, run through the big crystal and brass revolving door, and face the Münster from the front! All joy returns, my blend of youth, God, and rebellion, light streaming through the rosette as I enter the calm church. The coolness of stone on my soles, stilling the outcast, the stranger, embraces me. And back is the memory of Lebanon. The touch of the old carved door, as old as the sixth century. The door to the chapel of the embrace, Saint Catherine at the foot of Mount Musa. To enter that chapel-church in the desert, the Greek monk will lead you and stay with you. Very young I knew this embrace. A kind of absolute the young yearn for. A burning bush outside. Something that flowers from the day the sun shone for the first time. The Romanian-Greek monk is with me from that day on. He leads me, opening the door to the chapel; the carved-relief geometry of celestial perfection, that door of cedar with the intricate key. And my soles touch cool stone, on a burning day. All is before me: each step, each touch, recalls through sandal, naked foot, and leather the love of a mother unequalled. Recalls a morning rise to see the stone gleam red on the desert mountain; recalls the straining up the clumsy brown steps of element-rock, to reach the tiny chapel on the summit. Israel present in mind only. The law handed down, forever branded on you, my Christian lover, as well. My sweet. Hands in the hands of the other sisters untouched by men and sperm, free of the earth, looking into my eyes for communion – and down again to earth-desert-earth to live through a night of the stars above. There is no night like the desert night. There is no silence like it. And a full reality of God. If chosen or destined, God is here.

And entering the Strasbourg Münster, soles searching for the stone and receiving it, Lebanon cedar returning, and love; Sweet Prince, my day has begun well.

DIPLOMAS IN HAND, I return from France. 1936. My goals have to change. What to do? Entering the labour force, earning my rightful piece of bread, seems more like a chasm in front of me than a challenge. My undergraduate dreams of equality, women's rights, world revolution, lie around me like Master Manole's stones. After the Spanish Civil War bloodletting debâcle, there is betrayal on all sides, especially my adored Soviet Union. The swastika flies from all the rooftops of Germany. Which way, God?

So I enter my father's lab and pharmacy as hired labour. Well, not exactly – I am the boss's daughter in the eyes of my colleagues, who keep their distance. But hardened by the competition in France, where every student entering university knows as much as our graduates, I have learned to deal with clever people.

I enter the lab every morning with a grim face. Twelve hours a day of routine, the practical world, no fancy thoughts. I apply myself to do it right, because in pharmacy, no margin of error is permitted. No mistakes are allowed. At night I drop dead, my feet burning as if seared on embers. And there is not much thought beyond the working life, no goal. So far from the ideals and yearnings of my youth. I do not look any more to the other side of the street; Max is not there. I miss his love for me, as I miss my teenage years. I owned him. Could do, say, misbehave as I wished, he was there. I went after love on my own terms. Prince. This also is in the past. On my return from France – as on my return from Prague – I ran to him. But did not find him. I saw him at the Musikverein with a stately exotic lady, carrying a violin case, stood in the chocolate shop around the corner before the concert and watched them enter the hall, chatting. Too intimately, it seemed to me. And I "sat Shivah," as the Jews say, when mourning a loss. It was over. My Prince had taken the position of conductor with our small orchestra, the Collegium Musicum, and "she" was his concert master. I knew I couldn't compete, and it hurt. Not the unrequited love so much as the wounded vanity. It cut deep, and not a slick cut, but a serrated wound that stays with me as only hurt pride can. It shoots through the soul unexpectedly, provoked perhaps by a piece of cream-filled chocolate from the sweet shop. Prince always had one waiting for me at his flat, along with the first notes of a Bach partita.

But work is good. My messianic nature is returning full strength: I'm helping others, I heal wounds. Peasants enter the pharmacy and I bind their sores. I know what to do. They thank me. And one day, after two years, Max stands in front of me. Just before locking up one night, trying to close the rusty iron grill in front of the pharmacy, I feel the weight taken from my arm. We pull the grill shut together and he walks me home. He has studied in Göttingen, mathematics, physics, all theoretical. Trailing his long legs as if they belong to someone else, he succeeds in adjusting his step to mine, "to regain our teenage rhythm," he says. The rhythm is there but a little heavier, less carefree than before. But walking next to him, it is I who adjust to him now to be closer. We walk as if it were our last walk, each aware of the other. Surprise at the intensity of my joy at finding myself so close to Max makes me blush. We arrive at the gate of the old house, not having uttered a word, and we're about to say goodbye when Max starts to talk. He had no plans, other than to return to pick up his diplomas. He recounts matter-of-factly how he witnessed the November *Kristallnacht* in 1938, describing the mood in the streets, the silent terror. Among mathematicians he felt safe, he said. "Truly Süssel, they are a better lot than you ordinary scientists."

"Yes," I retorted, "I always suspected you to be of a higher species." Oh, it's good to laugh, and seeing Max again, a little taller perhaps, his neck longer and his forehead higher, but essentially unchanged, made me giggle, girlishly.

Barely touching, he turned to face me and said, "The war is almost here, we still have a moment's peace. Look out for yourself, stay well, Süssel. Never will I love anyone but you." He nearly took me into his arms. Then he left. The world had found its bearings. Max had returned.

Süssel

Down the Residenzgasse

They drive up the hilly Bahnhofstrasse, in full armour, tanks at the spearhead, to the acclaim of the Jews, who line the streets on both sides. Flowers and smiles. It is June 1940. Hitler has brought all of western Europe to its knees, and Jews tremble everywhere. The Soviets come as saviours, it seems to them. But very soon into the winter of 1940, they show their communist colours: taking all property, playing the colonial masters, making lists of the owners of businesses or of the "bourgeoisie," which could be anyone, a small cobbler in his cellar shop or an apple vendor.

This has been the Russian year, when servants, often lifelong servants in Jewish or bourgeois households, are suddenly forbidden to serve there. All are made to leave. Only Marusja and Dmitry are allowed to stay, since they are not living in the master's quarters proper. Father and Mother are disempowered, robbed of authority, Grandfather's mighty stone palace reduced to a transitory residence now. Beautiful Mother, Felix so visible in her features, takes an apron from the kitchen cupboard and cooks the midday meal. With her long filed and painted fingernails, she tries to make a fire, but it will not burn. A petrol lamp rescues her. She smiles, as she always does when we look at her, her glorious trademark. She smiles and says, "It will be good, you'll see."

It was good, but for the first time the four of us found no word to utter. I set the table for her in its usual style, with crystal, silver, porcelain, and damask. But we knew, the earth had trembled, we would never again walk on it with a sure foot. Still we were comforted by the familiar motions; the sound of cutlery against porcelain, our irritation for Father, were silently overlooked. A few familiar endearing words and we left the dishes for Mother to do, and hurried away to pharmacy and laboratory. Russians were guarding both places, waiting. They dismissed all three of us. The pharmacy and lab were expropriated but kept to inventorize. Soviet thieves, recording only half of the inventory, putting the rest into their own sacks. Thieves. "Do not tell a Russian how to inventorize," they said sternly, schoolmasterly. I understood: all dreams are at an end. And so a world broke into pieces. Dreams of socialism, of brotherhood, equal work for equal pay, and above all the end of exploitation of man by man. All things changed hands, furniture, buildings, pictures on the wall. Everything either looted or sold for bread. The *Bösendorfer* still sat there in lonely glory, for the moment.

Yet we all went about our daily lives as if all this was entirely routine. We developed a gallows humour, laughed at the mighty Russians with their proselytizing, false ideologies, and dogmatism. Stealing like schoolboys, unashamedly, right and left. Their women, party members in uniform, mannish monsters, lecturing my father.

The twelfth day of June, 1941. Almost a year to the day after the Soviet-Russian arrival, a nightmare of unfathomable dimension unfolds. Tatars ride through the town. Small horses with small riders; Asiatic soldiers with slit eyes, but speaking Russian. The town falls silent, stricken by terror. Shutters come down by soundless magic, you can feel all the eyes behind them. Doors are bolted with a gentle turn, as if not to wake a slumbering child. No dog barks, all life is stilled, as the evening descends and the stars rise. The Tatars ride, hoofs beating the cobblestones, and we tremble behind the shutters. The town, lightless and soundless, does not sleep. Big trucks join the horses in the streets, fists pound on doors, shouts of command force our doors open. And the heavy hand of God comes down on us. "Because of our sins," says my grandmother.

It was strange, disconnected, as if a dream, happening to someone else, somewhere else. Five Russian-speaking men, with five-cornered red stars on epaulettes and cap enter our house. They read from a senseless script, condemning my father, mother, and grandmother of offences no one understands. They tell Father, Mother, and Grandmother to pack what they can carry.

Their limbs still, heavy with dream, they move to collect a few things, to pack them in four-cornered sheets, and knot them at the top. "What you can carry," the soldiers repeat. And so the three of them go down, three stone stairwells of my grandfather's house, at one o'clock – or was it one-thirty? – into the dark of the night to the waiting trucks. Shouts, commands, the five men heaving Mother and Grandmother into the truck. Shouts of *Move, move, sons of bitches.* There are men and women, packed densely, body on body on the wooden benches of the trucks, their bundles beside them, their night faces showing total incomprehension.

Three days and three nights on the train tracks, city and country folk, strangers, packed into a cattle car. A cackling hen under the arm of a withered *Hutzul* woman from the high mountains, the only property she could think to take. Shouts and fists, to remove the hen from the small babushka, make my mother take the woman's defence. Mother's lens pops from the frame of her eyeglasses, is nearly lost. A fast alignment of the powerful against the helpless....

Forty or fifty in the cattle car, and just one small window, criss-crossed by iron, high up near the ceiling. The "heavies" have taken possession of the little rectangle of air and light. So fast, the bullies up there, on the shoulders of the meek – mothers, grandmothers with hens under their arms. Only two hours after the doors are bolted, they are already eating the provisions out of others' bundles. Standing, sitting, crouching in the car, everyone seeks a bit of privacy, that simplest of animal rights. In the middle of the car a square has been cut out of the floor to allow relief. But there are too many jostling bodies, and no one can hope to get there in need. So they shit where they stand, sit, or crouch – it does not matter. But one very young woman refuses, shouts, screams, beats her neighbours with her fists to push to the square. She takes a sheet from her bundle and, spying a hook in the ceiling, crawls over arms, shoulders, and heads to fix the sheet to the hook. Pulling the sheet around her to form a small chamber, she relieves herself inside. There is a momentary stillness, an echo of human dignity, while the young woman finds her way back to her own people.

Suddenly there are shouts from the uniformed guards: *Geller! No, it is Heller!* the crowd shouts back. And it was my father's name, indeed. The name shouted outside, that released him from the cattle car with his wife and mother, my mother and grandmother.

They had seen the world in those three days in a not-yet-moving train. They looked ashen when I saw them, my mother's fiery-gold hair now ash falling to her shoulders, without her tortoise-shell comb. The cascade of gold I longed for was there, but dulled into ashes, and I buried my face in it in bitter tears. A sweet, crooked smile around Mother's mouth: *It is nothing, my child, it is nothing, we're home.*

Sodom and Gomorrah, the home appeared to me. Books, money, currencies of the world from sterling to Swiss, my King-Lear-flowing-hair-in-the-storm box broken, scattered on the floor. Five officers of the Russian state police asleep on the floor, all drunk on perfume, *eau de cologne,* and any other spirits they could find. My father, he too ashen, unshaven and silent, said with utter derision, *Look at your communistic liberators, just look at them.* I understood, he spoke to me.

He too had seen the world, men in uniform doing hateful things without malice. Felt the pressure of the next-to-you, had his free will taken away. Felt the immediacy of need, accommodated it, and heeded the orders to "Move over, this is my place, you are not the rich man anymore, not here." My father's taut skin stretches over his cheekbones, shortening the slits of his almond eyes, the smile more his victimizers' than his own. Yes, he had seen the world in three days. His vest crumpled, the last buttons still holding somehow the golden chain and watch. His familiar smell, the aroma of sweet lavender and tobacco, has left him in three days and three nights. His underpants are full of his waste. I fall to my knees to undo the laces of his shoes.

He slept on the chair he had fallen into, next to my mother's bed. The five officers lay among papers, empty perfume bottles with labels of lilac, rose, and lily-of-the-valley. Scattered doctoral theses, chemistry research papers, money hidden in books, encyclopedias, and *Meyer's Lexicon* – the Asiatic officers too ignorant to identify them – among the leftover bread and sausage. The Russian officers insensible on the floor.

A scenario, wonderfully absurd, from a play so incongruous and irrational that I sat down in the middle of that set like an actor trying to think of his next line. When I heard my father cry out from his sleep, a savage sound of grief, I ran to him, startled, grabbed his hand, held his face that was wet with despair, and he told me his dream:

"It was a small place," he started, his almond eyes closed, his voice barely audible. "I'm sure it is a small place. A small craft, a hut, or something. There are men, lots of them, packed in tightly, so you can feel the breath of the one next to you. A door? There are no doors, just a small window high in the ceiling. Are we guests? Whose guests?" I touch my face to keep my tears from flowing. Shame, guilt, what was it? It is the morn of the eve of things to come. How small it feels. I can see the hand that holds the axe to strike, like fate.

Father's voice, louder now: "There is fire, a wild fire!" he shouts. "It eats my eyes, eats my skin, dries my hair, my nails, crawls up my shins to scorch my sex. Who brought me here? and how? I can see no road, no path, only dense wood – thank God for oak trees, they stand high and forever. I force my way through the sea of flesh, kicking and punching, not caring if I hurt myself or others, to try to get to that square of glass up high, to that light streaming in, to that oak, that blue sky...and then I am hung on the cross, on the iron cross of that small window."

The strength of my soul lies in my father. With the image of him on the cross I felt orphaned suddenly. The power of his law, the cosmic order of things by which my world moved, the simple right from which I deviated, to step into the forbidden joys of early days, vanished with the image of his crucifixion. An orphan – like a wild animal on a dark mountain pass – has to find his way alone, to tread with care.

But for the moment, oblivion. I lifted my father out of his chair, carried him like a child to the bed, laid him next to my mother. His beloved body, unwashed and reeking, slowly stretched into rest. The gentle smile, so longed for always, returned to the corner of his mouth. "Come my child, lie by me." And I squeezed myself in between them, to hold them both.

Felix came, sat in my father's chair, and waited until I woke. I rose and sat down beside him, took his hands in mine. And we sat close to one another, as if on a shore after a shipwreck, and he said: "Love has saved us. Ludmilla Bunin, my love, has brought them home for us. She has contacted Kiev and had them released."

I looked at a piece of paper, wasn't able to read it.

Love had triumphed against the Soviet might. Ludmilla Bunin, a Soviet officer in uniform, a soldier, a party-member-*apparatchik,* had fallen in love with brother Felix, as all women do, with his simple elegance. Bunin had met him in the first days of her party's dominion over us. The political officer in charge of health departments, including pharmaceutical production, she had in her young life seen "love" brutish-fast and was overwhelmed by my gentle brother. They met clandestinely all through the Soviet year – she was not to "fraternize" – and on the night of the twelfth of June, 1941, he ran to her apartment, fell to his knees: "Ludmilla, save my people, telephone the Minister of Health in Kiev, tell her my father is absolutely irreplaceable in his plant. Guarantee for him that the workers will march, tell her they adore him. Ask her to give him a year, or whatever it takes to groom a successor." And Ludmilla Bunin, dressed in her

Communist regalia, rushed to headquarters, found the Minister of Health, and offered her guarantee that my father would not sabotage the plant in any way. And thus she assured Father's and Mother's and my grandmother's release. Three such cases among perhaps ten thousand deportees. Bunin did it for Felix. Love, healing and redemptive, can drive a wedge into the sightless, conscienceless machine of destruction where all other powers fail.

"ANOTHER MALE CHOIR marching down the Residenzgasse," my mother remarks, her humour returning to deal with life in her female fashion. "But this time it's High German – *Hoch Deutsch,* not Russian, *Hoch Deutsch,* mother-tongue with a strange tinge. And the shade they wear is brown like you-know-what, but it is strong, wonderful singing." Young men singing in German, the language of our lullabies, of *Guten Abend, Gut Nacht."* My mother laughs. "Oh well, men," she says, "how stupid they are, dressing up in the same garb, their stripes of power on the collars of their uniforms, marching in formation, and feeling their sex rise in a crazy camaraderie powered by machine guns. How crazy they are, but how stirring their rhythmic dark voices." And we look through the shutters and tremble again. It is only a short, tense two weeks since the other male choir had marched, with horses and trucks, through the Residenzgasse, singing in sonorous and harsh Russian voices. And a fortnight later, at the end of June 1941, the Germans invade.

As evening falls, rifle butts pound the doors, windows break, splinters are everywhere. Shouts of *Juden-raus!* reach the two lower floors of my grandfather's house. Uncles, aunts, little cousins, all in my grandfather's big house, are pulled, pushed, and dragged away by these still beardless beautiful young German boys in boots, buckles, and helmets. On the third floor, we freeze. We hear shots echo. "The last judgment, no more days to come," my mother says. Then there is eerie silence. Total darkness descends, offering us camouflage. We descend from the third floor into the street to find the bodies of our people from the first and second floor. We find old Lev-Jossel Green, the grocer who rents a ground-floor shop and a basement vault from us, with his children in his arms, all covered in their blood. The seven of us from the third floor – Uncle Saul and Ruth, Felix, old grandmother Esther, Father, Mother, and I, carry the bodies, still warm, through the high gate into my grandfather's garden. Under the walnut tree, we lay them in a heap, some hardly bleeding, as if still asleep. My father carries Lev-Jossel Green the grocer. I loved old Green. And I loved his shop, where herring in barrels and cartons of chocolate wafers – the unlikeliest neighbours – found themselves next to each other, the herring smelling of vanilla and the wafers smelling of herring. Lev-Jossel let me weigh things behind his counter. I knew barley from buckwheat, the different crystals of salt, and all the sugars. And by putting one of those golden half-kilogram weights on the scale, I could judge how much it took, how many shovels of rice or flour. Oh, I felt like Anton Chekhov in his father's shop in Taganrog. In a similiar underground vault, with all the smells mixed up, and young Anton, weighing things out. My brother Felix and I read his stories together and found ourselves sobbing over his father's cruelty, as we saw it.

And now my father is carrying Lev-Jossel Green's body. Father had to free him first from the entanglement of his youngest child, Lisa. We heaped them under the walnut tree, to let them rest. Our massive walnut tree, its branches broad and outreaching, sheltering, its top branches touching the clouds, a dreamworld lost in its foliage, now all these dreams lying under it. We did not see the blood until the sun rose, the blood on our hands, faces, clothes, and soles. We washed as well as we could and without a murmur descended into the garden to dig the mass grave under the walnut tree. It was not easy. The tree resisted, its roots rebelled, opposed our shovels and spades, did not want our bodies. The tree knew these people as children, climbing its mighty branches, almost to the top. Knew the sound of their playing, laughing, teasing voices, and now it resisted their muted forms. So we moved the bodies, carried them into the open of the garden. Christian neighbours, from across the wild-vine-covered fence, came to help us dig and bury the bodies. No cloth, no linen, just earth to earth and covered with earth. We said the *Kaddish* and our gentile helpers repeated the ancient Aramaic words with us: *Praised be and glorified.*

Nor linen
Nor lace
Nor stone
Or rose
To heathen Gods
On altars sacrificed
A son
A lover
A breath
Sweet breath taken
Not offered
Love and limbs
Entangled
Hope and feces

Intermingle
On the altar
Nor linen
Nor lace
Nor cross
Or rose.

So we buried them in the open garden, as the faithful walnut tree wouldn't have them between its roots. Blood and walnut don't mingle, it seemed to tell us. And we walked up the stone stairwell to the third floor of my grandfather's house, heavier with each step, to start our seven days of mourning, the Shivah. On the floor, stripped of shoes, the ancient seven days. No ashes in our hair, too modern for that, perhaps. But the holy seven with its Sabbath at the end was the flight, the fleeing into the stillness of prayer. And my childhood intensity and my craving for God, the Hebrew, returned with its power. Words we spoke, words incomprehensible as the days we had seen; we sat close to one another, moved only to the rhythm of the necessary, held our bodies close. Our Greek Orthodox neighbours from across the wild-vine fence brought soup and bread and joined us on the floor barefoot. We felt lucky to still have the Sabbath, an inner smiling peace. Like retarded children, we smiled, having erased pain with prayer, to go on to the next meal.

GHETTO: EARLY OCTOBER, 1941. All hell breaks loose. Shouting and barked commands, objects are to be collected and put into sheets, bound at four corners, holding all you can carry in two hands. Doors are bolted, keys handed over. At dawn, down the long "Holy Trinity Street" to the collection ghetto –

Umschlagplatz. I watch my father's and my mother's backs, walking down that old street with the Christian trifold Godhead name on it, and my heart sinks. I watch their bent backs, watch them occasionally put down the heavy bundles, change them from hand to hand, sit down on the curb, watch them being chased by a brute, shouted at to *Hurry you lousy swinish Jew.* My mother and my father. There are no words. Again to the Turkish quarter. Three, four, five interconnected medieval streets, all the fifty thousand of us. Pets are left to grieve. We leave our mongrel Mary in front of my grandfather's house, tears welling in her eyes. Have you ever seen a dog cry?

BIG OR LITTLE, ALL GIRLS LIKE HATS. They are so wonderfully exotic, with names like *summergarden, beanshop, aviary, desert wind,* or *cherry harvest,* with a story behind each name. Huge plumes of ostrich, catching the air in their fibers, lie across the front of broad-brimmed hats, whipping gently. Ribbons, all colours of the rainbow, *soie changeante,* are bound to stiff enormous bows at the back. They are fantastic. They have veils, they fly in the wind, they need huge, frightening pins to hold them down.

On the second floor of my grandfather's house is my fairyland. There sits my aunt Gilda – a Polish princess married to my uncle Nathan – in the middle of my dreams. She makes all my dreams come true. She has nimble fingers, sings and speaks to her hats. Here I take refuge from piano lessons, Latin, Greek, and big fat bully brothers.

Stuffed ladies without faces, with bulky bosoms and derrières divided by tiny waists, stand on a single leg in the front room.

Some heads, without bodies, sit on little tables all of their own, their golden, black, or chestnut curls flowing down or piled up high. My aunt interweaves metal pins, mounds the stiff organza, builds and builds until it is time for the story. Today it is the cherry harvest. She piles the cherries in doubles, in triplets, on branches with leaves of green hearts, until they tumble all around the hat's inner body in yellow, black, and sour red. They speak of summer games, of sunshine, sweet tastes, and wicked boys.

My sweet princess from Poland is pinning another daisy to the summergarden, swivelling a form about to watch the grasses fall like golden sheafs onto the back of the mannequin. The grasses never sit still. She scolds the poor naked lady and places a delicate membrane of net across the summergarden, to veil the eyes a little, she says, mystery in her voice. My aunt Gilda.

Then suddenly boots, buckles, helmets. Brutes at the door. Truncheons, rifle butts, and heels kicked into the belly of my nimble-fingered Polish-princess-aunt and my uncle Nathan, sweet, straight, and honest, godmother and godfather to my fanciful childhood years. Down, down the old stone stairway, bundles bound in sheets by her beautiful hands. Driven, chased, hounded into waiting trucks. To the *Umschlagplatz,* to the trains, sealed in a railcar. Across three rivers, the mighty Prut, the Dnjester, and the Bug. She peels potatoes for the German war effort, for the officers in charge, the SS and the dogs. He digs the ditches to hold the Russians off. Nathan's arm breaks, he begs for his life on his knees: I can work, he says, it will heal. Look at the Jew begging for his life, the uniform answers. Vermin, not worth another bowl of soup. *Genickschuss.*

My sweet aunt Gilda, she ascends to heaven. Straight up. It cannot be otherwise.

JEWS HAVE NO PAST, REALLY. Things do not move forwards and backwards for us. It is always now, yesterday and tomorrow the same. Job is alive. He is with me, speaks to the Lord. We ask the same questions, unanswerable questions. Address Him: this is what we yearn for, oh Lord. Old words in different rhythms. New old questions.

My mother can't cross the room, there are fifty people between us, sitting on suitcases and bundles. Instead we speak to each other in sign language, with hands, eyes, and bodies. The ghetto doors are locked. What we know comes through the air, windows, keyholes. Information flows, fed by rage, hope, caught by antennae on our skins. Through the windows we see the trucks leave. We can't believe our eyes. It can't be true.

Resettlement – Palestine, Ukraine, somewhere. I am pushed around by my neighbour, who polishes his dentistry gear, totally oblivious to us. He is concerned only with a space of ten centimetres, the ten centimetres he has secured with growls and shoves. Polishing and straightening out and counting his drills. He is going somewhere, he knows. My dentist is unaware that God is not answerable to Job, or to him. A room full of dentists, fighting for ten centimetres.

The doors fly open. In come Romanians behaving like Germans, masquerading as the masters. It is bad theatre. Romanians, they are no masters, poor and earthbound, they are serfs, slaves, underlings. Here and there you will see one Jon or Petru do it well, but rarely. They are so ill-suited. A twinkle in their eye, they like their wine and women, they do not cherish murder. Orders? Commandments? Romanians do not obey orders easily.

But now they are here, brothers in arms, taking on like all slaves the trappings, the forms, of the master. The Romanians bow to the powerful to save their own necks, and sometimes also ours. So, in the middle of all that desperate chaos, the shambles of hunger, thirst, the loss of simplest civility, they, the Romanians, come up with a proposition to the *Oberkommando:* use these people before they die. It is not new, of course, the Nazis have done it elsewhere. But here it is new. So doctors, pharmacists, and engineers are selected, separated, and kept back for other uses.

My yellow star is clearly displayed on my white coat. We are requisitioned – my father and I – to work in a hospital. I serve the German boys – shot, amputated, delirious, young, dying for a madman. Our Jewish team works silently. No talk is exchanged, no holy words are pronounced. Who dares? My boss, my hero, my victimizer, the German doctor, has entered the makeshift laboratory. We are short of everything, so we have to invent, improvise. New casualties arrive from the front, boys with bullets in their chests, arms, bellies. We have no morphine injections, so we make our own solutions, sterilize it in stages, so as not to destroy the tender morphine, which can't stand high temperatures, and give it to the master, the doctor in charge, to inject. We are as good as any I.G. Farben research laboratory, the doctor says, coming very close to me. *Sleep with me tonight. You'll have dinner, cigarettes, and wine, and I let you rest in my quarters for a day. You are clever and you know me now well enough, you know I will be good to you.* Yes, I say, but may I respectfully ask for a favour: bring my fiancé out of the ghetto.

Walking between two strapping SS guards, dogs at the side, I recite the Lord's Prayer in my head, lighting one version on the other like a chainsmoker. It serves me well. From the Latin *Pater noster* to the Romanian *Tatal nostru,* with the *Vater Unser* and the *Notre Père,* I speak them wordlessly, as I did at the first hour of each school day, when the teacher came in and we rose to recite the Lord's Prayer.

Rumours are that the ghetto is emptying fast. Whispers carry messages; they travel on underground paths, from ear to ear; are heard by those afflicted, those whose days are numbered, who glean the truth from the horror tales with the finest of sieves. And numbered days infuse a strength beyond the ordinary, an inner tuning of the finest discernment, a high alert. So you hear what no one else can and your body makes decisions in seconds.

The ghetto is soon to be annihilated. Poor sweet Max is in there. The sweet idiot of my teenage years, walking in long strides, his shoelaces trailing. In my hand I carry the letter that will release Max. I pray he has somehow heard the rumour, that Dr. Bauer succeeded in granting his release. I think back to our adolescent years together, when love was undefinable, just a vague waiting and melancholy. *Our Father....*

I'm made to hasten my step. *March,* the two SS men say, *march.* The dogs look more human. But solace returns with oblivion, prayer, and past. Oh, the sweet, sweet boy under my window.

My name is Max, he said, and ran as if stung by a tarantula. I saw him hiding behind an eavestrough of the school principal's house, day in and day out, until one day I crossed the road to ask him his name. A slight slap with the back of my hand brought him back to this world. Max, he said, and ran. Oh, the sweet boy, lanky, gauche, not yet grown....

We were both fifteen or sixteen, and one high summer day I took his hand and said, let's go to the river. Down the ill-named, ill-fated Saint Trinity Street, leading to what is now the ghetto, down the Train Station Street – the Bahnhofstrasse, into the river valley. Through ripening corn, standing high, golden-stringed hair, into the endless stretches of sand, pebbles, and tall, tall grasses. The river was almost out over its banks, after a stormy rainfall the day before. I felt reckless and more so because of the tender timidity of the boy, who hardly touched me as we stretched into the sand. Let's go swimming, let's swim down below the bridge, I said. "No," he said, "no, I do not know how well you swim. It is too dangerous, especially past the bridge, where the river drops down, and there are crests of white foam, spiralling, pulling you down." I smiled. Of course he'll go, he loves me, he stands for hours under my window just to see me come out of the old gate. Come, I tell him, and glide down the high bank. Come! And in my summer cotton I dip into the mountain stream. Not as clear this time. Swollen, slightly cloudy with debris, the stream takes me fast beyond the bridges to the foaming falls. Water in my ears and throat, I can't fight the river, my feet are caught – when I feel jostled and then carried on Max's back to the lower bank. He has seen me sink, kicked his runners off, and jumped in to rescue me. Breathless, we stretched out on the heated stones, and I hear him say, in a very ordinary, everyday voice: "Will you marry me, Süssel?" I smile. "I will have to, because you saved my life. Yes, of course I will."

But we were more like brothers than lovers, wandering along the river dunes or hiking the seven kilometres to the Cecina mountain, in one day there and back. And I called him my fiancé, mockingly. But we are not for each other. The sweet innocence, the thoughtful adoring soul at my beck and call! I'm too wild. I have to find love on my own terms. I have to be the one who chooses. Love just given to me will never be enough. *Our Father, who art in heaven....*

He is my brother and we hold hands, walk, and chat. He tells me that men often stop and tell him how pretty he is. That men would take him to the river when he was five or six, to sit by them. They would carve whistles out of hazelnut wood, bind them together with grass, and play for him. Tried to put their hands inside his shirt to stroke his nipple. And Max blushed and said, I should not have told you that, but you are my friend, and I can't tell it to Moritz or the other boys – it would make them laugh and I would want to cry. I am not a pretty boy. I wish my hair would not fall in curls over my forehead and my beard would grow and change the peach-skin. But you will wait for me, Süssel, you will wait for me. And so we are engaged, he said, and he took my right hand and with his pencil drew a circle on my ring finger – to remind you of me, he said. Oh, dear, how will this be, what will I do not to hurt him? *Hallowed be Thy name, Thy will be done. Help me find him, Father.*

But he does look like a young girl sometimes, with his regular features, a breath of peach in his cheeks and hair falling down to his brow. Poor sweet boy. Oh, I have to take him out of the ghetto, or he will die. He is so defenseless, numb, unaware of the desperation around him. *Thy will be done on earth....* And Dr. Bauer. There is no escape for me. I knew it from the time I saw him dipping his eyes into mine. I am nothing, just a Jew in servitude, and he could take me by command...*on earth as it is in heaven.*

Sweet Max. At the *Umschlagplatz,* I saw a whirl of Jewish men and women jostling him, separating him from his brothers. He had never been separated from them, especially from his famous athlete brother, Moritz, of whom he endlessly talked on our walks. I got a glimpse of Max's face: fear, sudden abandonment. This almost Greek-sculpture intelligent face, wanting to undo the heavens with a piece of paper in his hands. Calculating, thinking, linking his thoughts with truths of the past, through ways of his own finding the truth of the moment. One that makes his face shine and relax for a little. Oh, the sweet boy! *Give us this day....*

As we hiked up our Cecina mountain, resting on stones near the thousands springs, he would take his steady companions – pencil and paper – and show me how simple truth can be, a shape like a triangle, a circle, or a rhomb. And talk about Galileo or Copernicus – the Polish father of astronomy, or his adored Johannes Kepler. "Without magic," he said. "The truth is here, I will show it to you, Süssel, without incantations or the priestly swinging of myrrh. Just beauty in itself. Forever." Then he smiled. "Unless modified and changed by the moving times." I did not comprehend but knew I was his kin in other ways. "Yes," I said, "I'll marry you. You're too beautiful to leave." And we blushed without kissing, holding hands and straining up the mountain. *Give us this day....*

Our town at the foot of the northern slopes of the Carpathians, nourished by fertile fields and by the waters of mountain springs, fed us with the myth of being chosen. All mountains touch the sky, as does the Olympus of Greece, the Sinai of the Law, and as does our Cecina for the little people at its foot. Next to the Gods. We sweated up, stone by stone to the top, just to get the sight of the river valley, the Prut, looking out at German and Ukrainian villages and further ranges on the horizons. I would want to stop, put my hurting feet into the springs, listen to the rush in the grasses, and rest after an hour's march. And he would come down to me, throw the rucksack onto the ground, and say, Look, I want to explain this to you. And he went on about Johannes Kepler, who made a living as an astrologer – pure nonsense in Max's view – yet laid down the most basic truth about the revolution of the earth around the sun.

No, I do not think we could marry; oh, it would not work, but he looked at me with such longing that I took his arm for support. When we descended, almost rolling down that mountain, the stars were up and we hurried away. So he remained my fiancé. A contract-brother – his face of fear and abandonment in the ghetto crowd – *Forgive, forgive us our trespasses, as we forgive....* Dr. Bauer will take me and I have no way out. Sweet Max.

He stood there and watched me. I did not like to be watched. I imagined all the boys commenting on me, in their minds. I could hear them say, her legs are too long, too thin for a fifteen-year-old, her hair is in strings, curled like shedding snakes, she can wear a hanger-dress, tied around her neck, because she wears no bra, there is nothing to put inside there, no flesh anywhere. So they all seemed to say.

When I am fifteen, he stands there, hiding in the chestnuts in bloom guarding the entrance to the Evangelical church. He melts into the trunk of one of them, covered by pink candles, watching me. Oh, go away, stupid boy – let me just sit on the rim of that magic fountain and let my naked toes touch the slate on the ground....

I can sit there now, a dream come true. I never could before. I was either too short yet, or it was strictly forbidden for other inscrutable adult reasons, which I dismissed with the superiority of the delinquent child. I don't like to be watched, it makes me claustrophobic. Strange that I can tolerate this stupid boy staring at me now out of his chestnut tree, almost glad he is there. *Father, forgive....*

Fifteen. Sitting on my fountain of fear, the horror of Ahi's encircling arms giving me gooseflesh. I lean against this many-armed body of cool iron, resting on the fluted spouts. Ahi's arms, the Turkish henchman's powerful arms, spewing water. Do not sit there, Ileana screams, do not sit there, Ahi will grab you by your hair from the back, encircle your body, and shout with joy when you drown. And no frog-prince will kiss you in a thousand years. *Father, as we forgive....*

When I was seven or eight, I would sneak down in the evening, after piano practice and homework were done, and wait for the copper arms to move, exhilarated by the danger. One day, I touched a fluted arm as if calling for water, and it fell by its own weight and I was left holding it, the end-face grinning at me. Too frightened to cry, I ran into Ileana's lap. Stories are true, Ileana said, you defy them at your own peril. He'll get you next time. He knows you're Süssel! Let's fix the damn thing to give him his arm back. I do not like his anger. Dear, dear, it's hard to work for Jews, they have to prove everything, they don't believe the simplest thing. If people say Ahi lives in that fountain, for me he lives there. And it is dangerous to play with it. If you need water he'll give it to you, but do not play with it. What a naughty, naughty child – *who trespass against us....*

After that I would not go near the fountain until I was fifteen. But at fifteen I feel grown, adult, above superstition. I sit on the rim touching the deep-green slate with washed toes. I sit there, legs trailing, watching this strange boy watching me. He comes cat-like through the chestnut foliage. I see his light brown hair. Unusually handsome, thick glasses sitting crookedly on his face. I fancy him pushing them into position. With his mannerisms, childhood habits, shirt hanging out of his brother's trousers, belt too loose, he stands there tall and still.

Does he love the fountain as I do? The way it occupies the crossroads dead centre between the Archbishop's Residence and the Evangelical church and, cutting across, binds Holy Trinity

Street to Gallows Hill. The henchman in the middle, Ahi, the multi-armed Turk, who can string up three men at the same time, growing new arms when he needs them. He swings the knotted rope around one man, holds the others with newly-sprouted arms. Three he can hang at once, cracking their necks, making music almost, Ileana laughs. Do not go near that hill, Süssel. No grass grows there, no tree, the earth refuses seed, for all those tears have salted the earth and made it barren. Do not go near it, bad girl. *Father, lead us not into temptation, lead us not....*

But at fifteen I do. I go up the hill without fear, or just a little horror in my veins. Up the cobbled road, past the vaulted houses from Turkish times, dark, menacing, low, arched cellars, where the poorest live. Ukrainians and Jews, speaking a Yiddish-German, Ukrainian-sounding, the proverbs and lore of the Slavs. A singing sound, crying and laughing. A local code of complicity and cheating. Merchants of coal by the piece, winter vegetables, and kerosene, poor, very poor. Selling lighting or heating oil with ancient measuring means, like the Dame-Jeanne, a huge-bellied lady of green glass or tin – the *damigiana*, as Ileana called that crazy bottle. All these cellar merchants, reeking of wet-pounded earth. Here and there a winter-apple shop, a little more respectable, sporting shelves, apples, and dried fruit. The east side open, precipitous, with a view of the chestnut treetops.

Up and up the hill. No blade of grass here, no moss, no creeping brush, no hazelnut bush, no tree. A small gust lifting surface earth, the taste of tears covering my tongue. The air remembers, carries its truth to those tuned to hear. No gallows to be seen, yet they are there, cannot be erased. Just for a short moment my eyes graze the valley, a German village, orchards – and I run back home. Enough, enough. *Deliver us from evil, Father, deliver us from evil....*

The stupid boy. Now he stands there again in the shadows of the eavestrough beside the principal's house. Hidden, he thinks. This overhang, forgotten by time, seems useless, except for stupid love-struck fifteen-year-olds. I have grown to want him there, behind the eavestrough, by the dirty ochre-coloured stucco – pretend Italian – of the house that holds my personal enemy, the moustached white-haired school principal, who locked the door one time to kiss me, "a honeybee tasting the sweet nectar." Oh, how I hate that house! But there he stands, my stupid boy, and I love to turn my eyes away from the setting sun to see him trailing his body out of his cavern for a last look up to the third floor. I am the cruel sort. Let them want me. It's sweet revenge for all the thoughts of derision and critique I suspect.

But when we first held hands, to walk up the mountain, I knew he would always be there for me. He would wait. I would go my way, love whomever I wanted, and he would wait. Dear and dreamy, a thinking boy, who feared my green eyes. I learned to look through his eyes, and saw a world in balance, held together by forces other than moral ones.

Just fifteen or sixteen, I wanted to live, gain the world by plunging into it headfirst, as into the river. No other thought than sensation. Then there was Max, learning life through thought, holding hands and waiting. For me? Heavens!

For Thine is the glory, for Thine is the glory....

Multi-layered, from bread to sin to the glory of God, the Lord's Prayer answered a desperate need, and carried by my chain of *Our Father,* in timeless trance, I arrived at the ghetto gate. It was eerily half-empty by then. He was there.

The Phantom Ship

THE TRUCKS HAVE STARTED ROLLING IN THE STREETS. Outside, the howling of dogs, men, and women mingling. We are forty in a closed room, but I have secured a "window seat" for myself. Gauche and *Weltfremd* – unworldly – as I am, it astonishes and amuses me how enormously successful I have been. How in heaven did I secure my few centimetres under the window? Where did I get another piece of paper and a pencil to boot?

I'm a strange bird here, who has had my shoes laced by my twin brother and my bread buttered by the other two boys just to get me through breakfast and off to school. Son of a very just mother, who cut her torte into pieces of geometrical precision, and was only occasionally outwitted by an indulgent father undoing her strictures. I grew dreamily between them, pampered and a little disdained. For not doing anything right, for eating with my fingers, stroking the cat with fatty hands, getting up from the table before permission was given. I was agitated with destinies of my different heroes. True or fancied, all of the past. Shouts of *no dessert for you.* My brothers ganging up to partition my torte. But generally there was solidarity. "Oh, let the idiot have it, come sit down and forget Karl May, *Old Shatterhand*, and *Winnetu on the Warpath."*

The ghetto room is dense with Jews, some I know and some strangers. Slowly, without realizing it, I gain more elbow-room, more breathing space, and suddenly I miss the pressure, the bodily closeness. Someone says, "You haven't eaten," and shares an open tin of sardines, while I look through my window, watching the trucks leave. Faintly recognize the woman I slept next to on the floor. There is no escaping the sardine smell. I hear the man say, "Drink the oil from the can, it will keep you for a while."

The group falls silent. By a summary count, there seem to be just twenty of us left, a little more space to collect one's thoughts. Yet there is lead in bones and muscles, and one sits passively on one's suitcases or bundles, waiting for the door to open. Sardine-man says, "Oh I wish we would move," and fiddles with a Swiss Army knife, clicking it open and shut. "It will save my life," he says. "Look, it can do everything, it opens sardine cans, it pulls a cork clean from the bottle, it can pull a sliver of wood as finely as a needle would, and here are the nail clippers, the files, the scissors." I smile at him. How strange we all are. How easily we adapt to life, as long as there is someone to explain our Swiss pocket-knife to. I do not like knives. I never cut my own bread, or the throats of other people. But I smile at him out of compassion for an idiot.

Rumours, down below a commotion of some sort through the window. A sudden tension in me makes me rise, give up my corner under the window. Sardine-man takes over, saying, "I'm holding your spot." I dismiss my furtive fear as he eyes my belongings. I desperately want to go to the door, not even knowing why. There is total silence around me. Children are still. Mothers with blank faces, leaden-gray, hold the little ones. How do they know not to cry?

The door opens, the guards in Romanian uniforms start counting, all Jews are on their feet. Standing by the door, I slip out unseen and run along the corridor on the ground floor onto the street. Trucks are assembling, guards pushing Jews into them, heaving the old ones up. A dear friend of mine, gentle and tubercular, by the unusual name of Trojan Freud, is being helped by his mother into the truck. I manage to almost reach the ghetto's gate when I hear my name called out. I move like an automaton towards the voice and enter the so-called "ghetto office" to present myself, when I spot Süssel standing between two SS officers and a dog. She waves a document at me. The bureaucratic face at the table hands me a paper to sign. It is my release from the ghetto, on orders of Dr. Hermann Bauer, Süssel's boss at the hospital. There is no time to rejoice; she disappears between the SS men as she had appeared, flown in like the carved angels on her grandfather's gate, wings spread, with a piece of paper in her hand. I am holding it now, standing outside the ghetto gate, not knowing which way to turn.

I WALK DOWN THE Bahnhofstrasse – the Train Station Avenue, but soon find myself inside milling, noisy crowds. Townspeople bringing wares to the market, peasants smelling of rancid butter, put on their hair to protect against lice and the devil, lining the sidewalk, and trucks moving towards the train road. I turn on my heels in the opposite direction and find a quiet street, so quiet that I shiver. Totally deserted, doors and windows blocked. If the crowds and noise were fearful, this is frightening to the core. And yet amusing: to be outcast from the multitude – it makes me laugh to find myself so abandoned. Especially by my Moritz. My brothers were always around me. I never slept, bathed, or ate alone. We four boys were close in that winter town-house; only in the summer, in the country, where father oversaw the waterworks, did we spread into many rooms and gardens.

As in a dream, I am falling, falling, I walk faster and faster, almost running down the empty side streets. Like an apple plucked from the branch rolling on the ground, waiting for a stone to arrest it. It is night before I find myself in front of an industrial building, not far from the bridge over the river Prut, and I recognize it. It was the sugar factory of the town. And I hear my name almost whispered from a slightly opened window. It is Ernst Springer, a classmate, a young engineer at his first job. Turn left, Max, he says, around the corner you'll find a small gate open. Hugs, handshakes, hot coffee, bread and cheese. Ernst is in charge for the night.

A German ethnic, whatever this means in our mongrelized Eastern world, with a Ukrainian mother. Soft to touch and fleshy, he was not anxious to play soccer; instead we played chess, and he beat me often. He also sharpened my pencils. I have refused to handle knives or scissors from the age of four, letting Moritz and other willing victims do it. Ernst was my friend.

"How did you get into the ghetto, you're not even Jewish, with your German mother?" We talk for another hour, my head drops down on my breast, and my saviour Ernst beds me down on sacks of sugar, with empty sacks for cover. There is no better heaven.

Ernst shelters and feeds me. He looks out for danger all through his three-day work shift and at night we drink wine and talk. "You're not even Jewish," he starts again. "How did you get in there?"

"Well, my father is, all his folks are, and he will not let them down. Foolish, of course, but my mother felt the same. At the collection point, near the Turkish quarter, we got into a melée and were separated. I lost sight of everyone and found myself in a crowd flooding into the Hormuzachigasse – all within the ghetto. In a room of strangers, forty of them. Locked in."

Ernst too is a lone wolf. Ideology cut straight through families of German or mixed-German heritage. Most embraced the Superman ideology, parading armbands through the Herrengasse – young men and their girls. It gave them a feeling of youth power, superiority, a tribal high, an old-renewed blood-related tongue to link, bind, and consolidate the ranks. Excluding their brothers who doubted or turned inward with their private dreams.

Ernst tells of his brother Edgar, who brandished a gun in its leather belt, showed off words, songs, and shiny boots, pulling the youngest, Helmut, along. Father, mother, and the two sisters, Lotte and Eva, too young, too homebound, understanding nothing and fearing everything unknown. *Heim ins Reich* they went. Except Ernst. A call went out to the ethnic Germans, to leave the old Austrian – now Romanian – homeland; to leave livestock, ploughed fields, houses, take what they could carry and move over to Poland – called the *Warteland* under the Reich. Ernst tells me, "We are not better off than you. We're on the road, like you. We left our dogs with tears flowing – I do not know where my family is, in whose beds they sleep. My mother shouted, 'I will not sleep in Polish beds or eat their sausages – I have no business to be there!' Poor Mother, she had to go, what else was she to do?"

I kissed and thanked Ernst, we clasped hands, cried together, and parted. We had all left our dogs with tears in their eyes. I have seen them. They do not move from their masters' doorstep. They do not take food from strange hands and their eyes shine with welling water, waiting to die. I saw Süssel's dog Mary, in front of the old house, stretched into near death.

I am driven once more to my lookout corner across from the old stone house, my hiding place under the eavestrough, where I saw Süssel – was it for the first time? Having said goodbye to Ernst, not knowing where to turn next, I go back for a furtive visit. To a town without location. A dispersed town, in the winds. A town of memory, taken along on pilgrimages, its beauty exaggerated, endowed with charm and the echoes of early days. No memory of poverty, tribal fights, and fears; just its glory remains. What myths we make to face the strangers: I come from fairyland. Not on the map. Not extant officially, under its true name or its many fake ones, but there within you.

The town is lifeless now, the Jews gone, the non-Jews not showing their faces. Not even a town but a ghostly sea, where ships sail without crew. As a child I was afraid of the oceans. In school we read *Das Gespensterschiff – The Phantom Ship* by Hauff – and I broke into uncontrolled sobs at the image of the unmanned, darkened boat, its sails torn. To the mockery of class and classics teacher Herr Niemeyer, who replaced the regular German literature teacher for the day. *"Das Pünktchen"* or "the little point on the *i.*" Herr Niemeyer – so named because of his size, his big head on Humpty-Dumpty legs – could not establish order. The class roared. *There goes Max, baby Max, shedding tears over a stupid story.*

Yet, now, facing this old burg, like the pirate ship sailing into the coming night, I could not cry. I looked up to the windows on the third floor, where Süssel always sat, watching the sun descend. And then turned west where her eyes used to rest and wander along the crenelations of the Residence carved with coal crayons into the sky. I stood just for a short moment to take her vision with me – then I looked down to the old gate, to the light angels and the devil above, for a short goodbye. Tears now, mingling with Mary's dying at the gate, ran down my face.

Slowly coming to my senses, I slid by the unlit houses, past the fountain where she had sat on the rim, cotton hanger-dress flaring, legs apart, dangling like a pre-adolescent boy. Took one more look at the many-fluted spouts, rising from the stone body in the centre and its copper snakes' arms, and Ahi's head at the top. Legends sprung up through changing times and occupiers – from the German holy-order of the Templars through the Mongols, the Tatars, the Eastern hordes on their flying horses, to the rulers of the Ottoman Empire – masks and faces, all on the fountain. And then there is Ahi, the Turkish henchman-executioner. A grisly face, an arm like a rope, growing out of the centermast. The townspeople, all of them – Ukrainians, Romanians, Germans, Poles, and Jews – call it "the legend of Ahi." It is built into the local daily talk. Terror, disgust, or fear will make them shout *May Ahi strike!* or simply *Ahi,* as a curse. I pass Ahi and his fountain, make fast across the open road to the entrance of the Evangelical church guarded by the two enormous chestnut trees – candle-blooms extinguished now, green fruit browning slowly. Like a thief I hide in the hedge at the side door of the pastor's residence. I knock, and he lets me in, without a word. An apple, some bread and butter, a glass of milk, and a small bedroom in the back. It is my mother's church.

I've been here often. Not willingly, but with a Lutheran one does not argue. My mother took me there, all the boys and my singing sister Cornelia. My singing and slapping sister Cornelia, in charge of us rowdy lot. She had a ready hand that flew so fast into our faces, and more into mine than anyone else's. Because I was the idiot of our close family-village. But I loved her. She sang like the angels. Our oldest brother was Süssel's brother Felix's classmate and co-conspirator. The two of them, with innocent faces, on their best behaviour – please-thank-you-holding-coats-and-doors to the adults – went as accomplices to Süssel's kitchen maid, Ileana. I know because I heard them talking about it. There is an attic in the old house, high up under the roof. It is hot in there in the summer. I heard them say Ileana, smelling of marinated herring, made them go wild – and so I know without knowing.

But Cornelia sang like a bird, a high coloratura bird-song. Our oldest brother Hans – Felix's friend – took her to Süssel's house, where everybody sang, and where an enormous nine-foot Bösendorfer grand stood in the salon, lid always open.

I did not see Süssel then, I really saw her for the first time when she sat on the rim of Ahi's fountain, her legs trailing. I will likely never again walk up the Cecina mountain hand in hand with her or talk to her about Orion, or lie at night in the fields for a short rest before parting, the sky brilliant with stars. Or drink from the earth-cool springs of the Carpathians with my bride.... Where will I sleep tonight and where tomorrow?

The pastor lets me sleep. A dreamless rest, and my morning eyes fall upon the illuminated east side of the old stone house. Glass three stories high, molten golden mirrors of the eastern sun. I haven't seen it before. I know every shadow of each angel's wing, how they float unsupported like autumn leaves in the wind, eight times over in each panel of the gate, beneath the dark and brooding evil devil, from the hours I spent in my stalking-watching hollow beneath the eavestrough. But I have never seen the eastern wing fully, not from the outside. I once charged up the three-floor stone staircase after my brother Hans to find them all, Süssel, her mother, singing with my sister Cornelia, and Hans and Felix on the Bösendorfer grand. Frightened, I sped away like mad.

But I never saw it from the outside. The whole back of the house turned east, glass walling each floor except for a stone support that just gently interrupts the flow of light, now fully ablaze. It makes me want to live. All is aflame. It towers over the two mighty chestnuts at the entrance of the church and lights the space between them. I hear the fruit falling, cracking the green to reveal a horse-chestnut in its shiny youth. Reddish brown, a shimmering eye of the newborn deer, it lies in its broken shell. Some litter the grounds within their slowly decaying green. It makes one want to live. So beautiful a world. A marble so round in my pocket to mean a wedding ring, and a round return of the sun. To be promised and fulfilled. Just coming 'round in an order devised – speaking of powers, for us to contemplate and separate, discern from chaos. Like the eastern tall-lit morning torch. And I pray, to my mother's God this time, to grant me one more and one more night's sleep, so my eyes can fall again upon this order-symmetry of return. One more gaze upon the slowly lightening fountain, the snakes of the Ahi, the copper spouts, and the Turk on arm and top....

The east side of the old house darkening slowly, I hear the pastor at the door, with bread and coffee. The local German bakers have left town to go *"Heim ins Reich,"* leaving old established bakeries to ruin, their homes, farms, and family links broken. There is still flour around to get in barter for pillowcases, silver, or tableware. But for the moment life is almost extinguished, with the Jews gone and war in earnest. I smiled at my intense joy of life. At my praying to live another morning like this one. At my just being half of everything – Jew and German. "We'll talk," the pastor said, "we'll talk at night. Go to the attic room – you'll find books. And don't venture out on the grounds – there are *Razzias,* soldiers and police of every description."

I stretched my limbs onto the spartan bed, so good a moment! My eyes on the old house greying now, the memory of Süssel's hand waving a paper, quietly musing about my hero, Johannes Kepler. Speculating on what it takes to break the mould, leave the trodden paths to find truth with a piece of paper and a pencil in hand; looking through a ground-glass lens into the universe at a starry sky. What does it take to think one's own thoughts? To drive a wedge into the thousand-year-old assumption that we are the centre of it all? Geocentricism, the idea that the universe turns around *us,* everything lives to serve us. What does it take, to stand alone against powers that have paradise for sale and hell if you do not buy? What kind of man does it take? How mysterious, how cunning, and how exultant a man to go out and find another to share a truth so dangerous to the dominant church and state! The wonderful letter Kepler wrote to Galileo about the findings of Copernicus – oh! I smile at the thought. Heavens, a German, an Italian, and a Pole thinking that the world is *one,* as in my father's faith, God is One. I like my father's faith. A credo with a number in the center: *One.* With all the abstract thought to follow. Who can define a number? A tongue that speaks through itself, like music, so beautiful. And here we are fighting. Killing one another.

The pastor does not want me to go into town, not now. Rumours are rampant. Straggling women, picked up wherever they are found, taken into trucks and sent behind the front to serve as "comfort women" to fighting men. Everyone else grabbed – Jew and sometimes non-Jew – put into formation, sent to the collection camp and quarry. So the pastor tells me, Do not venture out.

But I was beckoned by this strange silence, this eerie town without locale. It had lost its place on the map – become mirage, spun fantasy, uprooted, packaged into memories and carried in the heart. Now it was like a sea, with its empty ships, walnut, chestnut, elms, poplars swaying in the storm. It was October 1941, and my birthplace was being lifted from the ground. The raging sea taking over and pirate ghost-ships roaming....

I could not be held. I had to go out into this yonder worldscape. I promised the pastor to be on the lookout for danger and to be back before nightfall. I did not wear the David double-upside-down-yellow-triangle. It was in my pocket. I smiled at it, thinking, to mock the world, I should partition it and wear just one yellow triangle, for the half a Jew that I am. Which half of me, I wondered, the lower? God! – the laughter, idiocy, and perverted thinking – if only one could be Kepler! Maybe I will be, will think a glorious truth, escape into a crystal world without birth. I hope Moritz is alive.

The skies were dark when I closed the door of the pastor's quarters behind me. October leaden-grey, hanging low with foreboding. Nearly copper-brown, the foliage still clung to the branches, sounding metallic as the wind swept through. I used to collect the October chestnuts on the ground. Moritz the eternal classifier, organizer, sized the heaps for barter and weaponry. Shot them through a homemade sort of blow-cannon at whomever he hated, a bully on the playground. Admired and feared, my protector walked the battlefields, standing on the hills of command – the *Feldherrnhügel* – with the assurance of a warrior. Now I collect a few of the chestnuts in my left pocket – the right one is for Süssel's marbled wedding ring. Chestnuts are my amulets. I touch their silky surfaces, dipping into hollows and rising to an uneven round, a sweet familiar superstition. I rejoice in it, ashamed as well, for my scientific mind does not allow it easily. It mocks and disdains. Yet not even Johannes, my Kepler, could or would want to shed the medieval hold. Everything overlaps, in a weave of many-coloured strands. And his irrefutable laws of such beauty and balance shine golden through that weave. And so I turn and twirl this uneven round chestnut between my fingers as an anchor to my fears.

Along the bridges, ducking at moments, passing the University grounds and into the Goethegasse, I suddenly freeze, startled by a knock and Rebecca's face at her basement window. A gentle knock, but a wild gesture of urgency makes me turn into the gate of the six-storey stone building and down into the cellar world. Rebecca's world. A labyrinthian underground, a vaulted cellar world of interconnecting doors and tunnels, throughout the foundations of the block. She, the mistress-amazon, and her women, no pimps. I have seen her before. Moritz walked down with me one day as far as Süssel's pharmacy on the corner of the block, facing the National Theatre. And he told me, Everyone knows Rebecca.

"Come with us next time, Max. Come, silly boy. Rebecca will teach you gently. You've earned money with your math tutoring. She is not expensive, and she gives it on credit, too. We'll go tomorrow morning at five o'clock. You'll be amazed how sweetly she removes the – and she talks incessantly to cover your silence – you won't be embarrassed. I know you're a genius. But this is the real world. All those stars in heaven with your ridiculous heroes, all dead, won't get you anywhere. You're a stupid dreamer and I won't be around forever – besides, *she'll* never marry you. She is arrogant and cruel. I was at this studio dance-ball, and all the boys wanted her. Just to show her off in their arms, looking around for admiring glances, having carried off the prize – and you are just a shy, learned idiot of sixteen."

I start down the broken cellar steps. A reek of brick, mould, urine and Lysol hits and blinds me, makes me lose my foothold. Rebecca runs up a few steps to get hold of me, helps me over the loose bricks at the end of the stairs in the blinding dark, and guides me into her salon.

"I have a German officer, unconscious, in one of my girl's bedrooms," she says. "A gentleman, he paid ahead of time; we always have the money of the day, you know, in times of trouble, changing masters and soldiery." And she laughs a self-satisfied laugh.

"I do not want the police. No, I do not fear them, get me right, I have them all in my pocket, they get their cut, no matter what currency. But they also have changed, and this is not for them to handle. It is too big. Too many hostages have been taken. Hundreds of them are down the Schillerpark in a high school, awaiting the outcome. South of here, in the village of Rosh. Max, surely you have heard! They'll shoot every tenth one tomorrow at dawn if Lieutenant Gerhard Schneider is not found. What am I to do, Max? Should we go to the German headquarters, tell the truth, that he had solicited our services, paid us in German marks, and had suffered – God only knows what, a stroke maybe, exhaustion or whatever? Come with me – I need help. Someone clever to talk to."

I'll marry Süssel. I'll wait. I will not to be bullied, not any more. Often I have walked by this cellar-kingdom to get to the corner pharmacy for a glimpse of Süssel in her white coat, blue-embroidered collar showing against the flame of her hair; I leaned against the wall of this house, aroused, wild, ready to run down the cellar steps – But no! I thought, I'll wait. I'll marry Süssel...a lying coward, of course.

"Max, I know about you, Moritz always chats about his genius-twin." Rebecca talks on, she does know a great deal about me, little everyday things, my eating, my gestures. My arms are shorter than anyone else's and she knows it, the laces of my shoes are trailing and she knows that too. She knows me better than my good mother does, it seems.

So she drags me with her. Cellar to cellar, through corridors, doors – I could not have suspected that these stately bourgeois, utterly respectable buildings rested on this vaulted world of inter-connected cellars. There is no light, air, or windows. Only when passing from one house to another does an inner court open up, closing as soon as you enter the next building. Rebecca talks incessantly, while pushing me ahead of her. We walk on wooden boards over damp earth, skirting the holes she knows how to avoid.

"There is no one around," she says. "The streets are deserted. Our doctor, whom we are obliged to see every week to get our booklet stamped, the famous so-called 'whore-doctor' Landmann, went *'Heim ins Reich.'* Now we work without our checkups. You could not bribe Dr. Landmann. If we were not well, we did not get our book stamped and had to take the cure. I am not upset," she says. And she is not.

"I always keep my head cool. Just to keep everything running. Things are not always smooth. The girls – well, it's different in this business. I prefer the young trade or the very old, widowers, bachelors. The fat bourgeois I avoid like the pest! Their wives appear here, in their fabulous hats and with their fashionable umbrellas, break my few windows. Who needs it? The girls – not girls really, Mitzi is thirty-five, I do not tolerate twelve-year-olds – they know nothing. I hire them between twenty-five and fifty. Sometimes they are mothers. They are serious: learn the trade, know the customer. They don't want men for themselves. For love they come to me or to each other. I want them also. We haven't seen good things from fathers and uncles. For love we cuddle and hug. If men want us, let them pay for it!"

She speaks without pausing. We pry open crude doors and slam them shut behind us. She knocks coded rhythms on the pillars that hold the brick arches as we run over earthen floors to find Mitzi and her officer. There he lies, as we enter, on her square bed, still and handsome in his uniform, his fly open.

"He just fell off me, like a brick," says Mitzi, "Just fell off me onto his back." Quite unfazed, the two of them. Strange, such a lack of hysteria. Rebecca has seen them fall off her often enough, knows everything about pumping the heart by pressure or mouth-to-mouth resuscitation. This time it did not work, she tried all her tricks after Mitzi had stormed into her salon.

The women solve their own problems, most of the time. They are tenants, rent their rooms from Rebecca, don't really work for her. But she selects her tenants, refuses or rejects or grants favours, like an empress, or one of those mighty Celtic princess-warriors who fought Rome. I smile at my schoolboy memories, looking for the warrior Boadicea in Rebecca's whore-empire. She sits there now in Mitzi's room, quite unperturbed, a high stool supporting one of her mighty thighs. Enormous thighs crowning long legs and fine ankles, skirt falling in gipsy ripples into her middle, wrapping the upper leg. A petrol lamp gives spare smokey light to this eerie triumvirate. Though they disdained and cursed men, they expected them to spring into action when needed – "like real men," they said.

Mitzi's room was aclutter with objects. Dolls were scattered among scarves, cups, teapots on a table along the wall. A Mother of God above, flowers in her hair that looked mauve-purple in the candlelight. Mitzi was Polish, it seems; she looked at that Mother steadily, her round little body holding a four-year-old boy that could not be hushed away, holding him sweetly between her legs, stroking his hair. We had to come to a decision. Rebecca, the queen, asking the opinion of her minister, Max, who could only think of evasion. *Run.* I forced my brain to consider the options.

"There is a way," I said. "We need to enlist the help of the pastor." It was evasion on my part, of course, yet this time, without Moritz beside me, I simply knew I had to act. Rebecca, a good head taller than me, descended from her throne and took my arm, almost swallowing me in her embrace. She guided me out, towards the south side of her nine-block-square dominion, to a back door which led to the entrance of the Schillerpark, bordering the church garden.

"Hurry my darling," she urged, "hurry. I'll never forget this. You can come anytime and I'll reward you. Not my girls, I will do it myself, I'll teach you gently, as I do all my virgin boys. Go, hurry now." The sign of the cross and a squeeze for parting.

The fool I am, the fool. A citizen of Chelm, an idiot, one of those characters my grandfather's legends are made of. My father's father, a man who wears a silken sash around his middle to part the holy God-imbued body from the lower, a storytelling working man without a trade, lending a hand for a pittance to the rich and telling endless tales about them. He loved me because I am stupid. "You're so dumb and without brains that you could be from Chelm," he said. And once the name of this mythical locale is uttered, people, poverty, their puns and jokes, pour out of him. "Come, idiot, come my Chelmite-wise-man, come my Max-Mordechai. You have a Christian mother, poor thing, but I forgive you. It isn't your fault. We do not have a say, whose we are. God pairs us up there and we suffer the consequences and endure. Oh, she is a good mother, don't get me wrong. She works late in the night to sew and mend and she treads that sewing machine endlessly. Oh she is good – but, well...." And he holds me between his legs for a little while longer, searching in his pockets for the cube of sugar he has saved for me from his tea. I watch him sometimes sucking tea through his sugar cube, samovar on the table, small brown-betty crowning it. Glasses for tea, no cups, always glasses. One holds them scorching hot in both hands, good on a winter's day, and glass is kosher, pure!

The poorest of the Jewish poor, my grandfather has the dignity of the lettered man. A collector of double-tongued tales, which tell one thing and mean another. "Like the wise men of Chelm. Like you, like all idiots," he says. "You see, when God gave wise men and fools to the world, He in his just greatness wanted to parcel them out equally. So he called his angels, took one bag of the wise and one of the foolish, and asked them to fly over our world. But unfortunately, when they flew over Chelm, one of the bags broke and" – and he laughs – "Well, Mordechai, where do you think the Chelmites get their foolishness from? It is all God-given, my darling, all God-given." And I take his sugar cube and run, afraid of another of his endless Chelm-heroes. Is it because of him, with his Gimpel-the-fool, his Herschel-wisdom, that I turn a coin to read it on both sides, that I am so slow to act? Is this why I am so different from my beloved Moritz, who has no time for the slow-witted?

Instead of hurrying, I slow my step. The clouds are low, rain and heavy chestnut branches hide me, and I drag my feet. My only pair of shoes is full of clinging earth and pungent Lysol slowly rises to my nostrils, makes my head pound. The immediacy of the past hour. Whirling lights of greenish-blue curves and angles throb at my temples. I have always suffered from these flashing cartwheels. Only my grandfather listened to my headache stories, from the age of five. "Moritz never sees wheels of fire," my mother says. "Just Max with his head on fire."

"Max, would you please just help me with the shelling of the peas?" And Mother sits me down with the pressure of her flat hand, next to a green heap of pea pods. I love them, but I have no stomach for it. My head is full of green-blue-and-yellow, I can hardly count the peas in the pod. I'm blind, nearly totally blind, until a corner lifts on one side and slowly frees my sight. Coming back from a hurting dream, I try to break a pea pod open, can hardly move, when I hear my mother call, "Moritz, bring a cool wet towel and take your brother to the sofa, remove his glasses, and cover his head. Oh, it's nothing, just one of his eternal migraine headaches. Moritz, sit by him, please, a little." And she returns to finish the peas for supper herself.

My back against the chestnut trunk, I lean as if paralyzed:

lights, turning wheels of fire, a slow pounding rhythm in the hollows of my eyes. A misty rain gently cools my head and I feel Moritz's loving hand and hear my elder brother: "Max, what is it that plagues you? You do think too much! What will become of you?" And he presses his strong fingers against my head, playing a tune on the towelling.... Tears in my throat. Such longing for his love. So irretrievable. Oh, I remember the German officer. And I take the courtyard in a wild dash to the church door.

Under cover of that misty fog of weighted-down chestnut foliage, the pastor follows my lead towards the back door of the cellar-world. We retraced the steps I'd taken before, not speaking. I told him all I knew, how I had heeded Rebecca's call for help, and the pastor saw the hand of God and his Christian duty. No fear, no recriminations, he was a man of simple theology. He followed me, through the muddy path I'd made, the grey pebbly earth softened by the steadily falling rain, clinging to the soles. Past the hedges of the churchyard and behind the University grounds. Not far, but every step hard to take, avoiding the street. The pastor whispering, "Where have all the dogs gone?"

"They are shot or lying in front of their houses. Their masters are gone and they have no reason to live. They will not eat from anyone's hand."

The pastor: "How far yet?" as we were right in front of the low cellar door. It was half open, Rebecca in the frame of the door, grabbing my hand, a broad smile on her face. She pulled me in with her experienced bazaar gesture, the client-grabbing gesture of her trade. The pastor hugged by her encircling arms, trying to free himself.

We enter Mitzi's room. The officer is seated, his fly closed now, his uniform in order. He sits pale and motionless. Mitzi bubbles with the story of the officer's gaining consciousness and slowly, painstakingly, trying to recall where he was. He said at first it was lightless; frightened by the candle under the small figure of Mary, he thought it was lit for his deathbed. He slept a little longer, woke and saw all the dolls, dressed and grinning around the teapot, saw the used cups in disarray, and could not recall having come here. Mitzi, touching on small memories, bringing back the last few hours, speaking a German of the famous Ukrainian-Yiddish mix of Czernowitz, with Romanian words thrown in for good measure. They speak everything, thinking it is German, and it is! Yiddish, the *lingua franca,* elevated to a kind of German that can be understood by an officer of Hitler's army.

Mitzi told us the officer had hesitated at first at Rebecca's invitation. It was just ordinary sex he wanted, some release, mainly to be with women and away from the company of men, away from the horror he had just lived. They had entered a second-floor Jewish home uptown, and he had watched his friends take the women forcibly. His superior had handed him the baby from the cradle, had pushed him towards the window, told him to throw it out like a playing ball. Saying, We must not waste a bullet on something one can squash like a bug. It is forbidden. Out the window. That will do the trick. Before he could think, he had done it. And his superior, mockingly: See, you can do it, there is nothing to it. He felt sick, vomit rising, he asked and was given leave for a few hours; the unit was not moving until next day. All this Mitzi recounted now.

He had read the street names, some of them still German from Austrian times, most of them Romanian now. And he had walked down beside the university grounds, in the direction of a pharmacy he had spotted the day before, that sat next to a very

Austrian turn-of-the-century theatre-opera house. Turning into the Goethegasse he saw the women, ready for work, leaning against their gates, house after house on that huge interconnected block. And the older one, not whorishly dressed, but in an elegant skirt to her ankles, calling him, *Ah, Liebling, komm doch, wir brauchen Dein Geld und Du, brauchst uns.* True, I need you, he thought, I need you more than you need my money. He did not ask the price, pulled German marks out of his pocket uncounted, and followed Rebecca, who put Mitzi in charge of him.

Mitzi went on and on, embellishing the story, interrupting it with giggles; relieved hysteric laughter, after the crisis had passed.

I knew little of surrealism, the concept was new to me. Moritz read more than I did, finding in the unusual fertile soil for his derision, always looking for his own angle. But I recognized it, it was here now. Dark yet discernable. Objects became superimposed, melted into each other, took on forms not their own, moved inexplicably. A colourless room of petit-bourgeois respectability with crocheted doilies on worn armchairs. The officer sprawled, legs outstretched, arms limp, in one of the chairs. An elongated table along the wall. The tablecloth hanging, fusing into a carpet whose fringes melted into the pounded-down earth floor.

A naphtha lamp on the table was the only form that was clear and meaningful. I am the light, it seemed to say to me. I did not see the flickering candle under the holy image from my corner. An expert in hiding, "running from the scene," as Moritz would say, I found a spot behind the cabinet and the door, which Rebecca had left slightly ajar. Vying for escape, yet rooted to this surreal world, I stood very still and hoped the officer had not noticed me, that the pastor was slowly coming to terms with it all.

Mitzi's account of the officer's recovery, the sound of her crazy-Slavic-Yiddish voice, and the silence of the other three gave this tableau the surreality of *déjà vu.* I felt that I had been here before, waiting for the dream to run its course, to its last scream and wake.

The pastor made signs – the back of his hand waving me away – and I understood. I am free to save myself, his eyes told me, he would take care of it. I slid out the door, to rush to the safety of the church.

Süssel

Two Cardboard Triangles

TWO TRIANGLES OF CARDBOARD COVERED IN YELLOW cloth, juxtaposed. They are to be worn on everything one wears, and are predominant now on my white coat. I am preparing a makeshift autoclave to sterilize syringes and needles. I am in charge, I run a medical lab: six prisoners, my father under my command. Hungry and trying to smile, he looks young. Our hospital has been evacuated to accommodate hundreds of wounded German boys from the front. They come on trucks or tanks, shot, shelled, or in shock. It is my father who invents and prepares *ad hoc* anaesthesia, some chloroform, some ether *pro narcosi,* or just a soluble barbiturate. He distills water in a contraption made of two Jena bottles of neutral glass and an end of rubber hose, sterile enough to inject. And Dr. Bauer, Major Hermann Bauer, operates. I am under Dr. Bauer's command, so to speak. Six prisoners looking after all these young German lives. We are too bruised, broken, hungry to think of sabotage, of poisoning them all, or setting the hospital on fire, or fleeing. Slaves do not think – we jump at the raising of an eyebrow.

There are new beds to improvise, barracks to be built. Jewish prisoners from Moghilev arrive to put them up. I recognize my uncle Saul. My lighthearted, singing, printer-typesetter uncle, the youngest, called Shmul. Tell us a story, Shmul, tell us the story of when you set a whole page of the *Vorwärts,* our socialist daily, with wild Jewish stories of ghosts, dybbuks, possessed screaming brides, and dancing, exorcising rabbis, instead of the news of the day. How you got drunk with your buddies, draping yourself in the red flag of the "party," playing revolution, got fired and then rehired, for there was no other typesetter as skilled and fast as you. Tell us. Tell us!" He is stricken by typhus now, he can hardly move. None of the thirty *muselmen* – Jews at the end of their strength – are able to build anything decent. But triggers are loose, and they do what they can. I approach Dr. Bauer cautiously, humbly, to see if I can be permitted to requisition that particular Jew for the cleaning of our latrines. No, he says, not from that team. They are full of fleas and typhus.

Rumours are that in Moghilev four incinerators with some thirty-two *creusets* have been installed, to deal with the disposal of corpses and typhus-diseased flesh. "Not from that team," Dr. Bauer says. "I'll keep your father and you, but watch out." And he pokes me in the ribs with his *Reitgerte* – a small sharp leather whip – and then bangs it rythmically against his own leather shank, in front of prisoners and patients about to be operated on. Yes, we know who is God, no need to enforce it. No rebellion, we know.

It is *so* absurd. A Jewish child, pious, singing to the Lord and hearing His voice in reply, in fetters now. Total corporeal confinement. Yet with an end of muscle left in my face, the smile is there. It is there because of the sudden pleasure at the absence of our daily companion: guilt. It just isn't there. Everything seems acceptable, feasible now. The law, the centripetal law of living amongst others, is gone. Could I smile, undetected, I would. Of course, I will keep my end of the deal. Dr. Bauer has freed my fiancé, my so-called fiancé, my sweet, adorable, otherworldly boy, my teen-years companion, Max. I can see him standing across the street from the old house, hidden by an eavestrough's overhang, waiting for me. I imagine the two of us sitting on the Ahi fountain and chatting, as fifteen-year-olds, tackling the big questions: the meaning of existence, the search for God, the intellect versus the heart.

Dr. Bauer expects payment. He passes my father, still so young, a picture of himself as a young officer in the Austrian army, *Zwicker* – pince-nez glasses – on his nose. My father, moving among his test tubes, touching me sideways with his flared coat.

I am the sole woman among the six prisoners. As the head Jew, foreman, coordinator between lab and ward, my whereabouts are uncontrolled. Or so I think. In a tight hungry universe everyone senses the life-flow of the other, the state of pain, an occasional better day. One knows...here, silent anonymity is best. Nose to the ground, guts at high alert! They all know: I sleep with the boss. And I find myself in a state of hilarity. Guilt? Where has it gone? Theatre, absurd theatre. And this total absence of guilt gives me a strange freedom: no law! Nothing matters, not one of the ten commandments! Maybe the fifth, honour your father and mother. Because the surge of blood to my face, seeing my father at work, looking like a very young man, and his silent acceptance of the cigarettes or chocolate which I smuggle into his lab-coat pocket, make me still human. It is the only thing.

I made a deal. Dr. Bauer has offered me a day of rest, and I accepted. This first day in total seclusion is the first day of my life! Windows are covered, there is warm water in a tub, apricots, chocolates, and dried prunes in small dishes, and a field-bed made up in white linen. His barrack is fifty metres from the hospital, somewhere in heaven. He says he will not come until I have rested. I sleep countless hours. When he enters he watches me, takes me like a child to the tub, scrubs with a surgical brush my arms, legs, and back, with medical scissors he cuts the nails on my toes and fingers. He says nothing, until: "You have beautiful hair." I smile, of course. My head is bare and so is the mound below my navel. At the last delousing all that has disappeared. I smile at Dr. Bauer. He takes me to his bed and leaves me there. He returns to wake me at four-thirty in the morning, my sterilized prisoner's garb in his arms; he has operated with the help of two *Feldschers* all night. There is coffee, bread and butter, and vitamin-complex chocolate. We share it.

Five o'clock, I am on duty again, through the wards, my face stern, my movements machine-like. During my absence a shipment of gauze, bandages, potassium permanganate – the purple disinfectant of old, and live mercury has arrived. Intense joy pervades my team – to feel human, to work with purpose. All seems forgotten: hunger, sleepless nights, the occasional strap, and the eternal rush to the latrine with loose bowels. One thing matters, to escape into purpose. My father gets at the live mercury, commands everyone around to find some vehicle. He'd like pork fat, lanolin, but he settles for third-grade Vaseline. He fashions pestles out of wood, constructs a tub to mix it in. To start, equal quantities of mercury and Vaseline are needed to achieve a homogeneous mixture – mercury runs away on you otherwise, partitions itself into millions of small silver balls. Slowly he incorporates the rest of the Vaseline, and he and all the others glow at the successful mercury ointment. It combats everything, including venereal disease.

It was a good day. We are rewarded with soup from the hospital canteen and we all fall to our bunks, oblivious to the world. Guilt? Funny what people can think of, when they are warm and their bellies filled with bread and butter.

Dr. Bauer appears on the ward. Shaven now, rested, he drops his key into my white coat pocket. The new *Feldscher* takes over, and I go out into the night. Not really hoping, but expecting, Dr. Bauer to be there. He is not. I undress. There is warm water in a bowl, an old-fashioned ceramic bowl, with red tulips, blue tulips, looking at me with strange eyes. I remember white tulips on white on my mother's damask-covered table. Where? When? Flowers blooming everywhere. On the Ukrainian bowls, more tulips, and green leaves on the handles of the pitcher next to it. Dried prunes, dried apricots to chew. One chews here.

Key in lock. Dr. Bauer enters, with fried sausage, sauerkraut, in a covered army dish, and the smell of bread. It is to lose one's mind. One camp chair for Dr. Bauer across from me on the bed. I eat little and none of the cabbage. A slave knows her moment. She does not have a morrow. It is all now: if there is food, she eats and if there is warm water – well, it is simple. What does it matter who sees you? Where is the all-seeing eye, the laws to follow and to transgress? Where are the small loose bricks at the foot of a Moorish wall to swindle yourself into a secret mystery? What mystery – where? It is simple.

Dr. Bauer inspects me for lice and fleas, says *sotto voce,* a voice never heard on the ward: "Your hair when grown again will be beautiful." And he leaves me to my apricots and prunes, to the sucking of their pits like the comfort of a baby's thumb. At four-thirty he appears with coffee. No word is spoken. At five o'clock I am out in the cold that feels like minus forty degrees Celsius. The lab and ward.

After three days he comes and stays. Four o'clock in the morning, he undresses, kneels by my field-bed with coffee in his tin army mug, sweetened with thick milk, and a light-aired slice of loaf, the crusty sort. It falls in crumbs, and he collects them with his mouth. For the first time he touches my skin. Rises to put away the cup, and also for the first time, I see him naked. He is unaroused. Funny to look at. A dog's tail, between a man's legs, no wonder Germans call it *Schwantz,* meaning just that. How he handles every object from coffee cup to scalpel. Knowing fingers, all tipped with brains of their own. They know things, perceive and move, seemingly undirected. Innate elegance, in the fingers and in the palm, hanging from the wrist. I have watched these hands sever legs from the knee or hip, sewing and suturing, pushing bones into place. All with the tenderness of strength, joints moving on their own, yet in unison. I have seen beauty of such nobility in Johann Sebastian Bach, and I see it here. I watch those dangling, glorious fingers as he approaches my bed. Still unaroused, he kneels by me, and raises his left arm to cover my eyes, forehead, hairline with his whole flat hand. Fingers, imperceptibly moving, close my eyes, as if for the last time. With his right arm he moves across my body to press my left arm and with his body he holds my right one. Stretched and stilled now along hip and flank. Limp all muscles, limp as in death. No breath audible. Breasts fall in. Mine were never there. They are negative breasts. They make hollows and go the other way, inwards. I looked at my face in his shaving mirror a few days ago and saw a boy's face looking back at me. A hint of pink hairline, rising cheekbones, and green eyes. My father at eighteen. A young man, gaunt.

His breath is closer now. Barely touching my nipples, he warms them and brings them out of the hollow, with lips as clever as his hands. Taking time, his hands move down, calling for stillness; fingers entering the hairless sex to find the labia. A sharp stroke, repeated without gentleness. The thrill of small death. Tears rise to my throat.

It's almost five o'clock. Hundreds of Soviet prisoners have arrived. Do not go near them, he says, they are full of typhus, lice, and fleas. There is no facility to delouse so many, I have to keep what I have for ourselves. The prisoners huddle on the outer edge of the compound against the shed, on the frozen earth. He says, "They will die soon, and if they do not, we'll help them to it."

Out into the night. To the job. Sucking prune pits. Some in my pocket for my father. Guilt? Avert your eyes, oh Lord!

Gogol's Coat

I REGRET NOT HAVING GONE TO THE STRICH – THE strip where girls – old, very old, and prepubescent – offered their flesh for hire. I regret it, not having gone at sixteen, with Moritz my twin, my older brother Hans, and their friend Felix. I regret it now. I know so little, not having ever done it. One has to learn how to do things, and the Strich was just around the corner from Süssel's pharmacy, on the Tempelgasse and the Goethegasse – restricted areas, accepted by the bourgeois. But I could not do it then. I wanted to marry someone beautiful, of my heart. My body was not separate from my heart, as it was with other boys.

Well, yes, I went along with some of the stupid things, like aiming to the ceiling to see how far one could "spritz" the stuff, when I was ten or twelve years old. But I would not go to the Strich. There was an old whore there, ancient, Moritz told me, Rebecca – of all names, who was the best instructor a boy could have. She had lived in her basement in the Goethegasse for decades, and specialized in young teenage boys.

Just wash yourself, darling, she says, with that pink stuff – manganese she calls it. In her chipped enamel tub she washes you, inspects you, and says sweetly, *You look lovely, darling,* then goes on top and teaches you. You come before it is time, of course, but it does not matter. *Ante portas,* as the boys call it. I am a coward, an ordinary coward, or maybe just longing for Süssel. So I haven't learned anything yet.

IT ALL COMES BACK, after such a winter. A Ukrainian winter, when the earth freezes and your naked toe, sticking out from your torn boot, glues itself to the ground. It tears your flesh when you try to free yourself, keeping a piece, not letting you go. You feel nothing at all. A totally natural thing, not to feel anything. A good thing too – who wants to feel?

Shovel in hand I worked on a "strategic encampment." On what? Even the earth laughed at you as you tried to splinter its frozen surface, to stack it into heaps, lift it into small wagons, and carry it to the other side. I was one of a thousand Jewish men under German-Romanian command, set to the task of building useless fortifications on the eastern bank of the Djnester – or was it the Bug? – some river.

Romanians were in charge, along with some Jewish deputies. No one cared what we did or how well, as if the work was designed for torture only. We had tepid water-soup made from grass, potato peels at best, when there was fuel for cooking. So who cared? Lice everywhere. Who wants to feel anything?

Lucky as I always am, I found – is it possible? – in the middle of that naked plain – or was there once an old village there? – a three-legged table lying upside down. We had all been sleeping in the mud. An upside-down table made a three-poster bed, dry and luxurious. Joey and I, to the envy of everybody else, occupied it.

But of course our comrades, our fellow-Jews, would seize it if we were just a moment late for it. It was everyone for himself, kindness not invented yet or killed by the system.

It is the winter of 1942-43. Dreams are far away, love is in a potato peel. There is no grass except in the soup, when we are lucky, and days are long. Who has a brother here, I wonder, or a sweet Jewish grandfather? My grandfather sometimes appears, comes to me, no mistaking his presence, it is he. When I am at the end of my strength, towards the evening, he speaks to me: *All work is futile, do it without thinking. Just carry those wagons from one silly spot to the other. All is senseless, imposed by robots for their own might. There is only God to serve. Think your prayers.* I smell his tobacco, his unwashed gabardine, he is here, he is here! But it is December, 1942, and his *Mordechai, think of God,* does not keep my fingers from frost. One after the other they turn as white as the snowfields around us, and I lose control of the shovel. It falls from my hands and I fall next to it. I could cry then, and my grandfather speaks to me, consolingly: *Here is a cube of sugar. I saved it from my tea, God has chosen you. Sleep my Bubbale, my darling.*

"What do you do for a living?" the Romanian asks. Good-natured, full of wine, but impatient. He had given me up for dead and is slightly annoyed to see me return to the living. "I am a mathematician," I say, "and an astronomer."

"You can count, right? You will stand near the ditch, count the wagons as the other Jews fill them, and report the exact number to me. But not today. You have twenty-four hours rest." Watching me tumbling, trying to stand up, the Romanian guard smiles.

How lucky I am, twenty-four hours in the three-poster bed under my coat, a heavy, rough Russian army coat I have acquired somewhere, my own stolen long ago. Coats disappear as fast as one can steal them, being the most important survival item of all. Not even boots can compare. A coat can have lice in it, but lice can become your companions, you can talk to them, curse them, squash them between the nails of your two thumbs for entertainment. A heavy coat in a Ukrainian winter on the back of a Jew is a status symbol. It means you're strong enough to defend it, fight for it with your fists, you're a winner. It shelters you, it can be a *Baldachin* – a glorious roof at night. It has pockets to hold snatched pieces of iron, wood, or stone. And all sorts of wonderful hiding places, inside the lining, in the shoulder pads, thick with wool where pins, needles, or God knows what precious thing can disappear to outside inspection. Only you know. Even something that seems trivial might turn out to be extremely useful, a thread, a string – one can never predict what will come in handy and how inventive a Jew can be in extremes.

Well, it isn't Gogol's coat, let's face it, sporting a fur collar, shiny bone buttons, silk lining through the sleeves. A coat where every seam is straight and fortified, where pockets are lined with plush for the sensuous touch on your fingers. A coat tried on, watched in the making, expectation rising as it grows into its final beauty. Walking out into the centre square of a Russian small town, a simple clerk becomes a high official, a nimbus around his person, and the *mujik* falls to the ground in adoration. No, it isn't Gogol's coat, definitely not. Mine is threadbare on the sleeves, elbows, and hem. Greenish in colour. Pockets, heavily used, have torn through, and I have bound the hole with string. But an ankle-long Russian coat is heaven on earth, coveted, and almost as grand as Gogol's.

I know, I like to lie to myself. I like to say I can't remember, I can't remember where I found it. Lies. How would a Jew not remember where he found the coat that saved his life? Of course I know exactly where I found it. I took it off a Russian soldier who was almost frozen to the ground. Gently removed it from the stiff body. As gently as I could, for it wasn't easy to unbutton the coat, turn the poor wretch on his side and pull it off, as if from a mannequin. It wasn't easy, but no luck is easy. So I said the Lord's Prayer for my mother and the *Shema,* that God is One, for my father, and put the coat on my shoulders, slipped into its sleeves. It fitted like a dream. I had been sent to look for firewood and came back with power on my back. I had matches in my pockets – or rather in the hem, as they had fallen through – two boxes of them, a beautiful file, sharp at the edges, and a flat army vodka bottle. I was a rich man, a made man. Able to exchange, barter, and give for free. For love. To my twin – whomever.

So I had my coat and I stretched onto my table. Slowly, holding onto the up-in-the-air legs to ease myself down. I had not eaten, I do not know for how long. But how lucky I was! "No marble palace, steps leading into the sea, trade winds cooling your brow" could compare with the comfort of a dry board in the Ukrainian winter of 1942.

Fever shakes me like an aspen leaf, cleanses and frees me from the unbearable. I am floating, beyond food and drink or ablution, I feel my brother near. Hold his hand, look into Moritz's eyes of unclouded blue sky, feel a wet towel, pressed by his strong hands against my temples. And hear my mother joke: when the good Lord in his wisdom parcelled out hands and feet inside my womb, He simply made a mistake, and Max got two left hands and two left feet, and Moritz got all the right ones. *Sit by him, Moritz, do this for me,* Mother pleading, *Max has fainted again.* And I sip water from his hand, as he holds my head.

Who can live without his twin? So I fashion a new twin, and love what is near me. I embrace my coat, my Russian ankle-long body-hugging coat, and talk to him. I make my brother out of feverish dreamy stuff. I see Moritz high up in the top branches of the chestnut tree by the Evangelical church, almost in the clouds, pounding our enemies with the shiny brown horse-chestnut grenades. My heart jolts with joy, to have him as my own. I hold his hand and whisper, *Moritz, my tongue is on fire, my eyeballs are jumping from their orbits, give me a drink.* And he does, sip by sip.

And it is Joey, that is my twin now, who shares my table-bed, lies under my Russian coat with me, holds my head up, feeds me the soup he has saved, and speaks gently and reassuringly, *You have come to, Max. You're better, your fever is down. Tomorrow you can work again. Just don't die on me. Don't die.* Joey my twin. My new adopted brother. Mine own.

Süssel
A Divine Blessing

THESE ARE THE DARKEST DAYS, BETWEEN NOVEMBER and February. Stalingrad is raging. Russian prisoners flooding in, not enough guards, food, or water. Machine-gun shots – rhythmical savage dancing – as I emerge at five o'clock from the barrack of my lover, my true lover now. I love him furiously. His face, his duelled sharp *Schmiss* across his right cheek, his distorted upper lip, his eyebrows, those celestial arcs, are with me everywhere. Fed and rested, I can love. With my team for sixteen hours of the day, I am pursued by this face.

In a deputy role again, self-imposed, I order everyone around, fearing for my life. They'll get me somehow. They'll stab or strangle me, they'll poison my tea or catch my foot in an iron trap like a wild animal. And he'll rescue me. Mad, mad. I love him. Afflicted.

He has come to me fully aroused one morning at four-thirty and taken me without warning. The key in my pocket the night before, I arrived to a spread of cold meat and red wine prepared for me. Drank and ate at a small pine-box table he had improvised, an army towel with crest for a tablecloth. I washed in the tulip-ridden Ukrainian bowl, saw that my hair had filled in a little, smiled in his shaving mirror, put on his army shirt, and stretched my limbs long, stiff, free of muscle as he wants them. And was wakened by the sharp parting of my upper thighs and his brutal entrance. Catatonic as he wants me, the thrill will ring through my life. He came upon my navel, lying in his juice like a newborn from the womb.

Indomitable snowstorms, elemental blizzards of the Ukraine steppe as far as the Urals. The plains, from the Carpathians to the northern horizons, open to their wild roaring gales. It has snowed all night, white against the night skies. There is no light to guide the foot. Only the sudden burst of machine-gun fire, that rhythmic ritual dance. Ploughing through the soft virgin blanket, it would be easy to lie down to die. So tempting. But bodies go on as programmed.

These were bitter days. A small commando unit stripped the prisoners of war of their good heavy coats and covered the bodies with snow. Their coats we used as extra blankets. Boots piled up high. Here and there a ring no one had seen before turned up on a German finger. These were dark winter days, with typhus the ultimate equalizer.

We were unspeakably lucky. My father and another Jewish chemist had devised a sulfur volatilizing chamber, where the coats and woolens of the dead POWs were deloused, and we all wore them, Jew and German. There was now total dependency. Without us the German soldiers would simply die of shock, bullet wounds, and gangrene. They knew it and we knew it and our régime changed. There was more collegiality and banter, and we ate from the same pot. Always hungry, none of us or them had enough. But latrine cleaners and Jews brought in from Moghilev for rough work had nothing at all. They died before our eyes. The recovering soldiers took over some chores, postponing their return to duty. I would catch them rubbing their thermometers under the blankets with fingers or linen to bring the temperature up, so they could have another week away from action. They were just boys, hardly any beards, children almost.

Frontiers blurred: my father was suddenly everyone's father, a hero of stature. Only once in these bitter months did I hear a wounded officer call him a swinish Jew, for not having rushed to his command. Yet we never stepped out of place. It felt easier now, less menacing, but as Jews we knew better. Things can change in a moment and you are against the wall. We beat the system. We were a team. And this alone was the major victory.

Camp is calculated victimization, each prisoner a desperate single unit, everyone spying for the victimizer, serving the torturer, identifying with the master. I did it, for such small rewards, for a bowl of something called tea. In these barracks now, we almost seemed human. Dr. Bauer and his two new assistants, permitting it.

A strange, timeless, placeless reality, surrounded by a wall of winter. Another theatre set as absurd as any. Actors sent to play roles, transforming them miraculously, subverting the master-slave design. Young men, wounded soldiers without weapons, bleeding, no stripes of rank, all animals now of a different race. The six of us that hold their lives acquired the stature of parent, there was almost love. We were the masters for a moment. Changes in a classical play, in the unity of time and place.

This was still January, the famous month with two faces of God: Janus looking both ways, watching the gates of Rome, to keep order in the city, and looking outward into the world for approaching danger. This was *our* January, where every day had to be lived and none could be skipped; each day lived through, bitten into, as the hours stood still, all limits set. Our bodies moved with destiny. This was our January of 1943, a date just for the record in history books. This was our January, that stuck to our soles like Russian mud in spring. Heavy, black, and sinking. No sense of time.

Yet, one incomprehensible day in February, there are orders from Command. Strike the set. Most of the prisoner-Jews are shot at dawn. One night at midnight, Dr. Bauer calls in my father only, not me. Orders us to run in groups of two. Three times two, at intervals. He will be on duty. There are no dogs any more. My father: "The sick German boys?"

Dr. Bauer: "They will be shipped on trucks, tanks, and on foot. It is none of your concern."

My father: "It is my concern."

Dr. Bauer: "It is not. Look out for yourselves. Here is a small rucksack with what I could spare. Take your daughter. Take the Russian coats, the fur hats, and the boots. In thirty minutes you move silently in twos, out of the compound, direction southwest. Hurry. One moment more – shake my hand, I have never before seen a war hero of your stature." And he buried his head in Father's shoulder in a moment's embrace.

We walked at night, sleeping or lying in hollows by day, hidden from friend and foe. Two unlikely figures from an improbable world. We rationed ourselves the absolute minimum of biscuit and sausage, a little plum brandy and prunes, snacked out of the rucksack. And matches, thank God for matches. I found a spade under the snow somewhere. Everything can be done with a spade – snow piled into heaps for protection; if the earth permits, a fine bed can be fashioned, branches brought down for a fire in a hollow.

On the third day a huddle of houses, huts appear, still and dark. With roofs above and sheds at back. Small, almost square Ukrainian windows, a kerchiefed figure in one window frame. She seems to be there, part of the winter landscape and moves away to open the door. A gesture so natural and simple, as if for expected guests, who arrive just a trifle late. She looks at us, two ghosts. No questions, just: "Go down into the cellar, there is straw and sheepskin. You'll find soured milk in two open trays. Eat your fill."

She comes down to us with heavy bread, black like the earth and sticking to the palate, two bowls, and wooden spoons. She says, "Eat, my babes, may the Lord be blessed, that I can help those that have less than I have." And she makes the sign of the cross. "Sleep, sleep, my children." We stretch into the straw and I fall upon my father's breast. Tears stream down our faces with the warmth of the sheepskins and the woman's blessing.

DR Hermann Bauer

Letter From The Condom

February, 1943

Forgive me. This is my letter to you. I am writing it on toilet paper and will roll it into the condom. For protection, condoms are the best. We German soldiers have rolled diamonds into them, gold coins we found, and messages, sometimes. We hide them in toothpaste – easy! If you open the bottom part and reclose it, and hide it on the body somewhere, condoms are the best.

This is my letter to you. A letter of penance, maybe, but also of confession. You will read it, if you find it in the inner lining of the rucksack, should you survive the winter of '43. I fear you will not. Your father's strength waning and you yourself so close to the end, the rucksack will rot in the Ukrainian mud.

This is just an outpouring, coming from the need to speak, to tell. No *mea culpa*. I did not make that war. I am just like you but on the other side of the barricade. A victim with more luck than you. But it is time for penance, too, a trial of self. More for what is than what was. And what is is the night before, when we received the order to annihilate the Jewish prisoners. Mostly by *Genickschuss*. The order is: strike the barracks, pack the German wounded as well as possible, take the trucks – not enough or big enough – some fuel, some tanks. Ludicrous, not sufficient for any such operation in harsh winter conditions. Pack, leave, and burn the rest. We are to shoot you first. All of you. Oh God! You are the flesh of my flesh, your father is my father. It must not happen, not by my command. Your life might end in the Ukrainian snow or mud, but not by my hand.

I know you from a very long time. Two years in the war is an eternity. You may not believe me, but I knew you from the moment your green eyes met mine. And you have remained mine.

Jews were nothing to me, I had never known one. I am a German. They said Jews harm our very social fibre. The Bible seems to say that. I come from church-going Catholics, grew up in a forester's home in the Sylva Nigra, the Schwarzwald. I was clever and sent to medical school. My father said, you are a surgeon. You can split the finest branches, plant the tenderest sapling, with these hands of yours. I was five years old. He took me on wanderings in the forest, rescuing fallen birds. Come my young doctor, he said, build me a splint for the leg of this beautiful young bird. We'll take it home and watch it heal. I was a doctor from the age of five. I was the eldest of eight, and there was always something in somebody's eye to be removed, a knee to be caring for my youngest sister, who could not and would not ever walk. Hospitals were far away and God's will was accepted in our home.

Jews, Protestants? I did not know any. Nothing of politics either. Catechism, Mass on Sundays, very early, all nine of us.

Prayer, work, and the sublime forest, touching the clouds, rooted. A home to keep in order, I beside my father. Old trodden paths to repair, fallen trees, some to leave for the forest floor, some to remove for order and convenience.

In her eighth childbed, my mother died. At her grave, by then, I was my father's *Stellvertreter,* his deputy, for prayer, decision-making, and care. I fell in love with the newly-born. Of such utter beauty, rose-petal skin and eyes green as emerald, hanging from the beech branches. Your eyes that strike me suddenly in the nightmare-unreality of a ghetto.

Who are these strange robots, running to my will at the merest twitch of my *Reitgerte?* I used to slap it against my boot or high leather shank just to see – will they really jump? Creatures of that sort, they did not seem human. It was the summer – fall of 1941. I was already in uniform, and had to leave my beautiful new home and surgery on the Rhine. It was war in earnest and I had to do my duty. I am not saying orders are orders. But they are. Given in command of something one has never seen nor contemplated, there is not much abstract thinking. Just application to the task and everything of circumstance. A ghetto, what is a ghetto?

The steady incoming contradictory orders, the enforcement of harsh work, and the sudden appearance of convoys with instructions to move. Hospital, equipment, personnel, and Jews. Thousands of them. I was in command of my own Jews, a few hundred of them. These were men with their wives and children. They had to be separated. I made a list of fifty doctors, nurses, pharmacists, and cleaning personnel. They were loaded into trucks, into trains heading east. We passed the river Prut, the Djnester. By the time we had reached the

Bug, of my fifty Jews I had ten left. We threw the dead onto the open ground, sometimes from moving trains, sometimes in a station. Did you ever wonder how you, a woman among those men, how it was possible – not even I can answer this. It is God's will. What one calls circumstance is God's will. Jews were meant to wander. They did not accept Christ and they will wander, staff in hand, until they do. Or so I saw it. No one is permitted to think – to really think, we have to stop, arrest the flow of days, or we can't go on.

And why did I free your fiancé, take you along wherever I was stationed, let you get away with it when you stole alcohol and hid it in a flat bottle under your prisoner's pant? Why did I let you get away with it when you fraternized with the soldiers, took chocolate and cigarettes from them and gave them to your father, or exchanged them with other Jews? There was underground black marketeering. You were part of it; being a woman, you had other ways than men; being more intelligent, fast, and, I thought, cunning, you seemed to do well, as well as a Jew can possibly do.

It must be that God directed, God led my hand. I do not recall consciously making a decision. But once, I had to put an end to your flouting of authority. You were, a law unto yourself, showing a brazen disrespect, wearing your upside-down triangles, your yellow David's star, like a medal of valour. I saw some of your looks. It was derision, mockery. The more successful you were in work, bartering and dealing, the better fed you were, the haughtier you became. I felt you treated us – me in particular – as idiots, to be tricked, stolen from, and my blood boiled. But of course, I thought, she is a Jew and she couldn't show it more clearly. Behind those green eyes lives her dark soul. And her father. Experts at what they do. Pretending to be what they are not, they move humbly, silently, like cats. But I couldn't punish you, couldn't harm you. If it is God's will, so be it. You were in charge of my lab and ward, and assumed the position with an air of superiority. I was astounded. You could hardly stand on your feet, unwashed and unfed. I also watched that tribe cling together. You passed by your father all the time and he, without visible reason, hurried by you. Just to touch, make contact, be reassured by the other's existence, I don't know. I watched you, all six of you, when the sulphur came in, or the mercury. Getting wild with excitement to make sulfur cream out of nothing, to cure the itch, the *Krätze,* scabies, that afflicted our soldiers between their fingers and toes. How you asked for permission to go out into the fields, with guards at your side, all of you, to collect frozen rosehips from under the snow, where you had noticed them before. Waited for the *Hagebutten* to defrost, then crushed them and boiled them into a thick extract and made our soldiers eat it, for there was nothing fresh and your father said, they need their daily dose of vitamin C. I just succumbed to your superiority, simply. Acknowledged that I was told lies as a child. You are flesh from my flesh. The trials God gives us teach us to live better.

I know nothing of your religion, how you practice, what you do. I know how you are. You are mine, and I will make you mine, slowly. I am not a very sexual man. I dream of things, but I do not make them come true. In my first year of medical studies I fought duels, for stupid reasons; a first breath of freedom, away from parental eyes, responsibility for siblings. How stupid freedom could be! All of us, groups of young "foxes" going to the Freudenhäuser – homes of joy. No joy, really, just relief of tension and loud bravura about one's virility. All pitiful. And playing troubadours, serenading the "lofty lady" of your heart, under her window. Heavens! For the rest, study, work, go to Mass, and keep away from politics. But even if I only tangentially absorbed the philosophy of the superior race, it felt good. After all, I was a doctor from the age of five. I am able, a problem-solver. German. My fatherland. What is there to think about?

Then, as if heaven-sent, in a no-place-no-time no-man's-land, I was taught to love. By circumstance, by God almost, I learnt love. Sexual desire, as never before, but I could not give in. It took days and nights, while I was operating. And I don't know if you recall. Your father had made a sodium barbiturate solution. You helped me inject it intravenously and, dosing it carefully, by intuition almost, weighing the necessary amount, you kept the patient motionless and unconscious. You had never done this before. The operation was over in fifty-five minutes of anaesthesia. Whatever we did, it was a wonderful success – I think it was a severed finger. And it was then that I offered you that deal of a day's rest and you asked me to free your fiancé.

I wanted to earn you, as an equal would. I could have ordered you to my bed. But I wanted to see if you were honourable, in a curious sort of way. I took my time, to prepare myself, to dream about you, to fantasize. I am not a wildly physical man. I need a yielding partner, because I am easily frightened and can't get aroused easily. Why did I tremble, shiver, before a slave whose life I could extinguish with a wink of my eyelash? Would you allow me to take you on my terms?

It would be a test. If you loved me, you would guess, comply, answer my needs. You would understand I do not suffer resistance, the power of the other, gladly. It frightens me to the core. Not just in sex, at work, too: competing with colleagues, detecting manipulation, conspiracy, or just dislike, I would become as cold as ice, until I had bent men and circumstance to my will.

With you it was for the first time different in a not unfamiliar way. I waited. But there was no time, the war was moving faster now, and those Stalingrad months from November into the New Year were crucial. This time, which curtailed itself so rapidly, was our time. Suddenly all the concerns of the world took on an eerie unreality. The world others lived in and fretted about did not concern me, I lived in my own inner world. But I functioned in the external world unsuspected. A stern face will hold inquiry at bay. And I did my routine duty and more. The intensity of my imagined world was unnoticed by others – German, I wear the mythological "tarncap" which hides your face – makes you invisible – but the scrutiny of your face, your movements, and the increasing evidence of my triumph made me almost delirious.

I hide well, I'm hidden within, compartmentalized. Tarncap. Not even you, who are at the innermost centre of my quest, had noticed. Or I don't think you did. But you loved me, loved me. You guessed what I was. That I wanted your body and soul, pure as virginal snow. Wanted to be found, rescued, and owned. Life created, exhaled into you almost, by me alone. And this stillness, which you understood, when I stretched your body out like death, when I covered your face, not to see the thrill when it came – my triumph was not a hunter's only, a victory with the beast at my feet, it was the end of all things achieved, creation itself. And as you became flesh of my flesh and let me pour you into my form, you allowed me my manhood. I know you paid the price for this, for I've watched you, you are not the submissive docile kind, you had to overcome your own urge to control. You gave me that gift. It could have been for a day's rest, for a meal of sausage and sauerkraut, or simply for a pitcher of warm water to wash in. But it was not, it was love. Love that allowed me to fashion you, so you could live within my fibre. My hand's artefact, my child, my newborn sister.

And so I take my leave. It is the night before. The letter has grown bulky and won't fit, even tightly rolled, into that condom. I will line the rucksack with my cerate-lining, you know, the one I use to hold the bandage in place to prevent wetting. I will put a sheet of it into the lining, flatten the letter against it, and cover it with the same cerate-linen. All of it, I fear, is totally futile. The chance that you will survive this bitter winter, run south or southwest, you and your father and the rest of that team, is almost nonexistent. These words, then, are just to relive, rethink, and give account. To face also the experience, the elemental nature of our love.

You may be robbed, beaten; robbed of your good Russian boots, long coat, and fur hat by hungry, murdering partisans, or deserters from both sides. Or you both may huddle against the small cove of a windbreak and just sleep in the snow. The rucksack stolen or abandoned. So it is a farewell.

Desert Stone

We sailed from Constanta. The most unlikely triumvirate: Helen, her little Elizabeth, and I in Joey's stead. Carrying his name, and his child on my shoulders. It was another *Gespensterschiff*, that ghost-driven ship of my school days.

Hundreds of us silently boarding the boat, whose steps broke under our feet. It unleashed a gallows humour, released the tension we felt at the prospect of the next few days of being so closely housed without proper provisions.

I have never felt comfortable crowded into closed quarters, but when we sailed, nothing mattered except the thought of freedom, freedom and getting away. Everyone shared bread, water, hard-boiled eggs, and the exhilaration of the Black Sea air. Through the Dardanelles, Asia Minor in view, past the Greek islands, past Cyprus, and through a Mediterranean tinged with the memory of Odysseus-Ulysses. We did not have to bind ourselves to the mast or put wax in our ears to shut out the Sirens; we were so densely packed we were bound by each other. But someone's sudden shout – *I see land* – made us turn to the one next to us, the one we had cursed a minute ago, to hug and kiss. We craned our necks and saw it. A shore, stretching golden and green. Elizabeth on top of my shoulders, and every other child, shouted with joy. We were euphoric. As the boat docked in Haifa, Helen turned to me: "I will never forget this moment," she said. And the exilic *Next year in Jerusalem is today.* The promised land, I thought.

I walk up to the hills of Jerusalem, through thick cedar woods. I find a clearing that opens up into a magical light. Bouquets of sunrays thrown back from the stone desert of Arabia. Heliotrope stone, mauve and pink, hiding shadows in its valleys like a thousand and one nights to come.

Süssel loved the western sun. She sat on her window seat every day to watch it sink behind the crenelations of the Archbishop's Residence. She told me this the many times we went up the Cecina mountain, holding hands and never kissing. Now I too, so far from her and so longing, watch the western sun sinking, thrown back upon the east. Changing flowers, fading under your very eyes, revealing the east in hot and slowly cooling shadows.

I never dreamt of desert stone. I knew of sand, rippling, driven Sahara dunes, but nothing of stone. These are not just boulders, but seemingly seamless surfaces, in the dying light now robbed of reality. Cedar and pine hold the night longer, and catch it first, as in the Carpathians. One shivers with the first onset of the caught-in-the-branches night. So dark. I move down from these hills into the city, a town divided, Jordanian soldiers parading in uniform on the partitioning ancient wall, speaking German. My ear catches familiar sounds: Jordanians, not speaking Arabic – Well, I recognize the voice of the one. But I am cautious. And I come the next day to the wall with my little girl Elizabeth, too heavy now but still riding on my shoulders, just to see this phenomenon of Jordanian sentinels speaking German.

Elizabeth is Joey's little girl. My sweet adopted-twin Joey's child. Came to me as things come to an idiot like myself, with two left hands and two left feet – God given. Like a Russian coat when it is bitterly cold, a twin brother to feed me, so did I find Joey's lovely young wife Helen with her Elizabeth.

Helen had been in possession of a passport, a ticket on a boat to the newly-established state of Israel. Well! I stood many a night in front of a police station in Bucharest to enter my application, but was pushed from the door when almost there or, not knowing how to bribe, left empty-handed. A passport is the most desirable and unachievable piece of paper! And so is a ticket on a miserable, unseaworthy, overloaded boat like the *Struma.* One steals a ticket if one can, one tries to bribe officials if one can get to them.

We're in Romania and *bakshish* – the Turkish word for bribe – is king. It's the greasing of the palm which opens doors, if you only get near them. No one passes through a door without a bribe of cigarettes, a sausage maybe, or good currency; from the man at the door to the last stamp on the passport. To me, a stupid, bungling idiot, all of it was given: a passport, a ticket on that shabby boat, and a lovely young woman and her child. A gift from heaven. Many a boat had sunk on the way from the Romanian port of Constanta to Haifa, as the *Struma* did. But Jews in despair for a homeland will travel on any two boards nailed together, flying any flag.

Joey had told Helen about our time together, our private war, the winter of 1942-43 and the months after Stalingrad. About my clumsy *shlemiel* behaviour, my incompetence at daily tasks, like tying shoelaces – I stretching my boot towards anyone who would be able or inclined to help, the love that we had for one another, our willingness to give our last strength for the other. Our true alliance.

Helen met me in the middle of Bucharest after the war, in front of the University, where exiles from our mythic town met and found news of one another, renewed old friendships, and made new connections. Where people with a town carried in their hearts recognized each other by the wonderful high-German they spoke, by the Ukrainian peasant-wisdom thrown into their conversation, by the Yiddish folk jokes of tear-and-laughter, and last but not least the Romanian experience. There was instant trust and recognition. A name alone would connect one to schoolmasters, dates, years, teachers, youth-wanderings-in-the-mountains, and oh, the Cecina!

Who did you say? With whom did you say? Of course. You're Helen, sweet cherry-eyed Helen, my Joey's Helen. And all of Joey's story emerged. And his bitter end. We went across the University to an old coffeehouse. In spite of hard times, coffee-houses still had Turkish coffee, the shelves were full of nutty baclava dripping with honey, savarins in rum, whipping cream piled high, and the ubiquitous *dobosh* – hard golden caramel on top of a torte. And I heard his story. My brother Joey's end.

We kissed and hugged and I stepped into Joey's place as if I had been there always. I knew every beauty spot at the back of Helen's neck. I knew her gestures, her tea-drinking habits, how she lifted the saucer with her left hand, holding cup and saucer midway between table and lips. I knew her black curly hair, cut to hide a rather ungainly ear, a little too big, not flat against the head. I knew her hand movement trying to cover it. The *Bubykopf*, a 20s fashion. I knew the perfume of her breath, the velvet of her voice, an even-dark timbre – misleading Joey said, when he spoke of her passionate ways.

One day at the labour camp, dried fish had arrived in the camp and potatoes, rotten but still edible. We ate our fill. Late, under my warm coat, memories of love come flooding in. Joey talked of Helen late into the night, though the five-o'clock roll call was pitiless. I learned then how she turned at night, what her pleasures were, how she laughed during lovemaking, giggled, speaking French. And once in those long hard winter months – the Stalingrad months – from November, 1942, to early February, 1943 – he spoke of her expecting a child and his strong premonition that he would never see her again, or the child. She is too beautiful to survive, he said, too vulnerable to face it all alone. Joey, I said, sleep now, or you won't be strong enough to stand on your feet at roll call. They'll shoot you if you cannot work. Sleep now, while there is still time to rest. And I whispered close to his ear, I will find Helen, and I'll look after them if you cannot. Sleep now, my brother. He had held me in my feverish typhus delirium and fed me his soup, and now I tried to comfort his angst. A strange sixth sense made me speak those words, that I would look after them – I who can't even tie my own shoelaces or cut a slice of bread. But it gave him ease and he fell asleep pressed against my shoulder.

It had come true. As if things were ordered, they fell into place. And I carry sweet Elizabeth on my shoulders now, her feet dangling around my throat like a collar, walking along an ancient wall in the heat of a Jerusalem day. Elizabeth letting her head drop onto mine whenever she tired.

I was in the truest sense of the word virginal when Helen and I became lovers, almost at our first encounter. I had known only of dreams, of school-boy fantasies. Romantic encounters in the fields, near running brooks, early morning, waiting for Venus to rise above the horizon, or declarations of love and longing, my fingers stroking the green-white mottled marble, my wedding band. Always Süssel. I would think of her small breasts pressing against her cottons as she stepped out of the old gate, or I would imagine her naked beneath her clothes. But physical acts – touching those little breasts, parting the upper thigh – no, it wasn't given to me. And going with Moritz to Rebecca or Mitzi, to "learn the trade" – I would rather wait. I fashioned my images and they remained the same. I would try slight changes in scenery, or a more daring hug, but would fast return to what always was with me: Süssel. Her flaming hair, her swelling lips, which night after night I kissed in my dreams, though I had never dared in waking life. So desired and so chaste a love. Yet Helen took me to her bed, Joey's bed, without any fuss.

The next day Helen and I married. With a small *bakshish,* which she knew perfectly how to handle, a justice of the peace was ready to marry us without dispensation. And I stepped into Joey's life, taking his name as my own, on my passport, on my ticket. Simple. Societal morality, dismissed quickly! She was mine and I became another, at least on paper.

All is stone in this mideastern world, gleaming white. Creeping up the hills, hidden under cedar-juniper carpets, or breaking through, stark white-ivory-yellow stone. All houses are stone, chipped from it or built into it. There is no other work but stonework, done with chisels, with hammers, almost with your nails. Everyone who comes to those shores works at the stone. Classic Yemenite faces, whole tribes of them, still polygamous, dark Africans and nomadic Iraqi, Jews, looking like the whole world. They come to the new-old shores, and there is no other work. So we chip the stone of Jerusalem. Stone dust, an equalizer of rank, class, and skin. We are ghost-like when we finally put the chisel down. I come back to the work camp at night, where I live with my instant family in a Danish hut. No water, no light, a Moroccan family sharing the one room. The man is black-Arabic, but looks just as white as I do returning from the stone in the hills.

But up in the clearing of the cedar-pine hills the sweat is lifted from your brow by the steady breeze, and you look across the waterway to the eastern stone-immensity in the early evening, and all is transformed into sheafs of golden grain, wreaths of roses, red wine flooding the crevices.

I am alone, always. I climb up, sit down on a petrified root, and look across that majesty. It is awesomely new, yet I know it. It is Cecina, our mountain, and I am there with Süssel. Night is falling and she has just said yes, because I saved her life. The rich matty green ground of Cecina, the birches and beeches above, is so much more to my heart, so much more accessible, than this hard grandeur.

Süssel. In a way now, interfering, making it hard for me to find Helen beautiful. Her ears disturb me more and more. So small and dark she is, so sweetly slavish to my needs, waiting to be told to do this and do that. I let her cry and seem not to care. I tell her I chip the stone for you and Elizabeth, but that is all I will do. The rest is mine. I lie on my back and watch the heavens, nearly palpable, and muse. We are stellar stuff, made of all that is out there. I long for a piece of paper and pencil, for the comfort, the logic, of mathematics. For the meditation that asks questions, seeks answers: are we all made of energy, transformable into matter, and vice versa? If we are that, then God is truly one, in all forms. Oh, if not forever, at least as long as the stone of Arabia reflects the light across for us to witness.

YES I'VE HEARD THIS VOICE BEFORE. It is the German guard from the camp beyond the Bug, on its eastern shore. I can't forget that voice. The voice and his stance, the way he brandishes his rifle against shoulder and midriff. He doesn't recognize me.

A hot, hot day. Elizabeth is asleep on my head, her hands and feet heavy around my neck. I sit against the wall, moving from time to time with the sun, from one crevice to another to escape the burning heat. The two sentinels up on top. The wall is wide enough to safely walk, or march on. I had never suspected that it would be so wide. The transparent air of Jerusalem carries voices as if whispered into your ear, so distinct. It is Shabbat. The fine stone dust has settled. There is no hammering now, all is still. I hear clearly the footsteps on the wall and the German spoken on top. One voice, harder-edged, from the Rhine Valley further north, the other one *badisch*-sounding, with soft diminutive endings.

"The Jew down there, has he fainted? Look down, the one sitting on the ground against the wall, with the little girl on his shoulders."

"No, no, he is asleep, the sun is murderous today."

"Why does he come here so often, almost every Shabbat, almost at the same hour, whenever we are on duty?"

"What are you worried about? He probably just likes this spot. I do not fear the ghosts of the past, I don't let myself be haunted by anything. But I'm more comfortable with my past, I'm a Catholic from the Breisgau. We are less unhappy, less frightened, we from the south, than you Protestant northerners."

"No, it has nothing to do with religion, the Pope, or Luther, it's got to do with the fact that his face seems familiar, a nightmare face. I dreamt this face, it looked at me from a dream, not speaking. And this little girl was on his shoulders. He wants something if he comes in the daytime and at night like a ghost. I have to shake this or I'll go crazy."

"Oh, forget him. Come to our church, confess, you'll be absolved. You Protestants from the North are all tied up in knots. You do not have anyone between yourself and God to talk to. You're all silly. *You* didn't invent that war, did you? It's not your fault. They sent you there – for the Fatherland, super race, and all of that."

"No, it isn't that. We from the North are not as easygoing, happy-go-lucky, as you are, all of you from the other side of the Main, but we also have consciences and do not mock things as readily as you do."

I hear him call down, clearly stressing each word: "Mister, you speak German, don't you? It is so nice to speak to someone in your mother tongue in a strange land."

"Yes, it is," I say, looking up, and he throws me an army bottle filled with cool water.

"It is such a terribly dry day, with the *chamsin* blowing from the desert," he says. "Keep the bottle, it's insulated inside to keep the water cool." Elizabeth nearly catches it as it is flung down. I look up to say thank you and can't. In my throat, I feel again the kick of his boot, making me spill my soup and drop the bowl in the mud. I hear again the derisive laughter. The indentation of hurt, I did not know it be so deep. Like Proust's *Madeleine,* a small bite of the little cake unleashing memory through the senses. A water bottle and the wanting-to-forget. All there now.

We walked along the ancient wall towards the Road of Bethlehem, up to Talpiot, with its cedar woods and slender pines. We both sat down. Little Elizabeth awake and spry now, ready to play with Jerusalem's eternal toys, small stones, big stones, sharp and smooth pebbles, building stone houses held together with cedar sticks and overlaid with cedar branches. And I looked into the east, with the sun gleaming stark, swallowing the shadows.

On top of the monastery – a women's cloister now – I would hear them better next time, I thought. And so it was. Hidden among the chimneys – outlets for steam and other effluents – on the roof, I looked directly into the Old City, the monastery leaning almost against the wall, the dome of the rock in full view. I could move better on that roof without Elizabeth, who always wanted something – a kiss, a glass of water, a sandwich or banana. Next Shabbat I was up there. I climbed through a basement hole into the inner staircase at prayer time, and then out onto the roof, where Jerusalem, a dream world, was spread beneath my feet. They were there, marching in cadence, as expected.

Pilgrims, uprooted seekers with remnants of their home soil still sticking to their feet, return here a thousand times. Hidden behind a chimney on the roof of a cloister, looking at the white stone and the golden Dome of Jerusalem, I see them return. Suddenly I am a fifteen-year-old again, hiding behind an eavestrough, watching for that flaming hair to pass through the old gate. Waiting for the thump of his own heart.

Life within the tribe, sheltered by brothers, strict mothers, and indulgent fathers, was a game played by rules. Was a ball in the garden thrown to your brothers. But this sudden separateness, hiding in a corner, eyes fixed on the gate, waiting for your destiny, rips you from the vine. Frightening, that Süssel will be with you all the days of your life, will make you a wanderer – so dangerous to the promise I gave to Joey to comfort him.

Helen stepped into Moritz's shoes as I stepped into Joey's, with a simplicity and resignation worthy of legendary heroines. Yet I can't make love to her, not always. Small-boned, fragile, olive-skinned, she is wildly sexual. At first encounter, I loved her, knowing so well of her intimate ways. It seemed easy through Joey's eyes.

But that was dreamy stuff. This is real life in Jerusalem. A refugee life: state-owned beds and blankets, strangers sharing our room, Elizabeth sleeping in between us, a common latrine for African and Yemenite Jews, and days of chipping white hard rock. Washing off the stone dust, eating Helen's evening meal of eggs, olive oil, olives, and bread. Beautiful bread of rye and wheat. And Danish butter. All kind gifts. But lovemaking, without peace and romance, is hard.

"Come outside," she says. She has waited for me, washed with perfumed soap, and combed her black hair – much longer now and falling to her shoulders. "Come outside. The stars are brilliant and you like to talk to me about this sky – a different sky, just a little shifted from home. We'll talk. If you want me, we'll go behind the barracks. Come. I long for it – look, I'm just wearing this light shift-dress. It's days now – you say tomorrow and tomorrow – come my Joey, my Max." And I was moved, that Helen called me by my name, and we went out, sat on a boulder on the hill, and I held her close. She fitted so well into my right armpit. But make love – I couldn't. Dear she was to me, but not erotic. I held her lovely breast. Such a perfect apple, rounder and more womanly now. Tomorrow, I said, tomorrow.

But there was no tomorrow for us here. Jordanian villagers broke into the work camp, the *maabarah,* carrying huge blades –

the long broad knives they use to slaughter their sheep – and cut the throats of a family from Hungary, who had just arrived a week ago. Old and young. The Israeli boys – the newly-formed army – went back almost immediately, not murdering, but putting the whole village to the torch. The flames rose high into the air and lit the whole camp, so close were we to Jordan on the southern border of Jerusalem. The boys returning tell us they have thrown them out of their huts, they haven't killed but have burnt the village. And this is what this biblical "an eye for an eye" seems to be. There will never be rest. I want to run.

Helen wakes Elizabeth, wraps her in wool plaid – Jerusalem nights are cool – hands her to me, packs the few things we own, and we wander. We hire a small donkey, for thousands of years the beast of our burden. It carries our load, it watches, it picks its way with clever hoofs, surefooted, stone by stone across the hills, knowing the road, Elizabeth jubilant on its back. The two of us with a few bags in our hands, acquired somewhere, a pail – *à tout faire* – hanging from our load. An ancient picture, the three of us on the road to Bethlehem. All the Josephs and the Marys, all the babies, on the way to Egypt.

A kind family took us in, and we could cook and wash our clothes; we had one room entirely to ourselves. Again the intense happiness of having our own four walls, with a window, and a very large bed, just for ourselves and no one else. Again the eternal pilgrim's joke: no marble palace with steps leading into the sea could equal this. We could wash in our pail, with no witnesses. And we laughed and giggled and Elizabeth sat in her pail-tub shouting with joy.

I loved Helen this night. With my whole heart. I had not worked for a few days, had shaken the dust literally, had eaten a cooked meal of fish and rice, oranges from the tree. There is paradise. Oranges in Israel. Read a story to Elizabeth about bunny rabbits with white tails and pink ears until she slept. And the night was ours.

UP ON THE WALL, the two Jordanian soldiers, speaking German:

THE NORTHERNER: Why did he not say thank you?

THE SOUTHERNER: He may have and you did not hear it. Depends from where the wind blows, from the sea or from the desert. The sound gets carried away.

THE NORTHERNER: No, he has recognized me. He wants to accuse me – take me to court. I think I know who he is. He is that Jew that would not work, when I was in command of that work unit. There were several recalcitrant, impertinent know-it-all Jews. He is a professor or some egghead. Couldn't handle a shovel. I do not understand these people. I whipped them into shape. And now I see this face all the time. It looks at me from my dinner plate.

THE SOUTHERNER: Oh, come, you Protestants are unable to have a good time. Look, you have a good job, the Jordanians pay you well because you know all about the military art and you train soldiers well.

THE NORTHERNER: Soldiers, you call them. They are worse than the Jews. I had to put one of them three times into the hole before he understood. Lazy good-for-nothings. And in a Muslim country you can't even drink a beer and take a girl to a dance. The money is good. Nowhere to spend it, though. I can send it home at least. In part, of course. But, what do I do about that Jew? He'll get me in the end. You see, I couldn't let them all run away. This one did. I wish I knew his name. Around one hundred of them ran away. They somehow got wind of the order to annihilate the camp next morning.

THE SOUTHERNER: Don't worry so much. It will make you sick. So what if they ran away? Let them run. You're not God's policeman.

THE NORTHERNER: No, no, you don't understand, it is my duty. And I know, it was a Romanian officer from the other camp, who had no business coming over to my camp so often – his was a few hundred yards away, with five hundred Jews also. And I heard he had let them all just run away, when the order came to finish them off. He made some deal with them – you know Romanians, Latins, no morals, you can't trust them, they deal with Jews or anyone. I bet he made a million to let them desert camp. And I am sure this is why he came that very day, to see what money he could make and to meddle with my command. One hundred of them – including the Jew, who I see now without the little girl standing on top of the nunnery, spying on me – they broke camp around midnight and ran towards the river Bug. It was an open camp, you see – we had no time for electrified fences, nor the means, so they just got up and ran towards the river. Dogs and guards behind them, shouting and shooting. They threw themselves into the Bug river and swam. Underwater at first. We got a few but most of them were soon out of reach. That Jew was there. Now he is here. I will never have any peace.

THE SOUTHERNER: Honestly, can't you – oh, just forget it all. It's your paranoia. The trouble with you is you're not a Catholic. Come with me to our church. I know a priest, young and beautiful, a little on the – how would I put it – on the pretty side of men. Just so gentle and kind. He'll like you because you are a strong man, yet so troubled. He'll take your confession and you'll feel better. What happened to the rest of the four hundred Jews under your command?

THE NORTHERNER: We shot them at dawn. What else could I do with them? We shot them, when the work was finished. The graves were dug by them anyway, ready to go. Quite useless otherwise, to tell the truth. What else could we have done with them? Carry them along? They were supposed to be gotten rid of. That is what it was all about. Orders are orders. I am not one of these Gypsy-Romanians, you know.

AGAIN AND AGAIN to the foot of the wall of the Old City, and now to that high roof! I heard it all. I know it all. Why this self-inflicted pain, this watching at the keyhole?

The past returns full force through that voice on top of the wall, magnified and incomprehensible. The joy of recognizing Moritz in a shadowy figure as I enter the compound after a gruelling transfer from the Transnistrian camps – on land between the Dnjester and the Bug. In Transnistria everybody died of typhus, hunger, and the *Genickschuss,* when they couldn't work anymore. We were ferried across the Bug and then driven in a run to the camp.

Arriving at the camp, I see him immediately, shovel in hand, bent over. Moritz, my own, my beloved, my hero-brother, my idol. Our eyes meet, but he makes no gesture; Moritz has been there before me and has, with his finely tuned ear, quickly assessed the camp commander. I sense that I should give no outward sign of recognition. If they know we're twins, we'll be separated and harassed incessantly. At seeing Moritz, all exhaustion and hunger leave me. Intense joy in every fibre, I want to sing, to praise God. It is the most beautiful face on earth, the bones, clear of flesh, perfect, eyes of the blue sky, and the subtle smile of recognition, of love. My brother is with me.

Seeing Moritz changes everything. My joy is physical. I can eat the gross soup with fish eyes looking back at me without vomiting. My pants aren't full of loose feces. I can smile at the crude words of command, unaffected. My brother is with me! The earth is dry in August and hard to carve with the blunt shovels. I watch Moritz applying his discerning intelligence to the task, breaking smaller quantities and then pebbling it finely, achieving a full wagon in less time. I follow his example. It is for Moritz alone that I try not to be beaten, avoid the guards' eyes, keep my rebellious soul in check. So he will not have to suffer, to endure my humiliation. I know his temperament: choleric, fast to anger. Convinced of his own strength, he will react like Moses if he sees me hurt. He will strike the Egyptian master hard, and they will break his bones, the back of his nose, in biblical fashion.

He barters with the German guards, ingratiating himself,

though he has little to offer except a few condoms. Matches and condoms are the most valuable currency in the camps, the latter used by masters and slaves alike, for stashing away a piece of gold or concealing a dangerous note. And it is Moritz who realizes that the appearance of the Romanian officer from the other camp means something vitally important. Moritz was the first to know, through the Romanian, that the camp would be abolished at dawn. And he, our Moses, organized the breakout of almost one hundred prisoners.

We run for our lives and swim the Bug, the Egyptians – as I call them – in pursuit, with their guns and dogs. Moritz holds on to me in the river. I am a very good swimmer and even saved Süssel's life once, but he does not trust me. He holds on to me, taking me on his back at the deepest point in the middle. It is the end of August and the water feels chilly to undernourished, tired bodies. He fears my clumsiness and waning will to fight, knowing me well, as I know him. I want joy, delight, clear clean truth, the beauty and the road to it, one emerging from the other and retraceable. But Moritz also knows that I do not fight, moods can overwhelm me. Living is not worth just any price. He has watched me stand in front of Süssel's old house, waiting for her to emerge, not daring to speak of my love. Despairing of my inadequacy. Has watched me walk with her up the Cecina mountain, holding hands, dying to kiss her but fearing rejection.

Why don't you take her around the middle? he said. A young woman does not want eternity, she wants to kiss you now, lie next to you, feel your body as you feel hers. Don't stand across from her house, hours on end, just to get a glimpse of her – it is too upsetting. Moritz often smiled and said: my own twin brother and such a strange, helpless child. True. I often was ready for the river, just to float down it and not return. Süssel loves the river. She always talks of a house on the river, where she can see it eternally flow over the stones. But she loves the shores also, the life of them, with all that grows and breathes there. I want the stillness – the absorbed sound. Death transformed.

It all comes back, through the sound of the voice above the wall. All of that late August day, Moritz passes an extra piece of bread to me, where he had won it, only he knows. And at midnight, moonlight flooding the campsite bright as day, he gets up and says: "Max, keep close behind me. Those who want to join us, come." His voice is tense: "You are risking your lives by running, and you may be shot, but the orders are here for tomorrow morning. The camp is annihilated. None will survive." He jumps to his feet and I follow him and at once we break out. By the time the guards realize what has happened, we have gained distance and the river. Moritz: Kick your boots off as fast as possible, they are too heavy and encrusted with earth. Most of us do. Those who can't bear to part with their boots are drowned. Moritz, bootless and coatless, a latter-day Moses with his brother Aaron on his back, leads his flock across the river, swimming, sensing the undercurrents, wading in spots, giving us strength with his commanding voice. We make it to the other side, almost eighty of us. I don't know how long it takes to cross the Bug, an eternity, long and cold. We huddle on the other bank in a circle around Moritz. And he produces from his shirt pocket a condom tightly tied with string, dry matches inside. Moses unties the string, saving it. The matches are powder dry. A few of us go out to gather fuel, twigs for kindling, and we build a fire, a small fire that will not be noticed; we guard it, sit close to one another, warm our bodies, and think of God.

Heroes die on the battlefields. They do not make it to the promised land or to the other bank of the river. Legendary Achilles had a vulnerable heel, where his goddess-mother held him when she dipped him into the river Styx to make him invulnerable. Onto Siegfried's shoulder fell a leaf – was it oak? – while he steeled his body in the dragon's blood. Mythical heroes do not know the limits of mortal man. And so my brother Moses. With his limitless strength and foresight, multidexterity, and fast-flying cunning, he was successful from the moment he opened his eyes a half-hour before I did. But his self-reliance and relentless need to lead was his Achilles heel, his Siegfried shoulder.

It was still night when we fell onto the stones of the western shore of the Bug. We huddled close around our Moses, body on body, to make the most of our animal heat. Moritz shivered, felt his end. He commanded the young men around him to leave him, run – barefoot as they were – to swim the Djnester.

He fevered and died while dawn was in the east, a veiled Venus barely showing her face. I had always looked to her, at dawn and nightfall, for reassurance of balance in the universe, the eternity of things. Not for the omens, the stupid divination of the slow-witted. So different this morning. Now I feared her face, was threatened by her rising. And she covered her face for me. I knew I had lost my brother. An orphan is forever. No tears, no theatre.

I was left to guard Moritz's body along with a young Russian Jew named Grisha, a boy from the camp Moritz had adopted as his own. Grisha was beautiful, only nine years old. His people had been herded into a ditch and shot on the advance of the *Einsatzgruppen.* Bullets were not wasted on children, and Grisha crawled away unharmed. On the run and picked up by the SS, he was put to work next to Moritz. Moritz saw a guard eyeing the sweet apricot face and feared abuse – he had seen this guard molesting a very young Jewish boy. So Moritz protected Grisha, hid him, fed him, kept him close to his side, gave him easy work to do.

Grisha stayed with me and our dead Moses. We found branches to bed him on, fashioned a bier. He was light by now to carry. We picked up rags, derelict things, put them on the bier with our dead hero. There could not have been a more dignified mourning for Achilles or Siegfried.

Nightfall: I knew the stars so well, I calculated the distance to the Djnester and guessed where the villages were. I was good at that. Maps were my childhood games. Skyscapes of stars, shorelines of rivers, and the mountains touching the clouds, mighty Atlas carrying the world on his shoulders, I took to bed with me. My mother would find the atlas pages crumpled, as they fell out of my hands when sleep overcame me. I drew maps on pieces of paper like other children draw houses, a tree in front, a sun with rays shining, mummy and daddy inside.

Going up the Cecina mountain with Süssel; she knew she could trust me. I was as surefooted as a *Hutzul* donkey, knew the strength of every pebble to hold our weight at the turn of the path. And by the stars of every hour of the early morning, I could tell the time. Süssel would ask, how long yet to the summit? I would answer, oh, it is only two hours and ten minutes and we're there. Süssel always wanted to rest by the brook, cool her toes in the water. I wanted to get to the top, to have the world at my feet, three hundred and sixty degrees of endless mountain ranges around me.

So my calculations were correct and we found the village. And an old-old Greek orthodox priest, who looked at our half-crazed group, washed our feet, wounded as they were, fed us his corn bread, and buried Moritz with a Christian blessing. He fashioned a coffin, dressed Moritz in the best he could find, and put a coin on his forehead and a candle beside. He called a withered little woman from the almost-empty village to be the wailing woman – the *Bocitoara* – to cry and wring her hands.

Beans and onions and a wreath of almost-white bread appeared. Magic. Yet alien to my father's and grandfather's Jewish and my mother's Lutheran sensibilities: the open rough coffin with Moritz dressed, looking almost presentable, the priest's invitation to kiss him and accept that this was my brother, penny on forehead. Beans simmering-steaming on the red brick oven making my stomach cringe with hunger and Grisha nearly fainting with the hypnotic chant-song of the prayer.

We carried our hero on a haywagon made of two ladders with flat boards over the axles, drawn by a horse as old as the priest, and laid the precious body to rest in "Old-Stones" cemetery. And old stones they were. No crosses showed among the tall grasses. We found a spot. The earth was hard, but by then I knew how to handle a shovel. We listened to the priest, Church Slavonic. Its monotonous hypnotic beauty gave us comfort, as the Hebrew would. It was new to me, with my hubris, my gentle disdain of the unclear thought, always mocking the Hebrew or Latin, the appeal to emotion. This time was different. My own soul lay in the earth. How to part? The chant, smooth, almost liquid, the intervals close, the myrrh brought along by the priest, soothed me, helped me find an acceptance of God's ways that no Kepler, beloved as he was, could have given me. We stood a while, sat down next to the grave. I said the Lord's Prayer and the *Shemah. The Kaddish* I had not learnt. Until Grisha's "When are we eating the beans?" brought us back to the practical world.

Beans, onions, bread, and tea. Both I and Grisha – young as he was – understood the purpose of the wake now. The need to eat and get drunk, we on laughter, the priest on vodka. The need to overcome true tragedy, the death of a hero. To fall from so high.

Ludmilla Bunin

For All Our Sons and Lovers

It was early 1944 when the advancing Russian army, in pursuit of the disarrayed Germans, freed the few remaining inmates of a German labour unit on the east side of the river Bug. Süssel's mother felt herself lifted from the ground and laid on a truck. She slept a deep unconscious sleep among the few others still living, with no need of bread or water. Woke to the miracle of approaching Czernowitz on the left side of the Prut, to hot goulash from the army's *arrière garde* supply truck. And was left at the eastern train station to make her way to her father's house.

She had been lucky, beyond any expectation. Noticed for her high German tongue by a German officer who took her as his own servant. "Working in the kitchen saved my life, and above all my sanity," she used to say when asked about those camp years. As head cook for the SS management of that labour camp east of the Bug, she ate, if not her fill then enough to stave off hunger. Managed to protect her mother, Esther, who worked beside her, fed her with scraps saved. Seeing her mother beside her was sufficient purpose to keep her from hour to hour, she said. But grandmother Esther, as everyone used to call her, grew frail, and when typhus struck she succumbed to it. Strange, Süssel's mother said, how one goes on to the next task as if nothing has happened. "I saw her die but went on to the peeling of the next potato or onion. And I watched my mother's body swept away with all the other bodies and did not cringe. A totally natural event. So unnatural I had become."

The Russians occupying Czernowitz and area let her have, for the time being, one room in her own flat on the third floor. It had been looted. But the window seat was still there, and, lifting the small secret door, she found her purple velvet pouch she had hidden before going to the ghetto. Did not open it, but caressed the outside lovingly. Recognized by touch her rings, the few chains and the few pieces of gold. Held it for a little unopened in her palm and then put it resolutely into her big black leather bag, which had been with her through all the nearly three years of ghetto, deportation, and return. Made of once-shiny black calf leather, it was old and worn now, but its brass buckles still shone, and its clasp sprang open as if oiled yesterday. She smiled at the *click.* Looked at this companion, which had served as a pillow under her head, a seat to keep her off the wet ground, and a secret friend. She opened the invisible side pocket, undetectable by seam or button, and slid the velvet pouch into it. Locked the case again, seated herself on the window seat, the dear bag beside her, and waited, looking west, as her daughter Süssel used to.

On home ground now, she felt secure. Bereft of things, but it mattered little. She had time to wait for rescue. Marusja had opened the old gate, hugged her, had come with bean soup and the most fragrant bread, her little boy holding onto her apron. The world seemed in balance for a moment.

Blankets and some pillows were still there and the old kitchen had somehow been spared. Books. She was at home. The deep silence was unnatural to her, though, and she listened with sharpened senses to every sound around her. One day she heard a light step, a woman's step, getting louder as it approached the third floor. It frightened her. She ran through the vestibule to her front door to fall into the arms of Ludmilla Bunin.

They hugged and kissed. Closed the door behind them and sat down facing each other on kitchen stools. Bunin undid her dress and in there, between her breasts, was Felix. A small passport photo of Felix. The mother held this still warm and crumpled piece of paper with her son's face on it, holding back her tears. And allowed Bunin her time.

Bunin talked without a pause. Told how she had come from Vladivostok on the locomotive of an army train, across the Trans-Siberian, with two words to guide her: *Czernowitz* and *Felix.* The mother smiled in reply, hugged her again and again, said let's have tea. Busied herself in the kitchen trying to light a small alcohol burner that would not burn, and both women laughed at the state of the world they'd found themselves in. They succeeded in producing boiling water and had tea with real tea leaves from Bunin's bag. Army biscuits to chew on the side.

"Yes, it took months on the Trans-Siberian...." And while Bunin talked, the mother thought of her favourite short story by C.F. Meyer, about a Saracen princess trying to find her western lover, knowing only two words: *London* and *Beckett.* And managed to find him. So this is what love does; yet it is different. This is here and now, a Russian life. Bunin executed power like a robot, expected her miserable subjects to take it without a murmur, yet she could go to the scaffold and pay for her sins, with a love defying measure. How beautiful they are, how extraordinary. Obeying ancient laws of serfdom with a Christianity of the humus, the black soil. Christ taken to their bosoms only yesterday. What is a thousand years to people who work the earth, sleep on it, and have invented the fruits of it? What is a thousand years? Merely yesterday. They made their Christ, fashioned Him from the earth flesh that we return to. A God of their own, of inimitable perfection. Their passing hell – accepting this vale of tears to wade through. Just passing, to return to the golden glory of their icons.

"I have two days of rest," Bunin said. "Could I stay with you?"

"You're most welcome, and it will give me great pleasure, but I have no beds, everything is gone. My father's house has been ransacked. See, here Felix's and Sweetie's piano stood, and here was the library. They have permitted me to stay until someone comes to fetch me. But there are blankets and some pillows." And the two of them bedded themselves down on the leftover carpet, hugged, drank tea, and it was Felix and tears.

"He was so good to me," Bunin said. "He kissed my hand and called me his lady love, and I was getting prettier day by day because he said so.

"And do you know, Mother, it was I who saved you all from deportation on the thirteenth of June, 1941? Did you know that? Felix came running to me, at three o'clock in the morning, breathless and desperate on that fatal night – it was a week before Russia was at war – and cried, help us, help us, the Russians have taken my father, my mother, and my grandmother into the trains.

"I kissed his tears, and I ran to my office. We, the *politruks* – you know, Mother, we, the political officers of the party in the army, we have power. I phoned Kiev and managed to get a stay of the deportation, bringing the three of you home."

As Bunin talked on, the mother rose, boiled water for tea,

observed Bunin's intense love and wondered at the Russians. What people they are! She had seen them as automatons, the masked robots that took them to the trains in the middle of that night in June. She had seen them drunk on her *eau de cologne* in torpid sleep on the salon floor. She had seen them threaten one another with court martial, showing no emotion, as if punishment were equal to God's justice. *God,* a dirty word in Soviet life, had a residual power, it seemed.

For two days, undisturbed by the world outside, the women were held close by their sharing of love. They understood one another in spite of their different lives. Both spoke Russian. For the mother it was a learnt literary tongue, the Russian of Pushkin or Dostoyevsky. And it brought smiles of delight to Bunin's face, and she exclaimed, "I hear Felix's voice in yours. All books! So wonderful. We speak differently, today. You are from another world. I love you so."

Two days and two nights, the mother listening and Bunin talking of her love, her country, of God. She talked about how Felix met her after work, in the headquarters of the NKVD, that police institution, which changed its name with time and régime, to perfect itself under the Soviets. Bunin, key in hand, officer in charge. For three hours, they met, often night after night. "Mother," she said, "your son has loved and taught me; not just sex. He taught me love of my body. My ugliness vanished. He said, Ludmilla, I have had sex with the loveliest women, but Ludmilla, see your shining face! No one has ever given me that. And we laughed and laughed. He knew how to wait and what to do, and, Mother, he is my husband forever. I have been married to him!

"You see, in Russia now, we are forbidden to think of God. We are only allowed to think of Father Stalin, Father Lenin, and Father Marx, but Mother, not I. My people are Christians, the old Orthodox true faith. So I went to my own brother, a clandestine priest of the Russian Orthodox church, and I said, marry me to this man. But he is not with me, I said. You see, Mother, these were the Stalingrad days. Hard days, when men's lives were – well, Russians understand. Gregory turned to me, covered his head, took the liturgy in hand, set a crown on my head, spoke the blessing, and was priest and bridegroom for me.

"This is our custom. We are crowned to the glory in Christ on our wedding day. My brother Gregory took from a cupboard red paper flowers on green stems. They were there to beautify and honour a hidden icon of the Mother of God; he bound them into a wreath and crowned me to live in glory and faith to Felix. Our saint's image, beloved Chrysostom, was in my hand, as if in Felix's, and he is together with Felix, in my medallion, here on my heart.

"What you, Mother, have taught Felix is the true faith, even if you are not in the church: love will save the world. Mothers will save the world, you and *Mathka Bohu,* the mother of Jesus.

"You are my mother in truth, and if I never find my Felix, I'll work as long as my strength permits and then I'll give my life to God. My brother has found a Siberian monastery, unknown to the régime. A commune, true to the spirit of the Russian Church. Old style: a sharing of bread, of work, a holy place. And this is my vow. But first, this time, I cry before you as Felix did before me on that night to save you: Mother, help me find him."

They drank tea, hugged, held hands. They exchanged trinkets, a golden chain around Bunin's neck and a small enamelled icon of the *Mathka Bohu* on a string for the mother. Ludmilla Bunin. A Russian singing soul.

When Ludmilla left, Mother remained seated. There was nowhere to go. She listened to Ludmilla's receding footsteps echoing down the stone stairs of her father's house. The sound recalled childhood memories of playing in the stairwell, skipping, jumping, and counting – *How many can I take at one time?* – her brothers and sisters competing. All their lives in the stairwell, three floors, high ceilings. Six of them riding the mahogany railing like horses. How many were buried under the walnut tree – not under, but a little further into the garden, because the roots would not accept the familiar bodies.

She remained seated, wondering if someone had forgotten her, to fetch her to camp or across the border south. Or maybe she had been left to wait for Ludmilla. To be taught love. A simple mission, a single word. Perhaps Ludmilla Bunin carries the message from God to man: a mother must save the world. Through love, she will save the world. *Then, for all our sons and lovers, I will. Who will, if not I? There is no one left.* She rose and cleared the few dishes.

Süssel

Mother Courage

I see Felix often. How few we are now! Bucharest, 1944. Such a small band of wanderers. I see him often, his weathered, crenelated face like the ploughed ground. But his heart is light, assured of woman's love – Mother's, mine, Bunin's. Her icon in his possession, it will never leave him. Hidden, skin-close, he'll touch it from time to time, unbeliever that he is. What strange creatures we are; head and heart so far apart, never meeting. *God, where?* he always wonders, yet he holds it, touches it, senses with his skin a hallowed mother's presence.

War is still raging. Bandits everywhere, uniformed, armed with sticks. Ragged partisans to some presumed cause or simple vandals, smirks on their faces. Scum has risen, new fortunes are made. Vodka, army goods, the wonder drug penicillin stolen, resold for enormous profit to either side, German or Russian. Such a frenzy for the last spoils. Battlefronts are undefined, foes and friends indistinguishable, loyalties in flux. Small bands of wanderers we are. "Mother Courage" everyone, pushing the cart with her children, guessing from the gut which way to go. And often, a single wanderer, just a soul, an island, with no ferry.

She was sitting on a milestone, beside the road. I saw her sitting there, her black travelling bag beside her and her black Russian coat thrown across it, an island. Golden-red flame of her hair in my dreams, her smell of Houbigant. Passing a woman of the *nouveau-riche* Romanian class, the perfume triggers recognition: *My mother.* She was on the road. Left. Black old coat and the bag beside her. I have to hurry.

I took the last gold coin from its hiding place in Father's overcoat and I went out into that world of derelicts, black marketeers, alcohol-runners, to the money changers, barbers, who always have the latest currency of whoever was last to conquer the territory. A new class, surfacing in the turbulence, the nocturnal criminals who keep things running, always know someone who knows someone who can do the job. I changed my father's gold coin – a Napoléon – and hired two men with a truck. And went north between the lines, in this western style covered wagon, without mufflers. Looking out for waylayers, modern pirates, the hungry, the desperate, we drove all night on dark, wooded paths, avoiding the road. The truck heaved with every rock, lurched with every pothole. The two men knew their ditches and announced the hazards merrily. *Just wait for the hole.* Another drink of vodka from the same bottle, the three of us in a gallows mood. I went into the back of the truck, fell into heavy sleep, flat on my stomach, and opened my eyes in front of Grandfather's house.

Such is the honour code of the underground that they took my money and drove me north. No questions asked, no rape, no abuse, just sharing of vodka. In the jungle economy, the laws of economics work well. The word is given and the bargain fulfilled. One receives fair value for one's money.

A funny story Felix told me about the underground, promising me, "Sweetie, you'll have a good laugh over this one!" He had given rubles to one of the railroader-vodka-runners to change into the Romanian currency – the *leu,* with an arranged profit built in. The currency was to be delivered to him in Bucharest. Felix presented himself two and a half years later, with his name as his only endorsement, at the remembered address. The man said: Where have you been? I've looked for you everywhere! and paid Felix what he was owed.

We shook with laughter, both of us, having learnt the ways of the world. We laughed as we laughed, holding hands, in our teens, promising not to marry strangers who don't know when to laugh and when to cry, Süssel-Felix style. So we still hold hands and laugh, but the earth has been shaken and the soil has shifted beneath our feet. And we are homeless. The last family gold coin has been exchanged and there is no Archbishop's Residence on the hill, no parkland in the western sun, for our mirrored ballroom. Go, bring our mother, he said. The Lord only knows if you'll find her. I can't, as you know, Sweetie, he said, pointing to his crude wooden leg. Shot by bandits, hit at the knee, there was no way of saving it. The left leg had to be amputated. Dear, dear brother.

I open my eyes as the truck stops in front of my grandfather's house. Like the vision from the tail end of my dream, it lies there. A stone sphinx still, eyes split and silent, it hugs its long corner, unmoved. A world has washed over it, flags of all stripes flying. Rifle butts banging at its gate, uniformed men splintering its glass, my grandfather's house has withstood the onslaught and still towers over the crumbling brick houses across and beside.

I face it in the very early morning. Approach it slowly and

look for the golden-brass handle. Tarnished, I think, tarnished. But it feels morning-cool as always, and gives way under my hand. The gate hangs badly in its hinges, screeches when pushed, iron against rust. Its wood lusterless, the carved angels in their square frames hardly flying, wings gone now. And my heart is heavy.

A different return. So different from my first homecoming, after having tasted the rush of freedom like wine in my young veins. Returning, I felt secure in this enormous, solid house. Sure of love, sure of stability. With shouts of *Home, home,* I took the three stone floors in a wild dash. So different now. This return is parting, recognition of an irretrievable loss, paradise lost.

And memories come flooding in, unassailable. I welcome them, as if delivered. Memories of childhood love, and childhood guilt at stealing a coveted pencil from a classmate's wooden pencil box, stand in their power and presence alongside the murder of old Lev-Jossel Green, the grocer, whose shop Felix and I had compared to Chekhov's in Taganrog. With the floodgates open, memories rush in, important and trivial juxtaposed, each as intense as the other.

I face my childhood gate, feel the engraved surface of the turned brass, take a last look at Gabriel flying in his carved wood square. His wings have survived a little better than the rest and his smile is still visible, thank God. There are eight angels in all, somehow all still there. But no janitor. Nobody. Where are Marusja and Dmitry?

I turn to the staircase and climb slowly, stone step by stone step. To remember. I lean against the railing, letting the cast-iron arabesques paint themselves into my back, not to forget them. The sun is higher now in the east, breaking through the floor-to-ceiling staircase windows and warming the mahogany on the top rail to a rich brown glow.

One more step to the door on the third floor, my parents' flat. A light push and then the vestibule, older, dustier, the wainscotting nearly black, leading me to the ringed half-curtains on the glass salon door. Through the embroidered Madeira curtains – anemone petals around a stem – I see her, seated, fully dressed, by my window, looking west. Looking without seeing, hands resting in one another, the carrier bag and black Russian coat thrown across the bench, next to her.

How beautiful she is – her lovely head on that alabaster neck! White, yet gentle old rose glimmering on in her cheek a little. A Solveig waiting.

The golden ringlets on the Madeira curtain sound like the little bell on old Lev-Jossel Green's store, as I enter the empty room. Now she has seen me and I rush to bury my head in her beloved arms.

It was true, it was her on the road with her bag beside her. A moment of stillness, almost happiness, between us. She strokes my hair. Süssel, she says, I'm glad it's you. I knew you'd come for me. And she lifts my head out of her lap, recites our childhood-ritual words: *Look up my child, from your books, look up, there's a sky and moving clouds across the heavens.* And hearing those words, I would run and play as all children do, books scattering as I ran.

So different now in this empty room. My face in her hands, just for a little more. Then we rise almost at once. Another furtive glance around, another smile, and she says: "One can't take one's life along, can one?" I love her. Her making light of tragedy, her mockery of trouble. She bends for her bag. I take it from her but let her hold her black Russian coat. And hand in hand we go down her father's stone staircase.

MY MOTHER. Smiling at me, more than in my teenage years. Perhaps she sees herself reflected in me, can feel her own strong, rebellious youth returning. But she is weary. Crow's-feet are deeper around her eyes and her eyelids droop to shut out the world.

Felix and I both with her in Bucharest now. In shabby quarters, dense with northern refugees, infants and crying children sitting on mother's lap. She does not mind the confusion, it seems. But we know her sense of beauty, which is order, and her smiles are tainted. Out of her palace. At night, her hands folded in her lap seem to hold her displaced crown, but her queenly stance is unmistakable, as she sits upright in a straight-backed chair.

I know my mother. I know what she wants, but I'm not ready for it. She looks at me with questioning eyes, wondering when will I answer, will I have to ask? But I cannot speak about the death of my father. I cope by repressing memory, keeping my head cool for the task at hand: what kind of work is available – legal, illegal? Where are the markets now? Where are these small peasant enclaves that bring root vegetables, fruit, or whatever they can spare to town? This is how I deal with my loss. My father's death. I try not to think, I can't prevent the dreaming, but I won't easily speak about it. I did tell Felix, just to inform him, without offering details.

But I sensed, one evening when that whole refugee house had settled for the night, that her time was short. That she held on to life but barely. She waited and I had to respond. All was over for the day, dishes were cleared. We sat around a small improvised table she had draped with a triangular scarf for colour, and waited for our after-dinner Turkish coffee. I had acquired it at great expense, and it was now slowly steeping on the tiny corner hot-plate. Evenings fall just gradually on that southern plain, muting the passage of time. Every moment is too precious to relinquish to the next. And we sat, the three of us, on those straight-backed wooden chairs and I said, "Mother, you know I can't talk about it."

"I know that. I'll wait as long as I can, but Süssel, some things have to be said. They simply do not belong to you alone. Though they happened to you, they belong to Felix and me as well. His life was ours and so is his death."

"No, please don't, it is not necessary. Of course you have to know. You will forgive me, I hope, for hesitating for so long. And, indeed, how would I have felt had you not told me? You know me, I'm selfish – perhaps I need more time."

"Yes, my child, I should know, shouldn't I?" We all three smiled, thinking of the millions of misdemeanours I was or am capable of.

"I've told you both we found shelter with a saintly Ukrainian babushka, after we were released from camp. She kept us for several days, let us wash, eat, sleep, and restore ourselves. She told us where the villages were, and gave us more than she could spare, I'm sure, to take with us on the road. The day was clear when Father and I left, and we trekked two, three days, in the direction she had pointed out. But no houses appeared, and on the third day the weather changed. The sky got heavier, dark grey, and it snowed constantly. We were covered in it, but still ploughed on, through heavier and heavier snow. The wind grew into a blizzard, so the whirls of snow obscured not just the horizon but the next step. It was futile. The snow perfectly rooted us, so heavy it was clinging to our Russian boots. By early evening the temperature had fallen sharply; night was approaching. Father stumbled against something, which may have been a heap of boulders or perhaps a clump of stunted bushes. Beside it was a rather comfortable dip in the ground, and we settled alongside each other, as we always did, for nearness and for each other's animal warmth; we did not think of taking anything from the rucksack the old lady had replenished, we were so exhausted and wet with snow. And we just settled down in the snow. We had one more look around. "Where do you think we are?" Father asked me. "Near the Djnester?" We looked around, at a bluish-white expanse and a leaden-grey horizon, and all directions looked alike. So we settled in the snow. When I woke, it was day. Bitter cold, and the same sky as the day before. Father lay utterly still. His Russian hat had fallen off. I tried to rub his cheeks, did a few other desperate things, but I knew it was in vain. There were no tears, no theatrics. I sat by him. Took a few things from him I thought I could use, his pocket knife, the watch and chain Dr. Bauer had returned to him the day before releasing us. No Jew was allowed to keep valuables – as you certainly are aware – Dr. Bauer had kept it for him. I gave them to you, Mother."

"Yes, I have them in my jewelry pouch."

"I covered him in snow. Said the beginning words of the *Kaddish,* which I'd heard as a child; I'd forgotten the rest. Sat by him, with frozen fingers opened the rucksack to get the watch and chain, and took a bite from the dark bread and kolbasa the old lady had given us. Then I got up and started walking. Just guessing which way to go. So that is the story. Not very heroic, I'm afraid."

"Thank you," Mother said. "I thank you for it, Süssel." The

coffee was just ready, and I left the two of them to be silent for a moment. Mother smiled at the miserable cup I served her coffee in. But even if it wasn't served in gold-edged Rosenthal china, it was real Turkish coffee. "And we are who we are, no matter what," Mother said.

"Yes," Felix said, "no object matters."

"But one thing does," Mother said, taking a sip. "Love does. Dear Felix, here is the thing I owe to you. An almost incredible story. Ludmilla Bunin has come through the vastness of Russia from Vladivostok to find you, Felix. She rode on an army train, on the locomotive of an army train. She found me. We stayed a few days together, sleeping on the floor in our own flat, and she talked of her love. How it has changed her, and that if she cannot find you she'll go to a Siberian monastery. I have a small trinket for you, it is in my bag. It was perhaps one of the most beautiful encounters of my life."

"I loved her too," Felix said. "She saved us all."

So love will, I had thought then and still do. It was a solemn moment. And it was over. Coffee too. I turned to my mother and said, "Some things have to be said, you're absolutely right. It can't be helped." And she thanked me with her smile, which is her own and no one else's.

We tried to make her life bearable, ran to find fruit or vegetables – apples, perhaps squash from the fields, or a melon, but there was nothing to be had as 1944 moved into its winter. I dealt in clandestine drugs, made Felix carry dangerous suitcases – sulfa drugs, the new, rare, penicillin, or simply aspirin. He was aware of the contents, I think, but didn't let on, having my mother's elegance. Born to that crown and bearing it, unseen to others. Playing the game: we are who we are and no ugliness will make us descend. But Mother's crown was in her hands, too heavy on the brow. And as the days proceeded, in spite of all our efforts to even things out, prepare meals for her, take her for short walks around the working-class home where we had found shelter, in spite of all our love she stretched out on the sofa in the one room the three of us occupied to rest for longer and longer periods each day. Until one day, in late October, she took to her bed, refusing the cooked applesauce, the glass of milk. No urging would help. We understood, she had had enough. As we sat at her bedside, she put her hand under the pillow, pulled out the purple velvet pouch, and distributed the few things in it.

"Süssel, take my diamond earrings with the beeswax pattern. I loved them, they're from grandmother Esther." And, barely audibly, "my wedding ring too, of course. Father's watch and chain, that Süssel took from father's waistcoat, is Felix's, as is this small medallion. And yes, there is something for Marusja." And she handed me a few leftover gold chains and rings. We sat a little longer, as dusk fell. The house got louder, doors banged, children called out, cried, but it did not touch the room. It was silent, and she slipped away as if in her own lofty home.

We buried her with the help of the others around us. Felix looked at me and said, "Strangers burying our mother as if they're all sons, brothers, or daughters." How fast one learns – death brings things home like no other teacher. A simple box. Within twenty-four hours, according to the law. No rabbi. Buried in an old derelict cemetery not far from the airport. No permission sought, none granted.

We mourned for seven days, as Jews do. We sat hardly moving, Felix and I, mourning the end of her life. Or perhaps the silencing of her voice. Her voice gone, the hardest thing to fathom.

The sound of her so personal self. Where to? How is it possible? But after seven days, you rise. Pack things away, clean up and go out into the streets to renew contacts.

Felix had found temporary employment in a pharmacy and I did too, for a few days. But I spotted a colleague from Prague, in Czech uniform, or he spotted me. He brought me "merchandise" to sell and took me into the slowly-emerging underground. I signed up, went west in sealed trucks, Czech this time. Saw Germans on the run, who were allowed to run and were not shot. They ran barefoot with bleeding feet, having lost their shoes on their trek west. The Romanians who joined the Allies in 1944 – joining the winner as always – had attacked the German military base in Bucharest. The German soldiers who surrendered, barely fifteen years old, had fought to the end. I saw them come out, hands above their heads, or laid out on stretchers. Such was the scene. And there were no borders. All was no-man's-land, open to assault from unexpected quarters. The truck was waiting and I left.

Saskatoon
1951

Süssel

Your Haunted Face

Dearest Max, my little brother-fiancé, the last time I saw your beautiful haunted face was behind barbed wire. I had just been through a forced march, I do not know of what duration, and spoke the Lord's Prayer incessantly, saying Amen to the "Our Father" in four languages, as in the eight o'clock morning school devotions. I was able to ignore the two SS men at my side with their unimaginably-beautiful German shepherd, because I was as in a trance. With the prayer all our youth returned: memories of river walks over grass and sand, climbs up the mountain hand in hand, and always the image of your slender figure under my window. I wrote a poem about finding you at the ghetto gate. As you know, I wrote verse on scraps of paper, on walls, or spoke it to your desperation and everyone else's around me. But this is how I live my life. In words. They haunt me, wake me up at night, but they also transform despair into trance, or elevate routine into beauty, to make things bearable.

Dearest and sweetest friend, this will be a long letter, I'm afraid, to cover over ten years – but I must not go into small things, which I should leave for the day of our reunion. I hope you have come out sane on the other side of the slaughter. I tried to locate you through the Red Cross, suggesting Israel as a possibility, without success. But I still have hope through several Jewish organizations, which so far have yielded the address of my brother Felix, who is in Vienna at the moment. I'll include his address in the letter, next to mine.

Of course I have landed – where else? – on a river, very much like our own Prut. What a strange thing it is, to have landed on this icy river. I always land on rivers, sitting on high banks, watching the towns across, far beyond the rounding of the sky. I had never heard of either river or town and felt my years dissolve, carried by gusts of fierce winds. Naked branches hung in the blue that day, mobiles of silver, they moved almost free of the earth, free of trunks or roots.

There was no obstruction to the end of the world, the prairie heaved like the ocean and I was at sea. A river ran through the prairie sea, a gulfstream of ice, and I sat on that high bank, shipwrecked. It seems there is a busy domesticated world on the other side of the river, people live in homes, where points light up in windows and shine across.

But let me give you an outline, at least, of my trajectory, which was almost as unforeseeable and full of wonderful luck as were the bloody war years. My brother Felix and I had just buried my mother in Bucharest. For my grande-bourgeoise, stately mother, a simple fir box – unlathed, lowered into the earth, twenty-four hours after death, as is the Jewish law, with the Kaddish said by Felix, was fitting to her spirit. It was the end of 1944 and a Czech-resistance army unit had been formed. I was able to join, having studied in Prague and made my first pharmacy degree there at the Charles University. I left Bucharest with Czech papers, being again recruited as a pharmacist-chemist as I had been in the camps, but under much happier circumstances now. To my great chagrin my brother Felix could not join, he was disqualified. He had studied in Vienna and spoke no Czech.

Felix and I had met where all the home-town leftover people meet in Bucharest: in the University square; we spent as much time together as we could, but had to part so soon: such is war! But war was nearing its end. There was hope.

Dearest Max, I looked for you of course, asked whomever I saw, but had to leave with my small unit without an answer. I should not be so long winded, but oh, it's a long windy road. In Prague I was happy, I am always happy in Prague. But it had changed remarkably. The Germans were persecuted now, and hunted down as the war drew to a close. They did not show their faces, hid behind Czech names to deflect attention. I recognized German colleagues who looked the other way when they saw me in Czech colours, afraid of me now. The air was poisoned. All my Jewish friends, students, their parents, had perished in *Terezim-Theresienstadt,* and I walked on the shores of the Moldava, that golden river, and did not sing as I did before to the accordion. But it was not all tragic. I found Czech colleagues who had survived, non-Jews. They were overjoyed to see me, and as soon as I was released from the army they offered me a partnership in their father's pharmaceutical plant. A small industry, almost the size of my own father's. We flourished. From memory I patented a headache-antineuralgic pill, and developed a new line of antibiotica, which was new to me. There was such a dearth of everything, so we were hugely successful. Of course, the Russians had taken a hold of the country: the true economy flourished underground. It was hard to do research and bring out a good line of drugs in a double-accounting economy, everything done "under the table," and I was tired, tired of all the lies, the state having a hand in everything, and the constant inspection. Of course we cheated. All of that, so tiring!

So I would not stay, and after about five years of hard work I was restless. I got along very well with my workers and partners, we were honest and respectful of each other. But I was somehow unable to forge any closer personal relationship. To fall in love, hold someone close, take him into my arms – or even just walk hand in hand along the Moldava. I was too wounded, too guilty perhaps. Nothing was possible. I was alone, my thoughts assailing me, and I thought to leave it all behind and put the "big pond" between me and my past. But what was truly decisive was the atmosphere of strife. It brought it all to a head for me. It was Czechs against Germans, who felt unjustly persecuted, forgetting the times of Heydrich, the SS men, and their own actions. So I was restless. I had some difficulty getting a Canadian immigration visa, but finally succeeded. Sold my share "under the table." Interestingly, they allowed me to go. I was one of the few lucky ones. I had a good profession, a very good profession, was unattached. I opened up a big map of Canada, spread it across the table, and let my index finger fall where it might. And it landed in the middle west on a spot with a wild name that I had never heard before nor knew how to pronounce. I'd go west. Far.

But I did not anticipate the heartache I would feel at leaving the golden city. In spite of its politics, its Soviet masters, its lies and its ethnic miseries, Prague is with me as our home town is. It has a glow, a warmth in its day-to-day life, and the Hradcany dominates my horizon as the Archbishop's Residence did from my childhood window. My soul had adopted it and sung its tunes, but its soil is poisoned, as all European soil is, drenched in pain and loss. And I knew I had to go, before I became old. I made decisions fast, burnt my bridges – though the Charles-bridge is hard to sever – and left. Made a little visit to Strasbourg, also changed, perhaps for the better, but alien now. Paris, which I knew well from student days, eternal as ever, I enjoyed for a fortnight, then took *Le Havre* across the ocean, along with hundreds of others like me.

Everyone on that boat was a novel. Max, I marvelled. Old and young with future in their faces, going to Canada. I had seen in my life men and women emerging from despair, picking up the pieces, joined them as in a puzzle, but I had never before witnessed hope working miracles. This was just that. Going to Canada. Dreamland. And so was I transformed for the moment.

No one can escape the past, and I fear mine will be there, uninvited, hindering my first steps. It cannot be otherwise, for we're made of our past lives. But for the moment I was free. The salt air, the unknown before me, the first deafening sound of the foghorn, the hopeful faces, and a woman my age, Polish-Jewish, next to me, freed me of the past. And on that long journey we exchanged stories to make each other laugh: stories of cruelty endured were turned into amusing anecdotes, and each tried to outdo the next one. It was true friendship, if only for a time.

We docked in Halifax and parted from each other, and I

took the train across an endless land. Empty, virginal, it seemed to me. Lakes and forests for days, then the prairie, with its immense sky above. We'll talk one day. If and when this letter reaches you, write to me immediately. I'm just at this moment apprenticing as a pharmacist with a local Jewish pharmacist, who helps me with my English. He thinks there is no better worker than I am anywhere and promises to sell the shop to me when he retires. My degrees are in review and I will have to pass additional exams to get full rights.

Beloved Max, if you have survived it all – God had to be on your side to avert the bullets and all the angels from my grandfather's gate, which you so cherished, had to fly to your aid. You with your abstract, absent ways –

Dearest Max, do not hesitate to find me. There is room for you wherever I am. You and your own, if there are any. I will close with a hug and a kiss for you. What do you look like with so many years – dear God! – in between?

My Love, S.

DEAREST MAX,

The only fiancé I ever had! Brother Felix has found you for me. I am holding his letter with your Jerusalem address in my hand. I want to reply instantly but my eyes are blinded with tears. That you are alive! And in Jerusalem! Of course, it was war – nothing has to be explained, neither how nor where one went for rescue. But I love to think that you chose Jerusalem, and that it was partly for me. Aren't we women – men too – a crazy lot! It was war and you went where you could, and yet I feel you haven't forgotten my youthful search. In the Polish café called Kucharczyk – remember the wallpaper all roses? – we sat across from one another, *Kaffeekrapfen* oozing whipping cream on the table and our knees touching underneath it, and I said: "Go to Jerusalem, for me." Why did I send you? Why did I not go? I can't explain. But that you loved me as no one ever would, I knew. And that you would do it, if it was at all feasible. I offered you nothing in return, went my own way. Passion. Men. The workings of the heart. Yet you are the only one that remains.

Coming to the prairies – to that immense stretch of land that pins the sky to the ground in a perfect circle, I went to the river. Such solace, and homecoming! I had work. Earned money – as you know, I do work hard. I love the people here. All sorts of people, a near replica of home: Germans, Ukrainians, French. Remember, we did not have any at home, though we spoke it. And my new thrilling experience, the English. But love? Too much hurt to recall, it was a closed book. Or so it seemed. And when it came, by accident almost on the high bank of the river on a wintry fall day with icicles in the air, it ran its course.

It was not to last. No house, with foundations, a roof above, and a daily return after work. Not yet. No real property to my name. Though I had an extended stay in Prague after the war, I was not at home anywhere. Neither was David, this man I met by sheer accident. We had seen each other day after day walking a certain stretch of the high river bank, for recreation, taking in the riverscape and the wonderful champagne air. Bumping into one another – literally – one day, we laughed and recognized the homeless, the wanderer in each other. As one Jew does in another. And the stories started flowing out of us, like the river below. Where, when, how? The war. Childhood memories, yours and mine as well. I told him I had a fiancé but had never married. We parted several times, returned and parted. It was not to be, not with such pasts and David's character. A gifted, wonderful man, but footloose. So this is my story.

I have bought a piece of land, got a loan at five per cent to be repaid over twenty-five years. It is on the river, it was not cheap, and I had to virtually wrench it from a potato farmer, who kept increasing the price as I wanted it more. It is the spot of my dreams. Precipitous, with the low bank on the other side. A swelling river, sandbars and shores almost, not banks. It carries the most poetic name: Cranberry Flats. The air is fragrant with fruit.

I've laid foundations. Here they build fast, the soil being soft and sandy. With machinery and all of that. Beloved Max, I've built a house. For myself, my brother Felix, if he'll come, and, as I told you, not last nor least for you. I'll hurry to the post. It is early morning before the first pickup! A letter to Felix goes at the same time, by air.

Dearest Max, did you ever kiss me? I fear you didn't and so I dare now to hug and kiss you. I still see your beautiful face behind the barbed wire and I know you haven't forgotten me.

Your S.

Max

No Escape From Early Love

Süssel, my only beloved, my once-fiancée. Your picture is with me always. Not just one, but many, many pictures. Settings change. You do not.

Here in Jerusalem I chip the old stone for a piece of bread. It is hard. But I have two adopted children, a little girl, Elizabeth, and a seventeen-year-old Russian boy, Grisha. He is a young man now, who goes with me to the quarry and shares our room. Made fatherless a second time after Moritz died, Grisha stayed a while with a kindly old priest, but not for long. He kissed the old man goodbye, thanked him, and was on the road again.

One day he stood in front of our door, knocked and told me, "You're my father. I've come to live with you." And Helen and Elizabeth accepted him as their own. He is beautiful, young, Russian-looking, with a heavy Russian tongue that darkens and liquifies the sounds. Uninstructed. He has fought a private war against forces hostile to his little life. He is of a very pious nature, with an inbred ritual life, a self-directed morality, and has studied the Torah from the age of four. He found himself orphaned, running from the bullets of the *Einsatzgruppen*. Children were not worth the price of a bullet. So very often, thrown into the pit with the others, they crawled out from under their fathers and mothers, waited for the right moment, and ran. And so it was with Grisha. But he was picked up by the SS from a labour camp and put to work beside Moritz. You do know my brother Moritz, Süssel. There has never been anyone like him. He had a protective instinct, and the intelligence also to succeed. And so, God given, I have a son, as I have a daughter by Joey and Helen. I must do my duty. But there is no escape from early love.

Süssel, though I'm forbidden to follow you, there is no escape from early love. It's in the back of your eye. It is the way you hear things, how you pick them out, separate from the rest. It is a frame, holding your days. And it is almost a road. You'll choose to go this way, without decision or measure. It is your stance, the way you put one foot in front of the other, toe inwards or out. Predestined, written in Greek or Hebrew, not rational thought, just a direction. And you take that path, because there is no other.

We stand in front of each other's doors, without recalling how we got there. This is how I stood across from the old gate, day in, day out. One couldn't retrace one's steps, one simply was there. Grisha stood there, suddenly, and made me his father. We had put Moritz to rest together. Held the wake, ate beans, cried and laughed with the ways of the world. He was so young. He told us a little about his trying to find me, and it almost sounded like your mother's C.F. Meyer story, the story of the Saracen princess searching for her lover with only two words to help her: *Beckett* and *London.* And she found him. We find one another. Those who love us stand one day in front of our doors, hardly knowing how they got there.

Going to Jerusalem on that boat certainly was by necessity,

there were no other open roads for the uprooted with a town in their hearts. I am here, chiselling stone out of the Jerusalem hills with all the other nameless wanderers. But I am here because you, Süssel, said to me once, after a strenuous climb in a cool stalagmite cave deep in the Carpathians: I want to go to the Dead Sea caves. God speaks to the prophets there, and nowhere else. I want His voice. It is written on parchment or held by the ancient stone and released to those who yearn for it.

We sat a while in that dark hollow. Water dripping to mark time with the precision of ever-and-ever, and some light near the entrance. We bit into our apples, had bread, cheese, and almonds. Our longing came to rest. We did not utter one word going down – descending is often much harder than climbing. Muscles strain to hold your foot, like brakes, stones avalanche, making you roll with them. Precipices lurk where you least expect them, awesome and frightening. Suddenly you are facing a sheer cliff, you laugh with the derision of the exhausted, sit down, legs dangling, to recover your wits.

I am here because of you, my love. Your search for God is mine now. I have hired a shepherd boy, who knows clandestine routes across the border. It has to be at night. It is not hard to cross. There are no fences, long stretches are without barbed wire. Once inside Jordan and then to the Dead Sea shore, there is little danger, none that I cannot avert with a few *piasters*. The guides are so poor, money does everything. I will go alone. My adopted family I will leave in Jerusalem. You will meet them one day, if God is gracious.

Through the Old City, beyond the wall. Through the bazaar-hawkers, in their never-washed flowing garments, through mountains of honey-dripping sweets, smelling of coriander and pistachio, cuts of lamb hanging on hooks, covered with flies, beggars, legless or blind with trachoma, and with biblical scalp – *Parach* – baldness. I pass them, avoiding their glances, their open palms, for fear they'll stick to me like the flies on the lamb. Tourists, the world. No one sees me. Out the south gate, for a small price. A vehicle of sorts, donkey-drawn. An arduous journey, slow, with a killing sun above. The sun here, it does kill. It is not our beauty-sun, heavy, golden, benign, just hinting at its power. Here, on the desert slopes, it shows its intent. Its finality.

I am here for your truth, not mine. My truth is simple. It grows out of a seed, an idea only to be proven correct or false. This truth is a chain, and if broken has to be planted in other soils to grow, other minds looking to its proof, or disproof. Sometimes it is necessary to take another road or abandon the search. This is my truth. It stands on its own. It is about the universe and our place in it, as a conscious part of the whole. It has a beauty of God-like splendour. So different from your truth, Süssel. Yours is intuitive, from the gut, an inner certainty. I am here to find your truth, Süssel, to go to your dry, exhausted lands, along the red rocks, the pale ivory rocks with their hollows, to rest and seek.

My young shepherd boy, very young with the silken skin of green olives, is my singing companion. He hums all the time. He left his vehicle in the care of Bedouins, with whom he shares his profits. One camel resting. Wind lifting the tent sides: four naked poles. Who could live here? They had cooked a meal of mutton and rice, which rested on a wide braided board – branches or hardened grasses? – and we ate with our hands. No money was exchanged, it was Bedouin hospitality of the warmest kind. This was our last meal, since then it has been hunger, the freedom from the body that you, Süssel, once thought might sharpen our senses.

From cave to cave, with the blinding sun in between. A lightness of foot and head, sounds trembling in the air. We found a very flat dark hollow, a comfort totally unimagined by people with three meals a day, a toilet, and a mattress. The boy Ahmed and I, leather sandals on our feet, my shoes around my neck – as you and I used to do when crossing the Prut or wading through springs rushing down the Carpathians – we climb into that hollow as into a mother's womb. It embraces me with the comfort of a heartbeat, a living pulse, a restful half-darkness. It is as if I have come home.

The voice now within speaks in letters. I see them in that half-darkness. Not on parchment. Signs and sounds overlapping. Thought clearing also. Almost linking into my own enchained truth. To find it *One.* Like yours and my father's.

I will try to swim, or not really swim but bathe, tomorrow, in the salt-thick oily waters of the sunken sea the world calls dead but for me is alive. And will return over the Negev, travel along the Jordan River crevice – not truly a riverbed like our own mighty Prut, but an elongated crevice swollen with water in the rainy season, hardly a trickle in the dry season – just to say I have been there. And over the sands, that you, Süssel, always thought held all the answers.

You're absolutely right, I'm a fifteen-year-old behind eavestroughs, forever watching, hiding. Keyholes are strange frames to watch life through, flat on the bottom and round on top. I saw my parents making love through that absurd shape, it made me think no, no, I do not want it. I'll marry Süssel.

Lying under my saviour Russian coat in the mud, or dry on

the upside-down table, I shared Joey's love for Helen. The smell rising from under the armpits, the crude French words she loved to say and hear, her habit of turning away, to feel his rising desire against her backside, all the little beauty spots on the neck and breasts, her night-smell, her dishevelled hair – all this I shared with Joey. I knew her well before I met her. Making love to her in Joey's bed, I was still a fifteen-year-old behind eavestroughs. But it is you that I watch, Süssel my love. It feels a bit dishonest, to sleep with Helen and long for you, but not entirely so. I love her too. From the beginning there was an air of familiarity, as if I had made love to her before. Her gentle manner, her love of sex, wild or demure. Always with a giggle. I knew her well.

Yet I stand on rooftops in Jerusalem. Behind the chimneys, behind the enormous solar panels which warm their houses and heat their water. Perfect hiding places to watch my torturers, the Germans in Jordanian uniforms, SS or camp guards, hired by Jordan after the war. But it is useless. I won't bring them to justice, there is none. I hide, watch, let them afflict me, pain rising in each muscle.

I will stand one day in front of your door. Like all desperate lovers, like all lovers. What will you find in me, or want to find in me? – No, no, I won't think in those terms. I must let it be – You're with me wherever I go, our wedding band, the green-mottled marble, has a presence, a reality more powerful than my work chipping the stone, the beauty of little Elizabeth, or sleeping with Helen. Because this reality is of my making, fashioned to my needs. Perfected with time, held dear, called upon when needed.

Jerusalem is your world more than mine. Indomitable, extreme. Cypresses move their fine-edged tops with desert winds or sea winds; Jerusalem stone looks eternal. The houses are made of stone, solid blocks of stone, hugging the hills of stone, with flat roofs for gardens and the contemplation of the night skies. Windows forbidding the sun, looking like fortress slits waiting for combat. Walls look inward to small courtyards. It is a murderous world too. Long broad sheep-slaughter knives curved like Turkish swords sit loosely in the belt. Makeshift huts burn fast and easily, high to heaven in revenge.

But there is a wonderful calm at the lowest point on earth, on the shores of the Dead Sea, on the sands leading to the caves. Murder, rebellion, and hate leave you. We walked, I do not know how long, one early morning after a night on the hospitable cooling sands, tried to climb into the first cave we reached. But the rock crumbled under our feet. My sweet Arab boy knows his way around though, and he pulled me along. I promised him more money – being the dependent one now, and he found an easily accessible way into a half-dark low hollow, where we came to rest. Relieved of corporeal weight, needs, and wants, I was inside, where man has hidden God's word. This time it was not for you alone, Süssel, it was also for me. I did not stand outside, watching others live or feeling sorry for myself. My companion wanted to move on, fearing the high sun, but I asked for a few more minutes of this unimagined bliss. The boy stretched out with a sigh, and fell asleep. And I had this moment all to myself, a moment of beauty, a partaking of the eternal.

I paid my little Arab boy, kissed the donkey goodbye, and on a Jerusalem day brilliant with its eternal sky, I came home to total despair. Helen had been struck, Grisha told me, by one of those tropical diseases that we from the north have no defenses for. Grisha crying because he could find no help and cursing the Shabbat in Jerusalem, when all work stops, no buses run. Grisha cursing this country, pitiless and implacable, with all his Russian fury. He saw her die before his very eyes. High fever, swelling of glands, Helen delirious. When he finally found an old Yugoslav doctor, who gave her a penicillin shot, it was too late.

I borrowed money and buried her. The religious law here is twenty-four hours and a crude pine box. The body is washed and wrapped in linen. Nothing else is permitted, no paint job to make her look alive, no clothes, no penny on the forehead, no myrrh. There is the *Kaddish,* which is simply a glorification of God's ways, as you, Süssel, know better than I do. So, no "dust to dust," just "glory be to God." We buried her, Grisha, Elizabeth, clinging to me, and the kind landlords at her grave.

But how am I to face Him, when such a price has been demanded of me? How am I to build His house of beauty, justice, and thought? Sweet Süssel, hiring the Arab boy was for you, but for me also, to learn the law to live by. But it escapes me again and again.

I am afraid. Afraid of the emotions that make men here fall down and kiss the holy ground or stand at the foot of the wailing wall and shake in trance. I am not any more just a silly coward, as Moritz said. But fear assails me, fear of the sacrifice asked. Helen has been taken. What further price will be demanded?

A schoolbook picture of the Curtea de Arges haunted my dreams since the age of twelve. The image made me restless in class, to the general entertainment of everybody, including my brother Moritz. No, I did not faint as usual, but came home pale and shaken. My mother saw me and understood, one of the very few times when she understood me. She held me close and told me, you're absolutely right to feel this way, Max. Senseless cruelty and the taking of life, especially the one you love best, is too much to ask, is not fair. She hugged me again and again, saying sweet things to me quietly, perhaps even sharing a tear with me. "What is beyond our strength is not to be demanded."

And you, Süssel, wondered about it too, even as a five-year-old, when Ileana took you in her arms and told you this ancient tale. What does it cost to build a house of glory? To find His markings, His engraved letters, His thought, which is the real house of God. What will it cost? Master Manole had it easy. He had command, the will and madness for sacrifice. I am not he. I am terrified of that price. I will not give precious life; it isn't mine to give. It has to be wrenched from me. My beloved grandfather was taken. On what altar? you would say. Master Manole's altar is not mine. I look into the word of God to build that house for Him. But what will it cost? The walls have crumbled, my Lutheran mother lies on the ground, so do my father and his people.

An innocent, my father. With a charming, easy, peace-making disposition. A true innocent who taught me the unearthly beauty of sine and cosine. "Look to the geometrical shapes, Max, look at the answers they give you and you'll find them valid everywhere." He held me between his knees to show me his drawings, his cuttings of paper triangles and circles, to show me the world. My hatred of fighting and confrontation comes from him. His stories of war were so vivid, I lay in the trenches alongside him in 1916. He made me abhor rifles with bayonets, he forbade guns in the house. He played the drums for the emperor Franz Joseph II, it saved father's life. It was the year of the great Austrian emperor's death, and by then my father had succeeded in getting into a drummer's uniform. Perhaps these stories would not interest you, sweet Süssel, yet they come back to me, I can't help it, when I think of him, too, lying on the ground.

So, beloved, what price ought to be paid for our wanting to be or not to be, our wanting to find purpose, or that supreme beauty that makes our being here so unutterably worthwhile? Why payment? Why sacrifice? Why Master Manole, everywhere? No answer, sweetheart. We can only observe, as we do in the sciences, that this is so.

All my walls have crumbled, they lie around me in heaps of dust. And there is no stone left, in Jerusalem, where there is nothing but stone. There is no stone left to raise. I would have to be Manole himself to fashion the stone to finish the last chapel. I will not offer a life. Helen has been taken and I can't build a house. Not to God, not to thought or beauty. Not my house, for the wish to think, the wish to know, are gone. Just Job's quarrel in the end.

This is how homeless we are, Süssel. Existential creatures, having to know why they live, all the time. Formulating questions, asking God for answers. Pressing *Him,* who hasn't spoken since Job. And this querying is also our true homelessness. We are truly rootless. So I'll pick up the staff, my wedding band, our memories of youth, town, in heart, and wander.

Simple things first. Daily things, eating and sleeping, shopping for bread, olive oil, eggs, and meat. Trying to cook. Taking Elizabeth to school and walking with Grisha.

Grisha talks incessantly: "I did everything I could for her and I could not save her. You were away and it was Shabbat, the blind doctor came too late. Helen died in my arms. I've seen everything already. Everything. They have died around me, of hunger and filth, of beatings. But it was for everybody, not just for me alone, a nine-year-old boy. It was like something we all had to endure. Suffering for one another, we Russian Jews know this very well, we're chosen by God for it. And I found Moritz, a second father, who used to whisper to me, *Be a man, Grishinka, there will be better days, I have stolen extra bread for you. Wait for the night, when the other prisoners do not see you. Keep close to me, keep close.* He was everything to me, and we buried him. But I accept this also, as one accepts a flood or earthquake. We all feel the same at such moments. But holding Helen in my arms, hot with fever, muttering German, which I do not understand, was beyond my strength. Father, you have to believe me that I did everything. There was not a great deal I could do. I cooled her body with wrappings of wet sheets, changing them every half hour; water is rare, I had help from the landlady, God bless her. I wiped Helen's brow, sang to her and prayed. But she gave up her soul, in my arms."

So the two of us took long walks along the old wall of Jerusalem, to work it through, to let Grisha cry, and perhaps to search for our own answers.

An autumn day in Jerusalem, according to the calendar, but not truly autumn. It is eerie, hot, the air is almost still. Not what we love, Süssel, far from our Carpathian-sheltered comfort. There walnut trees grow and turn colour slowly, gold creeps into the leaf, we're forewarned of change, feel the year folding. Leaves fall one by one, resting like brass nuggets on the still green. We are aware of the end of things, winter to come. In Jerusalem time stands still. There are few deciduous trees here, and the evergreens look the same all year. And when the rains start in Jerusalem, Noah better build a boat. It is not merely rain, but sheets of glass, impenetrable, in front of you.

We live at the bottom of the hill. When Grisha, with Elizabeth in his arms, tries to climb up, he slides further down with every attempt. Sisyphus. She thinks it is fun, he curses in Russian, as only he knows how. Ukrainian mud is better than this. Where are the famous Jerusalem stones when you need them? – there is nowhere to rest your foot.

This is not our Meridien, where a translucent mist holds you hidden, eases your breath, relieves you of civilization. As you see, Süssel, we will never break loose from the slopes of our Carpathians, the rivers and hills wooded to the top. This here is the Bible. God and His land. Desert wind is desert and rain is flood. How are we....

ALONG THE WALL AGAIN, Elizabeth holding onto Grisha this time. It frees me a little, loosens the bondage. There is a certain freedom in loss, but also the unrelenting burden of not having loved enough. Two Jordanian sentinels, parading on top of the wall as usual, Arabic, not German, this time. I do not care anymore.

Pulling the Russian coat tighter around the two of us, Joey's voice is in my ear: "Helen does not like struggle, I tread cautiously with her," he says. "She gives up, without a murmur. If life is not beautiful, she does not want it." Yes, Joey, yes. She did not fight. And not just circumstance, the absence of penicillin, killed her. Helen set conditions to life; modest as they were, they were rigid in the end. She gave up, gave it over to others to take care of things. Yes, you said she'd run and she did, Joey.

I am left with the burden of not having loved enough. I was not here to thank her. For heating the water in the cauldron to rinse the stone dust from my face and feet. For going to the market every morning, up the hill as far as the Ben Yehuda Road, to get fresh yoghurt, and a kind of unfermented cheese they make here. She found cucumbers, small and crunchy, like we grow in the North, tomatoes and eastern spices; I did not thank her enough. Joey's whispers are in my ear: praise her for everything; she does not live by bread, she lives by praise. Her eyes will brighten and with her hands she'll fix a strand of hair self-consciously, over her ears. Praise her, Max. I was not here to thank her.

This calendar-autumn day. I see no birds flying south. It's cooler at night in the seven hills, but there is no hint of a lengthening night. The sun sets and comes around, like clockwork. How much I loved the roundness of that return at home, with its slight shifts, hinting change to come, yet staying round. Jerusalem's return looks rigid. Perhaps the shifts are finer, not discernible to me. So I am a stranger in this land.

One more Christmas, to see the tree lit in front of the YMCA. A single huge Christmas tree for Jerusalem, familiar and out of place, Christian-pagan-northern. Elizabeth claps her hands, looks at all the angels, the coloured balls that sound the glass when swung. She gets a teddy bear. The church bells are ringing. I love the bells, each of a different note, such an ancient art. Now, they break my heart.

Grisha is in charge. He makes a *kutja* out of wheat, honey, and nuts, hours of cooking. I always ate *kutja* with the maids in the kitchen. Because we never had a proper Christmas, there were too many Jews around to allow it. I miss the real spirit of the season, knitted woolens, spicy cakes, *kutja,* tinsel and kitsch, snow on the trees, fire in the cooking stove, kettle steaming, my mother and her maids conspiring with the boys around a small tree on the kitchen table. No father, no Cornelia sneering at pagan ways, Christian as they may be. I miss it.

There is no water in Jerusalem. We stand in queue for a litre of water, bottles in hand. From April to October, no raindrop from heaven. A shirt on your back will do, except when the winds from the sea blow in. How could we not long for the beech country, the waters of the Prut? Our myth and measure!

Enough, enough. I will take my two children, return the government table, chairs, and beds, sell our few kitchen things, Lusja's – Grisha's pet name for Elizabeth – beloved pail-tub, the movable iron stove. I will leave everything else for our landlady, the most generous soul on earth, and sail on the fifteenth of June.

Will you have us?

SPRING IN THE HILLS. Irresistible. Every seed blossoming into pastels covering the slopes. There is water in the Jordan. The air is spiced with all the perfume of the East. And I have had a marvelous change of heart. I answered an ad in the paper, looking for a map-maker for the biggest photogrammetry institute in the Middle East. What do you know? they ask me. I make maps, by every means, I say. Triangulations, photographs from the air. I have always drawn maps, just for love, I am a mathematician-astronomer. I make maps, of the sky, of the ground. They hire me.

Jerusalem-stone suddenly looks wonderful. Now that I do not violate it anymore with my hammers, it has become solid ground under my feet. The three of us take bus rides across the land. As far as Lebanon, where the Golan Heights find the Mediterranean, and then inland over all these mountainous stretches covered in wild flowers. Elizabeth picks a few to make a wreath for her hair, when from nowhere a guard appears to scold her. This is strictly forbidden, wildflowers must be left to give their seed back to the holy ground. Elizabeth does not like to be scolded, like her mother, but bows to the fierceness of the armed guard, seeking cover behind me and Grisha. No trees here. The Romans? Probably.

But expanses of the tenderest palette. No cornflower-poppy-daisy mix, but poppies in all shades.

Past Lake Tiberias – or the Sea of Galilee, where Jesus walked on the water. I, the skeptical scientist, listen to the legend now with a different heart. Part of the land, it has its own truth. Grisha is happier. His Hebrew was always good, he has done his prayers, studied the Torah, from the age of four. But now he comes home full of excitement, goes to school properly, for the first time in his young life.

The three of us live close now. Grisha cooks for us. He complains only of having to fry perogies instead of baking them, since we have no oven. We shop together. He loves the Arab food – chickpeas, oil and garlic, pita bread, and these honey-dripping rolls full of nuts and cinnamon. Elizabeth sets the table and I come home to find the evening meal ready.

"I want to be an astronomer like you, Max" – that is what he calls me when we are alone. After supper we go out onto the flat roof. I have borrowed a small telescope from the institute. Grisha already handles it quite expertly. Elizabeth is not that keen, but she tolerates it because it is night and she does not have to go to bed. Of course, she is touched by the heavens. As we all are, without having to name all the stars in the Cassiopeia. By the mystery of it all.

"Yes, I want to be an astronomer, like you Max, but I'll go into the army first," Grisha said.

"Army? We are leaving on the fifteenth of June." This worried me. I know the young.

"No, let's not go. I like it here now. I'll go into the army. Just three years and I can study in between." I was ready for this fight, but I wasn't sure I would win.

"Army? You want to wear a rifle with a bayonet on top? Guns were outlawed in my father's house. Do you want to kill?"

"Max, for heaven's sake. In the army, I'm armed. I can defend myself. Never again will we permit ourselves to be slaughtered. Besides, I spoke to a young girl who is in the army. A little older than I am. I will marry her. Max, she is beautiful, dark. Yemenite. Hair cut short, the limbs of a gazelle."

"So this is what it is, you're in love. Grisha, I promise you, when you have learned a profession and you're a young man, you can marry whomever you wish. But for the moment I make the decisions." I could hardly believe my tone of voice. Deciding! For others to boot! Grisha did not like it, was silent for the rest of the evening. Would not go onto the roof to look at the stars; instead, sat in a corner and read. And we fell silent. Am I right to go? I like it here now. I was promised a *shikkun* – an apartment with electricity, indoor toilet, within six months. Elizabeth has friends to play with. Where am I going? Grisha lifts his head from the books:

"Where are we going, Max?"

"To the fifty-second degree of latitude north, and we sail from Haifa."

"Where are we going, Max? What is the town called? You haven't answered my question!"

"It's hard to pronounce. It is called – after a fruit, a berry."

"A berry? What do you mean?"

"A berry, a wonderful dark round berry, round like the planet earth or a water drop. In fact, it is a member of the apple family."

"Max, you're not serious."

"I am serious. The city lies on a great river. It is one of the longest river systems in North America, and it flows into northern waters."

"Northern waters?" Grisha is upset. "Who wants northern waters? I like it here. There is no winter. I've had, as you know very well, Max, every part of my body frozen. I'm not going there. What is the river called?"

"Grishinka, don't be so hard on me! It's hard to pronounce, an Indian name. It means a meeting place, perhaps. A long name. Give me a pencil, I'll draw it for you. I'm a map-maker, you know."

"Max, look, you have a job. This is a country for Jews. The future is open for me and Elizabeth. Sure, we'll have to be in the army. But my beautiful friend told me how much fun they have. Night fires in the hills, songs. The love of the country which is ours."

"It's all true, I love my job, but I've made a decision for the first time! And not just for sentimental reasons. Let us try the new world. Grishinka, ancient as this land is, there is war, all around us. Israel has to prove itself. It will arm itself and fight. It is small, there is no land, not enough people to defend it."

"We'll defend it," Grisha interrupts my argument.

"Let me explain. Be patient with me, I'm your elder. Hard times are coming. Grisha, I can't face it again. There was slaughter in the tents just when we arrived. The country is surrounded now, it will certainly fight. I can see the fervour rising, the feeling of national pride, the determination to never again be murdered unarmed in your beds, or, what is worse, to be dishonored, have your good name dragged through the mud. It's a young man's old land, I can see that, Grisha."

"So it is just right for me, Max. I am the young defender of whom you speak."

"But it is *I* this time who makes the decision. You need a profession, a trade, you have to learn things. If that dark beautiful face will haunt you, you'll be back for her. Trust me, I know. If it's yours, there is no escape. Not from young love, I've been there. Where are you every free minute? Grisha, where are you? You are not home, you're dreaming, lost in thought. Grisha, I know, if it is, it will be. You won't escape. You'll come back. Or she will."

MAY, OUR LAST MONTH IN JERUSALEM. I took the children out of school, and we played tourists. First to Talpioth, where all the Yemenites were, with their aristocratic long dark faces. They work the silver, and we bought some of their goods. Silver threads, filigree work, a necklace for Elizabeth, a beaten-silver dish for Süssel, and all their butter and eggs. They stand on the road to Bethlehem shouting K'hma, with butter in their hands. Denmark's gift to the young state. They do not eat it. Or eggs. Olive oil they want for their butter. Grisha loves them. They are exotic, he says, not like our *mujiks,* square bodies without necks. Delicate they are, like the kings and queens of old Egypt from his schoolbooks. Nefertiti, every one. Shiny skin, like poured oil. And this is what they want, oil.

Grisha asked a young woman – he speaks so well now, both Arabic and Hebrew – who came to help us in the house what food did she like best. Bread dipped in olive oil, she said, with olives swimming in it for flavour, and black coffee. Arabic-style tradition, joy, and comradeship. The nimble fingers, working the silver thread into armbands, legbands – exotic, he says. So different from us serfs. She worked very hard, scrubbed the floor, the walls. Grisha offered her a saffron-flavoured rice dish he made. She refused, thank you. "It is not clean. You are not *kasher,* you

Europeans. We don't eat from your dishes." And she asked for a glass – and it had to be a glass – for a little oil with an olive in it, and dipped her bread. Drank the coffee, black as heaven. Before she left, she looked severely at Grisha and said, "You must mend your ways. You do not live by the law, and this is why, says my father, that Hitler became the whip of the Lord. He did not come to Yemen or Morocco." Well, what was there to say?

Grisha cooks, prepares picnics with Elizabeth's help, and we are again on the road. It is hard to leave this place. Each day becomes more precious. Elizabeth wants to go to Hagar's fountain. Biblical stories have the presence of now. It is in the air. Abraham was here yesterday, so was King David, and Solomon, and everybody else down the five books of Moses. They are alive like the blossomed spring hills. It is taught in the schools, from grade one. Quite wonderful. All is alive. And so is Jesus.

We went to the *Via Dolorosa* at the Church of the Sepulchre. Of course, all denominations are fighting over the authenticity of their own sites. But I'm accustomed to human folly. The Spirit is there for me, and it suffices. As it did in the sands along the Dead Sea shore and through the caves and Masada. The truth is preserved and felt. The dry air remembers, as do the sands, and the stones walking up to Calvary. You need not fight. Dominion? So foolish.

Hard, hard to leave. We fill every minute of the day with Jerusalem. Fall silent, little left to say, trying to make this land our own. To carry it in our hearts. It is a first for the children. A little different for me, who saw our town lifted from the ground on an October day....

An empty room, nowhere to hang your hat. Freedom from guilt at not having done this or that. Objects interfere. An unwashed cup and saucer, a broom in the corner: another day to come, the planning and the guilt. An empty room, like the sands along a shore, allows a peace and a preparedness. You're free to feel your way back, link thoughts. Solid ground, as airy as a walk with you, Süssel, in the mountains, will surface. Memory is free on this day, with no object to remind me of the meal to cook, the potato peels to clear.

Suitcases in an empty room. Me in one corner, Grisha and Elizabeth in the other. She wants a story. A specific story. Grisha has a stock of village fools. She loves them all, but she wants Chajm, the idiot, who smiles all the time when wicked children pelt him with stones, call him cripple. He limps about saying "Oh, how good they all are, how sweet to call me cripple." Grisha invents the fools for her pleasure. Some are *Stetl* lore, about Jews living as islands in a vast sea, held by their law and a feeling of superiority.

Not today, Grisha says, leave me, Elizabeth. Let's wait for the bus quietly. No, no, tell me a fool's story. It doesn't have to be Chajm. It can be a Chelmite idiot or the little Moritz, who thinks he knows everything there is to know. Lusja, sweetheart, please, put your head on my shoulder and sleep. She does not relent – she is too young to turn to her memories, and he gives in.

It touches my ear only slightly. They speak Hebrew now with each other. She does not speak Russian and he does not speak German-Romanian. So with this whole world here. A Tower of Babel lifting the holy tongue out of the Book to talk to each other. Life breathed into ancient letters, the language of biblical text.

And I see you sitting on the rim of the Ahi fountain, after a sweaty run down the hills, to catch the caboose of a train. You walk up the hill of the Bahnhofstrasse, over the Holy Trinity

Street, and you rest on that rim. It is the hour of the setting sun, when time seems to speed up, and must be held or missed, when childhood emerges. Your grandmother Esther determined what Hebrew meant to you. It defined no object, no useful thing, of ordinary necessity, no table, no chair, no linen. No please, no thank you, to each other. Only abstract thought, the Glory of God, and the obligation to serve.

All of this comes back to me in this empty room, Hebrew floating across. Lusja shouts with excitement as Grisha begins the story of her favourite fool, Chajm the idiot-cripple, who limps through life thinking the world is good. So Chajm eats at every door in the village. He is told oh, go away, I have nothing for you, or come in, Chajm, warm your toes, have tea and sugar, or on Friday night sometimes, the head of the carp no one wants. And Chajm thinks the world is good. He has no father, no mother, he can't read or write. And who needs it? Yes, Lusja says, who needs it? Well, says Grisha, Jews need it, they are made out of reading and writing, it keeps their soul and body together. Oh, well, she says, tell me, Grisha, how clever Chajm is. You always say all fools are clever. Right, not just clever, but wise and cunning too. So when no one is looking, Chajm slips into the neighbouring Russian village and hides in Luba's shed, between the goats, who greet him noisily. He is, of course, deathly afraid of Luba's husband, who almost broke "every bone in his body" – but, the world is good, and Luba would kiss him and give him a big hunk of black bread greased with Christian butter. Christian butter? Yes, the most wonderful butter, Jews are not allowed to eat it. Russians keep it in big earthen pots, it is creamy white, smells a little burnt, sometimes of onions. Luba rubs garlic into the grease and says, God bless you, Yiddish child, you're poor. We're lucky to have enough to eat, to be able to share with you. And Chajm kisses her hands, runs away fast to avoid Luba's husband and sons. And no one will ever know what this Christian butter is made of, and why Jews are forbidden to taste it. Maybe Chajm does, the wise man, who knows the world is good.

An empty room. A few suitcases and a telescope, carefully taken apart and packed. Lusja asleep in Grisha's arms. All is silent. Until Grisha: Max, do you know what a *sabra* is? No, I say, I do not know what a *sabra* is. It is a prickly fruit that grows here. A fruit? Yes, a fruit, and all the young people here, boys and girls born in this land, are called *sabra.* Because they are proud and prickly, just like the fruit. Thorny, beautiful. Grishinka dear, I say, I know now that you'll be back.

And I remain with you, sweet friend, for the setting hour of the day. You, my Süssel.

Max & Süssel

Then Jacob Kissed Rachel

THE THREE OF US DUSTY PILGRIMS IN FRONT OF Süssel's house. Grisha sees it first. It stands against the western horizon, three stories high, with the river below. Wood and glass. Her grandfather's old house. No stone or carved angels, no Archbishop's Residence up the hill, but the western sun is there igniting the upper-floor windows with a flare of gold. An old, old gate, not fitting the fresh-cut wood, handles of brass, gently warming as the sun moves.

Nowhere to hide. No principal's house. Not even a tree. It has a strange splendour. Glass to look through from east to west, tall, demanding attention, no embellishment other than the fire in the window. A precipitous bank. Rippling sands following the river. Islands of the mirrored sky, turning darker as the sun descends. A wide-open land. I look for cover, as I always do, and hug Elizabeth and Grisha.

There is no one home and we seat ourselves on a stone bench overlooking the river bed. I have trouble holding my tears back. Süssel has found a spot where the river curls and bends, grass pushing through the stones, that echoes our childhood's river valley. There is where we went to swim, and this is what we saw from the southwestern slope of the Cecina. The river flows straight out of the sky, carrying the blue with it. Turns and twists to make its way through the sands, which hold the river, gilding its edges. A dream and a return. The bank is not merely precipitous, more a cliff and abyss. *Memento mori,* Süssel-style. I stand in awe. Wider than our valley, the bushes lower, aspen and poplar more gnarled and wind-tossed. But berries in the air, from the coral glass of the cranberries to the deep blue-black of the nameless ones. On this high August day, the air remembers. Rose-fruit scented, orange-tinged, heavy with the past.

There is no escape from early love. It directs your footstep, like fate. No escape for her. Nor anyone.

I hide between my two children when Süssel appears from nowhere, or so it seems, leaning against her bicycle. Hair red-streaked silver, piled high in a chignon, like her mother's. Eyes aged but resplendent, with a deeper green than I remembered.

"So, you have come," she says. "And these are your children. I knew you would. No escape from early love!" And she laughs, hugging my two children and pulling them towards her gate. As I slowly follow.

WE WANDERED AGAIN ON RIVER BANKS. On the higher one and down to the shifting sands to take off our shoes and feel young again. But the newness of my feelings surprised me. So old and so new. It seemed Max looked at me with the eyes of his teenage years, yet transformed by the in-between years into something not yet definable. I wanted to hug him, get closer, touch, but was held back by a sudden fear of rejection, or perhaps feeling he needs a little space. It is not my way. I do not wait. I show myself fast, impetuously. But perhaps the in-between years were the missing link to be sought out, searched, and wondered at. And I didn't want idle gossip or an account of events to test the old imprint of love. So we walked and held hands.

I'm old at love, no novice as Max was and perhaps is. I wanted him near, and it surprised me. I took his hand and he blushed. Started running, pulling me behind, all along the bank. Youthful he was, and jubilant, falling over old tree roots and laughing. I helped him up from the sandy ground and we were so near a hug but stopped. I would have fallen onto the sand in a swoon, my body on his body, losing consciousness, but Max did not allow it. And I had to wait, let the in-between years speak, show themselves, and see where I could link into that chain. On his terms, this time.

It seemed he had come to me from far away. As far away as the image of spiked rusty iron across his face. And though his letters had painted the scene vividly, a decade or more had passed. Compressed into the pages of letters, his past had become storytelling, and needed to be unravelled to show its core. But this was here and now. His teenage eyes returned, mirroring early love, but this was a new Max, with children and all that battle in between....

So this is the "now." Yet to be learnt. And images return to me of the Polish café, sitting across from Max, our knees touching under the small table, roses climbing up the wallpaper, whipping cream oozing from the *Kaffeekrapfen* and I saying, "Max, go to Jerusalem. For me." All of it returned. Distant images to be set aside as I try to see the mature man next to me. Down to the river sands through all that underbrush, years of decay and rose thorns, we come to rest near the water. Breathless. Which is so good, if what you have to say may or may not be understood. Shoes thrown to the sands, toes in the water for a little while. A shallow spot to cross to the other bank. Higher, more protective bushes here; we find a hollow, slightly damp but cool and comfortable to stretch out in. Branches intertwining, old leaves, smelling of last year's decay underneath. "Yes," he says, "we'll rest, Süssel, let's rest." Smiling, and with an unaccustomed quick and manly gesture, he nearly forces me to the ground. I had waited for it, and with a still, inner joy I let it happen.

The sun moving across the stream lit the waves as if strewn with broken shards of glass. There was a deep silence on the sands along the water's edge. Late-afternoon prairie stillness has an intensity and a beauty that exalts your heart. All activity subsides, melts into the pure stillness. Slowly, as if in the presence of God, Max took from his pocket a piece of stone or pottery. Pale ochre, it curved inside his palm. He looked at me with his teenage eyes and said, "This is my wedding ring. It is yours now. It has been a green-mottled marble – my amulet, my memory of you. It turned itself around my finger as if with life. But I could not hold onto it through war and slaughter. So it had to change. Perhaps into something more meaningful. I picked it up when resting in one of the Dead Sea caves you sent me to, Süssel. Here it is."

I was sitting up now in our hollow, chokecherry bushes against my back. and he took my right hand, put his shard into it, and closed my fingers over it. Wedding day, I felt. "When?" he asked. "Tomorrow or" – with a smile – "as soon as the law of the land permits. Will you take my children as yours?"

"If they want me," I said.

And Max whispered, thank you, and continued: "Grisha will go back to Israel, I'm sure of that. He is stricken – as I was, early

– with a very dark noble Yemenite face. But he will only go after his astronomy-mathematics studies are done. I'll see to this. He is very gifted. A religious soul, too."

"We'll help," I said.

"And Elizabeth, willful as she is, will go to school and be whatever she wants to be. A Canadian child, perhaps. We'll have them for a while yet."

"Yes," I said. "We will."

I'm holding that "marble changed into stone" and all this unearthly innocence of Max in my closed palm. We stretched into our wedding-bed hollow, our bodies close, aware of one another, eyes full of the dome above. And into that stillness Max asked, "How to speak of my love? A verse in Genesis speaks of that love better, or like no other: *Jacob kissed Rachel and broke into tears.* There is no line, anywhere, that holds that power. This affliction, that will not leave you, no matter if you labour twice seven years for it or not." And he stopped. Took a breath and then: "When you stepped out of the old gate, I broke into tears as Jacob did." Max had talked as if to the sky, but now he turned towards me, taking his time, and so gently took my face into his hands, brushed back a strand of hair, and kissed me. For the first time.

Czernowitz
1941

Saskatoon
1961

Marusja

It nearly hit her . . .

IT NEARLY HIT HER WHEN IT FELL AT HER FEET! "IT'S A pretty baby," she said. "I don't care if it's Jewish." Marusja, barren all her life, picked the bundle up. "It is bruised and swollen, the poor thing, and so still," she said, checking its pulse. Reassured by the beating heart, she cradled it in her arms. "I'm doing the Lord's work, I'll christen it. Let's see – was Jesus? Yes of course, he was born one of them."

She had been walking up the Residenzgasse, disturbed by noises, harsh voices, and the roar of motorbikes. An unexplainable fear had driven her out into the street. She had hesitated for a while, thinking how little and powerless she was against all the armed men in uniform, but could not hold herself back. Why did she not simply resist the urge to go out where she could only find trouble? She had always heeded Dmitry's advice: do not go anywhere when I'm not there to protect you.

But this time she could not resist, she felt called to go, God's will. Something important was about to happen out there. Something portentous for her life. She likened herself later on to the mother of God being told by Gabriel of the imminence of His coming. A little immodestly, she thought, but wasn't the mother of God called on to do the Lord's work for us all? This is how she liked to think later in life. Called upon. As she walked up the Residenzgasse, back against the houses, as a thief would, she heard German commando voices, women's voices, screams, commotion in the streets. She saw German uniforms, vehicles coming and going, motorbikes, and some tanks along the south side of the street. She froze.

It nearly hit her when it fell at her feet. Picked it up. Held it close. She ran as if pursued, along the north side of the street and down the cellar steps of the old stone house. She loosened the crisscrossed binding, wrapped like a Russian doll, and saw what she had expected, a little Jewish boy. "They learn a lot from us," she thought. She undid the binding, freeing the young limbs. He was unhurt, a lusty cry from the lungs fully assured her. She had found her son.

"I'll do the Lord's work," she said again, between her teeth. "Man is too wicked. And he'll be a priest. He'll read and write, like them. I'll do the Lord's work. I'll buy him books. He must be clever, being what he is. It's a holy people, chosen I say, while Dmitry shouts accursed, accursed! I don't care one way or the other, it's such a pretty baby." And she held him close, putting her little finger into his mouth to suck. Went into the next cellar room, found an apple crate, put an old fur jacket from the village at the bottom, a clean linen on top, and cradled the child into it. Cooked a little water on a primus, put a spoon of sugar into a bowl, poured the boiling water over it, and waited for it to cool.

Marusja and Dmitry married young. No one knows how old they are. They married in the village Caliceanca, right outside the big city of Czernowitz, where the Archbishop's Residence was. Marusja seldom went there, only occasionally on market days, in a horse-drawn carriage. She seldom ventured out. She was not curious about the world. Playful, she liked fables, fairy tales, not real life. Even saintly hallowed places with lacquered stones and gems, priestly garments with purple sashes through the middle, were not things to be touched and seen. She preferred to hear about them, imagine them, recall the smell of incense when peeling potatoes for the twelve or fourteen of them, stirring the huge cauldron of wash with tall wooden handles. She liked to sing or just hum those Slavic heartbreak melodies, listening to her toothless grandmother sitting next to her on top of the brick stove on wintry days or on the bench in front of the house on sunny summer Sundays.

"Useless Marusja," her six brothers called her. She was the youngest, a very tiny little child and the only girl. The boys carried the burden. They worked in the fields, brought the harvest in, gathered the firewood in the nearby forest. Marusja watched with delight as her eldest brothers cut the trunks of poplar or pine. Handy and strong, they placed the heavy logs on two oblique crosses, moving the saw rhythmically between them. Marujsa's tiny little body was always in their way, splinters falling into hair and eyebrows. The boys, Taras and Vasily, cursing her, chasing her away. *We'll catch you – you just wait.* But she laughed and went on playing in the sawdust falling from the trunk, picked up the bigger pieces and built the Residence of the Archbishop, the fabled faraway home of God. Pebbles of all colour and lustre she put into the ragged roof, and she made a gate from an upside-down hazelnut twig, a diviner's rod, through which all her processions passed.

Her middle brothers, only a year apart from one another, were as alike as twins, in both body and mind. Less strong than the older two, they inclined to see "things beautiful," as Marusja did. Reviled the elder two for teasing and chasing her. Vladziu and Cadziu. Two of her kind. They listened more than the others did to the grandmother on top of the stove, to the old stories pouring out the ancient spirituality of the Ukrainian soul. Marusja would sit with them when work was done, or let them carry her on their shoulders, such a tiny doll she was. The two boys truly loved her, played with her, carved dolls out of wood for her to dress in whatever rags she could find. Vladziu and Cadziu, they let her dream.

Hating sexual encounters from youth, she fancied Christ: a bridegroom with a halo, one that would not kick her or push her down into the fields. Young men, working on the harvest, sweaty with the day's effort, would chase her into the stubble, would try to pin her down on that rough dry bed, piercing her shoulder blades. A kick into the groin made them groan and run.

She fancied a German boy from the village Rosh, younger than her by some years. She had seen him on her way to the market, bringing potted cheese and soured cream to the regular customers. He was barefoot, shoes around his neck, straining up the hill to the Schillerpark. The sight of his halo of hair, spun from yellow light, his simple features and movements, kept her from looking at any other young men in the village, no matter how eligible.

In the kitchen now, waiting for the baby's water to cool, she suddenly smelled herring. Thinking nothing of it at first, she took a glass from the makeshift cupboard, inspecting it against the light. She had to strain her eyes to check for dirt, hair, or unwashed spots, because the small oblong window, barely above the ground, allowed in so little light.

"I do the Lord's work," she told herself. The water had cooled to be pleasant to the touch of her little finger by now. A teaspoon of sugar first, and then the water to dissolve it. Right! Pleased and smiling, she approached the cradle-box, lifted the child, who woke, crying with hunger, and Marusja slowly fed her son with a silver spoon she had been given one Christmas by her masters from upstairs.

This miniscule silver spoon, with its long violin-shaped handle, strings etched into it, Süssel's mother laid next to the tiny Turkish coffee cups, made of the finest china and cobalt-edged. The after-dinner ceremony of thick black coffee – *kaimak* foaming on top – seemed a children's game to her. "How foolish the rich. But how sweet and dreamy." Not really coveting it, yet fearing she'd put it into her apron pocket one day, she had held the tiny spoon in her hand for a moment, and Felix had said: Take it Marusja, take it. She refused: No, I won't. Give it to me for Christmas, under the little tree on the kitchen table. And there it was on Christmas day, wrapped in rustling white silk paper, bound by a red ribbon.

"I'll fight for you, I'll work. I'll see you grow and do me honour. You're mine. Wait little one, don't cry. I'll boil more water. Oh dear, dear, the Jews are gone, there is no one I could ask for help. Little One" – she would call him this until his christening – "wait, I have to boil more water. Oh, don't scream." And she opened the buttons of her blouse to let him suck her nipples until he tired and cried because of her empty breast. She cleaned and changed the little one, put him into his box, and watched his petal-skin, the perfection of his fingers, the tiny nails on his toes, as she let the small body, free of constraint now, find his own comfort. *Bozhe moje,* she said. "Oh, the greatness of God. Look at the little flower, like a budding rose in its two heavier branches." And she sat still and prayed.

Such peace a heartbeat. Such warmth, worthiness, and bliss. She knew now what the mother of God had felt for her son. She also knew the moment, the beauty and might of it, a moment unmoving. She was warm, all over. Life was good. Poor and looking for bliss, she felt the eyes of her favourite saint upon her. No need now to race away to the next thing and the next. She watched, contemplated the sleeping child, as if she had arrived after a long barefoot journey. Her nipples burnt sweetly, reminded her of her body, and she smiled with the pleasant itch.

Saint Cyril she liked. The one with the book in his hand. A gentle saint, who knew the Greek letters and wrote new ones for her people, for Ukrainian and Russian words. Marusja never learnt the Cyrillic letters, which would make her able to read the liturgy. It's all right, she thought, I don't need it, let the priests do it. She also liked Methodius, the icon with the book in front of him, but her heart went out to Cyril because of his eyes. Warm and penetrating, his eyes shone with wisdom. His icon hung in the village church across from the painted window, catching the morning sun. She always went early, waited for that moment when Cyril's eyes flared like flames into hers. Touched by God, she sang her prayer, made the sign of the cross, and left before everyone else.

Something shook her out of her musings. The smell of herring again. *Why do I smell herring?* Not trusting her senses – for she knew she had no herring! – she opened the door to the cellar entrance and saw in the spare light a covered barrel next to two sacks of rye flour and barley. She entered the two rooms off the entrance, the ones with the slits of window pane looking out onto the garden. Her heart stopped; she froze. Loot. Plunder. Mother of God, help! Dmitry has robbed old Lev-Jossel Green's whole store! Clothes in heaps. Hats and ties, shoes of all colours, trailing between wreaths of dry dates. And oh! She saw the ladle with the violin-shaped handle from the masters on the third floor, she and Ileana had polished to perfection, Süssel's blue summer coat among Felix's yellow shirts. The Jews were gone. How eerie it felt.

She was a simple girl and had known them from the first day she came into the old house as a *Hausmeister* with her Dmitry, right after a wild wedding. Her father had died in the last battles of 1918. Her six brothers were the masters of the piece of land, and they set the rules. Her mother obeyed and so did she. Except when she refused to go to the "girl's market," a village celebration where young men came from far to view the "merchandise." Pretty or plain, all the girls went, all done up in their embroidered blouses, skirts – *horbutkas* – and red boots. She refused. You'll be an old maid, they all said. You'll starve, you'll go to the big city and whore, you'll end up with your nose rotting away and city people calling you names. She smiled, went on with her work.

A small-boned child, but strong and good-willed, she was stubborn. "You will not get me to marry the wealthy neighbours' son!" But Dmitry came, and he turned her head. His father offered a piece of land to his only son, and Vasily and Taras put on the feast. After church, the meal and dance, happy and shouting, guests from both families waited in front of the bedroom window for the bloodied marriage linen. Only Vladziu and Cadziu stood a little apart, scorning the custom. But they did not leave the party, wouldn't be called "party spoilers," which they had been called before for their dislike of crude words and drink. After all, it was their beloved sister's wedding.... But she did not bleed, and Dmitry, out of pity for his crying bride, squeezed some cherry-juice from the *Vishniak*-pot into the linen and threw the sheet to the rowdy lot.

She was a virgin. A true virgin. Dmitry knew it in his heart and played the game. But it was a sad beginning.

OLD LEV-JOSSEL GREEN, the grocer and tavern holder, lying in his blood. Children, how many? Marusja hated him, when he stood on top of the staircase shouting, or came knocking at their cellar room door. "He wants his money for your drinks," she said to Dmitry who lay unwashed, unshaven, not risen yet from his bed. "He wants his money, Dmitry," Marusja said.

"I'll kill the Jew. He lies and cheats, I never had that much."

"But you were with my brothers and no one ever stops them until they're under the table."

"I'll kill the Jew." Dmitry said. But he didn't.

"Go," she called to the old man. "Go, we'll pay!"

Dmitry is a coward with knives, has never stabbed anyone in front of the church on feast days. He stands aside and watches; rarely carries a knife for fear he'll use it. But he watches and lets his anger take hold. He's always with my brothers, and they carry knives. Hidden in the trousers, tightened by the belt. They pick fights with the Romanians. The Jews – no, they just beat them up. Jews are cowards. They do not like a good fight, they just sell the liquor to us, make us drunk, and charge us double.

Dmitry may be right, Marusja thinks, old Green may cheat on the accounts, or maybe he doesn't. But if you owe him money, you should pay up. I know my brothers, the two youngest – they want liquor.

"I'll kill the bastard," Dmitry said. "He comes to my door on a Sunday noon to ask for his filthy money. I'll kill the bastard." But he didn't. The killing units did. The *Einsatzgruppen* of the *Wehrmacht,* the mobile killing units. It was summer then, early July, right after the Russians had been attacked by Hitler and made to run. There was a short week of peace. Marusja still went to help the masters, carried the wood Dmitry had split for all those tile ovens.

She loved to talk to Ileana, the maid from upstairs. Really a whore and Romanian, who slept with Felix and his friends in the attic among all the drying linen, she thought. Marusja loved Felix too, but who needs boys, or even men? What are they good for, except splitting wood and getting drunk? But she loved Ileana and her creepy Romanian stories. So different from her grandmother's lives of the saints. And the masters loved Ileana; little Süssel ran into her lap and the boys ran after her. Marusja just wanted to hear her stories. They delighted and horrified her, gave her gooseflesh. And she sat at the kitchen table to share Ileana's dinner after dancing on her brushes to shine the oak floor with her. They were a pair conspiring. Often cursing the masters, their arrogance and pampered ways, but mostly gossiping and telling naughty things.

She and Dmitry had both heard the marching songs, the rifle butts against Green's door, and the shouts of *Juden raus.* Dmitry locked their cellar door. "The days of reckoning have come," he said between his teeth. "Let them die, they're an accursed race, they killed Christ, they suck our blood." But he trembled.

Marusja and Dmitry had known the masters and old Green all their days in the city. Dmitry had often helped him with the heavy loads, carrying petrol, barrels of salted herring from the train station, and potatoes in season. The Jew paid him well, was jovial, gave the victuals on credit. Looked after Marusja when Dmitry went to help with the clearing and sowing in the spring. Dmitry was an only son, and his father was less and less able each year to clear the fields and prepare the earth. Dmitry went home, solicited the help of Marusja's brothers, and worked for the old man. Vladziu and Cadziu liked Dmitry now, had accepted him as family. They knew how hard it was for an only son to carry all the burdens. Dmitry in return was grateful and only gently teased their "noble" ways.

He came only sometimes to see her. And it was on that summer night – was it late June or early July? – when he came to sleep the night with her that the slaughter happened. All of Lev-Jossel Green's people, his wife and four children, and the rich Jews from the first floor. They seemed in a hurry, those killing units, Dmitry thought, hearing the shots so soon echo through the walls; so soon after the knocks of the rifle butts, shouts, and screams. They disappeared as they had come, like Armageddon fulfilled. After it was over, Dmitry heard the masters from the third floor descend.

They have been in a hurry, these marching killers, for they seemed to have spared all of the third floor. Dmitry paid close attention to the sounds from above. He heard them more distinctly now, as he opened his cellar door. Whispers, silent sobs, people rushing back and forth through the old gate, which did not screech any more, as he had oiled it the day he came. It was Marusja's job, but she could not reach the upper angle, the thick triple hinges that held the heavy gate with all the angels. Dmitry wanted to be good to her. He took a ladder from the garden shed, oiled all the three sets of hinges, and polished the angels in their squares. He wiped them with linseed oil, which Marusja said had to be done, because "God likes his angels to fly and their wings dry so easily." Today he cleaned the whole gate. Polished the brass-copper handle till he could see himself in it. A mirror of sorts, even if his nose was too big. An only son, he had been pampered and called handsome by his mother. Come, Handsome, she would call across the fields, and he would take his time coming. Full of himself.

Today he would tend to the gate for Marusja. He liked her body, small and narrow. And though she did not bleed on their wedding night, he was thrilled by her tight body. He did not like those wide lips that gave way like wet rubber. Marusja was virginal and she stayed virginal. He had to force himself in. Seeking the spot with his fingers and rubbing her gently to make sure there was some juice flowing, but not really wanting it, and certainly not wanting the smell of it. He wanted her pure, and failure to conceive did not bother him. This was his womb and he did not need anyone else in it.

That night he did everything for her. He opened the small high windows to air the room, clear out the musty odor, carried out the bedding to puff it up and let the feathers breathe. He washed the windows with ammonia first, then propped them open with small sticks, for they had no springs. *Malenkaya, Malenkaya, Malenkaya moja,* my little one, he hummed while working.

Yes, she was a small, sweet thing, his Marusja, letting him do what he wanted with her. If this was love, then he knew it. Only when drunk did he lose his temper. Then he would throw her on the bed and his fists were not his own, he would hit her everywhere, and she would cry out. But afterward she would say: How would I know you loved me if you didn't beat me? And he would crash next to her and sleep fifteen hours, until he heard her call: *Lubitchku,* come my sweetheart, come, I have baked *kolaczes* and there is coffee left over from the masters.

He wanted her badly. Lengthened the day by thinking how heavenly hard it would be, to enter her, and he stiffened in his city pants, derelict old castaways from the masters. He went into the yard, which was separated from the garden by the enormous walnut tree. The yard was cobblestoned, with a chicken coop, three-tiered, an overgrown vine fence to hold the chickens, and a scaffold to hang, beat, and clean the heavy Persian rugs. Dmitry always had to help Marusja, when twice a year the rugs came off the oak floor and had to be hung over that scaffold to be aired and beaten with a bamboo beater.

Today his own pillows and coverlet were hung there, and he went to fetch them. The sun was in the west, behind the Archbishop's Residence, which he could not see from the yard or his cellar. He stepped out of the old gate and, careful not to smudge his golden reflection in the handle, he glanced down the silent Residenzgasse, with the Residence at the crown facing him. The chapel on the left caught the end of the sun, and the sky turned green, announcing the night. He felt his pants again, harsher now, against his full member.

He rushed in. Called Marusja nervously. She took her time, that always made him angry. Gossiping with Ileana or avoiding him maybe. His voice tense, he shouted up the staircase: "Marusja, Marusja!" Hearing no reply, he rushed up the stone staircase, holding onto the mahogany rail, taking the three stories in a few leaps, and knocked at the master's door on the third floor, calling to her. Marusja recognized the threat in his voice and flew fast to him, out of Ileana's kitchen, whispering words of calm and comfort, like oil upon a child's burnt skin. Dmitry grabbed her arm, pulled her behind him down all three floors, threw her upon the freshly aired bed, parted her wrap-around *horbutka* skirt, freed his penis, and entered her with one thrust. And now she bled, heavily. For the first time a wedding night. Tenderness filled his heart and he kissed her all over, as her blood spilled. *Malenkaya, Malenkaya moja.* My little one.

Marusja

The Smell of Herring

The old house was empty, so without life that Marusja hugged her little boy over and over again for fear they were the last ones alive. It was good to be close to that little breathing body. There was no sound in the house, no doors closing, no children's footsteps. The stone staircase up to the third floor was a world of compressed echoes from her village hills. Her ears distinguished grandmother Esther's heavy movements from Süssel's frolicking. She often wondered how the iron rail stood up, how the mahogany railing remained untarnished. She was glad, of course, because it was her duty to oil it and keep it shiny. She knew the sound from the second floor of the Polish-Princess aunt, as Süssel called her. Princess, a king's daughter, her step so different from everyone else's. Marusja always knew when she closed her door; delicately, deliberately. When she started down on the staircase in her pearl buttoned-up booties with the pointed toes, Marusja had to sharpen her senses to hear the gentle grating against the stone, imagined the grey gloved hand holding the rail. Her flat was a paradise of hats, flowers, and ribbons. Marusja and Ileana helped from time to time to shine her oak floors on their dancing brushes. She loved the Polish sounds, so polite and soft. Of course she understood. Slavs are bound by deep roots in their speech, no matter how different it sounds. And this was Polish, sweet, sticky, and always with a smile.

All empty of people now. Such silence. One can't even breathe for fear to disrupt the silence, yet one feels like crying out loud. *I'll go home to my mother and grandmother.* All the men had joined the German army, joined or been pressed into service. Her brothers, except the youngest; Dmitry too. They are crazy, she thought, how will the Germans give them a Ukrainian homeland? My own people, singing wildly, joining the Germans, killing Jews? What for? It will not work.

And the silence, with only the little one's breath to punctuate it. With no masters in the house, no cleaning or sweeping to do, she sat down, hands folded in her lap. She does not read or write, but what she hears she knows indelibly. And she hears her toothless grandmother, on top of her brick stove, telling her that it won't work. *You do not touch the Jews, let them be. God has chosen them. God has chosen his Son among them. He has chosen them to crucify Him.* And Marusja hears her say, *For us, Marusjinka, for us. The Jews have done it for us, to lighten the burden of our sins.*

Marusja used to complain about her masters, how rich and cruel they were – Were there no poor ones? "Of course there are many, so do not touch them, Marusjinka," her grandmother told her. "You do not touch them, not with our curses and not with our fists, or the Lord will come down on us, heavy."

The herring, the smell of herring again. She gets up, goes into the two cellar rooms facing the garden. The smell of the herring had penetrated her thoughts, reminding her of old Lev-Jossel Green who lay somewhere under the walnut tree. She passed the barrels and the sacks of flour and entered the big room where the midday sun poured in through the small slits. And she saw all of the loot, the familiar clothes and shoes – she knew exactly whose, the trinkets, small boxes with golden keys. One box, inlaid ivory with a crazy old man on top, hair flowing in the wind, she recognized instantly, and she cried out, hands covering her face, cursing Dmitry. She was sobbing quietly when her eyes fell on some colourful cans. She could not read the labels but there were cows on them, and she remembered hearing Süssel's mother say, *This is milk from America.* And she had watched her take the powdered dust, add water to it. A little different, but milk.

She dried her tears, to herself said, *God sent, God sent.* And in the burst of energy that followed her despair she searched and found Dmitry's pliers and opened the can of powdered milk. Busied herself with lighting the primus, chattering to herself. Boiled water, woke the little one, glad of his crying. Sang to him, while waiting for the water to be pleasant to her little finger. Took a silver tablespoon that wasn't hers, filled it with the whitish powder, and mixed it in a cup, thinking *I can feed my baby now.* It went too slowly for both of them with the teaspoon, but eventually, Marusja holding him close to her body, they fell asleep. A sleep so deep and peaceful as she had never known before.

They woke after many hours, the little one screaming with hunger. Marusja tore a strip of washed linen from an old shirt, dipped it into the milk, and put the other end of the strip into the baby's mouth. His delight gladdened her heart: "How happy I am," she sang to the Mother of God. She vowed, I will not touch any of the Jews' things. I will package them. I'll bury them. I'll return them, when they come back alive. I swear.

When the baby fell asleep she went into the next room, and in the heap she saw the blue coat. Süssel's coat. She hesitated for a moment, then: I'll just try it on. She being so small and Süssel so slender, the coat was too long, but fit her nicely otherwise. She liked it; it made her feel townish. The lining was slippery silk, and it hugged her peasant blouse and skirt intimately. She told herself: I'm a Jew's mother, I can wear their clothes. I'll return it to her, when she comes. She gave it no further thought, went out into the garden, cleaned the chicken coop, and let the chickens run freely for a little while.

Oh, she felt blessed. Dmitry had provided Jewish goods for her son. God had thrown him into her way to look after. To save a holy life from all the murder.

Slowly he grew, with the warmth of her body and the American milk. And he smiled at her.

Marusja locked the old gate with the elaborate key that hung around her neck on a leather string. The key was the emblem of her power-at-the-gate, her *Hausmeister's* authority, and now she exercised it. Locked the gate and did not let anyone in. There were none to be let in really, with Jews now God-knows-where and the local Germans gone *Heim ins Reich.* Not always of their own free will. Many would have loved to stay in their beautiful village Rosh, where every dog's hair was brushed, every little girl had a ribbon in her hair, and cabbages stood like soldiers in the army, crisp and straight. Nowhere else had potted cheese like here, and the churches were so clean and fresh you could eat off the floor. Blond boys who wanted to stay by their darker sweethearts broke all bonds and left, suitcases in hand. The best horses, wagons with wheels lovingly tended by skilled wheelwrights, changed hands for a pittance. Marusja's brothers bought four magnificent Pinzgauer, heavy, hearty brown-white work horses with friendly noses. And Marusja never saw the saintly boy with the golden halo walking up the Schillerpark again.

The Christians only slowly showed their faces in the Residenzgasse. They were bewildered by events, found themselves mistrustful, even of each other. There was looting, mainly at night. Dark shadows carried mattresses, clumsy objects, grabbed randomly what fell into their hands. Marusja saw them. *You won't have my little one's things,* she said to herself, locking the gate for good. That beautiful heavy angel gate that Dmitry had polished and oiled for her in a burst of love. She locked it with the iron key, big as a man's hand, copper and bronze inlays forming a complex design in the handle. It was her sign of power and Marusja used it. She also bolted the gate from the inside by throwing a metal bar across; she had access to her cellar flat from the garden.

And she began to cherish her solitude. Her God-sent boy to talk to. Every day she tried out another name on him, parading out all the saints, but she couldn't settle on one, so he remained *Little One* for a while. I'm not in a hurry, she said, I'm not in a hurry to share him with anyone. No need for a proper Christian name, for me alone.

No one in the neighbourhood had food and she felt guilty, looking at all her milk powder, herring, and flour. She used it sparingly. Baked bread, sometimes at night, in the big wash-kitchen, where the enormous water cauldron stood on the brick oven. She was cautious, afraid the smell of fresh bread would make people envious. So she waited. Hid, as if she weren't in. *Let them rob the other homes first, before coming here.* But she knew there would be a day, eventually.

She was careful when she set foot outside the old house. She was wary of neighbours' suspicious glances, the tension bred by greed and the fear of losing one's belongings. Marusja made her face as cardboard and expressionless as everyone else's. The Jews were gone, the local Germans were gone, it was an eerie, lawless time. She avoided encounters if possible. Ileana was gone, a pity. She had to leave, having lived in their household on their premises. Things were different with Marusja and Dmitry. Though living on the property, they were considered independents.

Oh, she missed Ileana. She didn't like all Ileana's stories. Some were just too "Romanian," Marusja felt; she did not understand their idea of holiness. Like the Legend of Master Manole. It is too much asked, she believed in her peasant's theology: why build a monastery, if you have to wall in your wife? It was too much for her. Ileana belonged to the same church, with the same Archbishop in the residence up the street, and the same patriarch, somewhere in Moscow or God knows where, the same services at Eastertime, the same twelve dishes and Slavonic liturgy, but they were different. Our stories are different, she thought. Beautiful. Not all cruel. She liked her gentle saints better.

Yes, she'll call him Cyril. But no, not just Cyril. She'll call him Nestor, her mother's father's name. Nestor Cyril Michalenko. And the little one had a name.

So she started baking bread during the day in the big washkitchen. Openly. The smell pervaded every corner of the cellar, masking its must. Dmitry had loved that smell. "Oh, your heavenly bread, Marusjenka!" Dmitry had called out, coming home unexpectedly one day. "I have baked six loaves for my masters but this one is for you, my real master," she had said, handing the biggest golden-brown loaf to Dmitry, adding a teaspoon of salt on the platter. "Welcome home," she had said proudly. And he had ripped a corner of the hot crust, dipped it into the salt, and kissed her three times. Yes, those were good times.

He loved to toss whole-wheat kernels unto the fiery grate of the brick oven and eat them by the handful. "You're just a little boy, aren't you?" she had said to him. But he had always helped with the baking, whenever he could. Warm, humid, and cozy, the wash-kitchen was a perfect place to set the bread to rise. Dmitry punched it down again and again with his full right fist, while taking little Marusja around her waist with his left arm, holding her iron-gripped. But she pulled herself out of it with a woman's wily delight. "Stop it, Dmitry, soon you'll want to punch me, and I have work to do until the bread is ready for the oven." Yes, those were good times.

But they came to an end. War changed everything and everyone. Ukrainian youth in search of a homeland believed German promises and joined their army. Others, like Dmitry, formed a local unit. "I have a Ukrainian heart, I want a little glory for my people," he had said then.

"And what glory, Dmitry? What is this thing I've never heard of before? Except for the glory of God, all glories are for the devil," she had replied. And begged him to go home, work his father's fields, and hide when they came to fetch him. Tears and sobs: "Who will look after your Marusja?"

"I will, I won't let my little one starve, but I cannot stay home when all the Ukrainian men are joining the army, one or the other. If we join early we'll be in on the German victory, which is a sure thing!"

And Marusja: "How sure? All I can see is that the world is upside down. They're after the Jews now and the Ukrainians will be next. The Germans do not respect us, they'll treat us like dirt, they are not our village-Germans. They're different, I don't trust them. Dmitry, go home and hide!"

But one day he was back with a wagonful of wood. He said: "Kiss me goodbye, Marusjenka. Do not worry, my angel, I'll be back for you." In uniform with the three stripes on collar and armband, he looked taller and very handsome. Her heart swelled. But he was a stranger, suddenly.

With the help of another uniformed man she had never seen before, he brought the split wood into the cellar and arranged it along the wall. The two were talking, swearing, and laughing: We'll show them, Jews have plundered us as long as we can remember, now we'll take some of it back. She heard it all, and didn't like the *Damn Yids,* uttered with each throw of a piece of wood. But she kept quiet. "We must go, Marusjenka. I am the leader of a small platoon."

"Yes," she said, "I know." She felt his impatience in the presence of a stranger and lowered her voice, coming closer to him: "God bless you. May Saint Cyril and all the angels watch over you. And one more thing, Dmitry, swear you won't –"

"I swear," he said quickly, embarrassed, and kissed her hurriedly once more.

She did not go to the gate to see him off that day. Summer, 1941. It seemed so long ago.

Dmitry had left enough firewood for a whole winter. Dear, dear, Marusja thought, he was good and loving and has provided for my Nestor. There was gratitude in her heart, but not longing. She loved her solitude too much, her independence. The little one was nearly crawling now, was picking up everything to put in his mouth. Well, you couldn't scold such a sweet tiny thing, so she sang to him, as only Ukrainians know how. Straight from the heart, with all its tears and pleasures.

It worried her not to know his day of birth. She had to christen him soon – at least when he was a full year old – and she did not know the day of his birth. God sent him to me – oh well, I'll christen him when he takes his first step, she thought.

One day, it was summer by then, she put on the blue coat, just to feel townish. She washed with the soap that must have come from America, and bathed her little boy. "This soap is for both of us, not just for you," she teased Nestor flirtatiously, and they played in the big water cauldron in the wash kitchen. She dried and wrapped the little one in the linen from the heap in the second cellar room, dressed him in a little peasant outfit she had sewn and embroidered over the winter. He looked like Ileana's story prince *Fat Frumos din Lacrima* – born from a teardrop. He truly looked like a prince, washed and combed and smelling of American roses. She took his little hand and said, "Walk Nestoritchku, walk with me." And he took two steps, sat down and giggled, looking up at her. These two steps made Marusja want to fall to her knees, but she didn't. She made the sign of the cross and said *Slava Bohu, Slava Bohu.* May the Lord be praised!

MARUSJA SLOWLY TOOK INVENTORY of her riches. "I'm so happy God gave me Nestor. I should really call him *Bohu slav,* because He provided me with everything, all I need for my love, all for my little one." And she called him incessantly to come to her side.

A year passed since the baby's first step, then two. Now he runs behind her, hides in her skirts, giggling. "Naughty," she says, "naughty, you start early, little Jew-boy." Oh, she knew she shouldn't call him that, but he liked it, and *Jew-boy* became his third, intimate, name. Lovers they were, with no one to disrupt or spoil their intimacy. They waited for each other to fall asleep each night. Nestor, who knew all his mother's lullabies, sang her to sleep. He began again to suck her nipples, and she felt a little guilty because it made her breathe faster, feel joyous. The tense itch between her legs relieved itself almost of its own, without her help.

No, she does not long for Dmitry – he would just put an end to her bliss, but neither will she sin by wishing for his death. He has been good to her. All his hard work, the wood he has stacked against the cellar wall, the ladders he climbed to harvest the walnuts. Heavens, up in those branches at the top, making the green fruit crash to the ground, and filling four or five wash-baskets full of golden nuts. Distributing them from door to door in the old house. All that work! And he beat her only when drunk. But, that is man's love, she thought. That is how they love; they do not know any better, poor devils. Push that thing into you, beat you if you don't want it, pry you apart with it, just to fall off you with a grunt, turn and sleep for fifteen hours, or until you come like a turtledove with food, drink, and a wet towel to wash their faces. These are men, this is how they are. But I've never seen Süssel's mother black and blue. What do they do, when they make love? It may be just the drink that changes men. Why don't Jews drink? They only sell us the liquor, they don't drink it. I have to like them now, think good thoughts about them.

Now I know it all, she thought. Dreadful. They'd robbed and beaten and killed the Jews. How else would she have found a Jewish child in the Residenzgasse? By a miracle he was only bruised, so well looked after and padded he was. God will have to forgive the Christians or He may not. *It's the holy people, don't touch,* her grandmother says.

Marusja slowly and very cautiously opened Old Green's front shop door. Left it open for just an hour a day at noon and waited. She offered the herring for sale. Not showing the barrel, but letting it be known to the people around the corner in the Balschgasse that she was selling herring by the piece. What money? The Deutschmark did not go here, no one had any; the Leu – Romanian currency – was despised, and the Rubles – no one expected them back. She took anything in barter: cornmeal – two cups for a herring, one egg or two, even household articles, pillow slips, towels. The people waited now for her to open up, not asking any questions. Where did she get the herring from? No one wanted to know. People looked strange, not like themselves. They came out of their houses or cellars alone, walked with hurried steps, didn't stop to chat. Faces expressionless. You could tell the clothes on their backs weren't theirs; the women did not know how to wear them. No one asked: where is this dress from, this hat or handbag? It was a town demented. Everyone knew the truth and carried on as if it were the most natural thing on earth. And so they also came for their herring, wearing other people's finery. Thank you, please, and thank you as if it were an ordinary day like any other.

They did look funny in the Jews' clothes! But Marusja seemed to notice less and less. She herself took to wearing silk stockings with a garter belt and underwear. Pulling at the elastic, she invented a sweet game with Nestor, her lover. "*Malenko,* come help me close this button with your sweet little fingers." And he ran to her, did it shouting with joy. She had never worn underwear, culottes, bras, things like that. Peasants wore blouses, long shirts under the *horbutka,* embroidered on white-as-snow linen, but never panties. And Marusja longed for pretty things that felt soft to the skin, caressed her. She tried on clothes from the storeroom, paraded them in front of Nestor. "How about this suit in pepper and salt, Nestor? Could I wear a suit and a velvet hat?" And Nestor answered, "Yes, Marusjenka, yes." But she couldn't, not Süssel's hat and suit. There was a limit. She folded them up neatly and put them away. And she didn't like herself, for a moment.

But in her own eyes she felt justified. She had a son to keep and she didn't mind riches. She kept the store open for two or three hours sometimes, selling very cautiously just a can or two from America. She couldn't tell exactly what things were for. But she knew the biscuits, wafers with chocolate or hazelnut, from Green's shop; she sold these or gave them away to little children to make herself feel virtuous.

Rumours started flying: not just resettlement, they're killing the Jews, no one will ever return. Marusja went to the Ahi fountain, at the crossroads of the Residenzgasse and the Heilige Dreieinigkeit, the Holy Trinity Street, where all the women holding onto their children gathered for news, talk, and fresh water. Men, toothless and in baggy pants, also came sometimes, to buy tobacco and paper for cigarettes. The women wore Jewish things more openly now. "They won't return. If we don't wear it, others will." And a strange alliance sprang from common guilt. They watched each other, full of glee, judging the value of their possessions.

The women shivered when they talked about the killing of the Jews. They spoke in low tones, fearful of Ahi. He might see them in the Jews' clothes and with a huge grin, condemn them. The fountain with the Turk on top. People feared the Turkish henchman still. He is said to have come back some times in the past to do mischief, give warning, or even execute people. So they started to come by the Residenzgasse near the old house of Marusja's masters on the corner of the Balschgasse. They stood there for a while, catching up on the news or simply sharing the fears of their haunted imaginations. The empty windows and balconies of the old house bothered them a little, so they slowly moved around the corner towards the old barred gate with the eight angels and the devil on top, sat on the stone steps leading to the gate. They began to stay a little bit longer each time in Marusja's opened shop. They came to buy, bargain, trade, and to sit on the benches in the adjoining tavern room gossiping until Marusja threw them out. Marusja: "Go home, go home, enough. I have work to do." It had become too much of a habit and she was afraid.

IT WAS AFTER STALINGRAD, spring, 1943, that strange things happened. The news was that the Russians were coming closer, and Jewish faces began to appear in the street, timidly at first, but becoming more daring each day. No one had suspected they were there. Familiar faces and names, with their own clothes on their backs. There was whispered information, who had seen whom. They came out more and more, at irregular hours. The laws forbade them for most of the day to go to market, shop, or show themselves without the yellow star. But they seemed to defy the law, became more daring as the possibility of a German defeat became real. The authorities, mostly Romanians, looked the other way.

And one late evening someone knocked at the old gate. Insistently. Saw the light in Marusja's cellar and knocked at the window. Marusja's heart stopped. She recognized Süssel's mother at her window.

NESTOR REMEMBERS this day very vividly. It was his first powerful impression of his mother's face. He remembers it as white, her countenance changed, her body fully still as she turned quietly to her little boy and said, "Nestor, my darling, I have to go and open the big gate. The masters are returning." Her manner was grave, and as little as he was, he knew a time had come to an end. He followed her as she walked to the gate, took the big key from her bosom, put it into the lock, removed the bar, and turned the key. The lady came up the four steps towards Marusja and the burst of emotion, the embracing, Nestor took with him all his life.

Marusja never put the bar back up to keep the house safe from strangers. Somehow power slipped from her and she did not mind. Rumours increased that the Russians were near. Jews appeared everywhere – not in great numbers, but she knew the faces. Times were changing again: what's on the top, will be on the bottom, she said with her peasant wisdom. But she did not relinquish the shop; on the contrary, she now made it truly her own. Kept it open all day, brought out proper scales and started a business, selling groceries and any merchandise that came her way. She took things on commission, not asking their provenance.

At the beginning of the war Marusja had noticed people were greedy to accumulate things, and showed off sometimes by wearing a Jew's furs or jewelry. Marusja once clearly saw the priest's wife, across the fence in the Balschgasse, wearing a light-blue stone set with diamonds around it on her finger – it had belonged to the Polish Princess. Now, almost three years later, she saw the Christians wanting to sell or hide the loot. The war moved closer, German authorities seemed nervous, and the Romanians, early in March, 1944, stormed their own trains to move south.

Marusja became a businesswoman, and a good one. Astute, clever with numbers, relying on trained memory like all illiterates, she knew the value of every item and how much things in demand might fetch. But when the first Russian entered her shop, she counted her losses, played the poor peasant woman, mother of a child, the exploited servant; she closed the shop and dealt clandestinely. That was communism, she knew. Most of Green's possessions were gone by then, and she was glad. A pious soul, she did not like all that guilt.

One early morning, she heard the rumblings of an old Russian truck. She heard it stop in front of the old gate but, having decided to let destiny take its course, did not go to look. Someone was coming up the four steps, opening the gate, and very, very carefully walking up the staircase. It was not a heavy step: a woman's. And now Marusja could not resist, and followed slowly up the staircase. Got a glimpse of her and realized she was a Russian officer of the military police.

Disquieted and worried: her hidden merchandise! She had seen deportation and imprisonment for two bars of soap under the Soviets. And Süssel's mother! What did they want with her? Poor, sweet lady, by herself up there.

Barefoot, as Marusja loved to be, she was up the stone staircase like a wildcat. Reaching the top, she saw the two of them embrace. Bunin, thank God. She was Felix's love for the whole Russian year, 1940-41. Bunin had rescued them all from Siberia. When police, militia, picked them up that June night, Bunin had brought them back. She had power and used it to help. And now she was back. It was a sign that all the Russians would soon return with their police and their godlessness.

Marusja, thinking of Bunin and her mighty uniform, smiled. There was a heart in there. She takes the uniform off and she is a simple woman. But Marusja fears godlessness. That is what hurts most: feeding horses in churches, devastating holy images. We need our stories to make us better, to live like Christ, she thinks. Even if we fail, we need something holy from a better world, either one that was or one to come.

Night after night, Marusja sang to Nestor. She set her own words to an inner melody. Songs about her favorite saints, Chrysostom, Gregory, and always Cyril and Methodius. Nestor sang them back to her, word for word, tune for tune. This was their time of closeness and spiritual feeling. It was this time, he knows, that made him a priest. He learned perfection, devotion, the exclusion of self, here on her breast. He was christened late – at five or six, but he understood much, and Marusja had him instructed in the Cyrillic-Slavonic script by an old priest in the Archbishop's Residence – Demitrios, a holy man, accepting the persecution of the true believer. Every day, Nestor walked up the Residenzgasse on the hand of his mother. The street arched a little, moved, slowing the step, increasing the intensity, the joy, of entering a world so different from his cellar world. Strange lights playing on coloured stones, on which one was allowed to walk or skip. He had no wish to pick the small spring flowers lining his path, loving the order, afraid to disturb a place assigned to God.

Sometimes he had to wait for his old master. After kissing Marusja goodbye at the enormous entrance to the garden, he looked around him. He felt so small, so comfortably, so happily small. Like the trolls, dwarfs, and tiny men frolicking around him. He sat on a marble bench to wait. Crazy little urchins, carousing in the fountain before him. He scrutinized them, watching the water play around them and spout forth from their "little thing." It looked different from his own, or so he thought. He mentioned it to Marusja, who smiled and told him, no two things on God's earth are alike.

True, no two things were alike. All the stone dwarfs in the garden were different from one another, yet you knew they were all dwarfs. Little people like himself. He loved to wait for the old priest in that big empty garden.

In the back room of the chapel of the Archbishop's Residence, Nestor learned to read and write and sing liturgy. Whole passages by heart. And Marusja's heart swelled with the pride of a Jewish mother to hear her son read the holy script.

He was with his mother or he was with his priest. Children, Christian children, who slowly emerged to go to school, avoided him, thinking him odd: home-sewn peasant shirts, his hair longer than everyone else's – of a light brown shine and down to his shoulders, giving him a girlish look. Nestor himself did not look into the mirror. Why should he? To see what? Marusja took little Nestor up the staircase and Nestor, counting steps, adding and skipping back to subtract them, heard Marusja say: "Look after my master. Keep her company."

And Süssel's mother sat this little boy next to her at the kitchen table and looked after him instead. And taught him to read and write German letters. Every day. And they sang, in thirds and fourths as she did with Süssel. Time flew. Nestor remembers longing for the moment he could go up there. He had many songs to teach her too. And Süssel's mother learned like a child.

Having lived with the Slavs, she knew them well, but she learned different things through the eyes of this child, the eyes of the icons hanging in the chapel of the Archbishop's Residence. She had never been inside the Chapel. She had been in the garden several times as an adult, but married with children, she kept to her tribe. Jews stayed with their own.

She had suspected her daughter loved someone in that garden. She had seen her stand in front of the trifold mirror, in her early teenage years, changing her dress at certain hours in the summer, with a secretive guilt in her turned-away eyes. She feared her daughter's passion, her wild wishes, her desire to know. As the daughter sat at the west window, facing the setting sun, the mother detected a shadow over that not-so-pretty, rather angular and willful face. She had sat on that broad windowsill since very young, facing the Residence, which rose with the rising, slightly hilly, Residenzgasse to cover the west. "Come down from that windowsill, those flying-outwards windows are dangerous. You'll fall. It's the third floor." Stubborn, Süssel said, "No, Mother, I'm not a baby." And she sat there dreaming.

Her mother now had much to remember and little else to do. She could not go out, fearing the street. The house had been looted by now and did not contain much. The armoire with the trifold mirror, the bookcases, and the Bösendorfer grand were gone. But books still lay about. All of Shakespeare in the Schlegel-Tieck translation, the French – Verlaine, Rimbaud – she had read with her son Felix. Strange vestiges of a life. She was content to be herself. *Furniture does not make a home, books do.* And a child was given to her; an overwhelming need to nurture, to instruct, made her get up in the morning from her improvised camp-bed, groom herself a little, and wait for Nestor. *I am so vain,* she thought. *And this may be good – to please others.* She combed her hair, still thick and lustrous but all of silver now with only an occasional red thread.

Marusja brought fresh bread and coffee every morning. The kitchen cupboards had not been looted and half a Rosenthal service – cups and saucers of pure white and simple form – was there.

I'll give everything back that Dmitry has taken, Marusja vowed. She had done penance, served the lady, fed her, loved her with all her heart. A Jewish mother, her Jewish child. She was sure of it, and her heart grew lighter.

One day she came upstairs to share the evening meal, a chicken in the pot. Like a real family, three generations. It was Passover and Easter at the same time. No bread, just a potato pancake, Marusja knew the rules of Passover. Not that it mattered. But she took pride in respecting the law of others. Unleavened bread, *mazzoth* of sorts, and an Easterbread, a *paszka,* for herself. The three of them sat around the kitchen table, the mother reading the Exodus story and sharing the bitter herbs and the mortar, a symbol for the bricks the Jews made for the pharaoh. Nuts and wine. The story of freedom and deliverance. But the mother did not go to the Easter midnight mass with them, though Marusja urged her to. "Someone might come to pick me up," she said. "I may miss Süssel. I know she will come. Or my son Felix." She did not expect her husband. She knew, he could not have survived.

Easter Sunday. Tempted to wear Süssel's blue coat, Marusja took it out. Summery and small, long, almost to the ankles. She had cleaned and pressed it. So nice for Easter Sunday. But no, she said, I have no right to it. Took it up to the third floor and, holding it in front of Süssel's mother, said: "Here it is, I cleaned it, please take it back, it's Süssel's coat."

The lady: "Put it on, Marusja. Does it fit you?" The tiny slim figure of Marusja melted into the coat. "Take it, Marusja, it will not fit Süssel. She is much bigger now!"

Given to her, it was now her own. She wore it on Easter Sunday, with ribbons in her hair. Went up the hilly Residenzgasse to the chapel, Nestor on her hand, glowing with the joy of a spring day, the blue coat and the resurrection of Christ. Nestor too was dressed up, in clothes the two women had transformed from Felix's childhood wear. Nestor remembers this walk – in real pants for the first time, a city shirt, suspenders with buttons. A fiercely proud little boy, who would not acknowledge that he cared.

Russian uniforms in the streets! A very young army, it seemed to Marusja, faces flushed with youth and success. All signs of German-Romanian might vanished as if swept from the face of the earth. The town fell silent again as people closed shutters, peered between slits to identify uniforms. As people do in the uncertain in-between times. Marusja, Ukrainian and at home in the old house, kept to herself. After Süssel's mother's departing footsteps had finished echoing through the house, she knew she was alone to care for her little boy. She was determined and resolute.

At their last Easter meal Süssel's mother had suddenly turned to Marusja full-faced and said: "I thank you, Marusja, for your love. I fear there won't be time, when they'll come to fetch me. I may go without knocking at your door. It will be easier that way. Marusja, you showed me a love I had not expected and do not think I deserved."

Marusja rose and, with an index finger to her own lips, begged, "Please, do not...."

But Süssel's mother continued: "Marusja, dear, let me say a few words for something that does not need any." And with a light pressure on Marusja's arm, she made her sit down again. "This is a woman's bond. We give birth. We know about love. And love beyond measure, call, or duty. I've seen you in servitude to us but I've also seen your love for Dmitry. And it was truly incomprehensible to me at the time, because I'm proud. But I have learnt. And now I thank you, for that bond between us."

They both rose in a common immediacy of emotion, held hands for a little longer. Then they started to clear the table, Nestor between them on his little legs carrying a plate too big for his hands. They broke into laughter, chiding Nestor, "You'll break it, Nestor, it's Rosenthal porcelain." But the dish, however precious, meant nothing. They were taken up in the moment. The awareness of the end of things, in leave-taking.

Very early one morning a single truck stopped in front of the old house. The gate was open. Since Süssel's mother had returned, Marusja did not bother to put the long iron bar on the inside. No longer the *Hausmeister,* she let events take their course, looking after herself, her business, and her boy. She heard the truck come to a rumbling stop. Listened at the window, but did not go out to see or interfere. A very slim, tall, familiar figure emerged; she heard her try the gate, which gave way. She knew the sounds. Since Dmitry had gone away and never returned, the poor gate screeched on its hinges. She heard the steps advance very slowly in the quiet of the house. All the way up.

The footsteps on stone echoed through the house, replaying their rhythm on her ceiling. She heard the two of them, mother and daughter, come down the old staircase, resting from time to time against the iron-mahogany rail. There was a quiet moment, then a screech in the hinges of the gate, and she heard the swish of their soles against the last of the four stone steps. Marusja pressed her face against her small window, eyes dark with tears.

Süssel

Dear Marusja, remember when –

1952
Dear Marusja,

I hope you have my address by now. My brother Felix has it and promised to forward it – if regular mail won't reach you, he'll try through the Red Cross. But in any case, here it is, clearly spelled out, inside and outside the letter.

When I came to pick my mother up, I found her as I had dreamt I would, waiting. I had to come alone, in a truck, travelling between fighting armies, marauding lawless partisans. She had waited, sitting on my childhood window seat. I'm sure you have seen her there, all ready, carrier-bag at her side. Mother took her leave from you at Eastertime, she said, not knowing when or by what means we'd come for her and not wanting tears....

Remember that night when I fell into your arms, returning from the "big world" for the first time? I was so delighted to see you open the old gate for me! I had come from Prague by train and arrived at night, took a *fiacre* at the train station. An ancient coachman, with two horses – even older looking than he was – took one look at me and said, welcome home, Fräulein Süssel. All fear of return and the dark night left me. As we went up the Bahnhofstrasse and through the Saint Trinity Street into the Residenzgasse, my fear returned; who will be at the gate? And it was you, who said oh, it is you, Süssel. I stormed up the staircase and my mother was astounded that my fear of the dark had left me.

I always loved you, Marusja, and so did my mother. Your name was on her lips moments before she died. Yours and Nestor's. Like mine and Felix's. So dear you were to her. You eased her loneliness by sharing Nestor, you fed her when she returned from the camps, and you helped her to wait for me to fetch her –

I wonder if the beautiful train station, Austrian style, almost like the opera house next to our pharmacy, still stands. So many things to ask!

Cranberry Flats is a place of longing. No matter how much I love the open skies, the way the river seems to flow out of it, it is a place of longing. There is memory everywhere, no matter where you turn. Every newcomer feels it. I talk to them – newly arrived, used to cramped European quarters, they are bewildered. But we pilgrims learn to see. My friends who come from all corners of the old world will ask one day: "Don't you think, Süssel, this river here, looks like my Danube?" "No," I will say, "not like the Danube, it looks like the Prut."

And so it goes, with immigrants. We see what we know, what gives us comfort, what makes us feel at home.

Wise Marusja. I remember you so well. I would creep up behind you when you were having your dinner with Ileana, wanting to be part of this conspiracy of women. It made me jealous to hear the two of you laughing together. To be so young and so ignorant, it hurt. We both loved Ileana, wanted and feared her horror tales, not only Master Manole with his walled-in beautiful wife screaming for air, but also her thrilling ghosts. They inhabited our world, unseen but evident here and there in signs and sounds, frightening us with their power. You and Ileana spoke in whispers, grabbed the salt shaker to sprinkle salt over your left shoulder or made the sign of the cross. And you giggled like two little girls. I remember it well.

I know so much about you, dear Marusja, from the sounds, smells, remembered from childhood. Hearing your shrieks through the house and my mother saying Dmitry came home drunk and beat poor Marusja. And my mother holding me back not to run down to you. "It is between the two of them," she said. "We cannot interfere."

"But I won't have it, I won't have it!" I pulled myself loose from her. "I will beat him, I will murder him!" I was about twelve years old or so. Such was my passion. I rushed down the steps, leaving my mother shaking her head, and found you, literally black and blue and bleeding from the nose, and Dmitry beside you snoring. I ran to the wash-kitchen to wet a towel, to cool your forehead and eyes, and said, "Poor Marusja, poor Marusja. Come up to us, this is a terrible cellar, I cannot bear the musty smell, and if I stay one more second I'll punch Dmitry in the nose." And you said, "No, my child. He loves me, in his way. You're too young to know and I cannot move anyway now. Everything hurts." Or something like this you said – remember?

Beautiful, tiny Marusja, like a doll you were, no taller than me then, a fine-boned lovely lady! And I cried with fury at the ways of the world I could not do anything about. Do you remember?

And later on our whole world broke apart and murder was right in front of the old house, the grocer Lev-Jossel Green in his blood with his children! And all those from the first and second floors of my grandfather's house. You did not come out to help, neither you nor Dmitry. You were there, we knew. Other people came, Romanians, Christians from across the vine-covered fence. They helped us carry our dead and took spade in hand to bury them in the garden. You did not show your face. Why? I have to ask you this, because I have wondered about it, through all these years of wandering, homelessness, and immigration. Why? Did Dmitry hold you back?

One more question: Did you hear me when I came for my mother? I thought you may have. Mother said: "I've taken my leave. Let's not knock at her door. I fear I'll break down."

As you know, Mother did not go out. She wanted to keep out of sight, afraid of what hostile forces were in power. She is not a fighter like me. I go after things; she waits for them to come to her. She told me so many things I had never suspected: how afraid she was of my passion, my impatience, and my wild, unpredictable ways. So different from her. She and Felix were two of a kind. And, of course, you knew Felix well, from Ileana's stories and the nonsense in the wash-kitchen, dyeing his shirts yellow or purple –

This is a long letter and not to the point, of course. Forgive me, Marusja, but everything comes home to me now. Where we live the air is clear and bubbles like fermented wine. Remember we had wine in one of the cellar rooms and we said it is spoiled and you and Dmitry said, no, no, it is just lovely, it gives you a light head and lots of giggles – yes, that is like the air here. It gives you a light head, carries berries and blooms at the same time, the one coming, the other going. A fragrance and a memory. All is back, your musty cellar, the difference between all of us, the love and the bond. These are the Cranberry Flats. A place to live, the way you are with all the baggage you carry.

I hope someone will read my letters to you. Your priest perhaps. I remember your fabulous memory – once something was read to you, you could retell it almost word for word, my beautiful Marusja.

Love,
S.

ONE MORE LETTER.

I lost my mother in Bucharest. After a harrowing trip in a truck, the same truck I came in, the one without a muffler, she, elegant as always, smiling, resting on her black Russian coat. She did not live long after that journey. She had been uprooted, taken from her palace in the Residenzgasse, to a one-room furnished flat we shared with others, and she was melancholy. She helped in the kitchen, did her best to care for all the displaced children around her, but soon took to her bed. We cared for her as well as we could, Felix doing most of it. Father had not made it. I had lost him somewhere on the way southwest after being released from camp by a good man, a German officer, our saviour at the time.

She loved Nestor. He was gifted beyond the ordinary, she said. He draws and paints, reads all letters, with an ease no adult has. He was born for words, she said, they find him without him seeking. A little boy, knowing all the Slavonic liturgy by heart, and your melodies...so she said.

You lived with all of us, Marusja, brought up one of our own when his life fell into your hands. Marusja, come, come to us. There is room for you and Canada will welcome you. There are Ukrainian churches and people to talk to in your mother tongue. Come. But if you decide to stay in our homeland, the beautiful "beech country," we will send you the money to buy the piece of land adjoining your own, so you will have enough to live on. Let us know!

A little yet about my mother, what you meant to her. We have both, you and I, been so lucky to live with my beautiful mother, share her presence, for a little while. Too short, too short. It was such comfort to be with her, because she looked for the spirit, found poetry in everyday things. She turned away from the dark side of life, did not get frantic, found a laugh where no one else would. I was rough on her, in my teens, thinking her frivolous, fond of rings with gems and diamonds, instead of high science. She knew more than all of us, including my clever father. She knew how to live, how to celebrate a day, how to make the most of things. By smiling whenever you looked at her, she took the thorn out of everything. And her "frivolity" about buying jewels – it was the cleverest thing in uncertain times, wiser than my and father's "science": with her jewels we bought bread and cornmeal and sunflower seed oil. We always had oil – remember how tall our flowers-turning-to-the-sun were? We always had the best oil, except in the war, when it went underground. Mother knew how to live and what mattered. She sold her jewels and we ate.

And all my teenage sins; too many to recount. Seeing me once in front of our trifold mirror, she stood there and said: "Süssel, my child, come let me hug you; I want to hold you for a moment, I so long for it! Heavens, how grown up you are in your silk shirt. Come, take Father's green cravat, it will suit you." And I took it out of her hand, but impatiently, with a slight pull. Oh, God, too late to repair things. I am so intemperate, Marusja. I wonder if she knew how much I loved her.

And I did, always, with passion and longing. Not just for her joyous ways, but also for her physical beauty. You know, Marusja, that red flame hair, up in the chignon against her grey silk dresses – was there anyone more appealing than my mother? Forgive me, Marusja, it seems I'm returning to my childhood, taking an enormous leap across the passions, the search for God, and all the thousands of single days which become one day in the end, to return to that haven at her side. So we become children, growing older....

We sat at her bedside, Felix and I, in that one-room flat in Bucharest. Felt her end coming. A slow summer evening, quietening the senses and calming fear. We looked at her and she smiled; she had so few muscles left, we just guessed at the smile more than saw it. And she reached under her pillow and pulled out a velvet pouch, with her remaining jewelry inside: "My wedding ring with the three stones, and the earrings, are for you, Süssel. They are from my mother," she said, "not that good, but beautifully set. The watch and chain from Father's vest coat" – and she looked at me, perhaps remembering that I had taken these when he died in my arms – "are for Felix, of course." She smiled a little more: "It always made a tinkly noise when Father pulled it out. And the few rings and the two golden chains are for Nestor and Marusja – children, please find them both for me." A smile and then she slipped away. With your name on her lips. "It is time," I think she said.

All this is so far back, yet it is here with that power that loss carries. I know you understand. Though you always said I spoke in "high-faluting Süssel-talk," as you called it, I know you understand more in your peasant wisdom than all the so-called learned, including father and me.

You know now where we are. Write, with the help of your priest or whoever, so we know how life is and how Nestor is faring. Write. We're here for you.

Love, Süssel.

P.S. Write! Felix will have reached you by now. My full address is both inside the letter and on the envelope.

Nestor
My Little Orphan

Nestor approached the house in the midday heat. Rows of young poplars led him towards the three-storey house, only partly visible through the branches of what looked like a walnut tree. Just a hope! But it was not a walnut tree. The trunk was crenelated silver and the leaves fell into the kind of perfection flags are made of. It was a maple tree, broad, out-reaching, covering the back of the house. It softened the sharp contours of the house, changing the straight geometrical shapes into imaginative, asymmetrical, moving spaces.

He carried two suitcases, one heavier than the other, changing hands occasionally to redistribute the weight. He'd dismissed the taxi at the beginning of the pebbly road and pushed open a wide country gate supported just by two wooden stakes. Saw the post box and her name. Smiled at being in such a different world.

Close to the ground and cozy under the young poplar branches grew wild roses on low thorn bushes, spreading into the fields. They reminded him of his mother's rose confiture. Every year in high summer, when he was three and four and five, Marusja would take him by the hand and they would go into the valley at the foot of the Cecina mountain, baskets in hand. "Little boys' fingers are so much cleverer in picking rose petals," she said to him, and "*Little one,* watch for the thorns." Then they picnicked near the springs and dozed in the fields. At home she washed and sorted the petals, put them into glass jars – alternating sugar and rose petals – sealed and cooked them in the big cauldron in the wash-kitchen. Intensely pink, beautiful, and unforgettable, his mother's confiture.

He switched the suitcases in his hands, stood for a moment, and then started down the winding path hugging the silver maple. The house emerged, its east side exposed, both familiar and strange. Glass from top to bottom, three storeys high, a small balcony up there jutting into the branches. He hurried along the path, approaching the front of the house. It faced the river, a new-old house with an old gate and what looked like a square from an Italian church door set above it. It felt warm and welcoming.

He was expected, he knew that, but was in no hurry to shake the cow bells which hung here, knotted through a leather belt, from a hook above. And he sat down on the stone bench, set the suitcases on the pebbles, and looked down the berry-strewn slope towards this curling river, which felt eerily like his own.

He was tired. His head nearly dropped onto the stone table. He had come three thousand miles, on trains from the east coast. Across a land so limitless there was nothing to hold its rails; a world without borders he could not have envisioned.

So he rested on the stone bench like many a stranger before him, overlooking the valley. The sun was high still and he knew there would be a long wait. He did not mind, he was not truly ready to face future, immediate future and past at the same time. Took in the valley, murmured a Slavonic prayer between his lips, and recognized, like all river-children, his own. Different, yet the same. Less intimate, bigger, flatter, with less of a cadence, the bank too sudden, steep, frightful, but the berries were there on low bushes and there was a strange enchanting light. *Parfum de roses* in the air.

He gazed at the deep-green slate with its labyrinthine pink squiggles, saw himself playing on them as a four-year-old. Playing around the Ahi fountain, wanting to pick up the pink polka dots in the sea-green slate. He cried out to Marusja that he wanted those marbly pink spots. But they weren't pickable. "You are a beloved but spoiled Jew-boy and you can't have them," she said. Tantrum.

The stones here were round with convoluted pink lines. The same and not the same. But they were here, all around the stone bench and square table. Oh, one never seems to get to twenty. Such a tenacious hold, childhood has. His eyes full of dust and eight days on the train across an endless land, he took a greenish wide-brimmed hat from one of the suitcases, covered his head, let his head fall upon the table, and, supported by his arm, he slept. Deeply. As if on Marusja's breast.

HE LIFTED HIS HEAD from the stone table, having slept all afternoon. He faced a burning ball sinking fast into the bushes, into the red-tinged river winding at his feet. As if in a dream, he smelled rose confiture. But not just roses, there was also a tart fruity sweetness, stinging mood and memory. He had arrived at his destination. But he feared it now, wanted to run. Back home. To Easter Sunday on Marusja's hand, when he was no taller than the bottom squares on the old gate. The two angels were at the back of his eyes.

Leaving both suitcases by the stone bench, he took the slope to the river in a bold run. He pushed through dense bush to the edge of the river, and sat down in the sand. The river had the stillness of a simple line, drawn by a child into the sand. *So alone a man's soul, were it not for his faith,* he thought. Even when he was growing up, not yet a young man, the two angels in the lower squares, his eye-level angels at the age of four or five, were with him. They had a way of hanging in the square, feet and wings flying. And he always felt: they'll take me one day to heaven. There is lots of room in their folded wings for a little boy. He found a dry twig and drew his angels in the sand by the river.

He had been so sheltered. So loved, by both his mothers, the one in the cellar and the one on the third floor. But now he had to think, to find words. How to put twenty years into a sentence?

The river had turned a darker green, mirroring the cottony clouds in the sky. The clouds were becoming restless as the sands cooled. He wasn't ready to leave yet. He played with the sand a little, let it run through his fingers, doodled with the dry twig he had picked up. An ancient little twig, with small berries still hanging on. Did cranberries grow here? The aroma was so distinct, heavenly. He breathed deeply. What was it? He got up, looked for a winding path to take him up the hill. It was not yet dark when he found a trail through a farmer's potato field. And suddenly he saw the west windows of Süssel's house burning with the last sun. And he remembered why he had come.

As he approached the house he could see two figures, a man and a woman, standing beside his suitcases. As she caught sight of him, the woman ran towards him, arms outstretched, nearly tripping over the stones. He fell into her open arms. "You have come, you have come," she cried, hugging him, pulling him towards

Max, who was seated at the stone table. Max, used to Süssel's passionate ways and only slightly embarrassed, rose and gave the young man a hearty handshake.

"Come, you'll take the east room, where the sun rises directly into your eyes in the morning. You do not have to talk at all until you're ready. Only then."

"But this is heavy," said Max, lifting one of the bags. "What is in it?"

"It's a secret, a real secret, the reason for my being here," Nestor said in his book-learnt, deliberate, broad English. "I came to deliver a suitcase."

"Heavens, how did you carry this? It could be a bomb or a corpse from a closet."

"The latter maybe, with all its weight of memory," Nestor replied.

Max carried both suitcases. Süssel held onto Nestor's arm, turning him this way and that, examining him from every angle. Finally she looked into his face under the greenish hat and said: "You're beautiful, my Nestor." And they entered the house.

BEING A CELLAR CHILD, Nestor had never seen the rising sun shining through a window. He had lived in that cellar until Marusja had put him on his way to Süssel's. Practical and resourceful, she made contacts with all sorts of people, to sell, to barter, and to save her own skin when necessary. A master at greasing palms in right places, she knew a bottle of vodka went a long way!

After she received Felix's letter with Süssel's address in Canada, Marusja went into action. She ran to the priest's quarters, now in the spare rooms behind the Archbishop's Residence. A university had been installed in the hallowed rooms, all services abolished, icons removed to the cellar. Her priest, Demitrios, was philosophical about it, but Marusja cursed and cried out: "God will not suffer it, He'll come down on them hard! Even if it takes ages or an eternity, He will do it. Time is nothing to Him." But Demitrios let Marusja kiss his hand and said, "Let's not curse, let's pray together that these people find their way back to Him."

And now she showed him Felix's letter, with Süssel's address in Canada, told of Süssel's willingness to send affidavits, overseas tickets, whatever help was needed. And Marusja said, "I'll send Nestor away. It is a godless place, there is no future here for him, I'll let him go. I know the train stationmaster. Ukrainian from my village. I'll go see him tomorrow. He'll tell me when the trains run. I'll take him vodka, some dry Hungarian sausage, a package of Majorca tobacco – oh, dear, what a life!" But she was joyful. She let Demitrios bless her, let him thank her for the fresh-baked bread and the *vodichka* she had brought him.

The next day she had everything in her hand, all the papers, the permit to take along some private property. Marusja had her plans, but in her peasant way she waited for the right moment to implement them. *When he's twenty,* she thought. *When he's twenty, my Nestor will decide to be either a priest or a Jew. No matter. Then it will be time.*

Nestor had slept on Marusja's breast until his fourteenth year, when one day Marusja told him, you're a young man now. I will give you my bed and I'll move into the other two rooms. She had furnished the rooms slowly and painstakingly. A businesswoman by then, she had the means to transform the cellar into habitable quarters. The cellar was now a comfortable and attractive home.

Nestor had a writing table under the small window slit facing the garden. All his holy books and arithmetic texts sat on a shelf, along with an hourglass given to him by the masters. He did Marusja's numbers now, as she continued to deal in old Green's vault.

The Soviets had come and stayed. The war was over now, everything had changed. People denounced each other, again neighbours walked in the streets, eyes turned sideways to see what the other wore. Simple Ukrainian souls like Marusja worried about being falsely accused of collaborating with the Germans, which some had done. People disappeared overnight, in the Russian custom. I'll send my boy away, Marusja resolved in despair. He was born a Jew and that is what he is underneath his clothes.

The Residence had changed; God had to move out of it. The Archbishop fell ill, was sent to rest, the seminary moved into smaller outside quarters, and the old priest was barely hanging on. Bad times for God have come, Marusja thought. *Bad times and my son a priest and....*

They were all there, suddenly. Soviets, with Soviet trucks, ice cream, rubles, and arrests. Marusja always wondered that there was no bread yet there was ice cream. *The devil knows them,* she said. She, determined to survive.

NESTOR WOKE AROUND FIVE OR SIX in the morning, eyes full of the rising sun as Süssel had promised. Süssel was shouting up the stairs to him. "Come down when you're ready. There is coffee and toast. Make your own, we're off to work. Take the house, get acquainted. Go to the river. Bye." Süssel's shouts carried clearly up the stairs. The house was all wood, with no stone to muffle sound.

My school English is good enough for books, but not for fast talk, Nestor thought. He would go down, but not yet. A bathroom all to himself. He'd wash his hands and face. There were so many things here, strange objects, gleaming with metal. Too much for a cellar boy. The masters in the old house had an indoor toilet upstairs, separate from their bathroom. But for his needs Nestor always went into the back of the garden where, hidden by flowering mock-orange and lilac bushes, was a little outhouse.

He liked it, getting out of the cellar into a summer night, when jasmine and lilac released their perfume, to relieve himself with the doors open. Marusja had taught him how to keep clean and how to wipe everything down when he was done. With newsprint, the language depending on the conqueror of the day. Russian, when he was four. Cut up in four-inch squares, it hung on a nail in that lovely little private house covered in spring blooms. He went there mostly at night, too modest to be seen going there in the day.

Funny, that world! People did everything with newsprint, except read it. Too many lies, Marusja said. She shone the windows with vinegar water and the *Pravda,* used it to wrap the dried peas and beans she had weighed in her shop, used it to line Nestor's leaking shoe if the sole went through. No, she didn't use it for diapers, though others did, she said.

As he grew up and became more aware of his body, Nestor was glad that Marusja had moved to the other two rooms in the cellar; he was afraid he would fall into sin. It was hard to be a little boy with a mother only, harder yet an adolescent boy with an untold story. One divined, he suspected, more and more as he grew into manhood. His days spent with his devoutly Christian mother and his priest, without sibling kinship, not knowing anyone of his own age or interests, made him feel like the first man. Adam, with no father, except the Creator from the holy books, the first man to tread the earth to find out who he was. This is how he felt at fourteen.

The old house was suddenly overrun with Russians and Ukrainians, from the other side of the Djnester and the Bug, speaking so utterly different a language. One without God. It marked the Soviet people as different from him. The house overrun, all Jewish property once, now suddenly in the hands of strangers. Süssel's family's flat on the third floor occupied by a *nachalnik* family, all other apartments inhabited by three or four families each. Nestor heard them fighting, over every leftover spoon, dish, or dress. And their children. He would have played with them, but he was alien to them and they to him. After Süssel's mother left – he did not remember hearing her and Süssel go – he was suddenly all alone again. Just he and Marusja. Nestor remembers her face vividly, bathed in tears. Hugging him over and over and saying sweet things to him. "My little orphan, all your people have gone now. All the Jews have gone." Mysterious words of consolation, spoken to herself almost. She set the table for the two of them now in the next room, set it properly with tablecloths of white linen. And said, we'll live now the way Jews should, and one day you, my Nestor, will take this shiny tablecloth to Süssel and my conscience will be clear. The old echoes, etched in memory, added to the unresolved mystery of his being.

"My little orphan," she had said, "my little orphan." The words haunted him. Why did they affect him so strangely? He hadn't missed love, he'd been full of his mother's nearness, but the words stayed with him, looking for a meaning. Like the words of creation. The words had nothing to do with anything, not with his morning breakfast of Marusja's bread and the sweet thickened milk from America – Cow Brand, he had read on the label. Or cornbread with *povidla,* the thick prune jam. Nothing to do with his duties either, Marusja sitting him down to shell peas with his little fingers.

She was the only one that used the piece of garden plot behind the jasmine-lilac grove. No one else laid claim to it. The Jews had no time for it, and Marusja disdained them for it. *They do not like the earth. They just dream,* she thought. *They push their children to the books. Words, all the time. Work too, but not in the soil. Knead it, clear it, put a seed in it, watch it. Not for them.* But she taught Nestor to dig in the ground behind the outhouse, deep in the garden. She used a big spade to hack away the walnut roots that spread as wide as the tree's crown. She did not mind the nuts, but she cursed the roots. "Walnuts," she mumbled, "luxury they are. Not like beans, onions, corn...." Her peasant wisdom was wasted on these useless city folk, it made her blood boil.

THE SUN HAD LEFT HIS MORNING WINDOW, opening a view of road and eastern horizon. Nestor wondered again – as he had wondered looking through train windows across this land: how does one live here? It made you feel as if you were hanging in the sky. The endlessness of it....

But descending the staircase, this inner skeleton underpinning the body of the house, he felt reassured, surprised at this handrail so far from home. He was infused with a sudden warmth by the redwood top over the black iron, the way it wound itself down, slowly leading him to earth. Something to stand on. He turned and saw the river-valley landscape flooding in the top-to-bottom windows. A cellar child wants to pray. Thank God, he has learnt how. Ukrainian words tumble from his lips with the beauty of his home town. The river Prut resurrected, the memory of Marusja taking him there to play in its sands. He recognizes coffee in a pot, fills a cup; takes a soft piece of bread, so different from his mother's heavy loaf, and an apple from a bowl sitting on the table. He goes through a squarish vestibule to open the gate, sits on the slate steps chewing the apple, coffee cooling next to him.

My little orphan, she had said. *My little orphan.* The words rang with meaning long before she sat him down in her cellar-salon to take her leave, to hug and kiss him and tell her story. The words had meaning long before that. The rush of the Russians, Soviet soldiers and *politruks,* to occupy the old house bewildered him, after their long solitude. He was frightened by the children that appeared from nowhere, slept overnight in the staircase. Marusja chasing them, eight- to ten-year-olds, a kind of *bez-prisornije* parentless, roaming. Poor shoeless, hungry. "Nestor," she said, "go feed the orphans, but tell them not to come back into the staircase. That poor old staircase, they pee all over it. Tell them not to come back at night or I'll beat the hell out of them." But they did come back. Nestor heard them while Marusja slept. He was full of pity for those orphans. What is a boy without a mother? And one night he hid away his own evening meal.

A boy he'd befriended had tried to steal the fresh bread Marusja had left to cool in the big wash-kitchen. Nestor heard him, caught him, held him fast, twisting his arms until the boy shouted with pain. Nestor was stunned by his own unexpected violence, his know-how, the strength of his arms. "What's your name?" he asked.

"Dmitry," the boy answered. No patronymic.

"It's my father's name," Nestor said, releasing him. A slight pang in his soul made him shudder, that a thief should have his father's name. But the priest had taught him to carry the guilt of his brother. Like Christ. Nestor heard himself say: "Dmitry, come after dark, I'll have a meal for you." And so it was night after night. It was his first betrayal of Marusja. But such a delicious sin, to serve one's own, pleasing Christ.

Poor naked boy! The two of them laughed and joked, sitting on the cellar steps. An outlaw child, an orphan, no father, no mother. It was a sweet friendship until it was discovered. Dmitry was chased away, not by Marusja but by the new occupiers, the soldiers' wives now protecting their new territory, the old Jewish house. Every floor of the three floors was bursting with strangers. *Locusts.* Marusja's disdain in his ears, Nestor pitied the shoeless Dmitry.

Marusja: "I will not move into those places. The Jews have been killed and God would punish me. Don't mess with the people of the book. Let *them* sleep in their beds, not you and not I, Nestor Cyril Michalenko!"

Nestor, sitting now on the slate-green steps with all of the valley in front of him, sees his home river binding sky to land, like a page in a picture book. *My little orphan, my little orphan* is in his ear. Marusja's black rye bread, the smell of cellar-must, more real than the fragrance of the apple he is eating. Preparing to take leave of her grown son, now twenty and ordained into the old true faith, she called him away from his books to sit by her in her cellar salon, on her couch. It was not stolen, Marusja said. It was exchanged for goods she had given on credit and she had it covered with a carpet. Persian, Süssel's mother called it. "Come," she had said to Marusja. "Come after I have gone, come fast up the stairs, you'll hear me leave, and take the carpets; that's all that is left of the valuables. Come and take them before others do." "I have earned them," Marusja said. "They are all mine. Given to me by the masters."

On that early morning, after Süssel and her mother left, after all sounds died away, she had taken the three floors in a jump and entered the empty house. Shivered. She looked over what was left: cups arranged in the kitchen cupboard, good porcelain. Let the Russians have it. Except the terrine. Beautiful. Gold-edged. She set it apart. Signs of early breakfast. She resisted sentimentality. Allotted time for tears, gave them their due. When the breast is choking, a peasant will cry. But not for a few crumbs left from breakfast. She had work to do.

She inspected the salon, where Süssel's mother slept on her carpets, the beds having been looted long ago. She took three of the carpets she judged the best, rolled two of them up tightly and pulled them all the way down to the cellar. The third one was small and silky, depicting a shiny blue tree with its roots in other trees, each treetop interweaving the roots of the tree beyond. Strange birds sat on the tree branches. Silky, shiny, with birds of silver, gold, and copper, a mysterious world, framed in the pattern of a carpet. She had often looked at it, knew it well. Blue-silver and copper-gold. How rich does one have to be to own such beauty? she wondered.

It was a smallish carpet, no bigger than a good-sized mirror on the wall. Ileana had never liked it. Standing in front of it, or taking it down to wash or dust the wall, the two women had complained about the masters, their own resentment, the frivolity of the rich. Trees with golden birds growing in trees – what the rich will think of, Ileana said. Jews. No, Marusja said, they told me Persians. Ileana: Makes no difference to me, all Jews anyway.

But Marusja loved these linking shiny trees. They are forever, she thought. They make you tremble, but not like the Romanian ladies walled in for the glory of God, who scream for air and do not get it. This was different. Jew or Persian, this is what Marusja likes. Life from the top of the tree to the root of the next. With birds singing in their branches. She hears them sing. Oh, Ileana, stupid and beautiful.

Marusja stood for a silent moment in front of the carpet, now still on the wall, removed the five round rings from the wooden bar, rolled it fast and determinedly, tied a string around it. Hoisted it under her arm, against her body. It was hers. She smiled in spite of the effort of pulling two carpets down all three floors and the cellar steps.

They did not smell musty, Marusja told Nestor, when she sat next to him the day he was twenty and aware for the first time of their parting. So sudden and so real, what had just been words before. Ethereal, as the future was. He couldn't grasp it. But sitting there on her Persian-covered couch, the old metal springs making him shift to find comfort, nothing was within his grasp, not that they were sitting there on that carpet, nor that they would both soon rise to their immediate new day. He had sat on this big throw most of his young life, played with the running patterns which did not seem to end. He had put kings and queens on it, pebbles and marbles, but he found no faces on it, as in the icons, just squares chasing triangles chasing rectangles, birds chasing something that looked like an animal but wasn't.

Now he was sitting on it, maybe for the last time. Not in his grasp. Bewildering, not to know the next moment. As if the river came to a halt, not knowing its course. Like speech arrested, no word pushing the other, or a tune not knowing the next note.

AND SO NESTOR SITS on the green slate steps on this late August day, an apple in his hand and berries in the air bringing back the must from the cellar.

Yes, she sat him down next to her. *My little orphan,* she had said, and he knew what she meant. Not just yesterday but the day to follow, the blank day. Parting. But not yet. "Go find your roots, somewhere in the treetops," Marusja said, and pointed to the small shiny carpet she had hung across the window slit to make the gold-silver-copper birds catch the morning sun. "Go and find your roots. It's an alien world out there across all that water, but Süssel has written that she is willing to put you up, feed you in the beginning."

"Which roots, Mother, which root, what treetops?" They laughed and hugged. "We'll have tea," she said.

"Yes," he said. "No one knows how to make a *chai* the way we do." She spread the table with the tulip damask from the masters, to serve her son *chai,* Ukrainian-Jewish style, as she said. Marusja knew how to wash and press linens. The damask was crisp and deeply creased along the fold. Marusja laid porcelain to enhance it.

What root, what trees? he wondered. "Mother, you are all the roots I have and need. I did not know my father, Dmitry, but it was war. All your brothers except the youngest fell on some strange soil, Russian or German or Polish – who knows? I need no other." They broke the white *bulke* together, fresh butter spread with the violin butter-knife he had never seen before. With a tiny spoon, Marusja served her rose-petal jam on the side.

He finished his apple, rose from the green slate steps to follow the sudden burst of roses in the air. He followed the narrow road down, going south, then west. Pebble steps led to the river in serpentines, lined on both sides with the wild rose in bloom. Creeping in, as if objecting to the path made from stones, wanting to reconquer the land underneath. The river was cool in the morning, just itself, with little sky in it. But the world all around it was roses, a fragrance lined with must that brought home the truth of Marusja's words. Yes, he smiled to himself, slightly bewildered, yes, I am in the treetops looking for roots. Just hanging somewhere. A priest and no priest. One is a priest to someone else, not to oneself. But her words stayed with him. Sweet, aromatic, and meaningful.

"But all of this you'll carry to her," Marusja said. "Not only to ease my conscience but to ease the conscience of the world, to repay. To do what is right." And she hesitated, lowered her voice, said with intensity: "Because, Nestor, the Jews are your people. You are chosen by God, as they are. Taken from a cradle and hurled into my hands. I picked up this bruised and swollen baby, a beautiful bundle, and knew God had chosen you, given you life, lifted you from the multitude to the glory. And that He had found me worthy to be your mother, what made Mary so humble with pride. I know what she felt and I know what it feels to let you go. Find your people, the people you come from. I do not worry about the old faith. You will not desert me."

A grave moment. All of it he knew without knowing the details. So, he thought, I am a bruised and swollen Jewish child thrown through a window onto the pavement of the

Residenzgasse in full view of the great Archbishop's Residence. So this is who I am.

He descended the serpentine rose-lined pebble path and came upon the sands; the sun had changed position, glared into his eyes out of the river. The sands crept in, filled his shoes and socks. He removed them as if he were on the banks of the Prut. Sweet roses were still in the air but also a tarter aroma, dried berries, made him feel he was the first man on this unknown earth. Marusja's words returned, along with the musty smell and the golden birds in the tree of her carpet, and he wondered: Who is my father?

He slept. When he awoke, the sun was still high and his head ached. The sands felt hot in his hands. Dread of the hours to come brought him up with a jolt.

There were strange things here, electrical appliances he had spotted in the kitchen – what were they used for? So many things.... He had lived a simple life with God and books, dreamy walks up the Residenzgasse, skipping over every stone and picking out the blades of grass between them, the Archbishop's Residence rising towards him as he walked. The priest older now, the world around him changed after Ukrainians from beyond the Djnester, strangers, took the house of God from them. The priest moved to a backroom, no services in the chapel, and the big Aula, the Archbishop's assembly hall, now a lecture room. Thousands of students invading their silent world. The big temple in town now a movie house, and the Evangelical church, right across from the old house down by the Ahi Fountain, now filled with armaments. Marusja and Nestor watched the occupiers hack the branches of the two glorious chestnut trees guarding the Evangelical church, to get their equipment into the church.

The sun was hot above. Nestor's temples throbbed and he felt again that strange sensation of first encounter, as if he hadn't lived yet. He found a child's yellow pail, filled it with sand and water to bake a sandcake, again five years old on the river Prut. He worried about the next hours.

Those were hard times to live through. But that was just the outside life. Within, a boy's life was simple, contained. Some freedoms and some taboos. He was not allowed to go up the Gallows Hill. Ileana had told Marusja, beware of the fountain, Ahi comes alive, do not allow Nestor to go up that hill, where nothing grows and sadness overcomes everyone without their knowing why. A few commandments. But a simple life and a very slow realization of physical things.

It's hard to be Adam. How to know one's father and his world? Being fashioned from clay and having to move clay muscles over unknown grounds. What memory, what fragrance to call on? What past mattered? Hard to be that first man. His body heavy with indecision, Nestor sat on the stones, watching the river flow.

He had soaked Marusja's handkerchief in river water and covered his aching head to cool it when he saw two figures, shadowless, winding down the rose path, arms outstretched to him. A man and a woman of no age they seemed to him. Nestor had to make a conscious effort: Süssel and Max, of course. When they reached the sands, they removed their shoes and ran towards him with calls of old friendship.

"What took you so long? You do know that we expect you for dinner. I cooked all day, dishes from home, so you wouldn't be so bewildered, which I am sure you are." Süssel hugging him again and again, and saying: "You are a very handsome young man, I must say, with your dripping handkerchief." Her friend Max not saying much but looking at him with something that might have been pity. He didn't like to be pitied, but almost welcomed Max's compassion for his distraught appearance. He imagined what he must look like with eyes half-closed eyes, his temples visibly pounding, his countenance of fear.

Now, it was his turn to look. Süssel: different from how her mother had described her when he sat beside her on the kitchen stool next to the little table. All those hours of Greek and Latin writing, Süssel's mother suddenly dropping her pencil – little Nestor knew it would be about Süssel. And he sat and listened: how good a little boy he was, and how naughty Süssel sometimes, but how beautiful her Süssel was! Süssel's mother sighed: "I often wanted to hug her, hold her close, protect her, but she ran from me, pushing me, mocking my love. Or so I thought."

Nestor, looking at Süssel with his childhood eyes – water dripping from Marusja's handkerchief – saw her mother in her features, and said: "You look exactly like your mother, Süssel. May I call you that?"

"No, I do not look like her. My mother was accomplished and serene and I am just the opposite, full of faults and fighting." That mocking look her mother had told him about was there though, that teasing tone.

"Heavens, what pants, they hang on you like a scarecrow battling the storm! I love your Ukrainian shirt." He had never worn civilian garb until he left the old house. He was a priest, he wanted to be distinguished in the mob, wanted it to be known he was not one of them. And he stiffened at Süssel's remarks. "Well, if this is the game, so be it. I wish to be different from all of you. Besides, I won't stay one minute longer than I have to. I will do my duty and go home."

But Süssel took him around the middle, whirling him about,

calling out to Max: "Good Lord, Max, look at this innocent. I do not mean any harm. We'll just dress you in Max's clothes, they will fit you perfectly. This face! This high forehead, the light brown hair and eyes – Max," she called, "this is another one like you, good God what will I do with all you idiots? How do you ridiculous, maladjusted, lost souls find your way to my door? I wonder, I do wonder!"

"Simple; love will do it," Max said. "Every time. Conscious or unconscious, love will do it." And Max took Nestor's arm, held it close to his own, closer than Nestor had ever felt a man's body. "Come," Max said, "we'll give you dinner and we'll talk." Nestor let himself be led up the rose path like a child, grateful, not trusting the next hour.

NESTOR SLEPT WELL, but woke several times to call to Marusja. The dream that haunts him never stops. He wakes, falls back to sleep, and it starts again, proceeding in its unfailing sequence and ending in his desperate shout for Marusja.

He played in the Balschgasse, the small alley-street beside the old house. Shunned by the Soviet children, who now lived in the Jews' houses, he despised them in turn for showing off the Jewish children's pocket knives, watches, and slingshots – despised them and envied them. He longed to be part of the boys' games, away from his priest's judgmental thoughts, or Marusja's. He liked the Balschgasse better than the Residenzgasse. There were smaller houses there, more gardens, a few Romanians still there from before the locusts came. They were his own people in some ways, poor enough and Greek Orthodox, if not Ukrainian, it did not matter. Still his own people. Thinking of God sometimes and praying; not animals.

One warm Sunday afternoon he was digging worms in his Balschgasse hideout with a small knife his mother had given him. It was not sharp, but was good enough to dig between the stones; unseen he cowered in a corner of the old house. Leaning against the north wall, he had caught a wiggly living thing and was looking at it, wondering at a worm's life. Suddenly he saw himself facing four or five big boys. Soviet kids, newcomers. From where he sat on the ground they looked enormous. "Give us that knife, little punk," they said.

"No, it's mine."

"All right then, keep it, we'll let you have it. Come, we'll show you a fun hideout we have. But you'll have to pay your dues. Five rubles. We have seen you around. You know, being by yourself all the time, are you, you know, a leftover Jew? Let down your pants, we'll soon know who you are, ha ha."

"No, I won't," Nestor said. "I am to be an ordained priest of the old Greek Orthodox church."

"The better," they said, and laughed, pulling him up to his feet and pushing him towards the darker side of the Balschgasse. They walked a distance together into the direction of the Train Station Street, where the Balschgasse sloped gently, and stopped by a neglected garden Nestor had never seen before. They opened a rickety gate held by a chain and soon stood in front of a small summerhouse. It was overgrown with wild vine, green fruit hanging from twisting leaves and stems. It looked peaceful. The biggest, or eldest, of the four – the one from Süssel's third-floor apartment – undid the latch of the covered entrance and pushed Nestor ahead of him into the dark green space.

At first Nestor could not distinguish anything in the dark, but he heard a moaning sound coming from a corner. Moving closer, he saw the biggest of the boys taking his pants down. He heard snickering laughter from the others, who had entered and fixed the hanging lock shut behind them. His eyes adjusting to the light, Nestor saw a little girl tied with ropes to the boards of the summerhouse. A very little girl, no older than six or seven, propped up against the wall, dirty empty dishes around her. She seemed blind and dumb, only able to moan. The big boy pulled her flat onto the floor, cursed her for a filthy bitch, parted her thin legs, and pushed his erect thing into her. Again and again he did it to her. Nestor ran in terror, storming towards the door, rattling the tight latch, to the amusement of the crowd.

"Coward, idiot, do it to her! You're a Jew, that's why you won't show your thing to us!" And they tore his pants down with one strong movement; the pants ripping in their seams as he desperately tried to pull them back. You owe us five rubles, they shouted, opening the latch of the summerhouse to let him run, and don't you tell or we'll slice your Jewish thing off you. And he knew now, that he was a Jew underneath. He ran through the silent Balschgasse, holding onto his torn pants, sobbing all the way to his cellar. Thank God Marusja was out on errands. No one had seen him.

A little girl. She was in there, dumb, blind, and bound, and they all stuck their thing into her. Five rubles. Where would he get five rubles? Who could he tell and who would believe him? Thoughts of rescue and terror mingled. I'll take my father's knives, I'll cut their throats, I'll cut the ropes and let her free. Tomorrow. And he fell asleep in the middle of the day, at the end of his strength. The next day he fevered, could not go to his lessons, and no cool compresses, no sugared tea, cream of wheat with butter in it, helped. I just have to wait until he is better, Marusja thought. I'll pray.

It took seven days. On the last day he rose when Marusja was gone, dressed, and went through the garden of the old house. Jumping neighbouring wild-vine fences to avoid the Balschgasse, he came up to the summerhouse from behind. He broke a few wooden boards off the wall where rot had set in and went in. It was empty. There was no sign of dirty dishes, the door was locked, latched from the outside. He sat for a minute on the floor in the corner, thinking he was mad.

But the dream pursued him, night after night. The scene came back, all of it, all the time. The walk through the Balschgasse, the summerhouse, the flight. The worst of it was that he woke each time with a stiffened member. Then he screamed, *Marusja.*

And why now, here, in a new world, that scream? After the peaceful simple times of the last two years. His dreams had abated. Why all of it all over again? The river, fragrant with roses. The night before, a good meal of cabbage rolls, wine, and homemade corn bread, a deep sleep; and now the sting of nostrils full of the summerhouse.

He rose at last. It was five o'clock, early morning. Going down the staircase, so familiar, so closely built on the old one at home, steadied him. It was made of wood and not of stone, but winding, spiralling. He held on to the warm polished wood. Silently, on furtive soles, he went into the fresh morning.

SO THESE ARE THE CRANBERRY FLATS. Nestor ran along the heights, then southward and down to the river on a thistly path. His soles stinging, he recalled a run down to the Prut from the Heights of Hapsburg, the birchwood-garden behind the Residence. He was not alone, for the first time. She was a Soviet child, living in the Polish Princess's flat, as Marusja called it, one of the many children of three Russian families squeezed into three rooms, kitchen, and bathroom. Marusja felt disdain for these barbarians, godless and rowdy. Their fights spilling into the stairwell, the children riding the banister, scratching the mahogany with Jewish knives, and peeing in corners, made Marusja's feeling of superiority take root. Nestor had no eyes for any of them.

He passed by her as she stood at the cellar steps; too often for Marusja's liking. "What does she want from us? Spies. Soviet spies. Carrying information to the authorities – NKVD, KGB or whatever they call them now. Spies and thieves. Wanting a bribe." Whenever she saw her, Marusja gave the newcomer a glaring look of fury, a gesture with one arm as if to frighten a fly away, but the girl stood her ground. A young thing, fifteen or so.

On one first of May, ready for the parade, decked out in the Princess's summer-garden hat, shiny fruit and ribbons trailing, Marusja could have swatted her like an insect. But she just stood there, like all lovers of fifteen, oblivious to power. She stood at the cellar entrance, not daring to descend the steps, but right at the top. Waiting. Until she cornered Nestor, books under his arm. Grabbed his free hand, pulled him through the old gate into the Residenzgasse and around the corner to the Balschgasse. She knew his childhood hideout, against the wall of the house. She held him gently captive and said, "I loved you from the moment we stepped into this house. Will you talk to me?"

And they walked up a hilly road, not through the Residenzgasse, where he was known, but behind all the green-vine gardens, none of which ever ripened into grapes. A lovely dreamy path of his teenage years. Nestor was a God-seeker, who looks into a trembling vine leaf and sees Him there, a mystic like his mother, searching for a unity beyond. He did not permit sexual indulgence, not because he despised it, but because he feared its power over him. How to control himself and not fall into sin....

But now he looked into her eyes running over. Seeing him only, holding his hands. Both speechless, though she wanted to talk, she had said. Wordless, up through the hidden gardens, up behind the *Habsburg's Höhe*, where countless lovers had lain or suffered rejection, through the birch wood, looking southwest. They took their shoes off, as is the custom of the young wanting the earth, and he felt a thistle stinging his sole.... The same thistle here and there stings you into memory. Dreams run through your bloodstream and spurt forth, suddenly.

Now he sits on the sands washing the red trickle in the cool still river. No sun on the river yet. He had left it in his window, fleeing its wild burst. It's hard for a cellar child. Hard to look at all those utilitarian, unbeautiful things, so demanding of you. He fled that sun. With his back to it now, the thistle sting cooled, he sits motionless, like all migrants who land on rivers.

Such a big world, without borders, unknown stones on your road, if it weren't for the thistle. Very fast one knows its sting and the limits of your freedom. Nestor smiles, thinking of Süssel's wild hugs, how she held him closer than other women would dare. A sexual hug with intimacy and warmth, a welcoming only Süssel could deliver. It frightened him a little, wondering what was expected of him. Until Max put a gentle hand on his shoulder, said: "This is Süssel, dear. You'll get used to her. She has looked forward to your coming a long time. As she made all the arrangements – the tickets, money, the affidavit – she grew more excited by the day. You are the closest she will ever come to her grandfather's house...." Then, chuckling gently, moving Nestor a little away from Süssel: "Do not mind her ways, you will soon love her as I do. Of course, one needs to be a little wary, for her wrist is loose, and before you know it, flies backhand into your face. Never mind. She'll be here for you, body and soul."

Yes, it seems so. She wants to hear it all. How many baskets of walnuts come September? Are the prunes and the peach trees alive? How about the wild vine across the fence to the neighbours? It needs pruning, you know. Endless questions. And Nestor sits, cooling his toes and thinking how inadequate are his answers, he who noticed nothing. Living in prayer and liturgy, avoiding the Soviet grind of falseness and deceit, so different from what she knew. Still, they knew the same cobblestones in the yard by the chicken coop, exactly which stones one could skip on comfortably and which to avoid. "Is the jasmine-lilac patch flowering?"

"Yes," he remembers that. "It was just in front of the little outhouse in the back garden." He loved it, he said, and she cried.

Barefoot he walked upriver on the sands, avoiding the sun. He feels at home on these sands, slightly humid and clinging, still so early in the morning. He had walked the sands of the Prut with the Soviet child very early one morning. She had stood on top of the cellar steps, her *Komzomol* red scarf – emblem of the communist youth – around her neck. It was the first of May and she said, "I won't go to the parade. It's only speeches, lies, and fat generals. It will be a hot dusty day –"

"Good," Nestor said, surprised at his daring and initiative. "It will be a holiday from life, I have no study today – the priest, my teacher, said we have to heed the law, so I'm free. Let's go down the Bahnhofstrasse, through the poplar row, down through the cornfields to the Prut." And she ran up to the first floor, where the Polish Princess used to live – so Marusja told him, they had all been killed before his time – shouting to her mother that she was off to the parade.

They walked along the Balschgasse, but very close to the fences, avoiding spies and tattletales. She took her red kerchief off and put it in his pocket, and they ran down the hilly Bahnhofstrasse, past the green, unripe cornfields to the river.

A small changing-house gave them shelter from the rising sun, and they sat on the sand still and wordless. What to do with one another....

Nestor longed for her now, for the first time. All the sands...an hourglass, holding the Prut, curbing its flow, under his soles. An hourglass that measured his increasing impatience, his budding love. Turn it, restart the flow, watch each kernel fall again; the interval more painful as his desire for her grew, slowing time down. He smiled at the memory of her sudden appearance on the top cellar step. Her face, he guessed, only materialized as he approached where she stood.

Marusja's hourglass, inherited – or looted, who knows – from the masters, always there on his shelf above his desk. Back in his room, he turned it now, watched every kernel fall. His longing rose, choking him, and he cursed his loneliness. I'll bring her to this river, or I'll go home to hers. Tears ran down his face. He raised a sandy hand to wipe them away.

Nestor

The Mission

Cranberry Flats. September, 1961.

Elenitchka, my bride! May I call you that? There have been no declarations of love or discussions of future plans between us! But it was clear to me, from the moment you stood on top of the cellar stairs, red kerchief of the Komzomol for the first of May parade around your neck, that I had found my love. I did not know it then, of course. How could I have? I had never touched a woman's hand except my mother's. Girls were for other boys to chase, catch, tease. I watched them, full of envy in my own isolation. My games were solitary games. The boys derided me, I was the butt of jokes for the newly-arrived Soviet kids. No one played with me; no girls, no boys. The only people who came close to being my playmates were my two uncles in Caliceanca, my mother's middle brothers. She had six brothers, good men, but two of them, a little older than my mother and not married yet, were the kindest men and loved me. Marusja, my mother, took me down to Caliceanca as often as she could. Casimir, called Cadziu, the gentle, studious one, is my godfather. He and his brother Vladimir – called Vladziu – came up to town for my christening. So Cadziu and Vladziu were my friends and I always wanted to go there. There was a welcoming, a warmth, a family intimacy there, that I didn't feel anywhere else, except of course in my mother's cellar. There I was at home, I was not an abandoned child. And not only that, those brothers were my mother's moral support when my father Dmitry went to war. They were hard working and generous. Am I allowed to say it – without sounding prejudiced – the Ukrainian way: they had their hearts on their sleeves and would give you the shirts off their backs? Am I allowed to say that? Of course, they too went to war.

Here, after all that introduction, is the point of this letter: to say that when I saw you at the top of the stairs – were you fifteen? – I loved you with the intensity and the certainty of the young. So here is the reason for this letter: if you will have me, you'll be mine! And it is the most important point. The next is also important: you know my mother, of course, though she has not exactly favoured you; thinking your folk usurpers, looters of other people's goods, Jews and non-Jews, sleeping in beds that belong to others. My mother is illiterate. Your people, who come from beyond the Djnester, all read and write. And if I have anything good to say about your "invasion," it is that you make children go to school.

So, beloved Elena, I do have to communicate with my mother. Would you be our intermediary? I'll write to you, and will you please go down the steps from the first floor to our cellar and read the letters to her. It will mean a great deal to me. It will strengthen our bond, bring the three of us closer, and perhaps within a short time, make us a family. So, here are the letters. I will count on you even before I receive your approval.

With love and respect,

N.

Dearest Marusjenka, my true mother, only now can I speak to you. Forgive my silence. This is too enormous a land! I do not know yet how I'll live – I miss my little corner in that cellar room that held us; where sunshine comes in through small slits in the wall, where you and I wait for the hour when its heavenly rays light the silver-thread birds in the top branches, and then the roots, of your eternal tree. On the little carpet.

You hung it, as the early astronomers would, to establish the exact moment of the rising sun. To know when to worship, when to sow, and when to harvest. You knew the exact moment of the illumination of Saint Cyril's eyes, when the sun broke through the painted window of your little church in the early morning. And you knew the changing hours of the day, as the year proceeded.

I remember a very early morning when I was five years old, bedded into a hay wagon, two old Pinzgauer horses cradling me to sleep, and arriving in Caliceanca an hour or so later to enter your little church and wait for Saint Cyril's eyes to catch fire. "Wait, little one, wait and watch, one more minute," you said, "and you'll see heaven. It will be in your own saint's eyes, the one you're named after." And we stood on the stone floor waiting. Your mother had always told you, there is virtue in standing, we need no pews. If we wait for glory, we should receive it standing up. And as we stood there, the sun lit up the eyes of Saint Cyril.

You did not have to tell me to look for heaven. Heaven was in his eyes, I saw it. And you took me then, totally exhausted, to your mother's, and I slept on top of the enormous red brick oven where your grandmother used to sleep, and where all your holy tales come from. Like the Slaughter of the Innocents, that still moves me to the depths of my heart. All the little children, and Christ, and all of us. Because of you I will always feel for the lamb. For all the little Jewish children, thrown into the ditches or shot in front of their homes. Innocents, you called them, thrown into the streets, from a window.... Remember the last night, before I left? Don't rush around, I said, don't waste these precious moments, Marusjenka, don't pack, it's all done, we will regret the loss of these moments – *Marusjenka,* come back to me and finally tell me....

Yes, I nearly hit you when I fell at your feet, you said. It was up the Residenzgasse, just up the hill a little. You had been to see your priest and suddenly there were trucks, motorbikes, Germans in helmets, going into the Jewish homes, or shooting them in the streets. Yes, I was one of them, you said. One of these Jesus-people. Innocents slaughtered. And you picked me up, held me to your breast. Where I still am.

I have no home yet except that breast. This land is too huge for a cellar child, with all the saints inhabiting his mind. And I am told to go and find roots in treetops. Right now the winds are striking these treetops, I can hardly hold onto them, and climbing higher is hard and dangerous. Away from my comfortable haven, how will I find my roots? A Jew, what is that?

Süssel says, wait, you can't build Rome in a day. I laugh at her: why Rome? Because all roads lead there, she says. And Max – do you know him? – says: Nestor, don't mind her,

Süssel talks in parables. Just wait, it will take time, she's right. Rome was not built in a day.

I'll write to you. Go upstairs to the Polish Princess's flat and ask for Elena. She is the one who used to stand at the top of our cellar step when she was fifteen years old, a Soviet child, daughter of some NKVD official. You did not exactly like her – could I flatter myself a little to think you were jealous, *Marusjenka?* Go upstairs, knock at the door, and ask for Elena. She'll read my letters to you. Please, *Marusjenka,* also tell her that when I walk on the sands of this river – and I do this every day, I am on the banks of the Prut. She'll understand. *Marusjenka,* please try to like her a little.

Still it is on your bosom that I cry! For the loss of my homeland. Beloved mother, I kiss your hands.

Your Nestor

Second letter.

Marusjenka, it is five o'clock in the morning. There is no curtain on these huge windows. The sun is blasting me out of my mind. I woke with a shriek for you, in a sweat. You will recall my countless shrieks for you and your running to my bed to wipe my brow. It's time to confess.

What is it about this dry immense land, about this morning sun looking into all corners of our rooms? It is now a full month that I run from its cruelty. I turn my back to it, sitting on the morning-cool sands, in Max's jeans now, you should see me! – my toes in the river. I go there for escape. Of course, there is no escape from the river. Looking west it is always the

Prut. The land here often has great beauty, the faraway bushes, groves, and grasses imbedded into the western sky, making me smile and remember – how big a world.

But no. I won't run today. The nightly sweat, and your name on my lips when I awoke, made me face my sun-flooded room. It's so bright that I go for shelter to a desk that Süssel and Max have set in a darkened corner, perhaps a defence from the rising prairie sun.

Marusjenka, I remember my early teenage years, when you, poor soul, could barely deal with me. I called to you night after night. A persistent dream, it is still with me here in Süssel's house, and I have to face it. And I confess to you: I'm not any more in a cellar room, where lying is easy; in the Soviet world deceit is expected.

Remember when I went to bed one day and would not rise for seven days? You tried everything. You went to Caliceanca, to your mother's herb garden, and came back with dry and fresh herbs. You boiled chamomile, linden blooms high in season, mint, and the famous Centaur tea, "the herb of the thousand guilders" – bitter and dreadful. I sipped a little of the tea, sweated at night from the ground anise seed or whatever else you put in to take the poison out. You brought the priest in, with his myrrh, incense, and prayer. And you sat there, waiting for my shriek, wringing your hands.

I cannot tell you the whole story, but you will recall that I came home with my pants torn, buttons missing, seams ripped, and crashed down on the bed. Marusjenka, two bullies, sons of the general from upstairs, and a few other Soviet kids, took me from the Balschgasse where I played in my corner. They held me captive and made me witness a dreadful violence to a little mute girl. I tried to flee and they tore my pants down, calling me a Jew. It was then that I swore to be a priest.

When I rose from my seven-day bed, I was another person, hiding from you, not looking you in the eye. I was searching for answers in the holy script. I swore I would never look at girls, and I could not. But neither could I contain my dreams or my desire for them.

Marusjenka, I will not say more. Only that the first time I dared to hold a woman's hand – besides yours, of course – was when Elena stood at the top of our cellar steps. She just stood there and waited. It seems that is what lovers do!

I leave you now, mother. I must run down to the kitchen. I hear Süssel and Max, arguing over their coffee and toast. Lazybones, they call up to me, you have not gone to the river, what are you doing upstairs? Come, come, we'll sit together for a half hour, it's a glorious day. And I will rush down to them, leaving my confession and feeling so light and unburdened. So young, suddenly. I've never been young before. While these old people are, heavens, almost carefree!

My love, my mother,
N.

Next day, five o'clock, early morning. The whole eastern horizon, fields yellow against the pale blue, is right here in my room. I am high up, on the third floor, nearly touching the top branches of the silver maple Süssel has planted. The trees here just break up the fields a little, without diminishing the distance. Young drivers are speeding down the road. An air of prosperity and optimism, all through my eastern window. How grateful my heart is, how light today. I have not run to the river for the second day, because I still have a few things to say, that cannot wait forever. I will have to start thinking of English school, employment, and why I am here.

But not yet. I have not yet fulfilled my mission. The treasure is safe in the big suitcase, but this time I'll take my time – and do it right – for you, *Marusjenka.*

Why did I not talk to you when I still could, when you were with me? Your love held me like an egg in a shell and I could not break it. So many regrets – Oh, yes, remember the time my nose bled, I'd been beaten up blue-green, and I refused to answer? It was not you, of course. You never lifted a hand against me, though you threatened out of despair sometimes. Well, would you believe I was defending the honour of Saint Volodymir – patron of the Ukrainians – against the Russian bullies, our new colonial masters? You once told me a beautiful saintly story of Volodymir's baptism, where Sevastopol is now on the western tip of the Crimea, and how he succeeded to convert the Grand Duke of Kiev. The Russian toughs, like the ones who live now in Old Green's flat, robbers and plunderers all, called him Russian and *Vladimir,* and said: "We are going to show you what you Ukrainians here will have to learn the hard way, that we are the masters and you are worthless serfs." And the hard way it was for me. I was made to run the gauntlet; they had slender hazelnut rods and they beat me with them as I ran between their rows. They tried to make me say Saint Vladimir is Russian and I am a lying serf. But I wouldn't. I stuck by Saint

Volodymir and our Ukrainian myth.

They left me for near-dead on the cobblestones in the yard just behind the jasmine-lilac patch. I heard you call, shout my name, curse me for a no-good for making you weep and worry. I waited for the dark, to wash my face and cool my aching head. You came to me at night, with compresses and hot milk. Did you know?

It is a funny story in a way. I don't even know who I am – what was Saint Volodymir to me? I did fight your fight and stuck it out, insisting that they were strangers and occupiers and I in my ancestral homeland. Considering that I have to look for my Jewish roots in the treetops, it's a pretty funny tale.

Did you go upstairs to the Princess's flat? I hope you are friends with Elena by now because, Marusjenka, I will bring Elena here, or I'll return, if she'll have me. I smile when I think of her thick blonde braided hair, violet eyes, and altogether Polish looks.

I asked her not to wear the Jewish things, the fancy hats and plumes. She said, why not, they are mine, the Jews are all dead, they won't return. And I said, Elenitchka, my mother does not allow it; it hurts her to see you or your mother parade in things that belonged to people she loved, good people. I said that I would not see her in any of their things.

Dear mother, forgive them, you see they do not know right from wrong, they have no religion. The simplest things, that we absorbed from our faith so early, they have to learn anew. Yet I love her so....

Your son,
N.

REMEMBER WHEN you apprenticed me to the carpenter down in the Jewish-Turkish quarter? The part of town that became the ghetto, a few months after you found me in the street. There was another Turkish fountain there, not quite so wonderful as our Ahi fountain at the crossroads of Gallows Hill and Saint Trinity, on the Yiddishegasse not far from where the carpenter lived. It was damaged but not totally destroyed after the annihilation of the ghetto. I wonder if you remember that; to me the ghetto, the murder, and all that tragedy are second hand knowledge, but more deeply ingrained than if I had actually lived through it.

A leftover Jew, you said, a returned one from the other side. I wonder what he knows that I do not, you said, and if there are different heavens. You told me, oh, there is no hell yonder, *malenko*, my little one, they just threaten you so you'll be good and go to church.

I loved your common sense, shrewd mother. You saw my talent to cut wood into shapes, bring them to life. It was good to work with my hands, escape from thought and memorization, and you knew it. Hours and hours I spent in the almost-lightless back room polishing an oval piece of pine, at my desk under the window, painting one of the angels from the eight squares in the old gate. Remember the one I knew best, in the lower-left corner? I observed it in minute detail while sitting on the four steps waiting for you to take me up the Residenzgasse. My angel, with legs flying, wings spread. Like letters they flew. Told me things. Flying birds with children's faces whispered into my ear, and I drew these angels with coloured chalk on the sidewalk right in front of the old house. Afterwards I wiped my hands on clean trousers, and you scolded me, took me in to wash before taking me up the Residenzgasse to my lesson. But I couldn't help it: friendless as I was, angels were my only companions. I knew whence they came and the stories written into the flutter of their wings, stories full of rivers running over diamond stones, ruby roses on their banks – they were with me wherever I went, protecting me from sun, wind, and nasty boys.

So I painted my angels onto oval-shaped medallions, drilled a hole for a leather string, and hung one around your neck on your name day. You cried and held me close.

The next day my wise and practical mother told me: we have a gold mine, Nestoritchku. We'll be rich! Cut small pieces of pine into ovals, polish them, paint the prettiest Mothers of God, a sweet little baby if you like, and add a leather string.... Remember all of that? It was perfectly wonderful. We were rich indeed! You sold all I could cut and paint, to the godless Russians, mainly. Black market, serving God and fighting the state, Marusja-style! First you sold them in the old house and then up the street. Customers came in droves, wore them hidden on a string, so the Soviet bosses, the *nachalniki*, would not suspect them. It was hilarious. Remember, we could afford everything, with their rubles. Could not fill the demand. A businesswoman, my mother, my simple lady from Caliceanca with the sharpest mind on earth. You enlarged your business and took special orders, for Saint Gregory, Chrysostom, or the Saviour Himself. And Cyril for you and me. I became an icon-maker, and my teenage years were full of these images. We could afford true gold for background in the end....

That is when you apprenticed me to the Jew in the Yiddishegasse, a returned-from-hell Jew. Returned from the hell of Moghilev. And I learned the trade: how to use a plane, a turner's wheel, and above all a finesse in joining. He was fatherly to me and kind, saying there is no Saint Abraham so he could not accept one of my golden-blue icons. "Thank you, Nestor," he said. "But Jews have no images. We do not carve them, paint them, or draw them in any form. We do not sculpt them in wood, clay, or plaster. No disrespect, but God to us is in here." And he pointed to his head, and according to the law, looked towards the hidden Mezuzah on the doorpost. "No disrespect. We all serve as we know how. You and me."

He was good to me, survived all that man can do to man and remained loving. And I knew then that I would have to learn his law. Marusjenka, I will, and I know this is what you have hoped also.

With love,

N.

ANOTHER LETTER HOME.

Süssel found me a job as a carpenter, on the other side of the river, in the western part of town. There the houses are smaller, the people poorer but decent, painting their front fences and greeting a stranger. Passing the synagogue on the way to work, I wanted to enter, but it was locked. A janitor appeared, with beard, black hat, Jewish-looking – or what I thought of as Jewish-looking. He said I would have to talk to Mr. Aaron, the orthodox rabbi.

Süssel found the rabbi for me, and Mother, I am now a regular student! At what age? Heavens! But it goes well! Carpentry and study go wonderfully well together, one relieves and complements the other. After a day of sawing, glueing, joining, hammering, and sweeping the sawdust, my soul soars with letters, Hebrew letters, with their pictorial beauty and meaningful shape. Süssel agrees with me, though she simply sees them as mysterious. But I see them taking off singly, unconnected, each with a life of its own. I can talk to you, Marusja, because having no letters yourself you are unspoiled by learning and feel the deep significance of symbols, like the Orthodox cross cut through threefold. Remember when I taught you to print your name, and each letter in Maria made you sob? And, what meaning numbers have for you! My black-marketeer under-the-counter counting mother! So I can talk to you and you will understand when I say that the script of the Torah lifts me from the ground as the angel wings in front of the old house did.

I love the rabbi. He is a saint. He smiles and says: "You have saints, we have only sinners." God – what sinner? A man that holds the book in his hands with so much reverence and teaches without regard to time or recompense.

Mother, you will never be in want of anything. I will work here. This country is so big it seems to have no borders. There is room for people. They smile in the streets. To smile at strangers! A dependency, maybe, strangers needing one another in an elemental land. There is shelter in the smile of the other. And I feel at home in it. These are mothers' smiles, not asking, just giving; they do not mind my miserable English. Maybe their own isn't so good. I think I can live here, though I did not think so in the first two weeks. But the smiles on people's faces give me that protection, that refuge I have felt only on your breast. Of course I am a lonely, only child and do not interpret the world easily. I can't distinguish – sometimes do not wish to – friends from foes. It frightened me as a child, and will forever, probably. But these Canadian smiles in this empty out-west land are comforting to such souls as mine, fed by your silver spoon, the priest's heaven, and the carpenter leftover Jew, as you call him. What he gave me, apart from the joy in his skill, and that is mine now, is what Süssel is trying to tell me: that we are all one. Engraved in copper, parchment, or skin, the letters prove it. The word, the letter, the divine in us. That the Shemah holds it all: that God is One. And if He is three to you and me as well, he is still one. I feel it more and more –

I have met a neighbour from two miles away while walking on the sands. Learning my way around the Cranberry Flats, I often wander off the beaten path, and with the shifting river sands it is easy to get lost in the bushes. And one day there he was standing in front of me. Wearing just a shirt and bathing trunks. He said hello ceremoniously, as if dressed for a formal occasion. I liked him instantly, and he has become my new friend. I come back often in the early morning. I go to the one-room shack he has built on a dune island, on government-owned land. (One can do that here.) We talk, swim, and have picnics. (What you and I used to do on the river Prut.) He views the world differently from us. Of mixed Métis heritage, he has broken away from his people to make his way as an artist. He paints birds, insects, small creatures in an immense sky. Good and evil reside in us, he says. This is where Satan is – and God, he says – and he points to his breast. So much for me to learn. That it is possible to deny God. And I am not talking of the "phony" Russians you know, who wear crucifixes and my Madonnas under their tunics. This Tom wears no tunic, he is usually in jeans and shirt. He has that essential smile that reminds me of you, Mother.

And now to practical things. Do you still want to buy the piece of land adjoining your mother's? The war has taken such an awful toll on all of your people in Caliceanca. Do you want it, sweet mother? If you do, Süssel has offered to buy it for you, if you decide to retire there. To get you out of your cellar. You have money, options, Marusjenka. We are here for you. It will be your choice. Tell us!

And please go to my carpenter-father. Süssel wants to know how many of her people have survived Transnistria. Please find out how many have filtered back into our hometown, who is living there, how are they living, are they in need?

Elenitchka has written to me for the first time. She was overjoyed that you kissed her and called her your daughter. Which she is and will be forever. She will honour you, as you deserve. She is as clever as she is good. Tell her in detail what you want us to know and she'll write it down faithfully.

I could go on talking to you, my heart is so full, of that wealth, the dear people here...but I will kiss you goodbye for now.

Nestor

"I am looking back into my soul," Nestor said to Süssel one night. "But it is a short life yet, and my memory is second-hand, distilled through my mother's mind. I had to grow in-between, protecting my inner world from the intrusion of her stories. Some were so beautiful and mystical that I'll never break loose from them, but some are unreasonable; from a world of guilt and ready-made opinion."

Nestor had come down the staircase to dinner. Süssel had called, her voice carried by its echoes through the house: "I am alone," she said. "Max will be late, and we'll have time to ourselves." He feared this *ourselves.* Not so much the back of her hand, as Max put it, but his own wish to kiss her. She was ripe and poetic, uncompromising. He feared his thoughts in the morning hours. But he ran down when she called, excited and happy.

They sat at the small kitchen table, facing west. The skies were overcast, deep blue-black, the light just fading. Steady, protective, the river, darker than the sands, borrowing the blue-black of the sky, so one could follow its gentle incline. A child's drawing. No beginning, no end. It flowed through the house, one never lost sight of it. Connected.

Not needing church for the first time in his life, Nestor turned his swivel chair to face Süssel. In the half-light, her face, a little diffused, seemed veiled with a fine net. All the years between them dissolved. So beautiful she was, and so close that he could kiss her. But he took both her hands across the table, brought them to his lips and said, "I am a Jew like you are, born of a woman from that tribe. No baptism robs me of my ancestral right. But I will have to learn what it truly means."

"Good, my friend," she said. "A whole world will open to you. I do not know how easy this is, away from all your palpable images, where God comes to you through objects imbued with a specific legend or mystery. When I entered this spiritual territory

I was younger than you, totally unprepared, and it was my first encounter with physical love as well. I had to learn, and so will you. You will have to turn the other way, away from the golden heaven promised by the church, to rely on the Judaic creed that God is One. Abstract and beautiful. Within the word, the letter, you will find it. With my humble help, the community in town, and the help of Rabbi Aaron, a just man of the old school. I think – I hope – you will love who you are, a brother and a son to us, Max and myself.

"We'll talk, but we can't go down to the river now, there is a storm threatening, I can see it coming from the south. Let's go to the study. Look west, the river turns the south corner, a world drawn with a pencil at your feet," she said.

They sat down on a loveseat looking across that world and suddenly Süssel, pointing at the clouds, asked: "Do you see the Moorish crenelations of the Archbishop's Residence against the horizon? Look how clearly drawn, how mighty, beautiful and unchanged, right in that cloud." And Nestor saw them, clearly. He knew them better than Max, who saw them at all times of the day, morning and night, but not from inside. Never from within. He had stood in his corner beside the principal's house for hours on end just to get a glimpse of Süssel. But Nestor knew, from young, each lacquered stone, all the trolls and the funny mannequins, who sometimes pissed and sometimes didn't – and they laughed, Süssel and Nestor, being children together, albeit a generation apart. Walking the paths, often forbidden for Süssel but allowed for Nestor.

"Do you know where the loose bricks are in the east wall?"

"No," Nestor said, "I always went through the main rounded gate."

"But of course, you're a Christian," she said, and laughed.

"There are advantages to being a Jew in a Christian world. You learn to circumvent the law; the forbidden sharpens your mind to find avenues for your longings. I sat with my summer lover...."

And Nestor grinned: "At what age?"

"Never mind, young! I sat with my summer lover against the dwarf pine, watching the trolls frolicking –"

He said, "Yes, I know them well. Stone they may be, but I always had the feeling they might break out of their stone world into life at any moment, so lively their movements were. So mysterious, bewitched, and slightly evil they seemed."

And she: "No, not evil, just shrewd, knowing the ways of the world. Even those in black soutanes, priests to be, books in hand, walking gravely as if the world depended on the last parable, even these they knew. They looked at us, those trolls; stone they may have been and man made, but not entirely. Their wisdom, their wicked smiles, told us, *we know you, we were human once.*"

They sat all evening, until they heard the gate; Max returning, shouting to them that he had just avoided the first ball of hail. Let's go and look, Süssel said. But they did not have to move, the river and its turbulent air were right inside. Hail crashing down. "Tomorrow," Nestor asked, "will we talk tomorrow?"

"Yes," Süssel said, "it is time."

THE SUN WAS UP. But he let it shine in without rising for the first time since he'd arrived. He let it shine into his cellar-heart with no need to confess. Though truth lay closer to the surface than he'd ever known it to be. A lightness of being, a Canadian heart suddenly. Memories still surging, but unoppressive now.

He would not go down, not to the sands and the river, not to the percolating coffee and toast. He waited for the gate to fall into the lock. Then rose, opened his down-to-the-floor window-door, and stepped out onto the small eastern-facing balcony. A diversion, from her grandfather's house, he thought – how did she permit it? The floor-to-floor glass of that old stone house did not allow any break, except for support. He stepped onto the wooden terrace and almost into the top branches of the silver maple, the nearest thing to a walnut tree one could hope for here. Too extreme a land for walnuts! He felt a pang of longing for home, for his walnut tree. The Soviet kids, invaders all, felt no loyalty to the tree, broke its branches while climbing. Many a green fruit had hit him hard, and he was accustomed to watching the thick inner foliage, suspecting the enemy.

The sun rose above the tree, freeing the Cranberry Flats. There they lay, spread out in their grandeur, flat and endless. Country roads and ditches led away from the river, the earth grassy, vulnerable, the sands deep beneath. Homes emerged, unobserved before, and a car here and there. But mostly a God-like emptiness, the sky linking horizons, like the church dome in his mother's village. Yellow with gold, that dome made Nestor's Byzantine heart swell with joy; how true his faith, how telling of this morning! Saints in his heart. And he smiled at his own stupidity: it was only a country road, pebbles and fences, people pulling their cars out to go to work, a rider here and there, proud in his English fashion. A flat, straight, non-heaving world, where one could ride into the horizon without hindrance. He smiled at his mystery-seeking self. Stupid or not, he thought, this is my heart, eastern. Even if I am in a strange land, without our ancient hills or the holy Cecina mountain to shelter me, and the world goes on forever until it falls into the sea, this is my heart, eastern. And memory rose on Cranberry Flats, from the sands underneath the grasses....

A spicy air, rich with ripe fruit and a sweetness of thought today, the past emerging without pain. A day where existence is inhaled, savoured, with a conscious breath of ease and delight. Nestor seated himself on a bench, facing south, put his hands into his lap and rested.

To prepare himself for the day, he let the sun move on its own, thinking for a moment of his priest, for this was his hour of study – like clockwork, our hearts. But it was a fleeting moment only. He had traveled far, and Nestor smiled as if to a companion.

Winds rise on these cranberry lands at certain hours and abate at others. Now they are rising, lifting the flats. Sand flies into his eyes and he seeks refuge, re-enters the open doors, slowly descends the staircase in the empty house. He turns northwest on the first floor, where Süssel has built her dining table, almost hugging the corner. "I love the northern light," she told him the day before. "So calm, so diffuse, so just a light, doing no injury to anything. I always loved it, even as a child," she said. "No crude assault as the eastern sun does, and much more so here, forcing objects to reveal themselves to their core, illuminating every cranny, exposing everything. In the north wing of my grandfather's house, where the dining table stood, and where we both, my brother Felix and I, did our lessons, the light was benevolent, the colours and edges toned down, and above all there was calm, and things could live together without fear." She laughed. "Oh, sweet Nestor, do not take me seriously, I spin yarns of all sorts. Please forgive me! But live here a little and you will suddenly, while walking barefoot through the "Euphrates," want to get to the other side, suspecting – cranberries. You'll find twigs and petrified stones and small kernels that look like dry old berries, and fantasyland will take hold, a berry-flavoured past will rise." She laughed again, hugged Nestor, whirled him around, and said, "I'm nuts, do not listen to me." That was yesterday. But it has become true.

Oh yes, this is her mother's dining table. Nestor had seen it, when he came in the mornings for lessons with Süssel's mother. So little he was then. Yet he can see her still, leading him around the empty house. "There it stood once," Süssel's mother said. "It stood in the northern corner, where drawing and painting is easy because of the sweet light, light that does not make you sweat or shiver." Nestor felt it then and feels it now. A little boy knows as well as an adult, or better. Words come later, they serve the knowledge that is already there. Sometimes Süssel's mother carried a small leftover kitchen table into the empty northern room, to show Nestor what she meant, and he drew the letters so much better, he saw them with more meaning there. And the Greek ones, pictures all of them. Pages of them one could hang on the wall, so pretty they were and in close order, following each other. He drew well from early on, was an icon maker from the age of four. Every letter was an icon to be admired. And in his teenage years – heavens! Nestor smiles at the "fortune" he made selling the small painted icons to all the fat Russians who wore them hidden, close to the skin. And no draconian law of Soviet Russia could legislate them away. All that memory!

Cranberry Flats, this strange and most intimate land, makes you relive your life, or reinvent it, he thought. Measureless, all sky, how can it be intimate? But it is. It throws you back upon yourself. Upon your own pool, pond, or resource. Such a good land for an ambiguous child, conceived where and by whom I will never know. A good land for someone like me, an outcast through a window! I try not to think about it, as there are no answers, but it haunts me, here under this dome of blue and cotton, on walks through sands which hold no imprint, like the river itself. Here more than back at home, where work, duty, study and the authority of others suppress thought of who you really are. This is an interval, he said to himself, a slice of time in between, given to me by God or Süssel. To come to terms, to find not answers but acceptance. And these lands so limitless, so different from my in-between cut-out time! They are fruitful, so good for thought.

Today I'll bring the suitcase down. Set the table, as Marusja taught me the night before I left. Today. He looked around, pushed the table this way and that way, to the centre of the room, picked up the chairs and arranged them against the wall. Yes! It was a good light. Taking the staircase with a few jumps, he found the suitcase in its corner, lifted it up for the first time since he came, and found it heavy. Carefully, as if giving the last rites, he brought it down, resting on each step.

Memories of old. Mother's hand: the suitcase, well-sewn calf leather; she had chosen the hide from a tanner in Caliceana, had it designed by a leather tradesman down below Gallows Hill. The buckles were shiny, the leather belts a natural golden brown.

Nestor opened the suitcase, and the damask tablecloth emerged. He lifted it out, spread it over Süssel's table. It fell elegantly, still smooth and creased from Marusja's pressing. It hung a little too long on both ends, but draped and enfolded the long oval table beautifully. Nestor contemplated it for a little, pulled the ends this and that way, then turned back to the opened suitcase.

A sizable fir crate rested in the suitcase. Nestor untangled it with some difficulty; it was well padded between rags and papers. In his hands he now held an apple crate, the kind Marusja would use to fashion chairs, bookshelves, kitchen counters, a trivet for an iron filled with burning coal, walls to separate the sacks of victuals in old Green's store. But Nestor also held his own cradle in his hands. In one of these crates he had lain under clean linen rags, on top of a sheepskin jacket. My second-hand memories again, of course, he thought, but just as true nevertheless.

Nestor hesitated for a moment, and then, with a decisive gesture, pried the crate open: Süssel's soup tureen lay there nestled in wood shavings, tightly packed and safe. Rosenthal-white with Greek-gold edges, its monumental dome concave within the bowl, wood shavings streaming from its surface.

Nestor set the tureen at centre table, turning the cover right side up. He had heard Süssel say she had not seen it since the ghetto days, and it was the only piece of porcelain she regretted losing. Because of its measured perfection, its matte-translucent sheen that took on the tint of the light of day. The other pieces in the set, though beautiful, did not move along so perfect a curve as this *objet d'art* did. And yet it was an everyday thing, that was set upon the one o'clock dinner table, carried by Marusja, Ileana, or Süssel's mother herself. Containing something as simple and wholesome as potato-leek soup or chicken broth.... Yes, he had heard Süssel speak of the tureen with longing for the irretrievable.

Woodshavings covering the floor now. They held memories of their own for Nestor: carving holy medallions, painting them; Marusja's childish stories, telling Nestor how she built the Archbishop's Residence from the shavings that fell all around her when her two brothers pulled their saw through a log of beech trunk. Stories. They become true.

Next came the ladle. A violin, packed in plush velvet, to keep the engraved strings from scratches. Yes, it was a woman's body, with a waist, curving in around the middle, to be held. It shone. Nestor placed it alongside the tureen in the centre of the table. A few more things remained in the suitcase: a small ebony box with a wild-looking man on the cover, hair streaming, staff in hand, inlaid mother-of-pearl, a golden key beside it, and, at the bottom, leather-bound books – he had seen these in his mother's cellar, Shakespeare in German translation. But he left these other things be for now, did not lift them out of the case. Instead he sat down in one of the chairs he'd placed against the wall. *For you Marusjenka,* he thought, *to ease your conscience. For penance and return.*

Nestor sat still. Waited for the sun to move closer around the corner, to flood into the room. And suddenly the light flared up, expected-unexpected, making the table shine like heaven, and the tulips bloom, white on white. He heard Süssel's key turn in the lock, remained seated, his pulse beating in his temples. Max and Süssel came into the open dining room, the sun still lingering on the silver.... They seated themselves against the wall next to Nestor, without a greeting.

Max & Süssel

A Love. So Desired.

THE EVENING WAS SLOW. MOVEMENTS RETARDED. Dishes collected themselves as if animated, ended up piled properly and geometrically on the kitchen counter next to the sink. The damask tablecloth Nestor had brought Max and Süssel used now to celebrate the coming night. It shook itself out of its crumbs by the open front door, and laid itself into its own pressed creases on the table.

Süssel sat and watched Max putting things away. So beautiful, she thought, such benign order. All things have their own time, Max finds the order in things, so unlike me, smashing things into their places. Max questions things and guesses their laws. How beautiful! And her smile followed him around.

It was a good time to reminisce. Süssel saying, "I had no children, neither did I long for them, you know that, Max. But once Elizabeth and Grisha had come, I could not think them out of my life."

"And so it is with young life," Max replied. "I received them as a gift from heaven, truly undeserved, but once we were all with you...."

"Yes," Süssel said, "these five years that they were with us –

heavens! I think I've grown less selfish!"

"Oh, well," Max wondered, a bit sheepishly.

"It's true," she said. "I forgot myself suddenly somewhere. It surprised me. I've learned a thing or two."

"Oh, Süssel, you knew it always. It just needed time to show itself."

They had had a slow dinner on the tulip-embossed damask cloth. With white china, gold-edged, replaying the white-on-white. Max had taken to it, insisted that they use it, when Nestor was still with them. Süssel was thrilled that he had guessed her wishes.

He knows everything about me, Süssel thought; he looks at me and reads me like one of his symbols. How carefully he moves, holding a stemware glass or a bowl of fruit with no more strength than it demands! Yes, she thought, this is how he holds me too. Binds me and lets me free. Such measure. The evening was slow and silent. No doors banging, no Elizabeth dropping her school books noisily on the floor, no friends of Grisha's with their electric guitars wanting to "crash" on the basement floor.

Grisha had done well, graduated in mathematics and astronomy. One day he had packed his bags: "You promised," he had said to Max.

"Go to your *Sabra*, with our blessing," Max had replied, looking to Süssel for approval.

"I'll do three years in the Israeli army first, so you do not have to worry about my sustenance, and I'll bring you back my Sabra – to visit," Grisha had said, as if to placate Max and Süssel.

"And I want to go with him," Elizabeth had joined in. "I'll finish high school in Jerusalem and go in the army, as girls do there, for two years. Okay?"

"We'll see," Max had said, but there was little point in arguing with a determined Elizabeth. She and Grisha had their secret code: Hebrew. They spoke it fluently, Grisha with a Russian accent and Elizabeth with a Czernowitz second-generation inflection. Elizabeth relied totally on Grisha, could not bear the idea of seeing him leave. A teenager now, taller than her mother, Helen, and just as dark, Elizabeth had Joey's eyes: a mercurial green-brown, between serene and tragic. Max loved this child. He had held her on his shoulders, she had slept on his head in the heat of Jerusalem's middays, and she had shared his split seconds of destiny, whose marks never fade.

But Max could not keep her. She could tell Grisha's stories now: an imagination between the cultures, bound by the Hebrew bond. The fertile Russian-Yiddish world of Grisha, the "people from Chelm," crowding Joseph and Potiphar. She could not stay. She had to go, Max saw it clearly. He said at their parting, "We'll visit, and you know that we are always here for you. You're as close as the five cents for a telephone call to Süssel."

"I know," she said. "And thanks to you we speak English now, which will be of great help." Hugs and tears.

Bags to be made, shirts to be re-hemmed. A few small Eskimo sculptures – a mother and child so intimately carved that it was hard to tell the one from the other and a few seals in soapstone – had to be packed in felt and nestled among Elizabeth's clothes. Slippers, made of moose hide, beaded with an Indian design – "What will I do with them there?" – she packed carefully. Süssel was grateful for the many small tasks that demanded their attention, allowed them to hide their feelings. She avoided Max's eyes.

"I'll look after my sister," Grisha had promised. It made parting easier. And it filled Max's heart with pride to see his children on their way.

Nestor also was on his way. He had gone north with his native friend, to the land of the "shimmering skies," as his friend called it. The two men conversed in "English," small penny-dictionaries at hand that they hardly used. Release from "the word," its letter, sound, and meaning, was an experience Nestor never would have thought possible. A strange freedom. How to speak to one another?

Northern skies hung with coloured curtains, billowing overhead, deepening the silence below, intensifying life. The two of them sat in communion. No priest, no rabbi, no mass, no *tefillin* on the arm, just an awareness of majesty and the unifying experience of being. Sounds came to them clearer, sharper than they did in bright sunlight, and both knew they were not alone. Tom, the native man, would give a name to one or the other, but mainly let the skies talk in their green-blue and ruby colours. They stretched out under these skies until the light faded, woke to the loon's call in brilliant sunrise, and took to the boat. Tom took care of everything: fished, fed his "guest," as he called Nestor. Tom called him "his brother," and when they parted, Nestor felt his kinship. A spirituality without words or doctrine taught them who they were in simple terms. And Nestor returned to talk to Süssel and Max around the table at suppertime, as had become their habit.

"I have come to a decision," he said. "I'm twenty-five, you know."

Süssel laughed it away. "Don't tell me, you are going to leave us!"

"No, never leave you. But I've learnt I cannot be what I am not."

"And what is this?" Süssel, more aggressive than Max, had stopped eating, had put down her fork and fastened her eyes on him: "What is this?"

"It is that I can't live in the treetops forever. I've come to find my roots here and I've found them, but I have to return them and plant them back into the ground. I'll be a better Christian for knowing to be a Jew. And forgive all these parables."

"What treetops, what roots?" This time it was Max who asked. Max loved symbols, but they had to stand for something he understood.

And Nestor smiled. "It's between Marusja and me. She had a small carpet, with trees whose branches intertwined with the roots of the next tree – a tree of life, a symbol of connectedness, of the continuity of life. You, Süssel, should know it. It's made of silk and wool, with silver birds sitting in its branches, it was your mother's."

"Of course I know it. I remember where it hung on the wall. I could almost draw the centre trunk for you!" Süssel said.

"No need. I know you remember. Marusja always talks in parables. And this was her way to tell me who I am; that I should know who I am: You were born a Jew, she said, go learn for yourself what it is. This is the story. Süssel knows," Nestor said.

There was silence around the table, cutlery clinked against the porcelain. It was not a melancholy time, but it felt like a parting.

Nestor broke the silence. "Yes, I'll be a priest. A Jew, but a priest of the Orthodox faith, old style. And I'll go to Jerusalem, to study. The most renowned seminary is there, and your children Grisha and Elizabeth, of course. One can't be what one is not. This is what the northern lights have taught me."

All three of them now talked at once, Süssel and Max to offer approval, Nestor to give thanks. Süssel brushed it away, said: "When I was a child, every decision, good or painful, was made around this table. Everything was either discussed or announced here. My father would say, 'Süssel, would you please accompany me to the salon for a few minutes.' Feeling guilty, I would tremble. Meals, talk, questions, and consoling love, always at my mother's table. And so I hope it is here, and will be for you too, Nestor, whenever you'll come." Süssel's eyes were full of tears; she laughed through them, rose, and said: "Before we clear that table, I want to say to Nestor, go with God, with mine, yours, Tom's...." Looking at Max she added, "And yours also! Go with God, which is *one!* One more thing: this table would not be here without you, Nestor. You have made it the centre of our lives. It is here that we will come to one another for love and occasional quarrel."

"Yes," Max said. "Quarrel, but never without a smile."

Dishes were collected and stacked. Nestor said, "They look like the ones in your mother's house, when I was a little boy."

"Yes," she replied. "I tried to find simple white porcelain with a Greek gold rim, as our Rosenthal dishes were, but here things are all English, Minton and the like, roses everywhere! But I found these in a German catalogue, from the Hutschenreuther Company. Quite beautiful, if not the same."

Max said nothing. Sometimes he did not see what was around him, didn't pay attention. And things did not always mean to him what they meant to others. "A plate is a plate, one eats from it, washes it, stacks it into piles, so one is free to go on with one's thoughts when it is done."

"But Max, heavens! Aren't they beautiful?" Süssel would not give in.

"Yes, gorgeous," he admitted. "But remember, I do not know

your childhood dishes, dear Süssel, and so I am not moved to tears by their beauty."

"I know, everything has to be of a higher order for Max to take note of it. Something simple, always around you, handled every day, is too humble to be noticed."

And so it went. Banter, making light of things. But Max did say, picking up the ladle at its violin-carved end, turning it tenderly, "I must confess, there is such a thing as perfect form. A woman's body almost. A waist to hold." Smiles all around.

The cutlery was collected, washed, dried with a soft cloth so as not to scratch the sheen. Nestor shook out the damask tablecloth at the open door – "crumbs for the feathered folk," he said, and folded it up along its creases. Amazing that those creases were still there, after so many washings. The table assumed its after-dinner glow. And the three of them lingered for a little longer with one another. Days do not end with sundown in the western skies; light fades slowly in the long evenings. The three of them sat together in the twilight, gently slowing down their senses to prepare for the night.

"Too much sentiment; let's say good night," Süssel said as the sky darkened in the west.

Both Süssel and Max worked hard the next days not to think about Nestor's leaving. Max in particular had taken to the young man. "I never did understand saintliness until I met Nestor," he said. Süssel replied, "I always could, I saw it in the Hebrew letter, as a child in Hasidic singing. I respond to God, without truly knowing how...."

Max went early the next day to his studio. He had joined a mathematics tutoring studio and taught students at all levels. He did not like the work in the beginning but gradually learned to enjoy it. He was paid well and his English improved. He tutored first-year university students, helping them over the hurdle of the first year. His students loved him. And it became his mission to instill the desire for knowledge into their young minds. So he stayed with it.

Days of goodbyes, then a suddenly empty house. So still again. But the silence was different, now, it held the promise of fulfillment. Max and Süssel moved closer, their bodies sought one another, wordlessly almost. They talked little, as if afraid of disturbing an emerging truth. Max saying to Süssel, "I slept badly last night, jumped down from my bed. The floor felt cold on my bare feet, the brass railing too cool for my warm hand, and everything moved. I had to steady myself against the night table and nearly fell."

"It was Manole, wasn't it? The stones still falling and the price to be paid?"

"Yes," he said. "Manole, a legend! A schoolbook picture. A story! What is the power that follows you from childhood, and emerges ominously to remind you of something, you cannot tell what it is. And leaves you with despair."

Süssel ran over to hug him. Her hands in his hair, over his face, she held his head and said, "Let's walk along the river."

An October day, dark and chilly. Pitiless winds took the last remaining leaves from the branches, baring rose, saskatoon, and chokecherry bushes. It was early evening now, and both were walking fast, pushing heaps of brown copper leaves in front of them. Max took her hand in his and they found their teenage rhythm again, as if a life had not happened in between.

And "Manole" abated. The feeling of loss, failure, and the price to be paid.... The despair of the night before left him. He pressed her hand. Süssel held on to him. "Max, let's find a spot a little more sheltered." They went as far as the hollow, the one they called their "marriage bed." It looked very different now; the shifting sands had redrawn the landscape, built a new bridge of sand. But it was the very spot that Max had given Süssel his cave-pebble, his ochre Dead Sea shard. "This is it," she said. In the hollow, with the sandy hill at their backs, they were comfortable.

"I did not sleep well either," Süssel began. "Everything moved in on me. Though I swore I would never have a hatstand in my house, suddenly there it was, the one from my childhood, closing in on me. Choking me, its arms around my neck. 'Mother!' I cried, but the shout stuck in my throat. I woke in a sweat. I heard you getting up, heard the brass bed squeak, pushing against your night table, and I thought, poor Max, all Manole's stones are crashing down on him too! And the poor woman's last shout for air. I rose slowly, went across the hall, opened your door, and saw you sitting on the edge of the bed holding onto the brass rail and I knew we had both been shaken by Lady Manole's cries. Max, I wonder, do you know that twenty-five years have passed since the day I came to the gates of the ghetto, Dr. Bauer's letter in hand. Do you know?"

"Is it?" he asked. "Twenty-five years? To the day?"

"Yes, to the day."

"Dear Süssel, is it possible? How do we remember? How is it possible that a legend can have that kind of power over you!" Max said. "That it can't be predicted or controlled, that it can persist so unfailingly in the dark of your soul! It shakes me. It is hard to believe." Max smiled at being forced to come to terms with Süssel's kind of truth. But in his logical and honest fashion, he conceded to her, "I lay my weapons at your feet," in the idiom of

Czernowitz. They rose, not wanting the moonless night to come upon them, and with the river darker than the sky, they hurried home. They sat a little longer with a cup of tea and a spoon of honey. Suddenly Süssel jumped to her feet, ran up the staircase, taking three steps at a time, to Max's room. She collected his night things, took them over to her room, and called down to him, "You're moving, Max, into my room. Come help me carry."

It was the voice Max had heard in the Residenzgasse. Young, bold, not tolerating any contradiction. His Süssel. It thrilled him.

He had not anticipated the embrace to come. Slow and loving....

Max sat up, his back against the headboard. He watched Süssel stretch, curl up, and fall asleep. Her face – in the light of a dim bulb put there to chase away her childhood fears – looked young. Her hair, no longer red, shone black against the white of the pillow. Fleeting visions came of goodbyes, last sun-rays, the shimmer of copper in her hair as she stood at the old gate, of her coming out with a light, quick step, oblivious of him, her hair restrained under that *Herrenhut*...he felt again the sting of a backhand striking his cheek, but also the touch of her teenage breasts through the blue coat. And slowly slipping down, to lie alongside Süssel, he fought the coming sleep to hold on to a love. So desired.

ACKNOWLEDGEMENTS

I AM TRULY INDEBTED TO GEOFFREY URSELL, MY editor, and I thank him for his guidance, counsel, and help with every aspect of the book. It was a wonderful collaboration, and I accepted his suggestion for the title of the book. I would also like to thank Margaret Kyle for the countless hours she spent reading my handwriting, keyboarding, printing, and correcting, and her intelligent observations, which I found helpful. Margaret has been with me from the first pages of the book and I hope she will work with me in the future. Many thanks to my friends, who read the first drafts of the book and encouraged me to pursue writing: Henry and Susan Woolf, Ronald (Bingo) Mavor, Mavor Moore, Rosemary Hunt, and Christopher Scott. And a very special thank you to Irene Blum, my daughter, for her support, advice, and steadfast love.

MARTHA BLUM was born in 1913 in Czernowitz, Austria (now Chernivtsi, Ukraine). With the defeat of Germany and Austria in 1918, the city became part of Romania and remained so while she was growing up. Her studies included pharmaceutical chemistry, languages, and music at the universities of Bucharest, Prague, Strasbourg, and Paris. World War II found her family at the crossroads of warring and occupying forces, persecuted in turns by Soviet Russia and Germany. She immigrated to Canada in 1951, by way of Israel, and has lived in Saskatoon, Saskatchewan, since 1954.